LESS THAN HUMAN

Gary Raisor

All rights reserved.

No part of this book may be reproduced in any form or by any electronic or mechanical means, including information storage and retrieval systems, without permission in writing from the publisher, except by a reviewer who may quote brief passages in a review.

Cover Artwork © 2023 by Elderlemon Design
Interior Design © 2023 by Brady Moller

ISBN: 978-1-58767-946-9

This book is a work of fiction. Names, characters, places and incidents either are products of the author's imagination or are used fictitiously. Any resemblance to actual events or locales or persons, living or dead, is entirely coincidental.

Cemetery Dance Publications
132B Industry Lane, Unit #7
Forest Hill, MD 21050

www.cemeterydance.com

LESS THAN HUMAN

GARY RAISOR

*For Joe Lansdale, Dave Hinchberger, Kevin Peddicord.
And Kariann, always.*

Being a cowboy isn't the state you live in, but the state of your mind.

CHAPTER ONE

T he Greyhound pulled into Carruthers, Texas, a little after nine and unloaded seventeen people into the unseasonably cold autumn night. All had family waiting for them.

All, except for two.

Steven Adler was the last one to get off the bus. He was lean and blonde in a gray Stetson. On his left hand, he wore a glove, also gray. He sported Tony Lama snakeskin boots, jeans, and a white cotton shirt beneath a leather jacket that held a beaded image of a rattlesnake coiled to strike. If the cold bothered him any, it sure didn't show.

"You got the address?" Steven asked the older man who'd gotten off the bus with him.

"Yeah," Earl Jacobs answered. He looked like Randolph Scott gone to seed. With a grin he buttoned his ratty leather jacket against the chill. He too carried a case. "I got it here somewheres," he said around a cigar he was trying to light, "somewheres."

He fished out a scrap of paper, turned it over, then turned it back. "It's up a couple of blocks, over on Eighth." He didn't look happy.

"Cheer up. It's a good night for a stroll," Steven said. He took a breath, inhaling the night, as he shifted the case tucked beneath his arm. "You can't tell much about a town from a cab, Earl. You got to walk around if you want to get a feel for what's going on."

"I'm getting a feeling our throats are gonna get cut," Earl commented, looking around uneasily. "Course, that's assuming we don't freeze to death first."

Steven grinned. "You always were an optimist, Earl. That's what I like about you."

They walked across the lot, dodging potholes, watching their bus being parked behind a chain-link fence topped with barbed wire. Lights died, and the Greyhound was left alone. A pop from its engine cooling sounded like a gunshot. Earl jumped, his hand darting beneath his jacket. He saw Steven grinning at him and he grinned back sheepishly.

A few blocks later, Earl tossed his cigar stub and fished out the address again. "We should've been there by now." His breathing had gone ragged. Beneath his beard stubble, his face had taken on a slightly bluish cast, and when the wind chased some leaves down the sidewalk, he began shivering.

Steven took the piece of paper from his companion's hands. "I'm sorry, Matt. We should've taken a cab."

"It's Earl. My name is Earl. That's the second time you've called me Matt this week. Who's this Matt?"

"Matt Thomas, an old friend from a long, long time ago. I'm sorry, Earl, sometimes I forget. Are you all right?"

"I'll be okay. It's a little hard to breathe after that bastard kicked me last night. I think he busted one of my ribs." Earl pulled out a pint and tossed off a quick sip. "I always thought the game of pool was supposed to be a non-contact sport."

"You made him look bad in front of his girlfriend." Steven took the proffered bottle, took a sip, and made a face. "She was laughing at him."

"I coulda showed her a few strokes, too," Earl said, tucking the bottle out of sight.

"She was young enough to be your daughter."

"Granddaughter is more like it." Earl looked around at the crumbling buildings and weed-infested lots. The smokestacks from some long-closed factory cast a shadow across the sidewalk. "I think we're going the wrong way."

"No, we're not. It's up ahead about five blocks."

"How the hell do you know that?"

"Somebody's playing nine ball. I heard them break."

"Did they sink any?" Earl asked with barely masked sarcasm.

"Yeah, one."

"You wouldn't happen to know which one, would you?"

"As a matter of fact, I do. It was the nine ball." Steven looked at his watch and stepped up the pace. "Come on. I feel like playing."

Earl had to trot to keep up. Damned new boots were killing his feet. His breath was a sporadic white cloud that trailed along behind him in the night like exhaust from some engine that wasn't hitting on all cylinders. He silently cursed. His damned ribs hurt worse than his feet.

Flickering neon told them they had at last found Leon's Pool Emporium. A skinny old black man weaved out of the building, paused to drain the last of his pint before smashing the bottle against the door of a Bonneville sitting at the curb. On the car's windshield someone had written in large bright red lipstick: *REPENT! Before Jesus runs the table on YOU.*

This seemed to anger the drinker. He whipped out a .45 and began firing at the car, all the while screaming "Ilene, I'm gonna kill your ass!"

Finally the enraged shooter emptied his gun. Not a single bullet had found its intended target. The other nearby cars weren't so lucky.

"Ilene's got nice penmanship, don't you think?" Steven said.

"I guess getting a game in a nice place is out of the question?" Earl responded.

They watched the old black man stagger off into the night.

"Your problem, Earl, is you've got no spirit of adventure."

"I'm too old for adventure," Earl said under his breath. "What I need is a hooker, one of those big fat juicy ones who smells like fried chicken."

They pushed through the door, and halted just inside the dim interior. The place smelled of hard times; the booze and cigar smoke couldn't blot it out. There were four Steepletons squatting in the middle of the room, dotted with the rings of ten thousand drinks. One was being used by a haggard cowboy and a college kid playing nine ball. A mahogany bar ran along the back of the room, lined with men nursing drinks. They were watching football on a TV with the sound turned off.

One of them eased off his stool and fed some change to the juke.

N.W.A's *Fuck tha Police* blasted the room.

"Why don't y'all turn off that black-ass hippity-hop racket and turn up the TV?" Earl yelled, walking closer. "I got money on that game."

"Cause it's broke, that's why," the bartender said, as though the answer was obvious. "It's been broke since '89. We got to where we kinda like it that way."

Every face at the bar turned toward Earl.

Every face at the bar was black.

Earl halted.

The huge bartender kept on polishing glasses and studying them as though they were apparitions that would disappear if he just waited long enough. He showed them some yellow teeth. Someone had cut him bad years ago, leaving a scar that ran from his eyebrow down to his jawbone. When he smiled, only half his face worked. The smile didn't improve his looks any. "You gentlemen must be lost."

"Not if you shoot pool here," Steven said. He took a stool at the bar, and he and Earl laid their cases on the pitted wood. "You do shoot pool here, don't you?"

"Yeah, we been known to shoot a game or two. If the money's right." The bartender quit polishing glasses and leaned forward, his muddy eyes looking at Steven Adler the way a snake looks at a crippled bird. "You two sorry-ass white boys don't look like you got a pot to piss in."

"We got a little put back," Earl volunteered. "Mom don't know about it, but we've been saving our lunch money. You'd be surprised how it adds up after a while." He pulled a wad of bills out of his jacket pocket and laid it beside the case on the bar. "There's a lot of dead presidents there. I'm sure you recognize a few of them."

The bartender's eyes took in the money before shifting back to them. The teeth appeared once again. It was not a reassuring sight. "You two got a lot of balls walking in here with a roll like that. What's to keep us from cutting you into fish bait and dumping you in the river? Shit, I bet they won't find you til spring—when you float."

"Jesus, what the hell's happened to western hospitality?" Earl opened his jacket, let his fingers play over his busted ribs and the .38 he had tucked in the waistband of his pants. "We don't want no trouble. Word has it you got a shooter here by the name of D. A. Fontaine. We heard he handles a stick pretty good. My boy here is willing to pay to see how good."

"You two ain't exactly hiding the fact you're hustlers." Leon studied them, trying to place their faces. "Should I have heard of either of you?"

"No, we're kind of shy. If you don't get your player out here quick," Steven said, "these two sorry-ass white boys are taking their money and heading down the road."

EARL WAS TOSSING DOWN HIS THIRD SHOT OF GEORGE DICKEL WHEN the door swung open, letting in the cold autumn air. As he turned, he caught sight of Steven's face in the mirror behind the bar. It had a look of bemused amazement on it. He saw why.

D. A. Fontaine was a girl. A black teenaged girl. She was dressed in black leather pants that fit her like a second skin and a chocolate-colored leather jacket that was too big for her. Under her arm was a case much like the ones Steven and Earl carried. When she pulled her hands out of her jacket pockets, long golden lacquered nails flashed in the light.

"Is this some kind of joke?" Earl took in the slight form standing in the doorway. "Ain't it past your bedtime, little sister?"

"I guess I could ask you the same, gramps. Shouldn't you be getting back to the home?" She smiled sweetly. "Before you miss out on the stewed prunes. I hear old people get real cranky if they don't get their stewed—"

"You can't be more than fourteen." Earl's voice rose with anger. "We came all the way from Corpus Christi to play a fourteen-year-old girl. I can't goddamn believe this, a girl."

"I've got a name," she said, unruffled. "It's Dorinda, but everyone calls me D. A., and I'm not fourteen. I turned seventeen in July, thank you."

"How come we never heard you were a girl," Earl asked. His voice lowered but his expression was still suspicious.

"On account of I used to dress up like a boy when I played pool. The guys wouldn't have liked losing to a girl. But, as you can see," she said, peeling off her jacket, "it got harder and harder to look like a boy. Besides, I found it's a lot more fun to be a girl." She flashed a smile at Steven.

"You stop that, Dorinda," Leon said from behind the bar. "Ain't been able to do nothing with that girl since her mother ran off."

"She's your daughter?" Earl inquired, disbelief on his face.

"She kept her mother's name. What're you trying to say?" Leon cracked his knuckles and a scowl appeared.

"Nothing. I can see the resemblance much better now."

"I hate to interrupt this tale of marital woe, but are you backing her action?" Steven asked Leon.

Leon nodded.

Earl got up from his stool, looked over at the bartender. "Say, brother, you wouldn't mind letting me get a look at some of your dead presidents, would you?"

Leon reached into a pocket and came out with a wad of bills, which he laid beside Earl's stack.

"Looks like mine's bigger than yours," Earl noted with a wink. "Ain't many white men can make that statement."

The expression on Leon's face didn't change.

Steven opened up his case and lifted out his cue. It was a yellowish white, and wrapped around the handle was an intricate red snake covered with feathers. The stick was a rare work of art. "What's your favorite game, Dorinda? You like eight ball?" He put the cue together quickly. "Or maybe a little nine ball is more your speed?"

"I like eight ball. I always got the stripes when Daddy and I played."

"Eight ball it is. Rack 'em, will you, Earl?"

"You want to flip a coin, or roll the cue ball to see who breaks?" Dorinda asked.

"No, that's all right. You break."

Dorinda shrugged. "Okay, Alan Jackson, it's your money. I play for a hundred a game. That too rich for your blood?"

Steven smiled, shook his head no. For a moment Dorinda felt a slight tingle of unease when she looked into his green eyes. Something wasn't quite right about them. They seemed way too old for his face. And there was some kind of hidden rage swirling around in their depths. She looked away, and when she looked back, his eyes were okay. It must have been the light, she decided.

"Something wrong?" Steven asked.

"No, I'm fine, don't worry 'bout me, Dwight Yoakam." She was angry for letting this guy get to her. Taking a breath, she forced herself to be calm. "Say, Earl baby, you gonna get those balls racked tonight, or you just gonna stand there and play pocket pool?"

"I'm on it, little sister." Earl finally got the balls the way he wanted them, a good tight rack. He looked over at Leon. "Would you listen to the mouth on that girl. You let her talk to the customers like that?"

"Ain't been able to do nothing with that girl since—"

"I know, I know. Since her mother ran off," Earl finished. He was beginning to enjoy himself.

Leon smiled back. The effort looked like it hurt him.

As soon as Earl lifted the rack, Dorinda put all of her ninety-seven pounds behind her stick, driving the cue ball into the closely bunched balls. They split with a flat crack, scattering across the table, where they rolled around for a while. Slowed.

One teetered on the edge of a pocket. Fell.

"Looks like this is your lucky night, you get stripes," Steven said. "Just like when you played Daddy." Steven's voice was soft, teasing. "I bet your daddy used to let you win, didn't he?" He sat down on a stool and crossed his legs at the ankles, became motionless.

Dorinda walked around the table. "Daddy hasn't let me win since I was nine." She looked at Steven, anger in her eyes. "That's a real nice stick you got there, Tim McGraw. Too bad you're not going to get a chance to use it."

"Yes, it is a nice stick," he said. "I've had it for a long time." He caressed it softly.

She sank a shot.

"Do you know what it's made out of?" he asked.

"Looks like ivory to me."

"No, not ivory. Bone."

Dorinda tried to ignore him, to concentrate on the game. She sank her next three shots, but she was edgy, aware of his unwinking stare. Her nerve cracked. She missed.

"My turn, already?" Steven uncoiled from his stool and strolled over. He studied the table for a moment. Then, with practiced ease, he sank the seven ball in the far right-corner pocket, putting enough spin on the cue ball to draw it back to him. He sank the three. The two quickly followed. Within thirty seconds he had dropped every solid-colored ball on the table into a pocket. Only her stripes remained.

And the eight.

Steven rolled the yellowish-white cue between his hands. "I thought you'd be better." He seemed disappointed and slightly angry.

She stared at him, alternately attracted and repulsed. "Is that stick really made out of... bone? Or were you just messing around, trying to throw me off my game?"

"I never kid about anything to do with pool. It's made out of bone. Human bone."

"You're lying. Where did you get something like that?"

"I got it from the first guy I ever played against. When I made my comeback."

Everyone at the bar was watching them now. The TV continued on, soundless people cheering a soundless game. The juke dropped another record. Leon dropped a glass.

Conversation looked to be on hold.

With Public Enemy's *Fight the Power* thumping in the background, Dorinda looked over at her father. For the first time she could ever remember, he looked afraid. The sight filled her with fear, too. "He lost it to you on a bet, huh?" She licked her lips and tried to smile.

"Yes he did, in a manner of speaking."

"I bet it's worth a lot."

"Only to him. It was made from his legs."

The smile died on her lips, unborn.

Leon reached under the bar. "All right, boys, no more Hannibal Lecter bullshit." He came out with a double-barreled sawed-off twelve-gauge. "You and your friend get the hell out of here, right now. Go on, get!"

Steven looked at the shotgun, then turned back to Dorinda as though Leon didn't exist. For a second, the hustler's eyes caught the light and gave it back, shiny yellow, like some kind of animal. "Want to see a trick, Dorinda?"

Without waiting for an answer he tipped his Stetson over those eyes that weren't right and stroked the cue ball. It banked twice, then slowly rolled the entire length of the table until it kissed the eight, soft as a whisper. It fell into the pocket.

Leon spat, wadded up a hundred-dollar bill, threw it at Steven's feet. "There's your money, Mister, take it and get out. Go on now, I don't want no trouble."

"We don't want any trouble either, do we, Earl?" Steven said, raising his hat.

"Nope," Earl answered.

With a grin, Steven unscrewed his cue stick and laid it on the table. Turning, still not hurrying, he picked up the wadded bill, straightened it with maddening slowness. He walked toward the bar. Stopped as the gun raised. "We just came in here for a friendly game."

"We like to keep it friendly," Earl agreed. He stood up.

Two soft clicks as Leon eased back the hammers on the twelve-gauge. It looked like a toy in his huge hand. "I don't know what you came in here for, but it damn sure wasn't to shoot no pool." He swung the gun around, centered the two stubby barrels on Earl's chest. "If I had to guess, I'd say your friend is a crazy son of a bitch who gets his kicks out of scaring young girls."

"Well hell, Leon," Earl said, "you must be psychic. You ought to get you one of them nine-hundred telephone numbers and tell fortunes for a living. You see anything in my future?"

"Nothing you're gonna like if I ever lay eyes on either one of you again," Leon promised.

"Damn, I was hoping for money."

As the two hustlers looked down the barrels of Leon's shotgun, Public Enemy continued on.

Elvis was a hero to most
But he never meant shit to me you see
Straight up racist that sucker was
Simple and plain
Motherfuck him and John Wayne

Steven laid the straightened bill on the bar, started backing away. "Oh, we'll meet again," he said. "You can count on it." He turned to pick up his cue stick, the easy smile still on his face. "Come on, Earl, I guess we'd better leave. It looks like we've worn out our welcome." The smile left his face.

His cue stick was gone.

CHAPTER TWO

J ohn Warrick was a small-time hustler.

He'd given his life to the game of pool. It wasn't much of a life, drifting from town to town, trying to eke out a living in places where your feet stuck to the floor and you could get shot as easily as you could get paid. A very few people, who made it their business to know such things, said John might have been the best to ever play the game. They also said that he was past it now. That he'd lost his nerve.

Maybe that was so. Maybe it wasn't.

Last night John had put his nerve to the test. It had held. Not only had he taken a loud-mouthed college boy for three hundred of his rich daddy's bucks, he had lifted a pool cue, a pool cue with a red snake curled around the handle. Sneaking around behind those crazy sons of bitches messing with Leon had been risky. If that scattergun had gone off, it would have turned all three of them into hamburger.

But life was full of risks. This one had paid off.

John had his reasons for taking the cue stick. Those two hustlers at Leon's place, he'd recognized them the minute they walked in. Last time he'd laid eyes on them was down Juarez way, and that had been more than twenty years ago. Their clothes had changed some. Their faces hadn't. The glove on the young guy's left hand hadn't. The cue stick hadn't.

More than a dozen people had died when those two had come slinking into town all those years ago. A couple of those people had been friends of John's.

The authorities had chalked up the deaths to a local drug cartel. John wasn't so sure.

At the moment John was sitting on a bed in a cheap motel just outside San Benito, nursing a Lone Star that had gone warm ten minutes ago. In his hands was the cue stick he had risked his life to get. He was waiting to see if any images would gather in his head. Ninety percent of the time nothing ever happened. Sometimes it did. It always took a while, and he was patient, letting the pictures come. Waiting for the cue to give up its secrets.

John Warrick had one other talent besides pool. He was a little bit psychic.

After a few minutes the water stains on the ceiling were gone, replaced by a neon glare, the patter of warm rain in the night. John Warrick was now someone else, and he was seeing what they were seeing. He was walking down a street. Searching for something. Someone. Hookers came up to him, bright smears of color, soft honeyed voices, offering to fulfill his every sexual fantasy. He smelled their drugs, their diseases, and he rejected their offers. The crowds thinned. The lights were left behind. He walked on, still searching.

Finally he found what he wanted.

A teenaged boy.

They talked. The boy said his name was Joey. The man gave no name. After a few minutes, Joey motioned for him to follow. John felt heat in the pit of his stomach.

The boy led him through a winding alley, up some stairs to a room on the second floor. Money changed hands and the man pulled the boy close. Nuzzled his throat. Cold leather, warm skin. A hint of some cheap after-shave on a face too young to shave. John tried to wake up, but the images were too strong and they held him between waking and sleeping.

Suddenly John knew that whoever this man was, he wasn't here for sex. Not even this kind. This was something else entirely. Lips peeled back over teeth, and the hustler knew the man was smiling. A case was laid on the soiled bed. Opened. Something long was taken out. He couldn't quite tell what it was. Then he saw it had a red snake on the handle. And that it was sharp.

Everything faded for a moment. And John knew something had happened. Something awful.

The boy struggled, and John could feel every beat of a heart laboring to beat. Strong at first, then slowing. Slowing. It felt like a wild bird flinging itself against the bars of its cage, trying to escape, each effort weaker than the last. While the heart struggled to beat beneath the frail ribs, John could feel his mind merging with Joey's mind. He suddenly knew things the boy knew, his deepest wishes, his darkest fears. Fragments for the most part, pieces of nightmare coupled with dim memories.

With fading eyes, Joey looked up at the man holding him. The killer's features were hidden by the shadows. Only the smile could be seen. The smile told John the man who held Joey in his arms was watching the boy die. And enjoying it.

Still fighting, John was drawn deeper still into the mind of the dying teen hustler, Joey Estevez, as they both were pulled down, down, down… into the dying boy's nightmare… as… Joey watched the rats crawl from the gutted dog that lay sprawled in the alley.

Joey ran past the dog. He knew the rats had seen him.

It was impossible they could have found him so soon, yet somehow, they had. More spilled from the fire-gutted house on the corner. Just a few at first. But in seconds, the place was swarming with them, and they watched him from the stoop, making no effort to hide, jostling each other like a crowd of spectators at a parade.

Joey would have laughed if he wasn't so scared.

Agitation swept through their midst as though they were… expecting him, and Joey felt he should know why they had come, why they were after him. The answer taunted, an elusive secret that danced beyond his grasp, tantalizing him with its nearness, whispering words he couldn't quite hear.

Joey felt the weight of their eyes as he moved past. His legs pistoned, a sharp turn, and the rats disappeared from sight.

He listened for sounds of pursuit.

All he heard was the rain drumming its fingers across the rooftops.

And the jackhammer of his heart.

Few people were on these streets at this late hour of the night. A man with an empty shirtsleeve pinned to his shoulder leaned against a street lamp and drank from a bottle in a brown paper bag. He began dancing, a demented Gene Kelly who stopped now and then to gesture, to whisper vague threats to companions who existed only in his mind. A hooker limped by on her way home, oblivious of the rain, cradling five-inch spike heels in one hand, a glowing cigarette in the other.

"You better lay off that shit, Georgie-boy," she called out to the dancer. "It'll make you crazy."

A cab cruised down the puddle-filled street, drowning the man's laughter beneath the hiss of tires.

No one saw Joey, who was dressed in black, from a leather jacket down to the Air Jordans that hugged his feet. The dark clothes made him one more shadow on a street of shadows, and if you were a thief and hustler, that's the way it had to be.

Especially if you were only fifteen.

He'd been out, taking care of business. Now he was on his way home.

Home—

What a joke that was. Sometimes he wondered what it would be like to have a real honest-to-god home, the kind that came with parents who made you eat all the vegetables on your plate, who made you do your homework, who beat your ass when you stayed out too late.

Who said they loved you.

A vacant smile replaced the sneer. That dream died when a doctor up at County had walked out into a waiting room to tell him his mama had OD'd. Joey remembered a dirty white jacket, the empty blue eyes that looked right through him. The guy said it like he was talking about the fucking weather. Hey kid, it's going to rain today; hey kid, don't forget your umbrella; and by the way, kid, your mama used to be a junkie, but now your mama's dead.

Before she made love to the needle for the final time, she had laid a curse on him. She made him swear he would find his dad and get him off the booze.

Last month he'd managed to keep his promise, even though it had been by accident. It had been something of a tearful reunion—the old bastard had caught him on the nose with a wine bottle while Joey had been going through his pockets in an alley over on Collins.

Joey had been about to carve his initials on some unwashed skin when something in the old man's voice had stopped him. The foulmouthed swearing had a familiar ring.

So they were together now, he and the old man, doing their best to get along. To get by.

Joey did what he had to in order for them to eat: shoplifting, purse snatching, making pickups for the bookies.

When times were tough, he sold his body to men with a taste for young boys, his smile of defiance a bandage too small to cover the shame when he endured their cold sweaty hands, when they threw their money at his feet, when they roared away in cars that smelled of new leather and spent passion... to their big fine homes... where the rats never came in the night.

Tonight the city fought sleep, tossing and turning fitfully. Sounds, some loud, some quiet, leaked from the apartments he passed: an argument between a man and a woman, a snatch of Latino melody, a child laughing, an old woman praying, someone crying. Always someone crying.

Night music his mama used to call it, a lullaby made by souls in torment.

When he asked her what she meant, she would always brush the hair from over his eyes and hold him close without answering. Without conscious thought, he brushed the hair from his eyes.

He pushed the painful thoughts aside. Time to get a move on. The night had found him far from home. He hated the night, because that's when the rats came. They might try to get into the apartment. His dad was there alone.

He picked up the pace, his footsteps throwing echoes down the alley—pat pat pat—as he weaved around an overturned garbage can.

At first he didn't see the rats gathered around the spilled trash. When they saw him, they lazily abandoned whatever they'd been swarming, only to return like a swarm of blowflies disturbed on a summer day.

Joey made himself part of the wall when the biggest rat he'd ever seen crawled out of the trash can holding onto a gobbet of something bloody. The thing was a monster, a twisted, crippled mass of scar tissue with fur the color of pissed-on snow. Joey watched it drag its bloated body up onto a fire escape and hobble along, trying to flee with its prize. But the smaller rats were quicker. They surrounded their leader.

Drawn by the smell of blood, they crept onto the span. The sheer weight of them caused the metal to groan in protest. Hunger drove them on, made them edge closer to the bared fangs that waited. Their eyes that were wet with equal portions of need and fear. They knew they were sidling up to death.

They hesitated, working up their courage. And then, like a single-minded organism that knew a part must die so the whole might live, they lunged.

The white monster killed five.

It caught them by the throat, one by one, and flung their wriggling bodies from the fire escape like a child digging through a drawer in search of a missing sock. One bounced off the wall by Joey, and he recoiled from the wetness that splattered his face.

Anger overcame fear.

"You want something to eat? I got something right here. How about a little metal pizza, you fuckers!" He scooped up a garbage-can lid and flung it in a flat, vicious arc.

A squeal of agony followed the clang of metal. Caught by the edge of the flattened lid, the white rat had been disemboweled. It should have died right there. Instead it dropped to the pavement, leaking wet black stains, and began a frenzied dance, spinning around and around, becoming entangled in its own intestines.

What happened next was inevitable. Joey had seen it before—the writhing mass of rats descended the fire escape, a magician's scarf fluttering in the night.

"Step right up, ladies and gentlemen!" Disgust was in his voice as he broke into an impromptu impression of a carnival barker. "Only one show tonight, folks, so you'd better get your tickets quick." He scanned the imaginary crowd, getting into the part. "How much, you ask? It's a steal. One thin dime—yes, sir, that's right, ten cents gets you in." He ripped an invisible ticket, his eyes never leaving the rats.

"Watch close now. It's showtime!"

He swept an arm outward and the scarf of flesh parted on cue. Except for some claws and a few teeth, not a trace of the dead rats remained. Even the white monster was gone. All of them had been devoured.

"Rat magic, ladies and gentlemen. Now you see them."

He tipped an imaginary derby and bowed to the imaginary applause.

"And now you don't."

Joey smiled, but the fear returned to his eyes when he felt their eyes bore into him. En masse they rose to their back legs, noses sniffing the air expectantly. His fingers strayed once again to his face, searching until they found a small blemish, a scar that marred his features.

"What the hell do you want from me?" No sooner had his words died, then they came at him, claws scrabbling on the cobblestones.

"Oh man, something definitely weird is going down here," he said, "very weird." He turned and fled from the alley. His side stitched with pain as he raced on, doubling him over.

His building came into sight and he risked a quick look around before ducking in. A sign was nailed to the door. Only one word, it summed up the building: The word was **Condemned**.

The landing was pitch black, but that didn't stop Joey. He knew every creak, every loose board in the place. Taking the steps three at a time, he raced to the second floor. A rustling came in the dark. For a moment he was certain the stairs were covered with rats. Hundreds, maybe even thousands, of rats.

—that they were creeping downward—

that they were only inches away—

The thought that one might touch his face caused his heart to squirt sideways. He floated in the blackness, frozen by terror, when he recalled how quickly the rats had scrambled down the fire escape.

"This is crazy, muy loco." Muttering, he yanked out a book of matches. When he tried to strike one, his hands began to shake. What if it was true? What if they really were waiting?

On the third try the match flared, burning his nose with the stink of sulfur. He lit the entire book and heaved it up the stairwell.

Only shadows flickering on the walls.

Mocking him.

Then he saw a flash of yellowish white and, for an instant, he thought the huge rat had returned. But it was just a newspaper caught in a draft, flapping down the hallway like a weary ghost searching out a room for the night. His laughter died with the light. The sight of all those rats in the alley had gotten to him.

He bolted the remaining distance.

Softly he eased into the apartment and tried to swallow the soured cotton that clogged his throat. His eyes slitted before they adjusted to a kerosene lamp guttering in the corner. The glow barely disturbed the shadows. That was okay with Joey, because the place wasn't much to look at anyway, just a bare room with a stained mattress on the floor and a couch so old its bones poked through.

LESS THAN HUMAN

His dad was a pile of rags asleep on the mattress, snoring gutturally, and Joey breathed a sigh of relief. Everything was okay. He was home now.

Yet the fear refused to die.

Somewhere, out of sight, came the sound of claws.

He tried to locate the furtive scrabbling. He couldn't.

It seemed to come from everywhere.

"Come on, Papa," he urged, his voice cracking, "we've got to get out of here." As he reached over to shake the figure huddled beneath the filthy blanket, his foot bumped something. It tipped over with a clatter... and the scratching grew louder... grew frantic... as though a signal of some kind had been given.

With animal quickness, Joey's hand darted out and grabbed the object. He turned it over, fascinated by the dull oily sheen that reflected back. Then, without warning, his head began to throb, clenching his skull in a vise of pain so intense he was rocked back. In an instant the tremor passed. He gave his head a shake before turning back toward his dad, before smiling and hefting the object in his hand.

Flipping it high in the air. Watching as it spun.

End over end. Once. Twice.

Watching as it came to rest in his hand.

Staring at a wine bottle—an empty wine bottle.

"You said you'd quit," Joey accused, his voice going soft as he caressed the bottle. "When I took you in, you swore on Mama's grave."

Agitation swept across his face, chasing all other emotions before it as he yanked the old man up. Joey bit into his lip and a dot of blood appeared, the head of a black worm crawling out onto his chin. He blinked back tears and fought for calm. His eyes were those of an angel betrayed.

Only this angel carried more than hurt; he carried the fires of hell.

"You promised!" he raged, "No more drinking!"

The words were a spray of blood and drool that caught the old man in the face, making him stumble backward. The hunched-over figure kept stumbling back, pawing at his cheek. He never took his eyes off the bottle in the boy's hand.

Joey raised it as though he meant to lash out, but then the pain stretched him taut. He gasped and the bottle slipped from his fingers. It hit the floor with a pop and shattered into dozens of shards. Glittering in the light, they were wet shiny eyes watching him double over in agony. He spewed more blood and saliva, his guts on fire.

He ripped open his shirt, and his skin, crisscrossed with scars, rippled when a spasm shot through him, a spasm that disappeared and then reappeared, causing his face to contort into a skull-like mask.

The scars turned an angry red.

"Papa, it hurts—"

The vise that held Joey's head closed another notch, the pain adding tinder to the fire of his rage. He fought, even though he was helpless to stop the blackness filled with hunger sounds. It was consuming him. He listened to screams chasing themselves into silence, leaving behind echoes that taunted him, promising remembrance of things better off forgotten.

The black fire grew hotter. Hotter.

Devouring him.

Arching backward, Joey raked at the scars that puckered into hungry mouths. His fingernails ripped his flesh, trailed long white furrows. Blood seeped into the grooves, filled them to overflowing.

And now he could hear claws.

Lots and lots of claws.

Scratching.

Growing louder.

The sound was coming from inside the room, and yet he knew it couldn't be. The room was empty.

"It hurts," Joey said, gasping. "Hurts bad. Make it stop. Please…"

The old man reached out, but his hands were unable to complete their journey. They stopped short, two pale moths fluttering against an unseen window. He began to cry.

The claws grew louder. Filled the boy's world.

Joey struggled upright, his fingers groping outward until they found his dad's face. They began exploring the ravages etched there by time and drink. His touch was gentle. Soothing. He seemed beyond the pain that had torn him just moments before.

"Papa, you know you shouldn't drink. You've made Mama angry. Now she's going to make the blackness come." His voice was plaintive, tinged with sadness. "Bad things happen in the blackness."

Sighing, Joey pulled back and began tracing the eruption of scars that decorated his own young body, as though they were a road map that would lead him to understand how he had come to this place. His fingers undulated along. Rising over peaks. Sliding down valleys. Riding the huge, misshapen lumps that had appeared under his skin.

Then a sound came.

Indistinct.

Muffled.

An ice pick punched into a bag of wet leaves.

The sound came again, louder this time. A scar bulged, then burst open as a head emerged from the torn flesh and looked blindly around the room.

When the old man saw the head belonged to a rat, his eyes filled with fear. He scrambled toward the door. When he realized it wouldn't open, he tried to scream, but all that came out was a mewling noise, and then, after a moment, that too died.

Only his eyes moved, darting back and forth, flickering with incomprehension, blank, like those of a dog Joey had once seen on the subway tracks, pinned in the oncoming headlights.

Somehow knowing its life was forfeit.

Not quite knowing why.

Joey went rigid, and another rat burst free. And another. The illusion of life was peeling away from the boy, like layers of rotten bandages, to reveal the shrunken husk beneath. Dark things were swimming inside his stomach cavity, small, as though far away, slowly growing larger as they fought their way to the surface.

Then every scar on his body erupted, spilling rats out onto the floor. Faster and faster they came—crawling from Joey, blood slicked, spewing out with wet smacking sounds, an ocean of dark vomit that seemed endless until, at last, the room was covered with rats… a swirling mass, a whirlpool with claws and teeth that eddied toward his dad, slowly at first, then with greater speed, flowing over him, pulling the old man down.

"Help me, Joey," he pleaded, "please. I won't drink anymore. I promise." His mouth gaped open and a rat darted inside. A violent flurry of activity followed. It emerged with something pink and bloody in its jaws. The old man saw his own tongue and screamed, his straining mouth forming perfect oval after perfect oval as the muscles in his neck knotted in agony, but no words came out.

Only sounds.

Wet sounds.

"You can scream louder than that, Papa. I did. I screamed a lot louder, but it didn't do any good. You know why? Because there was no one to hear me." His voice was a sigh, a distant cold wind on the road of memory. "After Mama died, you said I could go with you. You said you'd never leave me, only you got drunk and locked me in the room. And when you went away… the rats came…"

The words tumbled out, tortured remembrances of a child with the smell of the grave clinging to him. "I tried to fight them off… but there were too many. Too many. They bit me." His eyes were reproachful. "They kept biting me, and then they crawled up inside of me. Don't you want to know how I know that?"

Joey stared at the feeding rats while bitter emotions raged across his face. Yet his voice was calm, devoid of emotion as though he were talking about someone else.

"Because I was still—alive."

A hand darted up from the midst of the wriggling bodies and grasped Joey's jacket. It was all of the old man he could see, the rest was covered over. He pried loose the bloody hand and held it for a moment. The gnarled fingers locked onto his wrist, clutching at him as they tried to maintain their grip. But the hand was too slippery. Too bloody. Inch by inch it slid free until it could no longer hold on.

The hand fell back, rose, fell again, each movement slower than the last.

One last time the twitching fingers broke the surface, a drowning swimmer flailing toward shore, the old man reached out for Joey.

His reach fell short.

And he was gone.

"Rat magic, ladies and gentlemen," Joey whispered, sorrow holding him in a cold, white embrace. "Now you see it…"

He tipped his imaginary hat, but, this time, there was no imaginary applause. His shoulders hitched and the sounds he made were those of an animal in pain. A single tear rolled from his eye and dripped to the floor, yellow and viscous as pus from a festering sore.

Suddenly he doubled over, struck by an unseen hand. His hands darted to his stomach and he felt movement. Something was still down there. It was huge and restless, and it had claws. His insides were being ripped and torn with incredible savagery. The pain was beyond imagining.

He was being torn in two.

Joey felt, more than saw, the thing inside him crawl out and drop to the floor. The body landed with a meaty thud, lay twitching. Then it gathered itself, began moving toward the feeding rats, leaving a trail of glistening wetness. With each passing second, the dark shape was growing stronger.

After a bit, it shook itself like a dog after a bath. The darkness sprayed outward in countless drops. Covering the walls.

Mesmerized, Joey stared at the huge, crippled monster with fur the color of pissed-on snow. The misshapen head swiveled and looked at him. Their gazes locked.

The leathery lips peeled back from the teeth, not in anger, Joey realized but in a smile.

And what Joey had been unable to remember came rushing in. He was overwhelmed by the flood of memories.

"Don't be mad at me," Joey pleaded. He attempted to tear his gaze away from the monstrous rodent, from the eyes that bored into his head and filled his brain with hot coals. "I wasn't trying to hide the old man from you. It's just that sometimes I forget how things really are… that they're not really Papa."

A silent communication passed between them.

"It won't happen again. Please… I promise I'll get more of them for you. The streets are full of winos." Joey backed away, his halting steps backing up to a wall. He reached out a placating hand.

The eyes pinned him there, filled his entire world, filled it with fear and pain. He began shivering, sobbing for a breath that refused to come. His legs buckled and he saw the floor rush upward and slam into his face. Blood trickled from his busted nose, and when he tried to climb to his feet, his legs refused to obey. He began a frenzied dance, around and around, leaking wet black stains onto the wood… slowing, slowing… until a final shudder wracked his body.

Until darkness began taking him.

The boy looked up and saw the huge rat studying the pulse ticking in his throat. Slowly it reached toward him with claws that could disembowel another rat… paused… and soft as a whisper, gently brushed the hair out of his eyes.

Only now it wasn't a rat. Joey saw the man who held him, but Joey's eyes were dimming and he couldn't make out the man's face.

JOHN WARRICK GASPED AND STRUGGLED TO SEPARATE FROM THE DYING boy, but he couldn't. The night sounds outside the apartment ebbed and flowed in time with Joey's laboring heart. Stopped. Came once again. And then ceased as the boy's heart beat for the last time.

There was silence, a letting go. It was like a sigh in an empty room. All that Joey Estevez had been began drifting away. His fears, his hopes, his dreams.

John again tried to separate himself from the dead boy. Again he couldn't. His mouth opened in a soundless scream while he was pulled deeper and deeper into the blackness that was Joey's dying mind. John felt himself being sucked down, free-falling away from the light. His own heart began to slow. Missed a beat. The will to fight was melting away, and he knew it would be so easy to go along for the ride. His heart stuttered again, stopped, and, this time, it took much longer to resume.

The light was far away now, no bigger than a dime, growing smaller. Smaller. Images and sounds from Joey's life rushed past John, a fast-moving endless train with scenes from the boy's life splashed across the sides of the boxcars: Dirty rooms, darkened backseats of cars, grunts of men having sex with him, some of them angry, some of them crying, his mother singing a lullaby to him when he was very young, a park on a winter morning, trees covered with snow, pristine and white, achingly beautiful. Rain pounding on the roof. A fire crackling. The distant echoes mixed, lapped over each other like rippling water.

And grew quiet.

The light was now a pinprick on the skin of the vast night.

His heart stuttered one last time, stopped. He was letting go, the train was stopping for John.

But something deep inside of John Warrick rebelled. He bit down on his tongue and warm saltiness flooded the back of his throat, choking him and he awoke to—find himself lying on the floor. Rolling over onto his stomach, he tried to crawl to the bathroom before he threw up. He didn't make it. He lay face down on the beer-stained carpet and waited for the shaking to subside. His body was soaked with sweat, acrid and stinging. His terrified mind tried to sort out what he had just gone through while images flashed in and out of his mind. The train was still running and it still wanted him on board.

After a while he made it to his knees.

Most of what he had gone through was symbolic, John knew that. It couldn't be interpreted literally. Even so, what he had just seen with Joey defied all logic. He could make no sense out of it.

When he finally found enough strength to make it to the bathroom, he found more than just his bitten tongue. His nose was busted and his entire body was covered with red welts. Some of them were bleeding. The worst injury was the oozing slash across the top of his forehead. He looked as though someone had tried to scalp him.

CHAPTER THREE

John was too keyed up to sleep, so he eased the cue stick under the mattress and left his room. At three in the morning the parking lot was dead quiet, with only a few shadows chasing after the cars on the interstate. In the motel lobby, the night clerk sat behind the counter, asleep, bathed in the soft glow of the Coke machine, settled back in his chair with a paperback perched atop his protruding stomach. It rode there, a small schooner on an ocean of blue.

The night was clear and it looked as though they were going to get the first frost of the year. John was glad he was wearing the denim jacket that Louise had given him last Christmas. For a moment, he thought about calling her up. She would know what to do. But he didn't. Instead he fired up a cigarette and tried to think. He touched his nose. It was no longer bleeding, although the cold air made it sting. The welts were almost gone; the gash on his forehead was still oozing red.

What in God's name had he seen back there in his room?

Most times all he got in his visions were a few vague images, feelings of fear, sadness, lust. Nothing so detailed as this. Nothing so frightening. He could still feel those damned rats crawling around inside of him. Worse, he could feel that kid's heart stopping.

Had any of it been real or had he just picked up a little mental debris from some psychotic? What if he had seen an actual murder? Jesus, what was he going to do? He knew the streets he'd walked in the vision. They were just off the strip in Vegas. A lot of rough trade went on there. If you had the money you could get anything you wanted. Anything at all.

From one of the motel rooms he heard a woman laugh, and he knew he wanted to be around people. All this quiet was getting to him. He crushed out his cigarette and climbed into his old Jeep Cherokee. The first thing he did was to turn up the radio, even before he turned on the heat.

Most everything was closed at this hour of the morning, but he knew that Pop Turner's doughnut shop would be open, and the coffee there was always good and hot. He wanted coffee, lots of coffee. The thought of going back to his empty room and trying to sleep was out of the question. Maybe he could even negotiate a little female company. At this time of night, Pop's primarily catered to two groups; cops and hookers.

Both groups were well represented when he slid onto a stool at the Formica counter. A couple of the girls gave him the once-over as he ordered his first cup, but he found he wasn't that interested anymore. One of them wore perfume that smelled a lot like Joey Estevez's aftershave. It made him queasy.

Pop came over, poured the coffee. "You look a little rough, son. You want something to eat?"

John tested his bitten tongue and shook his head no.

"It's on the house," Pop said.

"No, that's okay, Pop. I got money." He pulled out a twenty and laid it on the counter. "Just keep that coffee coming."

The sun came up while John was on his seventh cup of coffee and second pack of smokes. He stared out the plate-glass window with red-rimmed eyes as the early morning traffic piled up. He envied the people who had normal jobs, someplace to go, someone to come home to. His prediction about the frost had been wrong, but he had made up his mind about what to do. He hoped it was a better call than the frost.

Pop gave him an understanding look when he asked for five dollars in quarters and made his way to the phone. He glanced at the clock before he dialed the Crowder Flats number. It was a little after six.

It rang four times. The voice that answered sounded a little harder than he remembered.

"Hello, Louise."

"John, is that you?" She seemed faintly surprised.

"Yeah, it's me. Sorry to bother you, but I wanted to catch you before you went to work. I need a favor."

The line went dead and then filled with laughter that sounded a little bitter. "I've got to hand it to you, John. You're one in a million. We haven't seen you in nearly a year, and you call at six o'clock in the morning to ask for a loan. Things have been a little tough around here lately. I can't loan you any more money. Amy's got tuition to pay for."

"Listen, I'll try to send you something. I—"

"Look, John, what do you want? I need to get to work. Frontier Days are coming up. Things are busy here."

"I just need some information. See if you can get one of your police buddies to see what he can find out about a kid from Vegas by the name of Joey Estevez."

"What's so special about him? You owe him money, too?"

"No... I think he was murdered."

There was silence for a beat. "Jesus Christ, John, what've you gotten yourself into this time?"

"Maybe something, maybe nothing. I don't know yet." He hesitated, looked around. Nobody was paying any attention to him. "Shit, Louise, I stole a pool cue from this guy over in Carruthers. And

I picked something up from it. Really weird crap. Stuff I couldn't make any sense out of. All I can be sure of is the kid's name, Joey Estevez, and that he's an under-aged male prostitute."

"Do you know how crazy this sounds? I could get into a lot of trouble. I'm just a dispatcher. You want me to go poking around in police business, just because you had another of your so-called psychic experiences?"

"Yes, I do. I've got to know if that kid's okay or not."

There was a brief pause. "I'm not making any promises, I'll see what I can do. Where are you staying?"

"The Milner in San Benito."

Louise laughed. "I thought they tore that place down years ago."

"Nope. It's still here, classy as ever. I couldn't get room twenty-three, though."

"You still remember the number after all these years?"

"Sure," he said, "you were the first girl I ever liked enough to spring for a room."

"That's what I like about you, John, you were always such a romantic." Her voice had lightened a little and he wondered if she was smiling. "You sure knew how to show a girl a good time on her prom night. Warm champagne in a cheap motel room."

"Hey, I was only eighteen. Do you know how long I had to save up for that room? I was so scared your old man would find out about us. You remember how he said he was going to have you dusted for fingerprints after I brought you home? He threatened to shoot my ass if he found any of mine on you. He was a cop. I believed him."

Louise laughed and, this time, there was no bitterness in it.

A young woman's voice sounded in the room, asking Louise who was on the phone. Louise said something to her, then came back on the line. "Look, I've got to go. If I have anything, I'll call you at seven tonight."

He held the line. "Louise…"

"Take care of yourself, John." The connection broke.

John picked up his remaining quarter and eased out the door. In the bright morning sun, with people swarming around him, the darkness inside his head didn't seem so real. He thought about

Louise on that long-ago prom night. The room might have been cheap but what had happened between them that night hadn't been.

Pop yelled something at him that he couldn't quite make out. He waved as he climbed into his Jeep.

Before John could pull out, Pop ambled out into the parking lot and waved him down. The old man held a white sack in his hand. "You weren't gonna run off without taking some of my doughnuts, were you?" He handed the sack over to John, studying the younger man's face. "Hope everything works out for you, son. Quit leading with your chin."

"Much obliged, Pop."

When he got back to his room, he was too wired to sleep so he turned on the TV.

THE PHONE PULLED HIM OUT OF A HEAVY SLEEP AND HE HAD TO CRAWL across the bed to answer it. The room was dark, but he could make out a white shape on the sheets. Pop's doughnuts lay beside him, smashed. He mumbled his name into the mouthpiece.

"It's Louise. Damn it, you gave me a scare. It's seven o'clock. The phone rang nine times before you picked up. I thought something had happened to you."

"Slow down, Louise. I'm fine. Did you find out anything about Joey Estevez?"

"A lot more than I wanted to know. You were right, he was a male prostitute and he was murdered in Vegas two weeks ago." Her voice filled with sadness. "He was only fifteen... three years younger than Amy."

"How did it happen?"

"He was stabbed, oh God, John—he was stabbed fifty-three times. And then somebody scalped him."

John thought about the rats, the sharp pains that the boy had felt all over his body, the slash on his forehead. It was beginning to make sense. "Where was he found?"

"Let's see." She paused to consult something.

"It was in a second-story walk-up," John said, watching it happen again inside his head. "They found him lying on a bed, and he was dressed all in black. Black high-tops, black jeans, and a black leather jacket."

"Stop it, John. You're scaring me."

"I'm sorry. I didn't mean to. Something else happened in that room, something that I couldn't get a fix on. Is there anything else?"

"Well, there was one thing…"

"Please, Louise, I've got to know."

"I don't know if this will mean anything to you. There was too much blood in the room, even for a stabbing. But maybe they're wrong about that. They said," she hesitated, "there wasn't any blood left in him. It was all on the walls and floor."

"Are you sure?"

"Yes, the report said something blew every drop of blood out of his body."

CHAPTER FOUR

The bar was a cheap bar in a cheap part of town.

The bar was called The Watering Hole. The town was called Vegas.

Inside the bar, the cigarette smoke was thick enough to cut with a knife. Nobody seemed to mind. Three people, so old they were sexless, were feeding quarters to the one-armed bandits against the wall, making mechanical love to the machines. Their money went in. Foreplay began. The arm went down. Back up. Holding them at bay. No consummation between flesh and blood and metal this time.

The expressions on the faces of the slot players matched those of the machines they courted: cold, hard. They seemed to have no expectations of winning. And yet they kept at their chore with dogged determination, as though they had forgotten why they were doing it.

On a raised stage, three girls were dancing, moving in and out of the dimness with practiced indifference, thrusting their naked bodies at the crowd without any semblance of passion. They couldn't even fake it anymore. Their faces were slack, without emotion. Slack faces stared back at them from out of the dark. Most had more interest in their drinks than the girls.

All but one, Billy Two Hats.

Billy, who went by the name Billy T, was dressed in jeans, a white chambray shirt, and a denim jacket. A snow white Stetson rested atop his head, snakeskin boots adorned his feet, making him look like an old-timey Saturday matinee cowboy. Nothing could have been further from the truth—the only horse Billy T had ever been on was the kind you put in your arm.

Billy T was a full-blooded Apache.

And something rare for an Indian, a full-blooded psychopath.

Billy T was playing nine ball against some slumming yuppie, and Billy T was getting his ass kicked up one side of the table and down the other. He knew why, his concentration was off. The girls on the stage were the reason. Billy T hadn't had a girl in over two months; however that was a situation he hoped to remedy tonight.

A few of the female patrons gave him a speculative glance, and he could have had any one of them.

But Billy T didn't want his women willing.

Billy T wasn't bent that way.

The yuppie in the expensive suit sank the nine ball and smiled. Earlier he had said he was a banker. He had a banker's smile. It looked like the one on the face of the man who had evicted Billy T's mom from her house when Billy T was ten. It looked like the smile on the faces of the men who had come out of his mom's bedroom after working out a deal on the rent of whatever shithole they'd been living in.

"That makes twenty you owe me," the man with the banker's smile said. He motioned to one of the waitresses for another scotch-and-soda. "How about you, chief, more firewater?" He smiled to show he meant no harm by the remark.

Billy T shook his head no. "We gonna shoot another game?"

"You going to pay me the twenty?"

Billy T laid the money on the table.

"You want to raise the stakes?" the banker asked. The smile was back as though it had never left.

Billy T had already lost a hundred, a hundred he couldn't afford. "Fuck you," he said. "And you can take that to the bank."

The smile left the well-fed face. "What's the matter, chief, the stakes too rich for your blood?"

The Apache considered smashing his cue stick across the man's face, but he didn't want to get kicked out of the bar. One of the girls on the stage had caught his eye. He looked at the white man on the other side of the pool table and smiled. "You call me chief again and I'm going to cut your balls off." Billy T smiled to show he meant no harm by the remark.

The fleshy middle-aged man braced his back against a wooden column and gripped his pool cue. The five scotch-and-sodas he had consumed in the last hour gave him all the courage he needed. "Is that right? Well come on, chief, cut my balls off."

Billy T risked a quick look over his left shoulder to see where the bouncers were. Luck found Billy T for the first time tonight. They were busy trying to throw out a burly construction worker who had kept complaining the drinks were watered. There was plenty of time to take care of this white asshole.

Reaching down into his boot, Billy T produced a knife. Thin and sharp, perfectly balanced. Made for cutting. Or throwing.

He hefted the knife in his hand, his eyes those of a lover caressing his loved one. "Say good-bye to your balls, you white motherfucker."

The white guy raised the cue stick to hit Billy T.

Across the room, the construction worker got in a good shot and knocked down one of the bouncers. Blood spurted. The crowd cheered.

Billy T laughed, drew back his arm. And threw.

The knife was a smoky sliver of light, too fast to follow. There was a soft snicking sound as the blade buried itself in the wooden column. It was as though the knife had appeared there all by itself.

The white guy looked down at the blade that nestled in the juncture between his legs and then looked up at the man who had thrown it. His expression was one of wonder, like that of a small child who has just seen something magical happen. He reached down and touched the knife. His hand came back smeared with red. "You cut my balls off." He looked at his hand, covered with his blood, while he considered the implications. His blood was warm and red and he could feel it running down his legs. "You cut my balls off," he repeated.

Billy T stepped around the table and caught the guy a second before his eyes rolled up and he fainted dead away. Grasping him under the arms, Billy T half carried, half dragged him over to an empty table and sat him down. The banker slumped forward on the table as though drunk.

"Relax, pal," Billy T said to the unconscious man. "Your balls weren't as big as you thought they were. I only nicked 'em."

The fight with the construction worker was still under way and nobody was paying the slightest attention to what was going on in the corner. The crowd was still cheering the construction worker, who was beginning to tire. Billy T lifted the banker's wallet, then retrieved the knife and slipped it back in his boot. The whole thing hadn't taken more than ten or fifteen seconds tops. Billy T felt good for the first time in a long time. This was going to be his lucky night, he could feel it in his bones.

Finally the bouncers got the construction worker out the door, and the waitress came over to the pool table with a scotch-and-soda. She saw the banker passed out on the table. "Shit, what am I supposed to do with this?"

Billy T pulled out a twenty and laid it on her tray before picking up the scotch-and-soda and downing it in a single gulp. "Keep the change," he said.

The waitress regarded him with new interest. Her interest was, of course, fueled by the twenty he had just given her. "You need anything, sugar, you just ask for me, Josie. I know how to show a cowboy a good time."

Billy T looked at the slightly heavy body of Josie and felt a faint stirring of heat in his stomach, but she wasn't what he wanted tonight. He looked past the waitress, at the stage where the blonde with the creamy white body was gyrating for the drunken businessmen. Her eyes were hooded, her lips were moist. And her expression was bored, completely indifferent. There were ways to remove indifference in a woman.

The dancer was the most desirable woman Billy T had ever seen. He was going to have her. Tonight.

He placed his foot on a chair and adjusted his jeans over his boots, letting his fingers touch the handle of the knife, then the blade, sliding over the sharp edge until blood appeared. Touching his bloody fingers to his lips, he smiled.

Josie saw where Billy T was looking and her expression went hard. "She doesn't go out with the customers."

"Really," he said with feigned casualness. "Who does she go out with?"

"I don't know," Josie snapped. "Why don't you ask her yourself?"

"Maybe I will." Billy T produced another twenty. "Bring me a beer, will you, Josie?"

"How about your friend there?" She indicated the passed-out banker. "He need anything?"

"Yeah, a change of underwear."

It was a comment that Josie had heard too many times to find amusing. She snorted and went to get Billy T his beer.

The Apache who looked like a cowboy turned his attention to the blonde dancer on the stage. She turned her head, just the barest hint, and smiled. At him. Maybe it was his imagination. No, he was sure of it—she had smiled at him. Her expression went vacant again, and Billy T felt the heat in the pit of his stomach climb another notch.

The beer that Josie brought him only fueled the heat, like gasoline on smoldering coals. He hadn't wanted a woman this bad since Abilene. Images of blood and sweating, heaving bodies filled his mind, taking him far away from where he was.

Taking him back to Abilene.

The girl had been so young, so innocent. At least she had been before that night.

If only the girl hadn't screamed.

He had been hitchhiking outside of Abilene when the old Mexican couple had stopped and picked him up in a van that smelled like chickens in the summer heat.

They had a granddaughter, sixteen, pretty, on the verge of womanhood, and there was no way for them to know that Billy Two Hats had already killed nine other women, cutting their throats with the knife he carried in his boot.

They were simple, trusting people who went to church every Sunday and put their faith in God. A smile and a joke or two got Billy T invited to their house for dinner, a room for the night. It was easy. It always was. After all, he was charming and funny, and he looked like a matinee cowboy. Hell, even the family dog liked him.

Later on in the night, long after everyone had gone to bed, Billy T went to the girl's room. Her name was Maria. He stood there in the warm dark, savoring the moment, memorizing every detail, for he would play this night back in his mind for countless nights to come. Remembering was important. It was the only link to immortality. Even after Maria was dead, after he killed her, she wouldn't really be dead because she would live in his mind. Forever.

The room was a mix of innocence and worldliness—teddy bears and posters of bare chested movie stars, perfume and candy. Standing over her, he let it wash over him.

She had been fine after he cut her with the knife, really fine, doing everything he had asked. Anything to save her life. At the end, used and limp, she had seen something in his eyes. She had known he was going to kill her anyway, and that was when she had tried to scream. He had cut her throat while he held her close and kissed her, tasting her blood as it poured from her mouth.

Then he killed the grandparents. That hadn't been as much fun as the girl. They had barely struggled at all, departing this world with small bubbling sighs as though they were secretly glad to be going.

He made sure the dog was fed before he left.

Last call sounded, shaking Billy T out of his reverie. His eyes focused and he saw the dancer on the stage was staring directly at him. Their gazes entwined, locked, and for a moment Billy T was disoriented, almost paralyzed, by the cold he saw there. Her eyes were the color of winter ice. This was crazy, he knew, but he had the feeling she knew what he had been thinking about, that she had somehow seen into his soul.

The scary part was the feeling she approved.

Billy T shook his head, trying to rid himself of the fear that had unexpectedly taken root. This wasn't the way it went down in Billy Two Hats' world. Women were scared of him, not the other way around. Wiping the sweat from his lip, he took another drink of beer and looked again at the dancer. This time his eyes went no higher than her creamy white breasts. He told himself the reason was he liked her body. That he was committing it to memory. Not that he was afraid.

After a couple more sips of his beer, he came to believe it. Almost.

The lights in the bar came up and the dancers began exiting the stage amid a smattering of applause. The one Billy T wanted was the last to leave. She paused, her eyes scanning the crowd one final time, coming to rest on Billy T. Her face held no expression he could interpret, yet the mocking heat of her eyes taunted him. A drunken trucker in the crowd yelled something obscene at her, but she ignored him.

Billy T tried to meet her gaze, and yet he couldn't quite bring himself to do it. She was even better looking in the light. Flawless, unmarked skin. White, so very white. Compared to her, the rest of the dancers were coarse, beneath contempt.

The dancer turned to go.

Then she paused and looked over her shoulder. She silently mouthed a single word.

It was aimed at Billy T. It was clear and distinct.

The word was Abilene.

Billy T went cold inside.

The dancer made a slashing motion beneath her throat before turning and vanishing from the stage, leaving Billy T staring openmouthed after her. This couldn't be happening. No one knew about Abilene.

About the rape.

About the murder.

Committed by him. Billy T gritted his teeth, his jaw muscles bunching and unbunching in silent panic. They looked like snakes crawling beneath his skin. Rape and murder in Texas still carried the death penalty. He'd had to cut that Mexican girl's throat, it had been the only way he could stop her from screaming. If they connected him to her murder, her grandparents' murder, they would put him to death, and Billy Two Hats couldn't imagine the world without himself in it.

Things became clear; he had to kill the dancer. She'd signed her own death warrant. And yet her saying Abilene didn't make any sense. If she knew about Abilene, then she knew what kind of man he was. She had to know he would kill her. That not only didn't make sense, it was downright crazy. His head began to hurt as he tried to think. Suddenly he brightened. He'd simply misread what she had said to him, yeah, that was it. That was the only answer. Anything else was impossible.

Billy T watched the bouncers drag the unconscious banker to the door. A smear of blood trailed after him. Nobody noticed. "Hey, cowboy," someone called out.

Billy T turned, saw Josie standing there with a note in her hand. She walked over and tucked it in his shirt pocket. "It's from your friend on the stage," Josie said. Her voice held a touch of petulance that she was unable to hide.

Billy T fished the note out and opened it. *Meet me by your car*. It was in bright red lipstick. It was signed *Abilene*.

The room tilted, and soured beer crowded the back of Billy T's throat.

"What's the matter, cowboy?" Josie asked. "You look a little pale all of a sudden. This could be your lucky night. You should be flattered. Juliana's danced here a month and I never even seen her say more than three words to any guy, let alone ask one out."

This was going from bad to worse, Billy T decided. Now Josie knew he was meeting the dancer and she had read the note, which meant she could connect him with Abilene. He wanted to slash Josie's throat so bad that, for a moment, he could actually see it bleeding.

He reached over and brushed a finger across her neck. "Anybody ever tell you sticking your nose where it doesn't belong could get it cut off?" he asked in a quiet voice.

Josie tried to push his hand away. "You'd better save the sweet talk for Juliana. I'm not interested."

But Billy T's hand was not so easily dislodged; he gripped her throat and pulled her close. "I don't know what's going on here, but one thing's for sure, I'm not going anywhere with that bitch dancer. And I never been to Abilene in my life. Is this some kind of little joke you two cooked up? Is it?"

"Abilene?" Josie asked, confused.

Josie saw sweat beading up on the cowboy's lip. The guy seemed on the edge of a meltdown. A tiny push could put him over.

Josie, frightened now, shook her head no. The guy's hand was a steel clamp on her throat and she couldn't speak, couldn't breathe. His fingers tightened, steel cables that dug into her flesh. She felt darkness crowding the edges of her vision. Then as suddenly as he grabbed her, he turned loose. Josie stumbled back. Her leg struck a chair, knocked it over. The sound was a slap in the now quiet bar. There was no one to help her. They were alone except for the bartender cleaning up at the other end of the room.

Josie realized this cowboy could kill her if he wanted to. The crazy bastard was quick as a snake. She stood very still, her hand on her bruised throat, trying to breathe. "Mister, I don't know what you're talking about. I never said anything about Abilene. I—"

"Shut up," Billy T said in a voice barely louder than a whisper. "Shut up. For the love of God, shut up. I don't want to hurt you."

His white chambray shirt was soaked with sweat now, and he gave off the scent of a hunted animal—acrid, bitter—and Josie wondered how she could have ever found him attractive. She felt like he didn't even see her now, or maybe she thought, with a flash of intuition, he was looking at someone else. Someone from his past. Whoever it was, Josie was glad she wasn't that person.

By an inhuman effort of will, Billy T pulled himself together and tucked his rage out of sight. His face relaxed slowly. It was like watching ripples in a lake disappear, leaving no trace behind of the violence that had caused them. "Sorry, Josie." He smiled. "I didn't mean to scare you. I guess I've had a little too much to drink."

The sound of clinking glassware carried across the room. A gust of cool air pushed at the cigarette smoke that hung in the room, caused it to swirl.

Josie nodded numbly, trying on a smile for size. It didn't fit. Reaching into his jacket, Billy T pulled out another twenty and handed it to Josie.

She looked at the bill as if it might bite her, but she finally reached out and took it. "Thanks," she said, her voice a rough whisper. "What's this for, a bribe?"

"It's for doing me a little favor. I want you to tell Juliana that I can't meet her tonight."

At Billy T's words, Josie felt herself smiling despite her pain. The cowboy wasn't interested. She couldn't wait to see the look on Ms. Hot-Shit dancer's face.

The waitress headed for the dancers' dressing room.

Before she knocked, she cast a quick look back at the lounge. The cowboy from Abilene was gone.

THE DRESSING ROOM OF THE WATERING HOLE WASN'T MUCH BIGGER than a closet and it smelled of stale perfume, sweat, and sex. It had a sort of false cheeriness imparted by the bright lights that lined the U-shaped mirror. Two of the lights were burned out, giving the impression of a gap-toothed grin. Hairbrushes and cheap silver compacts lined the tables, along with a set of false eyelashes that looked like dead spiders in the dim light. A radio played country music in the background.

"Pretty glamorous, huh?" Juliana said, and laughed. The blonde dancer had a husky voice that came from too much scotch and too many cigarettes.

In spite of herself, Josie laughed back.

The other two dancers had already gone for the night. Only Juliana remained, waiting, brushing her blonde mane with studied indifference. She wore a sleek black dress that cost more than Josie made in a month of waiting tables. Josie tried to stop the resentment that seemed to color her life lately. It wasn't Juliana's fault that she was beautiful.

"What did the cowboy say when you gave him the note?" Juliana asked, studying Josie in the mirror. Most men found Juliana's voice sexy as hell, even when she told them to drop dead.

Josie felt a pang of satisfaction when she said, "He said he wasn't interested. He said he had to go."

Juliana considered Josie's words. "Did he say anything else?" She seemed slightly amused, slightly bored.

Josie hesitated. "He said something about Abilene, something about he had never been there before." Josie touched her still-bruised throat. "Then he got all worked up. I thought he was going to hurt me."

"I'm sorry," Juliana said. "I didn't mean to get you involved in this. I should have given him the note myself."

"No, he might have hurt you. I saw a knife in his boot."

Juliana lit up a Mexican cigarette, took a drag, held it; let tendrils of smoke curl lazily from her nostrils while she continued studying Josie. There was something reptilian and incredibly ancient in the hooded eyes. She exhaled and somehow managed to make it look elegant. "You're not making this up, are you?"

"No, I'm not. Look Juliana, I don't know you or anything, but if that guy comes back in here, don't mess with him. There was something wrong with his eyes. They were crazy."

"Do you think he's a killer?"

Josie started to nod then changed her mind, feeling faintly foolish. "You should have seen the way he looked at me."

"How many people do you think he's killed?"

Josie had the feeling Juliana was toying with her, that Juliana knew more about this guy than she was saying. She certainly knew enough to throw him into a rage.

"All I know is, he was fine until I gave him your note," Josie said. "What did you put in it?"

"Nothing. I simply told him to meet me later."

"Knock it off, Juliana, you put something in your note that scared him half to death. I don't know what kind of games you're into, but keep me out of them from now on. Okay?"

"You don't like games?" Juliana asked.

Josie shook her head no. "They make me tired. I had an ex-husband who liked to play games."

Juliana looked away and her voice was slightly wistful. "That's a shame, Josie. Games are the only things that make this long life bearable."

It was Josie's turn to laugh. "You talk like you're old. You can't be more than... what... thirty?"

"Oh, I'm older than that. A lot older."

The words hung in the air.

Josie wanted to ask how old, yet something stopped her. She had the feeling that if she asked, Juliana just might tell her. And Josie thought that might be a mistake. A horrible mistake. The hooded eyes peered at her from the mirror. This conversation had started out friendly enough, yet it had somehow gone wrong. Josie felt a slight tingle of fear. At the moment she wanted nothing more than to be back at her apartment, taking a hot bath, trying to wash away all traces of The Watering Hole.

"Look, Juliana, I appreciate you pretending to be one of the girls and everything, but I'm feeling kind of ancient, myself." Josie pulled off a high heel and began massaging her foot. "Twelve hour shift."

"Why don't you ask Ralph if you can be one of the dancers?" Juliana asked. "You're pretty enough."

Josie actually felt herself blush. "Thanks. I tried to once. I made it through the audition but I couldn't walk out on the stage naked. It all seemed so... so..."

"Cheap," Juliana finished.

"Yes, cheap." Josie's face went redder. Even so, she didn't turn away.

A definite trace of amusement crossed the blonde dancer's face. "You're very unhappy, aren't you, Josie?"

This time, Josie did look away. "Look, Juliana, it's getting late and I've really got to go."

"You don't like men very much, do you?"

Josie felt on uncertain ground. "What are you talking about? I was married for three years."

"It wasn't your husband's fault that he left you."

Josie turned to go, but the blonde dancer's words stopped her, pulled her around. She waited.

The dancer turned from the mirror and looked at her with icy blue eyes that saw too much. "Oh, you remember, don't you? You were in high school and your girlfriend spent the night, only your big brother came home from L.A., and he took the spare bedroom. So you and your girlfriend had to share your little cot in the basement. Shall I go on?"

"Stop it." Josie was no longer blushing, she had gone very pale. "Please, stop it." She stared in horror and her legs, which were so thick and strong, threatened for the first time to buckle. "How could you know that?" A mascara-coated tear, like a dark beetle, scuttled down through her too-thick makeup, leaving behind a ghostly trail. "No one knows about that night."

"Don't worry, it'll be our little secret." Juliana began peeling off her black dress. She wore nothing beneath it.

Josie stared, unable to look away from the naked dancer. She saw that Juliana had something dark smeared between her perfect breasts. Mascara? No, it wasn't mascara. It was…

"A feathered serpent," Juliana finished for her. "How do you like it?"

The dancer moved closer.

"What are you doing?" Josie asked. She began backing away, moving toward the door, which seemed a million miles away. "That was a mistake what I did that night. I was only a kid, a lonely, frightened kid. I don't go in for…"

"You can't even say it, can you?" Juliana grabbed Josie by the hair and held her. "You think I want to make love to you?" Juliana seemed amused by the thought. "I'm afraid you wouldn't be very good at it."

Josie tried to pull away, but the dancer was strong. Very strong.

Juliana pulled Josie closer. Until their mouths were only inches apart.

"Don't. Please don't," Josie said.

"I'm sorry, Josie, I have to." Juliana leaned slowly forward and brushed her lips against Josie's cold, trembling mouth.

Josie felt the caress of the warm lips, then a sting. She touched her throat. Looked at Juliana, wonderingly. She tried to speak. And couldn't.

There was a knife in Juliana's hand.

There was red on it.

Josie wanted to speak. She wanted to ask about the knife, about the red on it, the red that looked like blood. The words wouldn't form.

"I've cut your throat," Juliana said. "You'll be dead in about a minute or so. I'm sorry, but I had to do it. You know what the cowboy looks like. My mistake. I can't have you going to the police and giving them his description."

Josie again tried to speak, even though all that came from her mouth were wet sounds that didn't sound like words at all. The pain was a distant burning, not connected to her at all. Josie wanted very much to touch her throat, but, if she touched it, she might discover that the hurt was real and she couldn't deal with that. Her hands hung at her sides, limp, undecided.

Somewhere in the distance a siren came and went. No help was coming. No one would answer her question, the one small, stupid question that wouldn't let go of her. Why had Juliana taken off the dress?

Josie felt her heart beat and blood spurted out, splashing onto Juliana, rolling down the dancer's white breasts, down her legs, pooling at Juliana's feet.

Understanding came as Josie stared at the pool of red growing on the floor. Juliana had taken off the dress, not to make love to her—Juliana simply didn't want to get blood on it.

The dancer pulled Josie over to the sink, bent her head down and held her there like a sick child who's throwing up on the floor.

Josie wore only one high heel and her feet beat a lopsided, manic tattoo on the tiled floor as she fought to get away. Her struggles were useless. The sink was filling with her own blood, choking her. Her other shoe flew off and the tattoo went silent.

"Just relax," Juliana soothed. "It'll be over soon. If you fight, you'll only make it harder."

Josie began crying, and a strange gurgling sound caused by the hole in her throat filled the room.

"Don't carry on so. This is for the best." Juliana raised the waitress from the blood-filled sink and held her close, began rocking her gently back and forth. "This will be over soon, Josie. Very soon." Juliana began singing a lullaby, her husky voice surprisingly tender.

The blood from Josie's throat was coming out much slower now. Josie felt tired, very tired. She laid her head on Juliana's shoulder and closed her eyes. The dancer's skin was warm and she smelled of some exotic perfume, sandalwood and roses, very faint, very expensive. Josie felt Juliana stroking her hair like her mother used to do when she was little.

Out of dimming eyes, Josie saw something strange in the mirror, a woman covered with blood holding her. Josie decided it was all a bad dream. She had been scared for a moment, but she wasn't scared anymore. Her mother was holding her tight, just the way her mother always did whenever she had bad dreams. She laid her head on the warm shoulder and went back to sleep.

Finally, the blood slowed to a trickle. Ceased.

Josie shuddered, gave a small sigh.

Juliana gently sat the dying girl on a chair in front of the makeup table, looking away from the wound that circled the throat like a glittering black pearl necklace.

"You would never have been happy, Josie. Your guilt was unbearable for you." Juliana sat down beside the waitress and lit up another cigarette. "Guilt can be a terrible thing. Believe me, I know."

Josie took in one last dying breath, exhaled, and Juliana breathed it in, her eyes growing soft. Their lips touched for a long moment. Something passed between them.

Juliana arranged the dead waitress in front of the mirror. "You were so lonely, so frightened, Josie. I felt it the first time we spoke." She patted some blush onto Josie's white face, giving it a faint semblance of life. "Now you're with me. With us," she amended. She blended in the blush until it appeared natural. "You have to be careful with blush. Too much and you end up looking cheap." Working with a tissue, Juliana repaired the damage to Josie's mascara, blotting away the tears and the dark smudges. "There, you look much better now."

The radio still played softly in the background. The DJ came on and announced the time, 3:27 A.M. It was getting late; still Juliana took a moment to brush the dead girl's hair, arranging it so that it covered the wound on the throat. "Now you won't have to feel guilty anymore. Or lonely. You can be at peace."

Juliana stubbed out her cigarette in one smooth motion and stood. "But enough of this girl talk. I, too, have things to do." She stepped into the shower and let the hot water sluice away the red stickiness that covered her. Then she put on her dress and walked out of the bar and into the night.

BILLY TWO HATS SAT IN HIS STOLEN 'VETTE CONVERTIBLE AND WATCHED The Watering Hole with as much patience as he could muster. The side street was dark, thanks to the lights he had busted earlier. Leaning back, he listened to the night. He paid attention to what it said. The night was his friend and it whispered things to Billy T, things meant only for his ears.

In the distance the glitter of neon pulsed and danced to its own secret rhythm, fueled by money and sex. Billy T knew all about rhythms. They were tides in the blood, ebbing and flowing, carrying secret messages. All a man had to do was listen to them and they would tell him what to do.

They told Billy T to wait.

While Billy T waited, he did some thinking.

The knife in his hand sank into the leather seat beside him with monotonous regularity. There was a problem. Billy T was caught between the proverbial rock and hard place. He had to do something different, something he had never done before; he had to kill two women in one night. Changes in his normal operating procedure made him extremely nervous. Waiting wasn't helping matters any, either.

No one had come out of the bar in the last twenty minutes. The last one had been the bartender. That left only the waitress and that bitch dancer. What were they doing in there?

The time crawled by, making Billy T more nervous. He watched a starving mongrel knock over a garbage can in an alley across the street. Jesus, he hated to see a dog starve. He loved dogs. Another can went over. Bottles and cans rolled out with a clatter. Then silence resumed.

Billy T's knife sank into the seat.

The dog rooted through the scattered contents, searching.

The knife sank into the seat.

No food in the garbage cans. The dog came out of the alley, trotted down the street, disappearing.

The knife sank into the seat.

And Billy T froze. There was a second knife—pressed against his throat.

"Hello, Billy T, you waiting for me?"

Billy T slowly turned and looked at Juliana. "No, I was waiting for Josie."

"Well, you can quit waiting. I killed her about ten minutes ago. I cut her throat."

He weighed his chances of killing the dancer.

As though she were reading his mind, the knife in her hand sliced into his throat, just enough to bring a trickle of blood, but not enough to seriously hurt him. It slid down his collar, ruining a brand-new white chambray shirt that had cost him nearly a hundred dollars. He weighed rage against caution. Caution won.

His hand came away from his knife in the car seat and he felt naked, alone. "What do you want from me?" His voice trembled just a bit.

"Thrills, Billy boy, thrills." She reached across him, the blade at his throat never wavering, and scooped up his knife, threw it into the darkness. Her warm flesh was close and Billy T felt a surge of desire despite his fear.

Within seconds he had an erection.

"Is that another knife in your pocket?" Juliana asked in a husky voice. "Or are you just glad to see me? I guess in your case it's the same thing." With a laugh, she crawled in the car like some kind of boneless snake, but instead of taking the seat next to him, she sat in his lap, facing him. Her tight black dress rode up over her hips, revealing she wore nothing beneath. She ground her pelvis against the bulge in his jeans and the car was suddenly filled with the musky scent of her sex.

Billy T realized she was enjoying this, that it was turning her on. He stared at the creamy white flesh he had fantasized about all night, longing to touch it. The knife in her hand maintained its steady pressure on his throat.

Waves of desire rolled over Billy T, making his tongue thick. "Why are you doing this to me?" he managed at last.

"Think of yourself as Disneyland," she answered, "and you're the E ticket ride."

"Are you going to kill me?"

"Do you mean like all the women you killed?"

Billy T felt his erection die.

"You're wondering how I know that," Juliana said in answer to his unspoken question. "It's in the blood, Billy boy, it's all in the blood. I smelled death on you the moment your pretty-boy face walked into the joint." She continued rubbing her almost-naked body against him, causing him to groan with fear and desire.

Billy T started to reach for her, but the knife never left his throat. It pressed down harder. More of his blood eased onto his collar while his powerful hands lay by his sides, clenching and unclenching, unable to do anything.

"Are you going to kill me?" he repeated. This time his question sounded more like a statement.

She took his white Stetson from his head and put it on. "I'm not going to kill you... if you're a good boy. I've got uses for you."

He considered her words. "You want me to kill someone for YOU."

"Something like that." Juliana's body started shaking and for a second he thought she was frightened, or maybe just cold, but then he realized she was laughing. "I want you to kill lots of people for me, Billy T. Lots of people. But first, we need to get to know each other a little better."

Still laughing, she leaned forward.

Maybe to kiss him.

Maybe to kill him.

Billy T decided this was the best chance he was going to get. He grabbed her by her long blonde hair and yanked backward with all his strength. Her head hit the steering wheel. The knife flashed as she blindly stabbed at him. The white Stetson that she had taken from him slipped over her eyes and that was the only thing that saved his life.

Billy T jerked his head to the side and the blade slid past his face, grazing his throat again before he managed to get hold of her wrist. He twisted.

The knife spun from her hand, disappearing into the darkness of the car floorboard. He tried to hold on to her, but she was too quick. Too strong. Her elbow, or maybe it was his elbow, hit the power on the radio, causing it to come on. It was thunderous, loud enough to shatter eardrums. As they wrestled for the knife, her naked hip brushed the scan button, causing the stations to leapfrog, sliding up and down the band, country music, pop, heavy metal, an advertisement for weddings. "Don't live in sin," a sonorous voice admonished. "Quit your fornicating and come on down to Uncle Ed's Marriage Emporium and do the right thing, the Christian thing—"

She rolled off his lap, reaching down, hands feeling for the knife, and he again grabbed her by the hair, tried to pull her back into the car seat. He wasn't fast enough. Not nearly fast enough. She had found the knife.

His hand was suddenly on fire. She'd cut him.

This was beyond comprehension. No one had ever cut him before and this woman had cut him four times. The knife flashed again, turning his hand into burning agony. He held on, slowly raising up her head. Even in the dim light he could see she was enjoying this. Her eyes held a wild glow.

The knife caught his arm, cutting through his new custom-made denim jacket. Another three hundred bucks gone.

He punched her, a short vicious shot to the mouth, and he felt her lips spread across her white teeth. Her eyes went out of focus and the knife was his. He pulled it from her limp hand, held it beneath her chin.

"I should cut your throat right now," Billy T said. He was breathing heavily.

Juliana's eyes focused and she wiped the corner of her mouth, leaving a red stain on the back of her hand. "That's not what you want to do." She licked the blood off her hand, reminding him of a cat grooming itself. If she was afraid, it didn't show. In fact the rougher it got the more she seemed to enjoy it.

"I want some answers." Billy T grasped her by the hair and pulled her to a sitting position.

"What do you want to know, Billy boy?"

"Just one thing. How do you know about Abilene?"

"You wouldn't believe me if I told you."

"Try me," he answered, showing her the knife. "You'd be surprised at what I believe."

She smiled and he cut her to show that he meant business, nothing personal, just a small cut on her face. Women didn't like to have their faces marked. The cut should have been enough to wipe that smug smile off her face; instead it only made her smile wider. She leaned forward and pressed her mouth against his, and Billy T felt the heat from her, rolling off in waves. This woman was like nothing he had ever known; she was musk and exotic perfume, overpowering, and it was making the blood thunder inside his head, carrying him along on a tide of desire to some distant, unfamiliar shore.

He fought. Struggling like a rabbit in a snare.

Billy T had never wanted a woman the way he wanted this woman. He answered her kiss and tasted the blood in her mouth from where he had struck her.

Her legs locked around him as she pressed herself closer. They were almost melded together.

There was something frightening about her need, something that went beyond mere sex. He tried to pry her loose, but her long legs easily held him, tightening, until he realized she might break his back. He was having trouble breathing. She wouldn't release him from her kiss, holding his tongue with her teeth.

He jabbed her with the knife and she released his tongue, laughing. Her hands slid beneath his shirt, tearing it, stripping him to the waist.

Billy T wanted to be inside her, but she held him at bay, handling him as if he were some inexperienced teenager.

Her teasing was driving him wild. The radio was playing heavy metal, all bass and drums, pulsing to the blood tides that were crashing inside his head, so loud that he barely heard her when she spoke. "Do you know where sex takes place, Billy T?" She grabbed him by the hair and pulled his head back so she could look into his eyes. "Where it really takes place?"

Billy T could only look at her, unable to speak.

"In the mind." She stroked his dark hair. "It's all in the mind."

The cold night air caressed him, drying his sweaty skin, causing the cuts on his throat to sting.

Still gripping him by the hair, Juliana pulled his face close and placed her mouth against his mouth, biting his lip. Her mouth moved down. More bites.

For a moment, he thought something was wrong with her teeth. They were too long. Too sharp. Must be the light, he told himself. She smiled, opened herself.

Billy T entered her.

And found she was cold inside.

No, not really cold, just cooler than a woman should be, and Billy T felt a slight shock. Her skin was feverishly hot to the touch. He didn't find the contrast pleasant. If he wasn't more than a little drunk, he might have wondered why that was. It was like making love to a dead woman.

Then her hands were on him, touching him, driving all conscious thought from his mind. Her tongue probed his throat. Going deep. Deeper. And then still deeper. Warmth and ecstasy flowed into his body, causing him to groan. This was pleasure beyond drugs, beyond sex, beyond anything he had ever known or could imagine. Even killing didn't compare.

Voices he had never heard before cried out inside his mind as wave after wave of sensation shot through him. This was the best sex he'd ever had, multiplied by thousands, building, building, as though he were picking up on orgasms from the biggest gang bang in history, and it was all happening right inside his mind, that somehow he was wired into all of their nervous systems at one time and he was feeling everything they were feeling.

The pleasure fed itself, eating him alive.

Then it was beyond pleasure, beyond pain. He was drowning in white-hot sensation, of desire. Of insatiable need. His mind overloaded, began shutting down, and still there was no escape. His heart fluttered, stopped.

Her tongue went deeper still, bringing him back from his dark shore. Bringing him back from death.

Billy T gagged, tried to pull back.

But something connected him to Juliana.

Something black and shiny.

It had that bright, copper smell that Billy T had smelled on the women he had killed.

It was blood.

Billy T tried to scream. He wanted very much to scream. But he couldn't utter a sound. His throat was paralyzed like the rest of him, coated with fire, ice, and the taste of dead things. Whatever was inside his throat was alive. And now it was moving. Coursing through his veins. He could feel it. Like fire ants, it now left agony in its wake. It was alien and it was crawling around inside him, reaching up into his brain, exploring, reading all his secrets, knowing everything that made Billy Two Hats who he was. He tried to pull away, to hide.

There was no place to go.

Finally it found what it was looking for.

The part of Billy T's brain that held the memories of the nine women he had raped and murdered.

For the next hour, in the front seat of his stolen 'Vette, he relived those memories with whatever was inside him.

There was no pleasure this time. At least not for Billy T. This time, Billy T was the one being brutalized while he played the woman's part. He felt the laughter of whatever possessed him.

Inside his mind, he felt the violation, the humiliation, the incredible pain, as his insides were invaded, torn, and each time, at the end of the sex act, he begged for his life, but no matter how hard he pleaded, the knife always sank into his body, burning agony that took his life, time after time, until at last, his mind could no longer function.

While his thoughts retreated toward darkness, trying to escape, the thing that called itself Juliana raked razor-sharp fingernails down his back.

Leaving long bloody furrows in their wake as she finally climaxed.

Her body arched and she cried out. If Billy T had been capable of hearing her, he would have thought the words were merely the product of passion, instead of what they were. A language that hadn't been heard in over three thousand years.

They lay together the way spent lovers do after hard lovemaking. The night breeze dried their sweaty skins with gentle, cool fingers.

"You were the E ticket ride, Billy T," she said. "And you didn't disappoint."

Billy T looked at her with unseeing eyes. A small string of saliva trailed from the corner of his mouth, ran down his chin. He made no effort to wipe it away.

She lifted his face, their mouths joining in a final lingering kiss. Something convulsed in her throat, causing it to bulge like a snake swallowing an animal that was too large. The substance, dark red, shiny, left her to enter the Apache serial killer. His neck swelled. Receded.

Their kiss ended.

Juliana fell back.

In an instant, every drop of Billy Two Hats' blood exploded from the scratches on his back, his chest, exiting in streams that stretched out more than thirty feet. Propelled by incredible pressure, the slightly less than eight pints of blood hit the plate-glass window of an abandoned laundromat across the street. With the force of a fire hose, it cracked the glass, then sprayed the sign above. The one that promised to get your clothes snowy white was set to rocking back and forth, slowly coming to rest. The sign had a picture of a little girl in her snowy white dress, except now the dress was spotted with red. The little girl was oblivious of the broken promise. Her smile never wavered when the blood began its steaming descent toward the street, looking, in its evenly spaced rows, as though something had clawed the glass itself, causing it to bleed.

Flexing his powerful hands, Billy T slowly touched his body, exploring it as though for the first time. Looking down, he saw a rippling occur just beneath his skin, as something red began forming in the center of his chest, finally emerging. It was a small, feathered serpent. "A little something new, a little something old," he said, looking at himself in the car mirror.

Billy Two Hats raised himself up and stared at the unmoving body of the dancer. "Good-bye, Juliana," he said, "I'll never forget you." He leaned over and placed a gentle kiss on her lips. "I hate to leave you like this, but I've got to go." Pulling on his shirt, he gathered her into his arms. "It's a nothing little place, name of Carruthers, Texas. Something happened there, something I need to look into. Maybe Billy boy, here, can help."

He sat Juliana down in front of the laundromat and knelt in front of her. A breeze ruffled her blonde hair. The face of the dancer was calm in death, but whatever controlled Billy T saw a trace of sadness in the beautiful, composed features. "You won't ever get old, Juliana," he said. "Or lonely."

He arranged her so that she looked as though she had stopped here to rest and had somehow fallen asleep. "You're with us now. You'll always be with us." He stroked her face. "Always."

As Billy T drove away, he saw that the starving mongrel from the alley had returned and was licking the blood from the plate-glass window. Several of the larger dogs had joined the first dog. They were staring hungrily at the blonde dancer, waiting for her to move.

When she didn't, one of the dogs darted forward, tore a chunk of flesh from her.

The rest soon joined in.

Billy T smiled, glad. He sure hated to see a dog starve.

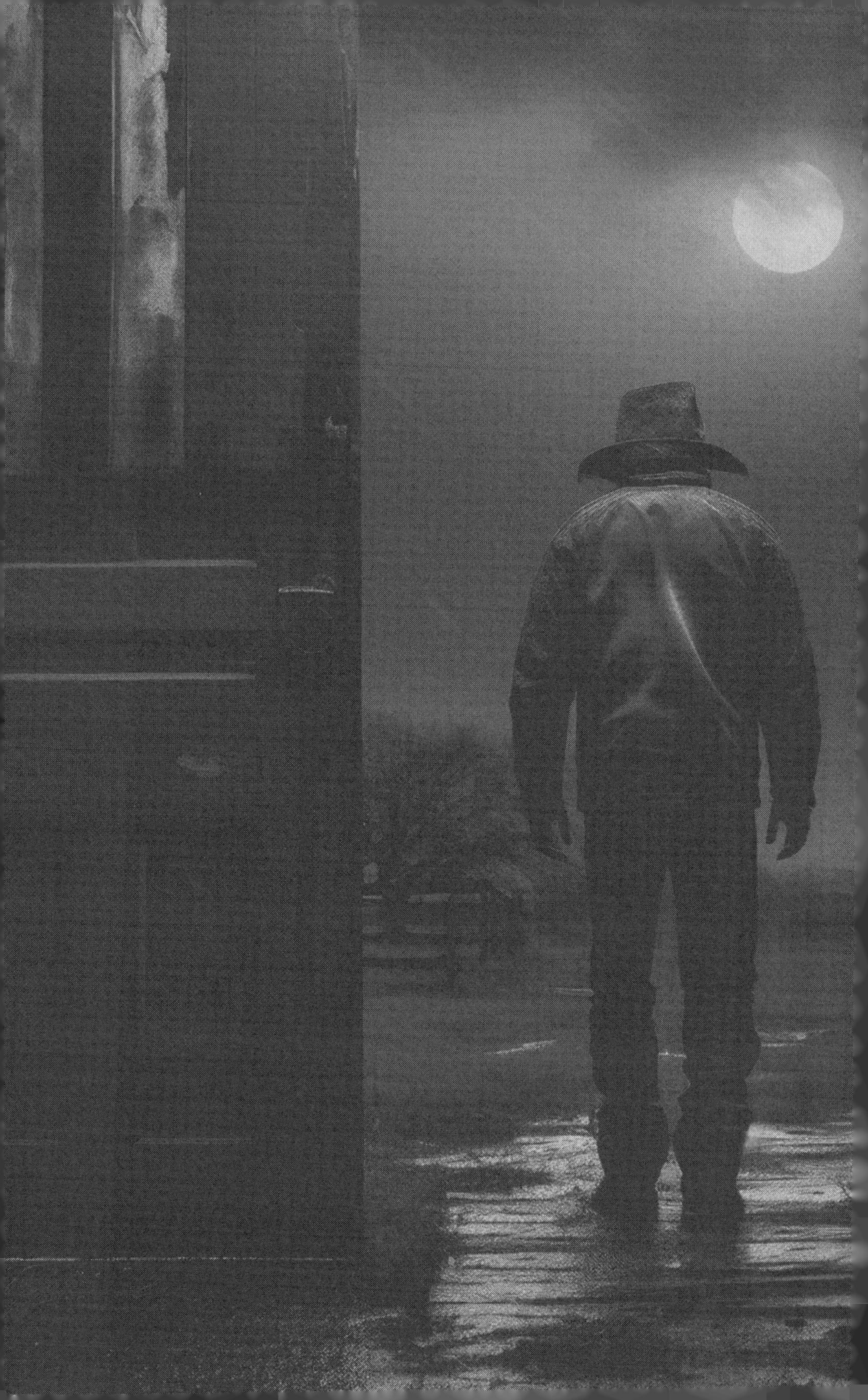

CHAPTER FIVE

Leon Francis Wilson, owner of Leon's Pool Emporium, sat upright in his bed, causing the springs to groan in protest. He blinked the room into focus. What he saw didn't please him. There were two guys standing at the foot of his bed, watching him as though it were the most natural thing in the world. He couldn't quite make out their faces in the shadows.

They seemed to be smiling.

One of the figures stepped forward. He was wearing a ratty leather jacket and holding a .38.

"Sonofabitch, I know you," Leon said. "You were in my place earlier tonight."

"I told you he was psychic," Earl Jacobs said to the other man in the shadows. "Let's see if he can guess why we're here."

"How the hell did you get in here?" Leon asked. "There's dead bolts on both doors, bars on the windows. I didn't hear nothing."

"I'd ask for my money back on those locks if I were you." Steven Adler peeled away from the wall and settled on the foot of the bed. "Sorry to come calling so late, Leon, but we need to talk to you about something."

"Look, I didn't mean nothing back there at the pool hall. I thought you was gonna start trouble. I can't afford to have no trouble. The cops told me one more time and I—"

"We understand, Leon, really we do." Steven patted him on the cheek, softly. "And we don't bear any hard feelings, do we, Earl?"

"Not a one. Not even after he threatened me with that big old scattergun." Earl smiled. "Not even after he called you a sick son of a bitch who gets his kicks out of scaring young girls. By the way, where is that tasty little daughter of yours?"

"She's staying with a friend. You leave her out of this," Leon said. "This is between us."

"You're absolutely right. We all make mistakes in judgment from time to time," Steven allowed in a quiet, friendly voice. "It's only… human. We've come to help you rectify a mistake you made last night."

"The money's over there on the dresser."

"No, no, Leon. You're not getting the picture here. We're not interested in your money. I want to know where my cue stick went." Steven leaned close and Leon got a glimpse of what Dorinda had seen in his eyes. "That stick means a great deal to me and I'd like to have it back."

"I don't have it," Leon said.

"Who does?"

"I don't know."

Steven rose from the bed, smoothed out the sheets where he had sat. "God, I'm so glad you're going to make this difficult." He traced the scar on the black man's face with his finger until Leon pulled away. "This is a very nice place you've got here. Earl and I were looking around a little earlier and we noticed you have a pool table in the basement. I'll bet it's the same one you taught Dorinda to play on. I'm right, aren't I?" He threw Leon his robe. "What do you say we go down there and play some pool? We can talk."

Leon calculated his chances of getting to the nightstand where he kept his .45. They didn't look too good. He shrugged on his robe and walked to the basement stairs ahead of the two intruders. The stairs creaked beneath his weight as he started descending into the pitch black. About halfway down he leaped to the floor and scrambled sideways.

If they hit the light switch, he was screwed before he started. They didn't.

Moving quickly for someone of his bulk, Leon bolted to the fuse box, hit the breaker switch. Then he began feeling his way toward to the small refrigerator where he kept extra beer and snacks for his poker-playing buddies. Way in the back was a .32 stashed behind a jar of pigs' feet. It should still be there. Nobody ever ate pigs' feet. If he could get his hands on that little baby, these two assholes would be talking out the other side of their asses. Nobody came into Leon Wilson's house and threatened him. Nobody.

He began edging away from the wall, trying to remember just exactly where the card table was. Didn't want to fall over it. And where were those two boys? What the hell were they doing?

The refrigerator kicked on and Leon nearly filled his size 42 boxers.

"Leon, come out, come out, wherever you are," Steven called from the foot of the stairs.

They were standing in a shaft of light that came from upstairs. They melted into the dark, the young guy in the lead. To get to the refrigerator, Leon had to cross the light.

Funny thing, Leon noticed, the steps hadn't creaked under their feet. Maybe he hadn't heard anything on account of his heart thumping so loudly. And maybe frogs didn't bump their asses when they hopped, neither. Something weird was going on here.

"I love hide-and-seek," Earl said.

Their footsteps were getting nearer and Leon had the distinct impression they could see him as plain as day, that they were just playing cat-and-mouse with him. That was crazy. No one could see in darkness like this.

And yet they were coming straight toward him.

Time was running out. It was now or never.

Leon had hoped for a few moments to check the pistol over. It had been in the refrigerator a long time. He didn't have a few moments. With a silent curse, he ripped the door open and shoved the jar containing the pigs' feet to the side. Something was wrong with jar. He looked for the .32. Looked at the pigs' feet again. Something was wrong. What? It wouldn't register. He slewed the contents of the refrigerator onto the floor. No gun. No goddamn gun.

He slammed the door shut and the room was once again dark. But only for a moment.

The light popped on, throwing the basement into blinding brightness. "Say, this is really nice," Earl said. "Steven and I always stay in motels on account of we do so much traveling. It ain't often we get to see the inside of a real house." He pulled Leon's .32 out of the waistband of his pants. "I didn't think this thing was ever gonna warm up. It damn near froze my balls off."

Leon grabbed the first thing he saw, a pool cue propped against the wall. He swung, caught Earl a good shot with the business end.

Earl whoofed, went down. But he didn't turn loose of the gun. He leveled it at Leon from the floor, holding it shakily before him like an inadequate bribe.

Only Leon wasn't interested in him anymore. The big black man dropped the shattered pool cue and looked past Earl, his eyes drawn to a flash of light on the floor. The jar holding the pigs' feet was rolling slowly toward the wall, spilling its contents along the way the way a dryer does with the door open. Most of what was inside was already on the floor, but one of the shriveled pink nubs was darker than the rest and it had something shiny on it that caught the light. Leon wished he'd gotten the glasses he needed as he tried to bring the jar into focus. Someone had put rings on one of the pigs' feet. Now, that was a real stupid thing to do. He would have laughed if he wasn't so scared.

Then he wanted to look away. Because all of a sudden he knew. He *knew*.

The concrete floor had a dip in it and the jar began rolling backward, coming ever closer to him. He could almost make out what was inside. It was gold, all right, but it wasn't rings. The jar bumped up against his feet, splashing them with coldness, then it began rolling back down the dip.

That was when Leon saw the golden lacquered nails peeking from the brine. "Dorinda," he whispered, and then with his huge hands curled open, he started toward Earl. It was apparent he meant to strangle the smaller man, gun or no gun.

Earl began scrambling backward.

"Why?" Leon said.

Steven stepped up behind Leon and hit him in the back of the head with a gardening spade. The metal made a dull, flat, whacking sound. Caked dirt hit the wall.

Leon staggered, but didn't go down

Steven hit him again, harder this time.

Leon grunted, went to his hands and knees. Began crawling forward. Still trying to get to Earl.

Steven hit him a third time. Blood and sweat shot from the black man's head, splattered Earl.

Steven raised the spade a fourth time, but Leon was through. His eyes showed white and he toppled over sideways, unconscious. The jar that had held his daughter's hand continued rocking back and forth for a while longer, finally coming to rest against his head. It looked as if the disembodied hand were trying to comfort him.

Steven put the spade down. He looked vaguely disappointed that he didn't have to use it again.

Earl hobbled to his feet and looked over at Steven. "Jesus Christ, did you see where he hit me? I can't believe it, he hit me in the ribs! The same ones that kid over in Corpus Christi kicked the other night."

WHEN LEON CAME TO, HE WAS TIED TO A CHAIR AND STEVEN WAS shooting pool. Earl was eating a pig's foot. "Is she dead? Is Dorinda dead?"

Steven nodded, shot. A ball fell.

"You didn't have to kill her…" The good side of his face was as dead as the scarred side.

"She wasn't a very good pool player," Steven answered, as though that explained everything. "I came to town for a game and I didn't get one. You see, I've got this problem with my temper. I guess I just got a little upset." He lined up another shot. "Besides, I wanted you to know I was serious about getting my cue stick back."

"What's so important about a cue stick that you'd kill a sixteen-year-old girl over?"

"I thought she was seventeen," Steven interrupted. Another ball dropped into a pocket.

"No," Leon answered, "she was only sixteen. She wanted to be an artist when she grew up." He looked at her hand on the floor and then at Earl, who looked away.

Steven stopped shooting and turned his attention to Leon. "You want to know why that cue stick is so important to me? It's because it has something inside it that I need, something that I can't live without. I've got a few spares put by, but none close by. But that's not the point. It's mine. I want it back."

He walked to the refrigerator and pulled out two beers, handed one to Earl.

"We came here because we think you know who has that stick." Earl hobbled over to the wall and took down one of the pictures hanging there. The snapshot was of three guys in the Army, one was Leon, a much slimmer younger Leon, the second guy Earl had never seen before. The third face was familiar—from Leon's pool hall earlier tonight. "Tell us about this guy." He pointed at John.

"You can go screw yourselves. I ain't telling you nothing."

"Steven, you see anything odd about this little group here?" Glancing at the snapshot, a smile tugged at Earl's face. "A black guy, a white guy, and an Indian. What the shit is this?"

"The Village People?" Steven said.

"Leon, looks like you put on some weight since that picture." Earl pointed at John. "C'mon, big boy. Where can we find this guy?"

"I don't know. We were friends a long time ago, that's all," Leon said. "The Indian's dead. I don't know where the white guy is. He just stops by maybe once or twice a year. He's a hustler, stays on the road a lot."

Steven finished his beer, crushed the can.

"If you go on and tell him where to find the guy who took the stick," Earl said, his voice dropping to conspiratorial whisper, "I promise I'll get Steven to kill you straight out. A bullet in the head. No torturing you first. It's asking a lot, but it's the best I can do under the circumstances." He spread his hands. "I can't hold this offer open long, so you'd better make up your mind fast."

Leon had the absurd feeling he was talking to a used-car salesman. "Something's been bothering me. You mind if I ask you a question?"

"Sure," Earl said. "What's on your mind?"

"I got the feeling you could see me in the dark and when you came down the steps... they didn't squeak. A cat can't walk down those steps without—"

"Can I let you in on a little secret, Leon?" Steven asked.

The scarred head nodded.

"We're not exactly human."

Beer flew from Earl's mouth.

"Did I say something funny, old friend?" Steven asked. He sounded slightly annoyed.

"You killed the guy's daughter, cut off her hand and stuck it in a jar of pigs' feet, and then you tell him that you're not exactly human. I think he's already figured that out." Earl tossed his gnawed pig's foot on the floor, turned to the bound man. "What my young friend meant to say is that we're not just a couple of psychos who run around killing people for the fun of it. Well, actually he is."

Steven smiled.

Earl was beginning to sound a little embarrassed. "What I'm trying to say is we're a little less than human... oh shit... show him the teeth, will you?"

"Why don't you do it?" Steven was laughing out loud now. Earl's face actually turned red.

"All right, I'm sorry, Earl. I didn't mean to hurt your feelings. I know how sensitive you are on that subject." Steven moved around into their captive's field of view, the smile still plastered on his face.

"Watch this shit, Leon, you're going to love it." Suddenly from behind Steven Adler's very white teeth appeared a second set of teeth, much longer than the first, curved, and sharp as needles.

Warmness ran down Leon's legs.

"God, I hate it when they do that," Earl said, wrinkling his nose.

Steven closed his mouth, cutting off the grotesque smile. "Let's see, where were we? Oh yes, why I want my pool cue back. It's because it has something in it I need. Dirt, very special dirt. It comes from my—"

"Grave," Leon supplied. "You're a…" He couldn't bring himself to say the word.

"Vampire. The word is vampire," Steven finished.

"You can't be," Leon stammered. "You're drinking beer."

"You're absolutely right, though I wouldn't call this light shit you drink—beer." Steven emptied the can on the floor and watched it flow toward the drain. "Look, I'm going to make this real simple for you. In the scheme of things there are species of animal who don't care for the light of day. They live, they hunt by night. Why should humankind be exempt?"

"Do you have any children?" Leon asked dully, staring at his daughter's hand.

The question seemed to amuse Steven. "Earl here is my son, in a manner of speaking. But no, we are aberrations of nature and we can't reproduce in the human manner. Think of vampirism as a disease, one that's very hard to catch, but still just a disease."

Leon opened his mouth to say something.

Steven raised his hand, cutting him off. "You've had your turn at twenty questions. Now, it's my turn. I need that name and address we spoke of earlier."

"I can't give him up to you," Leon said. "He's my friend."

"Last chance."

Leon spat in the pale face.

Quick as a cat, Steven bared razor-sharp teeth and Leon felt a sting on his neck.

"Now look what you've made me do, Leon. Didn't I warn you about my temper?" The tongue slid over red-stained teeth, leaving them pristine white. "There's one very important thing that popular fiction doesn't mention about us. Do you feel it yet? It works fast."

Something alien began stirring in Leon's blood, spreading numbness down his arms and legs. Much worse, though, were the horrifying images that began filling his mind. "What've you done to me?"

Pulling back, Steven said, "Tell us about this thief." He touched the face of John Warrick in the picture. "And maybe I'll answer you."

Warm stickiness slid down Leon's neck. Trickled out of sight. When the black lines came to rest against the inside of his white T-shirt, red stains blossomed one after another as if by magic, an impromptu Rorschach test.

"I keep looking for a bat," Earl commented as he leaned over to examine the stains. "Never seen one yet."

Their voices were fading and the images gathering in Leon's mind were getting stronger. Steven Adler and Earl Jacobs looked more and more like the kids who'd waylaid him on his paper route when he was ten.

The years peeled away.

Bringing back painful memories.

Once again Leon was lying in an alley, the smell of dog shit and rotting garbage in the humid air. His ruined bike lay beside him, two white teenagers stood above him. Their faces were devoid of all emotion except hatred. "My old man says we can't allow no niggers to have a paper route in our neighborhood. We warned you to get your sorry black ass on back to your own side of town. Guess maybe you need a little reminder."

There was a soft snick when the switchblade opened. A knee in the chest, a flash of pain on his face. Blood running down. He kept thinking how mad his mom was going to be because he had ruined his brand-new shirt. "Momma, I'm sorry," he had said, doing his best not to cry. They wouldn't see him cry. Not ever. His hand went to his cheek, trying to stop the bleeding.

Everything was exactly like he remembered on that long ago day. The pain, the humiliation. He could see the wheel on his bike spinning in the bright sunshine, a car cruising past, too far away to help.

Except this time there was one small crucial difference. This time old Mr. Saltzman didn't come rushing out to save him, and the knives kept on cutting and cutting.

Everything got all confused. His daughter, Dorinda, was there and she reached out for him, trying to help him up, but she couldn't. She had no hands. "They hurt me, Daddy," she said, and her eyes pleaded with him for help. She touched him.

He looked down at his shirt. Saw the bloody stains, left by his daughter looked up—into the face of Steven Adler, who was whistling softly while he shot pool. "Bad dreams? Talk to me, Leon, or we can do this again."

Though Leon was filled with shame at his cowardice, he knew he would do anything to keep Steven from touching him again. He told them everything he knew, except for one thing. John Warrick had a family. The image of Dorinda with no hands helped him to hold out.

They seemed to believe him.

"You should've taken our offer and told us where John Warrick was when we first asked," Steven said, placing a hand on Leon's heaving shoulder.

Leon tried to pull away.

"It would have been much easier for everyone concerned." Steven spoke as though he were explaining to a small child why it was being punished. "This isn't going to be very pleasant for you, Leon. You see, one of the side effects of getting bitten by a vampire is that a hallucinogen is released into the blood. That's what you were feeling. Its purpose is to immobilize the victim with fear. Makes it much easier for us to feed. How did it do?"

Leon didn't say anything.

"On the good side, it destroys short-term memory. You won't remember anything about tonight." Steven leaned close. "Time to go night-night, but don't be scared. Daddy always gives his children a little kiss before he tucks them in."

LESS THAN HUMAN

The refrigerator kicked on, kicked off. Then the only sound in the room was a hungry sucking.

After a while, Steven raised from the unconscious body of Leon Francis Wilson. The vampire wiped his mouth with the back of his hand, smearing red. "You want a taste or not?"

"I guess so." Earl looked hesitant. His eyes were fixed on the floor.

"What's wrong now?" Steven asked.

"Nothing."

"Come on, what's wrong?"

"I left something in my other jacket."

"Something."

"What?" Steven coaxed.

"Something... all right, my teeth! I didn't bring my fangs with me, okay? Damn it, it's not my fault you turned me after I lost all my teeth!" He looked away, his voice sad. "Cut him for me, will you?"

"Why don't you do it?"

"You know how I feel about knives and cutting people." Earl traced the scar on Leon's jaw. "You coulda got what you needed from him when you fed. You didn't have to torture him so much. He would have told you what you wanted to know."

"Kind of like the way old Cates told you what you wanted to know? You remember Cates, don't you?"

"Yeah, I remember," Earl answered. "I remember.

EARL JACOBS HAD STOLEN HORSES FOR A LIVING IN HIS YOUNGER DAYS, but that was a long time ago. Now he was getting old. He had never thought he would live to be old, since the fate of most horse thieves was to finish up on the end of a rope.

The year was 1919—he wasn't too sure about the month—and the meager living he made these days came from peddling snake oil town to town. A man wasn't as likely to be hung for selling snake oil as he was for stealing horses, though it was still a risky occupation. You might catch a rock thrown by a disgruntled customer if you weren't quick on your feet. All he could say for sure on the subject, it was a living and a man had to take things as they came.

On the good side, he had a wagon with his name on it; on the bad side, he had a temperamental rattlesnake, the two slowest mules in Texas, and a surly, one-eared dog that wouldn't do any tricks.

All in all, he figured he wasn't doing too bad.

He was standing in the middle of what passed for a main street in Jessup, Arizona, trying his best to interest the crowd in a bottle of his elixir. Progress hadn't quite managed to locate Jessup yet. There was a dry-goods store where you could post a letter if you had a mind to, a Baptist church where you could be saved if you had a mind to, and a saloon if you didn't. Most of the citizenry didn't look saved, which meant they had no intention of spending their money, unless it was over at the saloon. Some of the farmers kept gazing wistfully in that direction and rubbing their sunburned necks.

Earl's claims for his patented medicine were being met with a great deal of good-natured jeering. Most of the folks were more interested in seeing him handle the four-foot rattlesnake he claimed to own than they were in drinking his medicine, which was watered-down whiskey with a touch of laudanum. He was going to have to pull out the snake if he was going to hold on to the crowd, and he hated that. The heat tended to put the snake in a bad mood. That had already led to getting bitten four times this month. Today damn sure looked to be number five.

He was feeling more than a little put out and kept glaring at his surly dog, who wouldn't even shake hands with anyone in the crowd.

So far, no one was showing even the slightest interest in buying a bottle of his cure-all.

Already the crowd was beginning to get restless and some were drifting away. His chances for making a sale were getting slimmer by the minute.

Only one thing to do—bring on the snake.

He went to the back of the wagon and lifted out the wooden crate that held the big diamondback. There was an ominous rattle from inside. The onlookers brightened up considerably at this development. Earl was not particularly cheered by the sound. That old snake got bigger and meaner by the day. Maybe someday he would grow large enough to swallow the surly dog. It was the first cheerful thought he'd had all day.

One of the ranchers, a big florid man in a straw hat, was telling anyone who would listen about a preacher he'd seen down in Louisiana who handled snakes. "It was the damnedest thing I ever seen," straw hat said, playing to the crowd. "He had snakes crawling all over him. Said he wasn't scared at all. Said the Lord would protect him."

"What happened?" his companion asked.

"I guess the Lord must have been busy that day, 'cause one of them snakes bit that preacher right in the face. It wasn't no time before he got all swole up. He died before the sun even went down."

"The snake or the preacher?" a wag in the crowd asked.

Earl started to tip the box over, but he lost his grip and the snake tumbled out onto the dusty street. The old diamondback was thick as a man's arm. Before Earl could get hold of him, the snake struck him on the hand and held on.

Everyone saw that it was a serious bite.

"We ain't got no doctor," straw hat said. He didn't seem too sad about it. "We got an undertaker, though. You might be able to trade him them two mules for a fancy send-off."

"That's right neighborly of you," Earl said, grabbing the snake behind the head and dropping him back into the box, "but I think I might need those mules when I set out for Crowder Flats tomorrow." With that he opened up a bottle of his elixir and drank it straight down.

"You throw in a couple of bottles of that colored water and the undertaker just might put you up a stone." Straw hat was still playing to the crowd as he waited for the fancy-talking old man to double over and start swelling up. "But you'd best not wait too long. That preacher I saw get bit couldn't even talk before long. Tell you what, you give me them mules and I'll see you get a Christian burial myself."

"Friend, your concern touches me deeply, but I'm going to be fine. That colored water, as you call it, contains a secret ingredient taught to me by an Arapaho medicine man. A hundred years old last month. Still makes love to his squaw two times a night. Can't no snake hurt me."

"I'm giving five-to-one odds this old fraud is dead before sundown," the florid rancher called out. There were quite a few takers. The mood of the crowd was becoming positively festive. This was the most excitement they'd had in years.

They settled in to wait.

Every so often, someone would remark that Earl didn't look too good and more money would exchange hands. The saloon keeper, an enterprising fellow, set up a canvas awning to keep the sun off and managed to sell quite a bit of beer while everyone waited for the old man to start puffing up.

Once in a while, to show everyone he was feeling fine, Earl would get up and do a little dance for the children, even let out a whoop or two. The small boys loved it and some of the braver ones would shoot at him with their wooden guns from behind their fathers. The girls mostly hid behind their mother's skirts and cried.

The big rancher was suspicious that Earl hadn't swollen up and died by the time the sun began to dip. He demanded to see the snake-bit hand, which Earl showed him. Sure enough there were two puncture wounds and one even had a little blood oozing out of it. He looked closely at Earl, with hatred in his eyes. "Your little trick cost me money today, old man." His voice was soft, meant only for Earl. "I know you from somewhere, don't I? Maybe from a long time ago?" He tightened his grip on the injured hand, causing more blood to flow from the wound.

"I doubt it. I don't get through here very often." The grip tightened some more and the pain was bad, but Earl didn't let it show on his face. He smiled. "Mostly I stick kind of close to Missouri. Ever been there? It's pretty country, good place to raise a family."

Something flashed between them and the big rancher looked hard at him, as though weighing the chances of shooting him where he stood. "My name is Cates and I don't ever forget a face. Yours'll come back to me." He released the hand. "We'll talk again when it's not so crowded." Before Cates could say more, he was overrun by people eager to collect on their wagers.

Within a few minutes, Earl had sold every bottle of elixir he owned. Well, except for his personal supply. He was in such a good mood he even promised the snake a toad.

By nightfall, Earl was a good ten miles away from Jessup. Riding along in his wagon, he nursed his sore hand with nips from a bottle of his elixer.

All the venom might have been milked from that mean-ass old rattler, but where it had bit him still hurt like hell. The hand was going stiff, too. Come morning he wouldn't be able to close his fingers. Getting snake-bit was part of doing business, he was philosophical about it. What worried him more was that he could barely hold on to the big old hogleg Colt he kept under the wagon seat. He was going to need to hold on to it, as soon as Cates figured out where they'd met before.

And Cates would figure that out. Twenty-five years had passed since Earl had seen the massacre, yet it might have been yesterday as far as he was concerned. He had been running a herd of stolen Kiowa horses up Missouri way when he came across what was left of a dead family—a hunter turned farmer and his squaw wife.

They had been butchered by renegades. White renegades from the look of the signs. The man had been tied to a tree and gutted; the woman had been raped and strangled. They had been dead for several days because the animals were fighting over what was left of them.

Earl had seen death. He knew what was in that cabin was going to be bad. He braced himself before he looked in there. What he saw was worse than anything he could have imagined. There were two boys, no older than eight or nine, and a girl of about six, their heads bashed in.

Only the little girl wasn't quite dead. She should have been. She had been skinned alive and was crawling across the cabin floor on her stomach.

Trying to get away from him. Thinking he was someone who had come back to hurt her some more. She was trying to hide. Her own blood greasing her path.

Crawling...

Like a snake without a head.

He wouldn't have thought such a little girl could hold so much blood.

Knowing he was a fool for risking his life over something that was none of his damn business, he tracked the killers back to their camp. There were five of them and he fully intended to cut all their throats as they slept.

After night fell, he sent two straight to hell with gaping toothless grins carved in their throats. The second one had taken a long time to die, bucking and thrashing so hard that Earl had feared the rest would be awakened. It was just plain bad luck that prevented him from finishing off the rest of them. One had drunk too much whiskey and had gotten up to relieve himself. Earl sliced the man's throat while he was making water, but somehow the man slipped loose and got off a shot. That slug tore off part of Earl's lower lip. In the flash, he got a look at the renegade leader. It was only for an instant, just long enough to see a big man wearing a straw hat.

And for the man to see him.

The man in the straw hat called the other renegade by name, trying to direct their shots in the right direction. Several of their slugs came so close, Earl felt the air brush his ears from their passing. Luckily for him the killers had camped near a stand of cottonwoods or he would have been shot dead right there.

As it was, they tracked him for a week, causing him to ride his favorite horse to death. He managed to steal another one from a ranch and was finally able to lose them on the other side of the Arkansas River.

That had been a long time ago. Now he was driving his wagon across the Arizona flatlands in the dark, and it had been three days since he'd left Jessup, and it might be another three before he made Crowder Flats. He hadn't slept much in that time because he knew Cates would be coming after him. But then he never slept much anyhow.

This country was deserted, not much grass and even less water. Only lizards and snakes and bad men lived out here. There would be no one to interfere when the big rancher came after him. He took another pull from a bottle of his best pop-skull elixer and waited for Cates to come.

The only sound was the creaking of the wagon, the dog's snoring, as the mules continued on. The sound lulled him into a light doze. Still, he heard the man riding after him. That was all right. Earl was expecting him. He had been expecting him for twenty-five years.

Earl's eyes sought and found the old hogleg lying on the wagon seat. He stared at the pistol and remembered the little girl crawling on her stomach. Night after night he had imagined what he would do to the man who had killed her when he found him.

Now that the time had come, Earl just wanted it to be over.

Cates wasn't a man to put off a fight or maybe he was just plain crazy. He came in at full gallop, leaning low over the buckskin he rode, letting the animal shield him. His shots weren't even directed at Earl. He meant to spook the mules, which he did, because they went to kicking and bucking until they kicked over their traces. They bolted and Earl had to jump from the wagon before it went over on its side. He fell heavily, twisting his leg, and that old hogleg Colt landed in the dirt.

Before Earl could get to his feet, Cates came at him. The big man spurred the buckskin forward, meaning to run him over. Earl leveled the pistol—but Cates didn't seem to care. Beneath the straw hat, his face was dead calm as he guided the horse toward the man on foot.

Earl thumbed back the hammer and squeezed the trigger, and nothing happened. He tried again with the same results. The pistol wouldn't fire. Something must have happened to it when it landed in the dirt. All those years of traveling from town to town, looking for Cates, only to let him escape. A feeling of sadness crept over Earl.

He had let the little girl down. For a moment he saw her crawling across the floor, leaving a trail of blood.

The buckskin would be on him in seconds. Eyes on Cates, he was surprised to see a small white shape dart in front of the horse. Cates was taken by surprise when his mount pitched sideways into the dirt. The horse landed heavily, pinning the rider for a moment before rolling free. The buckskin climbed to its feet and stood there, trembling.

Cates didn't move.

The white shape came trotting over and Earl was surprised to see his surly, one-eared dog who wouldn't do any tricks. The dog had been scared by all the noise and had decided to make a run for cover. Earl was too numb to be surprised.

Quickly, the snake-oil salesman limped over and picked up the big man's pistol, stuck it in his belt. Almost as an afterthought he put a hand on Cates' chest, feeling around for a heartbeat. He found one. Earl pulled out the pistol and pointed it at the rancher's head, but after twenty-five years, he had to have some answers. He went to the wagon and returned with some rope.

Hooking the mules to the wagon, Earl righted it. The rattler didn't seem happy with all the commotion. Grunting with the effort, he dragged Cates over to the wagon and tied him to a wheel. The rancher groaned once and Earl clubbed him in the mouth with the heavy pistol. Teeth and blood spilled onto the ground. The big rancher slumped. Earl had to use every ounce of his willpower not to raise the pistol a second time. He went over and made a small fire and put on some coffee.

After an hour or so, Cates came to. At first he looked confused, but then as he recognized Earl, his face darkened with anger. He strained against the ropes with all his might until he realized his efforts were useless. He smiled, showing ragged stumps where his teeth used to be. "Mister, I got over forty men riding for me.

You're going to be one sorry son of a bitch if you don't cut me loose right now."

"Why'd you skin the little girl?"

"I don't know what you're talking about."

"We're going to talk a little bit, Cates, and then I'm going to kill you. Whether it's quick or slow pretty much depends on if you tell me the truth."

"You might as well go on ahead and kill me right now." Cates spat a mouthful of blood into Earl's face. "Cause I ain't talking to no goddamned killer."

"I spent half my life looking for you, Cates. So listen up, you're going to talk to me." Earl picked up the skinning knife, reached over, and calmly sliced off Cates' left ear. He tossed it onto the bound man's stomach. "Maybe you can hear me a little better now."

Cates looked with disbelief at his severed ear lying on his stomach. A big greasy tear slid down his cheek and landed on his stomach, mixing with the blood already there. "She turned me down," Cates said. "She was a goddamned Indian squaw, who did she think she was, turning me down? I hit her a couple time, but I didn't kill her."

"You're a liar." Earl sliced off Cates' remaining ear. "I caught up with the other renegade just outside Abilene last year. The last one besides you. We didn't get to talk all that much, on account of he shot himself. Trouble was, his aim hadn't improved any since the last time we met. He did live long enough to tell me you didn't have nothing to do with the squaw. He said you didn't much like women at all. At least not grown ones."

"He's a liar. It wasn't me."

"Here's what I think happened. Just nod your head if I get close to the truth."

Cates tried to pull away, thrashing against his bonds like a madman.

"You raped her, didn't you, Cates, even though she was just a little girl. Only you had to get around a problem first. She was an Indian, and her skin was red, and that made you sick to your stomach, but you found a way to handle that, didn't you?" Earl raised the heavy pistol and brought it down on Cates' leg. Bone splintered. "Her skin was the problem"—the pistol raised again, fell again—"so you skinned her."

Earl severed the ropes and Cates slumped to the ground. Somehow the big rancher had managed to hold on to consciousness, watching while Earl hitched up the mules and the buckskin was tied to the back of the wagon.

"You're not going to leave me here, are you?" he called out to the departing wagon. "It's three days' ride to the next town. I can't walk... my legs are broken. You promised you'd kill me quick if I told the truth."

Earl looked back once and saw that Cates was trying his best to keep up with the mules. But it was hard going for a man who had two broken legs, who had to crawl on his stomach across the sand.

After a while it came to Earl what Cates looked like.

He looked like a snake.

When Earl made camp a day later, he fell into an exhausted sleep. His dreams were peaceful for the first time in more years than he could remember.

The dog's yelp woke him.

Earl rolled out of his blankets to find a gun under his nose When he looked into the man's face who held the gun, he was met with a smile. There wasn't much friendliness in it, though. "Cates wasn't lying," the stranger said. "He never touched that little girl. It was three army deserters that did all that killing. One of them told me everything before I..." The smile widened just a bit.

"Who are you?" Earl asked.

The stranger's smile practically split his face. "Steven Adler, I'm your new partner." He moved closer.

"If Cates didn't kill the little girl, then why did he come after me tonight?" Earl tried to back away and found he couldn't.

"You hunted down and killed a lot of innocent men, Earl. They were Cates' friends. That's the reason he came after you. You spent half your life looking for the men who killed that little girl. I admire that kind of persistence, and I like the way you use a knife." The young stranger was laughing now. "I can use a man like you, so I've decided we're going to be together. For a long time. A long, long time," the stranger repeated, as though he had just said something funny.

Earl felt a sharp sting on his neck and for an instant he thought that old diamondback had gotten loose and had bitten him. He knew he was a dead man because he hadn't milked that snake in three days, but it wasn't the snake that had bitten him. It was the blonde stranger.

The last thing Earl Jacobs saw before he began his new life were the teeth covered with red, the teeth that were too long and caught the moonlight.

He wished many times since that night that the snake had bitten him instead.

Reaching into his boot, Earl pulled out his knife. The light reflected off the blade and caught him in the eyes. They were filled with sadness.

"Jesus Christ," Steven said, looking at Earl in disgust. He took the knife from Earl's shaky hand and prepared to cut Leon Wilson's throat. "You're not supposed to get sentimental over your dinner."

"No, I'm not getting sentimental," Earl answered, eyeing the knife. "It's just that Leon's a good man and I like him, okay? You're not going to kill him. We have a deal, remember." He stepped in front of Steven. "No more killing unless we absolutely have to."

Steven put the knife to Leon's throat.

"You do him and I'm walking," Earl said calmly.

"You're forgetting who's the boss here, aren't you?"

"No, I ain't forgetting. You kill him and I'm taking a walk in the daylight."

"You're bluffing."

"Try me."

"You'll die."

"Good. This ain't much of a life, no way."

Steven relented, pulled the knife back. "No reason to kill him. I scared him enough to get what I came for. That fake hand in the jar made him spill his guts."

"Yeah, it worked real good. He almost spilled mine, too."

"Sorry. He was quick for a big guy." Steven straightened Earl's jacket, slapped him on the shoulder. He smiled at Earl, searching the older man's eyes. "You're not going to take a walk on me, are you?"

"Not unless you break our deal."

"All right, we'll drag him over to the steps, and when he wakes up in the morning, he'll think he fell. Right now, you need to hurry up and get yourself a little taste. We've got to shag our asses over to Crowder Flats."

The knife went to work.

CHAPTER SIX

John Warrick eased the phone back into its cradle and lay back on his bed. Louise's words wouldn't quite sink in. An under-aged male prostitute in Vegas, mutilated and left to die, all his blood found spattered on the walls. What kind of man could do something like that?

Why?
Kicks?
The cue stick lying on a chair across the room caught his gaze. The red-feathered serpent curled around the handle seemed to peer at him with baleful eyes.

Accusing him.

The stick belonged to whoever had killed Joey Estevez. The boy had been killed for fun. And for something else. His blood? John didn't want to think about that. He looked away from the chair, his eyes straying to the ceiling. No good. The afternoon sun spilling through the window gave the water stains a reddish tint.

That room in Vegas where Joey had died had been covered in blood.

Those thoughts started the walls to closing in again, causing his head to throb. What the hell was he going to do? John didn't know the killer's name; he only knew what the guy looked like.

Okay, say he went to cops and accused the guy. It was his word against the stranger's. John knew his word didn't carry any weight, not since he'd pulled that job in Tucson. He'd been a kid at the time, but cops had long memories. Suppose they asked him a few pointed questions about how come he knew so much about the murder.

What would he say, that he knew the guy did it because he, John Warrick, was some kind of half-assed psychic? That he had just happened to pick up some weird vibrations from a stolen pool cue? If the cops didn't stick him in a padded room, they might arrest him for the kid's death.

John was in over his head and he knew he was in over his head. It was time to pack it in.

Yet the memory of the dead kid wouldn't turn loose. He had to do something.

Maybe Leon could shed some light on who those guys from the pool hall were. John fished a doughnut out of the crushed bag while he dialed the phone.

Marvin, the assistant manager answered. "Leon's," he said in his high, hoarse voice. The sound of clicking balls came through in the background.

"Hey Marvin, this is John Warrick."

"John, damn, everybody was wondering where you went. I got a message from Leon for you. He says you are one crazy son of a bitch stealing from those guys last night. He says he's gonna kick you right in your boney white ass the next time he lays eyes on you."

"I guess he's pissed."

"You got that right." Marvin's voice dropped a notch. "I was in the back. Did Leon really introduce those guys to old Stumpy?"

"You mean the sawed-off? Yes, he did."

"They said he cocked both hammers." Marvin sounded almost wistful.

"These guys were kind of scary," John said.

"Shit, man, I always miss all the excitement."

"You'd better be glad you missed it." John kept his voice casual. "I need to talk to Leon. He been in today?"

"No, he ain't. He better be getting his big butt in here real soon. I got some business to take care of over at Sharlene's house." His voice lowered again. "I think I might get my balls racked tonight, if you get my drift."

Somebody laughed in the background. "Rack these balls," a loud voice called out.

"Rack your own damn balls," Marvin yelled back. "Can't you see I'm on the phone?"

"Marvin, either one of those guys Leon kicked out last night been in?"

"No way. Leon said they ain't ever coming in here again." Someone at the pool hall said something and Marvin faded out, then came back on. "Hey look, John, I got to go. You want I should have Leon give you a ring?"

"Yeah, he knows where I'm staying. See you 'round, Marvin." John felt the vise that held his head tighten another notch. This had started out as a simple theft and now he was involved with murder. Everything was moving way too fast. He was alone and the night was on its way again. Already shadows were beginning to creep out from the corners of the room. A day had passed and he still couldn't decide what to do about this mess.

A siren sounded in the distance, a plaintive cry that rose and then died away, leaving him more alone than ever.

He dialed Leon's house. On the fifth ring he got Leon's answering machine and the gravelly voice came on the line. "If this is the jerkweed who keeps calling me about aluminum siding, I'm gonna find your ass and you're gonna need a can opener to take a shit." A slight pause. "Leave your message at the beep… and have a nice day."

A slight smile creased John's face and the desire to leave a message was strong, but he fought against it. He hung up without saying a word. Leon's bluster didn't scare him any. He couldn't really say why he stayed silent.

Where was Leon? The big man only went to two places when he wasn't working. The grocery or the liquor store.

"He's fine," John said to himself, yet he couldn't shake the feeling something had happened to his old friend.

The man who owned the cue stick was a stone-cold killer, and if he thought Leon had anything to do with its theft.

John struggled into his jacket, knowing he was going to Leon's house even though it was a dangerously stupid thing to do. He tucked the stick under his arm and closed the door behind himself.

Before he cleared the lobby, Tommy, the rotund night clerk, called out to him. "John, hold up a sec. I didn't get a chance to tell you, there was two guys here last night looking for you."

"One of them young?" John asked. The taste of fear brushed the inside of his mouth, drying it instantly.

"Yeah, the other guy was older. Had on a jacket that looked like he slept in it."

"They say what they want?"

"No. They said they was friends of yours. Said they'd come back tonight to see you. The young guy said you had something for him."

John felt sweat prickle on his forehead. "Thanks, Tommy." He stuck a ten in the chubby hand. "They come back, tell them I checked out this morning. You don't know me. Okay?"

"You got it."

"I mean it, Tommy. Don't mess with these bastards."

Tommy tucked the ten in his shirt pocket, behind a Snickers that already resided there. "These two gentlemen wouldn't be in the collection business, would they?"

"You know how it is, Tommy. I got a little behind," John lied with what he hoped was an embarrassed grin. He spread his hands helplessly. "I ran into a little streak of bad luck last week. I just need these guys off my back until a few things come through." John figured it was easier to let Tommy believe what he wanted. And safer too.

The lie seemed to satisfy Tommy, who waddled back behind the counter to fish out the half-melted Snickers. He took a big bite, smearing chocolate all over his chin. In the fluorescent light it looked like blood.

The bright sunshine hurt John's eyes after being in the motel, but he didn't mind a bit. He hated the dark, always had. Growing up, he had slept with a night-light on until he was damn near twelve. A quick glance at his watch told him the sun would be setting in about two hours. The drive to Leon's house would take about half of that. Plenty of time before dark.

JOHN PARKED A COUPLE OF BLOCKS AWAY FROM LEON'S SMALL RANCH-style house and walked. The area was lower middle class, sliding downhill fast, fueled by the meth trade, but still a few years away from bad.

Kids rode by him on their bikes in the gathering darkness. Four high-schoolers were shooting hoops in a driveway, yelling, laughing. Someone somewhere was grilling. Lawn sprinklers were doing their *shhhh-tik-tik-tik*. The odors and sounds of suburbia filled the smoky autumn air. Familiar sounds, smells. Almost forgotten. A feeling of melancholy washed over him as he made his way along the sidewalk . This was a piece of life he had missed out on, and now it had passed him by. He had given his life to the game of pool and it was a cold bitch of a mistress.

He looked around, trying not to be too obvious in case some of the neighbors were watching. Leon's old red Caddy was gone and all that was left of it was a bottomless oil stain on the concrete.

Pounding on Leon's door brought no answer, so John turned and went back to his Jeep. He drove around until he found a phone. Another quick call. Still no Leon at the pool hall.

This time Marvin had sounded a little pissed and more than a little worried.

That made two of them.

Indecision gnawed at John as he idly let his fingers play over the cue stick resting on the Jeep seat beside him. He knew the man who owned it would kill for it. A shudder passed through him. After what he had seen back in his motel room when he'd held the yellowish stick in his hands, he had no illusions about the man who was tracking him.

John parked on a nearby side street and waited for darkness to settle. There were too many nosy neighbors around for him to go breaking into Leon's place in broad daylight. Already he had attracted more attention than was smart by pounding on the door like a crazy man.

He didn't have to wait long. Night came fast this time of the year.

John had reached two conclusions while waiting.

First, Leon was still inside the house.

Second, and more important, if Leon was there, he could be dead.

The smart thing, John thought, would be to stay out of this, a quick anonymous call to the police, but hell, he'd never done anything smart in his life. Why would he start now? He was going to have a look around inside the house.

If his old friend was dead, John figured he was the man responsible for his death. He had to know.

For this trip, he pulled duct tape off one of the Jeep seats, reached inside, and pulled out an old Army .45. A little present left to him by his old man. It was the only thing his old man had left him. The glow from the dash showed it contained three shells.

The sliding glass door at the back of Leon's house popped off its tracks easy enough. That made John even more nervous, and he was already scared to death. This was too damn easy. There should be a bar on the door. And where was Fast Eddie? That mutt would bark at his own shadow.

John felt as though someone had left the door open.

A car cruised past, causing him to crouch down on the patio. His knee popped. In the silence it sounded like a shot, and when the car went away, he climbed to his feet, feeling old and faintly foolish. His shirt had gone sweaty and now it stuck to his back like a second skin.

John eased through the door, hoping he was wrong about all this; hoping the only kind of dead Leon was—was dead drunk.

Several years had passed since he'd last visited here and in the dark he couldn't tell how much the place had changed. He doubted that it had changed much. Leon liked things to stay the way they were.

He paused, just standing and listening to the house. Feeling it out. An occupied house had a different feel than one that was empty. It was more than the whisper of air, the faint hum of appliances running.

This was an empty house. Or, he amended quickly, a house with nobody alive in it. He pulled out his flashlight and swept it around.

Still only empty-house sounds.

The light was enough for him to see he was in the family room. "Jesus, Leon," he whispered, "where the hell are you?"

An old-style console TV sat in the corner. A small portable TV sat on top, and in the darkness, the larger TV appeared to have sprouted a head. A tray with the remnants of a burrito sat beside a well-worn recliner. The half-eaten burrito was as dry as a dog turd in the July sun, which meant it had been there awhile.

Everything had that slightly untidy look, like the place belonged to a man who wasn't used to fending for himself. Leon's wife, Darlene, had walked out a few years back. Now Leon ate takeout, drank himself unconscious every night, and did his best to raise a teenaged daughter all by himself.

To John's right was the kitchen. There were some dishes that needed washing stacked in the sink. They sat beneath a dripping faucet. He tried to turn off the faucet. No good, it needed a new washer. Leon had been deeply hurt at his wife's leaving, though he never talked about it much. Once, drunk on tequila, Leon said he would have given her whatever it was she wanted, but he had never been able to figure out what that was.

"Welcome to the club," John had said that night to Leon, and they had toasted in that solemn way that only the very intoxicated can.

Another right, a few yards down a hallway, and John was standing in Leon's bedroom. It smelled slightly of Aqua Velva and dog. And somehow loneliness.

The bed was unmade, Leon's clothes were spread out on the floor, his size thirteen shoes were lying on their sides. For an instant, John had the crazy idea that Leon was in them and had somehow crawled under the bed. He kicked them. They were just empty shoes.

Feeling like an intruder, John backed out and peeked in the other bedroom. Posters lined the walls. Shoes, posters, and clothes were a multicolored covering on the floor that obscured any trace of the carpet. Dorinda's room. Leon was trying his best to keep her off the streets and in school. Last night at the bar, Leon had been talking about Dorinda, said she blamed him for her mother's leaving, said she was going to leave, too. Just as soon as she was old enough.

Dorinda's bed was made, which meant she hadn't been here last night. That meant she was okay and John felt grateful for that.

The living room was untouched and he realized Leon was keeping the room exactly the way his wife had left it. Leon had never lost hope that Darlene would come back someday. On the coffee table lay an open scrapbook filled with pictures from the old days. Pictures were dangerous. Their flat, shiny surfaces were like glaring ice that blinded a man to the darker water that ran beneath. The past was a dangerous thing. It looked safe, but a man could drown in it.

The only place John hadn't looked yet was the basement. As he started down the squeaky steps he held on to the thought that maybe Leon was okay. That maybe he wouldn't have to be the one to tell Dorinda that her father was dead.

Because her father hadn't been too smart about picking his friends. One in particular. John Warrick.

The basement was empty and John breathed a sigh of relief. He had been wrong. Then he saw the dark lump lying on the pool table. At first he didn't know what it was and when he did, he didn't believe it was real. As he moved closer, as his flashlight caught the golden nails, he knew it was real.

It was Dorinda's hand holding Fast Eddie's leash. The dead boxer was arranged so that he was pointing at the freezer.

John walked across the room and opened the gleaming white door. The bulb inside popped on, but it was just a feeble glow. Something was blocking the light. John stared at the contents of the freezer for a moment before anything registered, and even then, his eyes refused to accept what he saw.

Leon had been stuffed inside.

All 327 pounds of him.

A distant part of John's mind marveled at how they had managed to make Leon fit into such a small space. They must have had to break a lot of bones was all he could think. Leon was holding a jar of pigs' feet in his lap and Dorinda's other hand was inside it. Her fingers were grasping the edge of the jar as though she were trying to pull herself out.

John backed away, until the edge of the pool table jammed him in the spine.

The freezer door, still open, yawned wider, gathered speed, slapped down. Absolute silence. He opened the door and the compressor kicked on. Cool air met warm and Leon was wrapped in a shroud of thin, white mist. Leon sat in the too small space, his limbs broken and twisted into impossible angles, and John saw there were trails of ice beneath the large black man's eyes.

He had been crying.

"I just wanted to get Amy something for college," John explained to his dead friend in a faintly pleading voice. "A little present. You know how girls like presents." His words faltered. Crushed beneath the weight of his guilt.

John stared at the ashy gray face. The warmth of the room was melting the ice tracks beneath Leon's eyes. A tear, frozen in place, resumed its trek and trickled down, splashed into the jar of pigs' feet. The dead man had become a mourner at his own funeral.

John touched Leon's cheek, wiped away the wetness there. Touched it against his own face. Felt its coldness. "Those hustlers, I wanted to know who they were. If they were killers. I thought I could find out from the cue stick. I didn't mean to drag you into this." John reached out, fastened one of Leon's pajama buttons before he realized the futility of what he had done. "I didn't know..."

The corner of something green protruded from Leon's mouth.

John realized it was a hundred dollar bill. He pulled the bill out, saw a message written in blood.

The words read:
BRING IT TO CROWDER FLATS.

CHAPTER SEVEN

Crowder Flats, Arizona, between the Fort Apache and Navajo reservations.
The Broken R Ranch.
October 26th.

Bobby Roberts was launched into the air.
Launched, there was no other way to describe what was happening. He swapped ends a couple of times while he was up in the air, his arms and legs wind milling wildly. His hat flew off. Drifted away like some ungainly bird. He kept rising, and then he hung in the air for a moment, suspended. Then he came down. On the wrong end.

Hard.

Martin Strickland, foreman of the Broken R Ranch, leaned against Bobby's old white Caddy and watched the action in the corral with a grin.

Dust geysered upward, followed by laughter from the ranch hands.

Bobby scrambled for the fence.

Today was Saturday and the men were fooling around, watching Bobby try to ride a huge yellow Brahma bull by the name of Desert Storm. Besides raising cattle, the Broken R supplied bucking stock to a lot of rodeos, and Desert Storm was Mr. Roberts's pride and joy. That bull had never been ridden. Today didn't look to be any different.

A couple of the hands herded the bull back into the chute. Bobby climbed on board once again.

The gate came open.

Desert Storm exploded.

And once again, Bobby went flying into the air, coming down on his back with a heavy thud. This time he was slow in getting up and barely reached the fence ahead of Desert Storm. A few good-natured catcalls greeted his sheepish grin. He was covered with dust. "Almost had him that time… I think he's afraid of me."

The bull butted the fence and charged around the corral.

"Yeah, he looks like he's about ready to beg for mercy," Martin said as Bobby limped over. "Son, you'd better save something for the rodeo Sunday."

Bobby's pal, Kevin Paine, an amiable twenty-one-year-old who had just started at the ranch, joined them. "You'd better save something for tonight, Bobby," Kevin said, "there might be some ladies at Jake's looking for a ride, too." He nudged Bobby with an elbow. "Course, I heard they're looking for someone who can stay on more than eight seconds…"

Boyce Gates and Nash Tippins, two older hands, laughed a little uneasily. Bobby had a temper. You could never tell what might set him off. Kevin didn't weigh more than 140 pounds with his glasses, saddle, and hat thrown in. Boyce and Nash hoped they could avoid having to break up a fight. They were already in their Saturday-night best, clean shirts and jeans, with boots shined.

Nash jumped in, diverting Bobby's attention from Kevin. "Shit, last time Bobby made out in that Caddy"—Nash took off his hat just in case Bobby took a swing—"his ass hit the horn, he thought it was the buzzer and bailed off."

Bobby sure looked like he wanted to take offense at the remarks, but at the moment, he was too out of breath to do more than glare.

Reaching down and picking up Bobby's hat, Nash handed it to him. He slapped Bobby on the back, causing dust to fly. "Come on, we don't want to keep the ladies waiting."

Bobby finally smiled and looked over at the foreman. "You coming with us, Mr. Strickland?"

The tall foreman shook his head no. "You boys go on. I got a little paperwork to take care of before Chester gets back. Besides, someone needs to stay here and look after things." He smiled. "It's about time for Amos Black Eagle to come calling."

"What's the matter with that old Navajo?" Kevin asked. "He do too much peyote like everyone says?"

"No," Martin answered, "he just gets drunk every once in awhile and chases off a few horses. He ain't never done any real harm."

"I'd have his crazy red ass put in jail if I had my way," Bobby said.

"Well you ain't got your way. You boys cut Amos some slack." Martin laughed. "Me and that old man go back a long ways. He taught me how to ride, how to shoot a decent game of pool. And a few other things, too. A lot of folks don't know this, but that crazy old Indian taught John Warrick everything he knows about the game."

That got their attention.

"Some say Amos's son, Thomas, was better than John," Bobby said.

"Don't nobody know that for sure. They never played. Thomas used to…" Martin caught himself and shook his head. Sometimes he forgot Thomas Black Eagle was dead. It always took him by surprise when he remembered. "Let's just say it would have been a hell of a game." Martin glanced at his watch. "You boys better shake a leg or you're going to be several beers behind."

Bobby saw that the conversation was getting under the foreman's skin and he decided to change the subject. "You change your mind, Mr. Strickland, you know where we'll be."

"Yeah, I know." A look of distaste crossed Martin's face. "Jake Rainwater's bar."

They waited for the inevitable lecture.

"You watch your asses over there," Martin warned. "A lot of bad shit happens at Jake's."

Bobby and Kevin nodded. The only bad things that had ever happened to them at Jake's were hangovers and broken hearts. Nobody, far as they knew, had ever died from either. Bobby walked over to the Caddy and started it up, causing a stream of blue smoke to pour from the tailpipe.

Boyce and Nash began edging away when the noxious cloud moved toward them.

Kevin watched the two hands take off their hats to fan away the smoke from the tailpipe. Somebody let go with a strangled moo, and Bobby's face went scarlet with anger as he turned to see who had made the offending sound. "Who did that? I'm gonna kick his ass when I find out, I swear to God, I'm gonna kick his ass. You see if I don't."

Boyce and Nash gave Bobby their most innocent look. "Jesus, Bobby looks like he's about to pop a vein. What's the matter with him, Mr. Strickland?" Kevin asked.

"I guess he don't like to be kidded about his car," Martin said. There was something in the foreman's eyes. It might have been a twinkle.

"Everyone knows what the exhaust from that old Caddy can do," Kevin said. "Boyce told me it caused Mr. Roberts' best long horn bull to pass clean out. I guess something like that could make a man a little sensitive."

"Boyce tell you that? He use the words passed out?"

"Yeah," Kevin said, warily. "He said Bobby was bringing a bull back from Holbrook last summer, towing him in an open trailer behind the Caddy. And when he got here, the bull was passed out."

Martin was trying to suppress something that looked a lot like laughter. "That bull wasn't passed out, son. He was passed away. There was a big ruckus, finger pointing, even talk about lawsuits."

"What killed him?"

Martin leaned in close, like he didn't want anyone else to hear what he was about to say. "The county vet was called in to see what killed old Sparky. That was the bull's name, Sparky. Damned good bull, that old Sparky."

"Can we hold up on the memorial to Sparky?" Kevin cut in. "What happened?"

"Well, the vet said that old Sparky had been asphyxiated. By fumes."

"From the Caddy?" Kevin supplied. "He was killed by fumes from the Caddy?"

Martin nodded. "Old Sparky had enough ten W thirty in his lungs to change the oil in a Toyota."

"Are those Sparky's horns on the front of the Caddy?"

"Yep, Chester put 'em on there. He told Bobby if he ever took 'em off, he'd cut his ass off without a cent."

"Man, that's hard." Kevin turned to look at the car and had to turn back immediately so Bobby wouldn't see the smile. Kevin wasn't fast enough.

Bobby saw. His face went bright red for the second time.

He revved the engine, causing everyone to move back a few more feet. "You shitheads can walk to Jake's for all I care. It was an accident, I didn't mean to kill Sparky. It could have happened to anybody."

There was another moo, followed by some coughing.

"All right, that tears it," Bobby said, climbing from the car. "At least old Sparky got laid before he died, which is more than any of you will be able to say."

While Nash and Boyce were trying to keep the car between them and Bobby, something occurred to Kevin. His expression went serious as his voice dropped to a whisper. "Mr. Strickland, what do you want me to do about the dogs?"

Martin stared at the boy, saying nothing, his smile gone now as though it had never been.

"Bobby said to turn 'em loose," Kevin said, reluctantly. "He told us he's supposed to be in charge while his dad's gone." Kevin hesitated, torn between his friendship for Bobby and loyalty to the foreman. He decided to plunge ahead. "Bobby said not to say nothing to you."

"He did, huh? Well, I don't give a good goddamn what that little shit said," Martin answered, anger contorting his normally calm face. "Nobody's going to turn those Ridgebacks loose on that old man. They'd tear him to pieces." Martin removed his hat and wiped the sweat from the band while he fought for control. "There's already been some dead stock up in the north pasture, ripped up real bad. I know those dogs did it."

The younger man digested this for a moment. "You going to do anything about it?"

"I can't prove anything." Martin replaced the hat. "But if I could, those dogs would be off this place—Bobby or no Bobby. You know what those Ridgebacks were bred for, don't you?"

Kevin shook his head no.

"They were bred to chase down runaway slaves. Hell, those dogs can even climb trees, did you know that?" Martin jerked his head, dismissing Kevin. "Go on now. I'll handle Bobby and the dogs." With that he started back to the bunkhouse.

Over by the car, Bobby had given up chasing the two hired hands and was back in the car.

Boyce and Nash walked over to see what was going on.

"Martin looked kind of serious," Nash said. "What's going on?"

"Man, I wouldn't want to be in Bobby's shoes tonight," Kevin said. "Mr. Strickland looked mad enough to bite a nail in two."

"Yeah, I never seen him this upset in a long time," Boyce chipped in. "You'd think Doralee was back in town."

That brought a few nervous nods.

"Ain't nobody can get to him faster than Doralee," Nash said. "You remember that four-day bender he went on last year? Nobody knew where he was."

More nods.

Bobby, over in the Caddy, was still beating the dust out of his clothes. It was down to a thin cloud now.

Nash stared at the departing back of the foreman. "That was when Doralee ran off with a car salesman from Dallas. She took Nicky up there to live with her. Whew buddy, that was when the shit hit the fan."

"Yeah, it did," Boyce said, remembering. "Me and Mr. Roberts finally found Martin holed up at Jake Rainwater's, crazy drunk. I didn't think nobody but Mr. Roberts could talk to him. Martin hit me when I tried." Boyce smiled, showing where two teeth were missing. "He don't even know he did it. I told him a horse kicked me."

"Well," Kevin said, putting an end to the talk, "it looks like he wants to be by himself. So I say we let him. I say let's get over to Jake's and spend some of this money that's burning a hole in my jeans."

"That sounds like the best idea you had all day," Nash seconded. "The wind's shifted. I think we can make it over to the car."

The three ranch hands, eager to be on their way, piled into the Caddy convertible, all scrambling for the front seat. Kevin made it first.

Nash and Boyce had to settle for the back.

Kevin looked at them and grinned his usual shit-eating grin. "You boys are getting slow. I reckon that comes with age."

Boyce grinned back and knocked Kevin's hat off. "You pups need to learn to respect your elders."

Bobby yanked the gearshift down into drive, punched the gas, and spun a rooster tail of gravel all the way to the highway. They were all in a good mood, ready to blow off a little steam.

"I still think Mr. Strickland ought to come with us," Kevin said. "He spends way too much time around here. You'd think he didn't like us none, the way he acts sometimes."

Nash Tippins leaned forward and said in his slow drawl, "Ain't that at all. He likes us just fine. I wasn't going to say nothing about what I found out this morning, but you boys ain't going to let it go." Nash paused to consider his words. And to roll himself a smoke.

The rest of the group squirmed impatiently in their seats, waiting for him to speak. There was no way to rush the easygoing ranch hand. Finally, when Nash had his cigarette rolled and lit, he resumed his story. "It's his boy, Nicky, that's got Martin all worked up. He ain't doing no paperwork tonight. He's waiting for Doralee to call and he don't want nobody to know about it."

"How come you know so much about what's going on?" Kevin asked suspiciously. "You been kissing up, bucking for a cushy job?"

"No, nothing like that," Nash said. "I was building a fire in the stove this morning. That's when I found this scrap of paper that wasn't burned up all the way. It had Nicky's name on it."

"What did the note say?" Kevin demanded.

"Well, most of the paper was burned," Nash answered, "but I could make out a little piece of it. I think Nicky's run away from home again."

Boyce Gates adjusted his hat in the rearview mirror. "Jesus, how old is Nicky now, thirteen, fourteen?"

"Yeah, something like that," Bobby said. "Anybody know where the kid went?"

"The letter said Nicky might be on his way here," Nash replied. He elbowed Boyce out of the way and adjusted his own hat. "I guess that's why Martin's staying home, in case Nicky shows up."

"Sounds like a lot of trouble to me. That's why I ain't never having any kids," Boyce pronounced solemnly, finally satisfied that his hat was cocked at the precise angle that would guarantee maximum female interest over at Jake's.

"I think we can rest pretty easy about there not being any little Boyces," Nash said.

"And why's that?" Boyce wanted to know.

"You gotta get a woman to have sex with you first."

Boyce let the remark and the accompanying hoots pass before turning his attention to Kevin. "Say, I heard you talking to Strickland about some dead stock over in the north pasture. What was that all about?"

"Mr. Strickland says those Ridgebacks killed a couple of cows up there."

"He gonna do anything about it?" Boyce asked.

Kevin shrugged, nervously watching Bobby out of the corner of his eye. "I don't know. He didn't say."

"You let the dogs loose like I told you?" Bobby casually asked.

Kevin said nothing, just stared straight ahead.

Bobby laughed at Kevin's silence. "Don't worry about it. I knew you didn't have the guts for the job so I took care of it myself." He cracked the knuckles of his right hand slowly, thoughtfully. "One of these days I'm going to have to show old Martin who's boss."

Night had fallen and Bobby reached out to turn on the headlights, flashing them at an oncoming pickup running without lights.

The driver shot them the bird as they passed him.

"Was that Jesse?" Bobby asked, looking into the rearview. "Yep, that was his own self, Jesse Black Eagle," Kevin said. "He's crazy as his grandfather. After we have a friendly game or two over at Jake's, remind me to have a talk with Jesse about road etiquette."

Nash grinned. "Jesse's pretty handy with his fists, but I guess you already know that since he kicked your butt in high school. He might teach you a few things about etiquette."

Boyce looked a little troubled at the direction the talk was taking. "If I find me a girl that'll talk to me, I don't want you to start no trouble, Bobby. You can't get no girl while you're in jail." At the thought of jail, Boyce's look went from troubled to apprehensive. "The last time I was in the lockup there was a couple guys that said they liked the way my jeans fit. One of them said I had a nice ass. He was a real big guy, too."

"They was just funning you," Nash said. "What did you say to the guy who liked your ass?"

"I told him I had the hemorrhoids real bad."

"Did that work?"

"He said that was okay, his old lady was always on the rag," Boyce answered. "All I know is that I slept on my back the whole night. And I got a bad sinus condition, too. It drains down the back of my throat, and I got a cold on account of that. You know how hard a summer cold is to kick…?"

Bobby took his eyes off the road, reached down to turn on the radio. He didn't want to hear any more about Boyce's summer cold.

"Bobby, watch out!" Kevin grabbed the steering wheel and gave it a sharp jerk. The Caddy swayed across the road, running off onto the shoulder before Bobby could react. When he did find the pedal, they spun around several times before sliding to a shuddering halt in the dust.

Bobby smacked the steering wheel with the heel of his hand. "Are you fucking crazy, Kevin? You trying to get us all killed?"

"There was somebody walking along the road. I didn't think you saw him." Kevin laughed, even though his face had gone pale. "I was afraid you were going to run over the guy."

Boyce dabbed at his bleeding lip where he had hit the headrest. "Kevin, I think you're the one who fell on his head today, not Bobby. There ain't nobody out there."

"Yes, there was," Kevin insisted. "I didn't get a good look, but there was someone out there. I swear it."

Bobby made a U-turn in the middle of the deserted stretch of blacktop and drove back a mile. Everyone in the car scanned the night for Kevin's hiker.

There was no sign of anyone.

Bobby made another screeching U-turn and headed back toward Jake's. "You satisfied?"

"I guess I was wrong. It's just that I was sure…" Kevin reluctantly shook his head. "Sorry, Bobby."

"It's all right. You were probably expecting to see Nicky. Watch it, though. You almost cost Boyce another tooth, and he ain't got too many left as it is."

MARTIN STRICKLAND WAS DOING HIS BEST TO STAY BY THE LANDLINE phone, though he was too keyed up to sit still. He didn't trust his cell, reception was spotty out here in the boonies.

The sun had gone down about an hour ago, bringing the familiar chill to the air. They might even get some frost tonight. Rubbing his arms, he got up, took a poker and prodded the fire in the potbellied stove. The chunk of cast iron sat in the middle of the bunkhouse like some silent and benign Buddha. A loose board squeaked when he walked back to his desk. The quiet was stretching his nerves to the breaking point.

"Damn you, Doralee, why didn't you keep an eye on Nicky?"

The thought of his son hitchhiking had Martin scared far more than he wanted to admit. The boy was thirteen and could take care of himself. Still, you never knew when you might get picked up by the wrong guy. There were a lot of sick sons of bitches out there.

Martin looked at the drawer where he kept the bottle. A drink would taste real good, but he knew if he took the first one he wouldn't be able to stop.

Pushing back the chair, he climbed to his feet and walked outside. Not so far he wouldn't be able to hear the phone. It was his habit to take a look around the ranch every night before going to bed. Besides, the dogs needed to be fed.

He got within twenty feet of their pen before he noticed the gate was open.

"Damn," he said with the fatalism of a man who is beyond surprise. The bag of dog food fell at his feet, splitting open, spilling on the ground. He gave the remaining contents a sincere kick, which made him feel a little better. "This has got to be a joke. If you turned those dogs loose, Bobby," he vowed beneath his breath, "I'm going to kick your skinny little butt, and your daddy ain't going to be able to stop me." Martin gave a shrill whistle to summon the dogs.

After a few minutes, he realized they wouldn't be returning. Not until morning. They were out on the ranch somewhere, five of them, running around in the night, looking for something to kill.

Martin pitied anything that met up with them. He'd gotten a good look at the cows they had ripped apart and it was one of the most brutal things he'd ever seen.

The night chill crept under his clothes, causing him to shiver. He was tired. Sometimes he thought about quitting the Broken R, but he knew he was too old to get on with another spread. The ranching business was about gone to hell, anyway. Mr. Roberts was renting the grazing land from the Navajos and his option was up next year. Word had it the Navajos weren't going to let him renew. Their strip-mining operation was a lot more profitable. If that happened, he would be out of a job anyway. He didn't have much put aside. He'd lived his life like Bobby and Kevin, and all the rest of the hands, spending his pay every Saturday night at places like Jake's, buying drinks for his friends, whoring, and gambling. When Doralee had taken Nicky, Martin had quit thinking about the future.

When he stooped to pick up the busted dog-food bag, he heard the phone ring. It rang five more times before he reached the bunkhouse, and then quit. "Damn it, Doralee, I told you to let it ring."

Martin pushed into the bunkhouse.

The first thing he noticed, someone had been rummaging around in his desk. Caught against the window was the outline of a figure holding the phone. As Martin's eyes peered into the dimness, he could make out someone in stained denim and a cowboy hat that looked like it had once been white.

"I think it's for you," the figure said.

CHAPTER EIGHT

Amos Black Eagle sat on his trailer steps and tried to find a position that didn't cause his his old bones to ache. He didn't find it.

In the meantime he watched his grandson, Jesse, work on the pickup. That old truck hadn't been much when the boy bought it, but a little money and a lot of hard work had made the Chevy into something real nice. The old man smiled when Jesse pulled out a handkerchief and wiped away some imaginary dust.

"That is indeed a fine vehicle," Lefty Thunder Coming said in his gravelly voice. Years of booze and cigarettes had honed it to a low rumble. "A truck like that would bring a man much pride. I used to have a nice truck back a few years ago, a Ford Ranger." He shrugged philosophically and spat in the dust. "But I lost it in a poker game up in Pagosa Springs. I had two pair, kings and queens, the other guy had three deuces. I thought the son of a bitch was bluffing." Lefty hung his head at the memory. "It is a shameful thing to get beaten by three deuces."

Amos was barely listening. He had heard this story at least a hundred times.

Lefty was an Apache from the San Carlos reservation whose wife had grown tired of his gambling and had kicked him out. Lefty had earned his nickname from welching on a bet; his right hand had been cut off as payment.

Every Saturday Lefty showed up at Amos's place with two bottles of whiskey, which they drank while playing pinochle. At the last estimate, Lefty owed Amos a little over three million dollars.

Lefty dusted off a spot on the steps and eased down by Amos.

They watched Jesse work on the back window of the truck. A huge black eagle holding a snake had been painted on it. "That back window's new, ain't it?" Lefty asked.

"Yeah, Jesse painted it himself."

"Did a damned fine job. He must take after you."

"I don't know who he takes after." Amos felt a heaviness in his heart. He had never thought he would have to raise another boy, or live long enough to see his only son dead. Amos was seventy-three now, seamed and bent by the years, and he wondered if he would be able to see the job through. He hoped so. There was no one else to look after the boy.

"Last night I heard an owl calling," Amos said. "Sounded like it was right outside my window."

"Is that a fact?" Lefty asked, impressed. He considered the implications for a moment. "Rudy No Horses over in San Carlos heard an owl. A week later he was dead."

"What happened?"

Lefty took a long drink from his bottle while he tried to remember. His face brightened. "Rudy was killed when he dropped half a joint down in his car seat. Set his fat red ass on fire. He was jumping around, trying to put it out, when the car door came open and he fell out. They say it was a hell of a sight, him turning cartwheels down State sixty with flames shooting out his ass."

"Did he really hear an owl?" Amos asked, taking a drink.

"Yeah, my ex-wife said she heard it from a woman over in Flagstaff, who claimed she heard it from her cousin, who got it from a very reliable source. She said Rudy's car went out of control and hit a Bible salesman in an S-Ten from Omaha. Killed him, too."

"You think the Bible salesman heard that owl?" Amos inquired, taking another drink.

"That's beside the point. The point is that Rudy heard an owl and a week later he was dead."

"I don't even know why I talk to you, Lefty."

"It's because I bring good whiskey," Lefty answered, unoffended.

They went back to watching Jesse work on the pickup. Over by the corral.

The corral was the showpiece of Amos's spread. The place wasn't much, ten acres of hardscrabble dirt with almost enough grass to feed his old U-necked Appaloosa mare and the three moth-eaten buffalo he kept so the tourists would have something to take pictures of. At last count there were eight nervous chickens, and that was two less than last week. This was a fact Lefty pointed out.

"The coyotes been sneaking up here at night and eating them," Amos said. "Custer there," he pointed at the dog, a blonde border collie sleeping under the truck, "is supposed to make sure that don't happen. But one of the coyotes is a female. I figure old Custer there is selling me out for sex."

"You mean he's looking the other way while his lady love is eating your chickens?"

"That's exactly what I mean. Old Custer is about the horniest dog I ever seen."

The dog raised his head at the mention of his name, then lowered it back.

"He does look like his ass is dragging," Lefty said. "I wondered why he ain't been doing any leg dancing lately. I was beginning to think he didn't like my leg no more."

"Well, you'd better enjoy the break, cause soon as the chickens are all gone, your leg's going to start looking good again. And I'd watch where I passed out if I was you. I seen him eyeing some other parts of your anatomy."

"Thanks for the warning. You do any business today?" Amos shook his head no. "Should have some tourists soon. Frontier Days is coming up."

The trailer that Amos and Jesse shared was twenty-three miles from the interstate, most of it on pothole-riddled dirt roads, which meant they didn't get a lot of company. Still, once in a while they would get some tourists who were looking for real Navajo Indians. Amos felt obliged to show them one.

For a price.

A sign out front promised authentic Indian souvenirs for sale, but the stuff was fake. Junk. Amos made a trip to Tucson a couple of times a year, where he bought the crap from an old Jewish lady who had a son who brought it in from Taiwan. Amos didn't make much of a living; still he managed to make enough to keep himself supplied with the only thing he ever wanted from the white man's world: *Jack Daniel's* whiskey. He took a sip of the sour mash and savored the evening. The truck radio was playing a sad song about lost love.

"We gonna play some cards tonight?" Lefty asked. "I feel lucky."

"You say that every night," Amos answered, his mind far away. "I don't feel lucky. I feel like something bad's going to happen."

Jesse had finally got that last speck of imaginary dust off his pickup. At twenty-one, Jesse was a lot like his father, and that made Amos proud. And a little scared. Jesse's father, Thomas Black Eagle, had wanted to make his way in the white man's world and it had gotten him killed in the end. Jesse wanted no part of his own tribe, either. He talked constantly of leaving, of going to Los Angeles. Amos knew it was hard for the boy, being half-white, half Navajo. More times than he could count, Amos had seen the swollen eyes and split lips that Jesse had brought home from school. But the boy was tough. He had never cried, never complained.

The old man turned his eyes to the hills in the far distance and watched as the sun began dipping behind them. A breeze sprang up, ruffling Amos's long gray braids.

As Jesse slammed the truck hood shut, Amos smiled, showing perfect dentures that flashed white as snow. They were a present from Jesse. His grandson knew he loved corn on the cob, but Amos would never spend money on store-bought teeth. Jesse said getting those teeth was the biggest mistake he had ever made, because now they had corn on the cob every night.

"The boy sure loves that old truck," Lefty observed.

"Yeah, he's gone every night in it." Amos thought he knew where the boy went. He had a pretty good idea from the pool cue Jesse kept hidden under the truck seat and the stash of bills he had under the mattress in his room. Hustling pool was a risky business. A man could end up only broke if he was lucky. Dead if he wasn't. Dead like Jesse's father.

Still, Amos knew a man was going to raise a little hell now and then. He'd done his share. The old man looked south toward Mexico, a good two-day drive to the border. That was where he'd get in trouble when he was younger. The last time had been nearly ten years ago. His wife long dead and gone, he'd gotten himself a scrawny young Mexican prostitute who looked like she needed the money.

A small sigh came from Amos as he thought back on that night.

The girl had been about twenty or so, tiny, with a bad complexion and good teeth. Smiling, she said her name was Amanda Oliveros. She'd only been in the business for a little over two years, she told Amos. This was a temporary thing, she explained with a shyness that wasn't feigned, just something to help her get by for a while. She had plans. Her sister, Carlotta, who was a maid in some big fancy hotel up in Phoenix, was going to send for her any day now. The only reason Carlotta hadn't sent for her was because the hotel wasn't hiring yet.

There, Amanda had assured him, she would meet some rich American who would take her away from all this. Despite the softness of her words, there was something defiant about the way Amanda Oliveros told her story. Something sad, too.

Amos said nothing about her plans. He knew, deep in his heart, the sister was never going to send for her.

They had sat on the bed in the small shack that leaked in the rain and passed a bottle of tequila back and forth until they were both gloriously drunk. In Spanish and broken English, amid much giggling, Amanda told Amos that he reminded her of her grandfather, who used to sit her on his knee and tell her stories when she was little. Amos was stung by the remark. The girl saw the hurt on his face and tried to apologize, but the damage was done.

Later, when he had tried to make love to her, Amos had been unable to do anything. Hurt by the grandpa remark, drunk, and filled with memories of his dead wife, he had ended up lying next to her on a cot in the dark, listening to the roof dripping into a couple of five-gallon pickle buckets.

When Amos had pulled himself out of bed the next morning with a head filled with wool and shame, he had put money under her pillow and let himself out quietly.

The last thing he'd seen that gray, rainy morning as he drove away was the girl standing in the window waving good-bye. She'd blown him a kiss, smiled bright and cheerful, a smile that seemed out of place on such a gloomy day.

Many times since that night, he wondered if Amanda's sister had ever sent for her. If he went back to that tiny Mexican village, would she still be waiting for that call, a little older, a little harder, her cheerful smile not quite so cheerful? He'd decided long ago he didn't want to know. Life was full of sadness enough without going out of your way to find it. He preferred to remember how her hair smelled like spring rain, fresh and clean. How she'd smiled when she had waved goodbye.

Still, it was a hurtful thing he decided, when a man grew old and could no longer be with a woman. Now Amos just ate corn on the cob with his new false teeth and drank *Jack Daniel's* whiskey on the porch with his friend of many years, Lefty Thunder Coming.

Lefty nudged Amos. "Earth to Amos, wake up, Grandpa. Your grandson is talking to you."

Amos blinked, took a drink.

Now that Jesse had finished his ministrations to the truck, he walked toward the trailer, his voice full of disapproval. "You need to lay off that *Jack*, Gramps. You know it makes you do things you shouldn't."

Amos ignored the remark. "You going out again?"

"Yeah, I got a little business to take care of."

Amos studied the boy before him. Dressed in blue jeans and a white T-shirt, Jesse looked more white than Navajo, and that hurt Amos. Jesse had his father's angular features, his mother's eyes, green and piercing. And slightly angry. The boy was all grown up and Amos felt like he didn't know his grandson anymore. The thought only added to his sadness.

"What kind of business?" Amos inquired.

"Just business." Jesse evaded Amos's stare and stepped around him.

"You want something to eat before you go?" Amos asked.

"No, I gotta get going. Got people waiting on me. Besides," he smiled, "I don't think I could eat any more corn." For a second the Jesse that Amos knew was standing in front of him, then the mask slipped back over Jesse's face. Amos felt as though he were suddenly talking to a stranger.

Maybe the whiskey made Amos bold, or maybe it was just worry that made him say, "Shooting pool for money isn't a very smart business."

"You been spying on me?" Anger made the muscles in the boy's face clench.

"No, but I hear things and I got two eyes. I seen that cue stick you got under the seat, the money under the mattress."

Jesse snorted, his laughter derisive. "How should I make a living? Like you? Selling junk to tourists?"

"You could go back to school. One more year and—"

"Fuck school! I'm not ever going back there."

The old man flinched beneath the anger in Jesse's eyes and had to look away.

Jesse saw the sorrow in Amos's face and his tone softened. "I'm sorry, I meant no disrespect, Grandfather. It's just that I'm all through with that. My father went to school. What did it get him? The best he could do was end up working over at the mine."

"It was better than dying in a bar fight," Amos said.

"Was it?" Jesse answered. "Was it?" His face hardened. "You heard the way he coughed after breathing that dust all day?" Jesse's fist clenched and, for a second, Amos thought his grandson was about to strike him. Instead the boy's hands fell to his sides. Helpless. "Getting killed in that bar fight was probably the best thing that ever happened to my dad. Nothing good ever happens to anyone around here."

It was at that moment that Amos Black Eagle realized Jesse didn't need him anymore. He was the only thing holding the boy here.

Jesse turned and walked away, his shoulders bunched beneath his T-shirt. He didn't look back as he climbed into his truck and drove away. Several of the chickens almost didn't get out of the way in time. Their raucous clucking was the only sound for a long while.

Amos watched the Chevy fade into the dusk until there was only a faint cloud of dust, and then that too disappeared. He sat on the porch of his rusted trailer and sipped whiskey and stared at nothing at all. Lefty had already passed out. After a while the moon came up and the breeze that blew in from the mountains turned cooler.

Amos reached over and plucked Lefty's bottle off the porch. "Lefty, you're a good man, but you can't hold your liquor for shit." Amos tipped the bottle and took a sip. By the time the bottle came down, he had an idea.

Lurching to his feet, he went into his trailer and came out with his saddle and a rope. He called out to his dog, Custer, who appeared as if by magic. The dog looked tired and hungry. He flopped at Amos's feet, his tongue lolling.

"Guess those jackrabbits were a little too fast tonight, old son?"

The dog laid his head on his paws.

"And I suppose you want me to get you something to eat?" The dog looked up, hopeful.

Amos indicated a bowl of refried beans sitting on the porch. The dog looked dubiously at them. "It's beans or nothing, Custer," Amos said, heading toward the corral. Custer took one disdainful sniff at the bowl and loped after Amos.

Amos managed to get the corral gate open. His steps wavered, causing him to have to lean against the corral poles until the ground stopped moving, yet his hands were steady. He managed to rope his old U-necked mare on the first toss.

"Come on, Amanda," he soothed the ancient appaloosa as she skittered around him in circles, "we got us some business to take care of, too." He threw the saddle on her and waited. Amanda didn't like to be ridden and she had a habit of holding her breath. Amos couldn't count the number of times he had walked home after the saddle had slipped sideways, throwing him into the dirt.

Amanda finally exhaled and Amos yanked the cinch tight. "You're getting old, girl," he sighed, patting her on the neck. "You used to be able to hold your breath a lot longer."

Amos Black Eagle rode off into the Arizona night, an ancient man swaying drunkenly on his ancient horse, his hungry dog trotting along behind.

DARKNESS CAME FAST TO CROWDER FLATS. ALREADY THE SUN HAD dipped behind the mountains and the desert seemed to pause, to take one final breath before exhaling the night. Jesse Black Eagle gunned his pickup around the potholes in what passed for a road in this shithole of a town, and smiled. The smile was bitter.

Dust trailed after him, a dun-colored ribbon that wrapped itself around everything, as though the desert was quietly trying to choke Crowder Flats. Sometimes, Jesse felt that the desert resented the town being here. Having had the shit beaten out of him countless times because he was a half-breed, Jesse felt pretty confident he knew resentment when he saw it.

As he drove, night settled in. He loved the night. That was the only time he felt really alive. The daytime was something to be endured, like his job at the strip mine, where he worked on one of the water trucks.

Even though only six months had passed since he had dropped out of college, Jesse knew deep down inside that this was as good as life was ever going to get for him. He had to get out of this town. Already he was beginning to cough from breathing dust all day, just like his old man had coughed. Jesse couldn't count the nights Mom had sat up with his dad, wiping away the blood-flecked spit that ran down his old man's chin, before they stuck what was left of Thomas Black Eagle in a box and lowered him into the hard-packed earth.

Two years later his mom had followed.

Every few weeks or so Jesse went out to visit their graves. They were in the pauper section of the churchyard, where no one came to leave pretty flowers, and the weeds were the only things that grew. Jesse had asked the council of elders to move his parents to the sacred grounds near the reservation, but his request had been denied. Thomas Black Eagle had turned his back on the old ways when he had married a white woman. In the end, neither the whites nor his own people had wanted him.

So Jesse ended up living with his grandfather, Amos Black Eagle.

The courts had been reluctant to hand over a twelve-year-old to a man with a reputation for drunkenness. The only reason they did it, Jesse figured, was the orphanage didn't need any more hungry red mouths to feed. They already had more than enough.

Jesse wanted to leave Crowder Flats. Hell, once he'd even done it. He had gotten as far as Tucson before word that Amos was in jail again had reached him. Amos had a failing for Jack Daniel's, and whenever the old man got tanked up, he would saddle up his U-necked mare, go raid Chester Roberts' ranch and run off all Chester's horses. Chester was a good sport about the whole thing. He never pressed charges when Sheriff Johnson put Amos in the drunk-tank to dry out, but someone had to be there to round up the horses and bail Amos out.

That someone was Jesse. And that meant Jesse was stuck in Crowder Flats.

Voiceless fury clamped itself around Jesse's chest and squeezed. He pressed down harder on the gas and the souped-up V-8 responded with a satisfying rumble. He didn't want to think. Thinking was stupid. Thinking was for people who were doing something besides marking time.

He checked his appearance in the rearview mirror as though looking for weaknesses. His face was all hard angles and planes and his dark green eyes were too old for his years. He was primed and ready for trouble.

Reaching into his cooler, he popped the tab on a Coors and drained it in a single swallow, feeling the brew slide down his throat like molten ice. "Oh man, gonna have me a little fun tonight. Some real fun for a change." His voice sounded a little desperate to his ears, so he stopped talking. Crushing the can, he flung it with all his might at a lonely cactus standing beside the road. A spark of satisfaction shot through Jesse as the can struck it dead center. The arm that had made him a starting pitcher at Lone Mesa High was still working just fine. And so was the temper that had gotten him booted off the team his senior year.

Jesse drove fast, without headlights, flipping the bird to a passing white Cadillac convertible that flashed its brights at him. His smile widened when he recognized the surprised face in the Caddy. "Shit, my old buddy, Bobby Roberts." Jesse's smile gave way to laughter. "Didn't recognize you, Bobby, or I'd have run your ass off the road."

He fished out another beer and this time he drank slower. Best stay sharp. He was on his way over to Jake Rainwater's, just outside Crowder Flats, where he was going to shoot some big-money pool. The game was against the guy he had just given the bird, Bobby Roberts.

Bobby was as white as you could get, but his money was plenty green and that was the only color that really mattered in this old world. Three of Jesse's running buddies would be there to watch, so Jesse would have to be cool. His rep was on the line tonight. And if things got rough, maybe more. Bobby got mean if things didn't go his way. To make matters worse, Jake was involved, and you couldn't trust that lying old bastard. He might be backing Bobby. Jake's favorite color was green, too.

A few more minutes passed and the darkness settled in quick and final, forcing Jesse to turn on his headlights. No matter how many times he watched the night come, it always caught him by surprise. This country was hard, giving little, and things could change quickly. He reached into the dash to make sure his equalizer was there. It was. Fully loaded, too. He gave it a kiss, slipped it into the pocket of his leather jacket.

He'd had to show the .32 when his last opponent had been a little reluctant about settling up accounts after the game. The guy'd had the audacity to call him a cheap hood, a hustler. Worse, he had suggested Jesse leave the money on the table. It was more than Jesse made for two weeks of breathing dust on that water truck, and he decided, right then and there, that no one was ever going to take anything away from him again. The way he figured, that money was his, won fair and square. Though he wouldn't even admit it to himself, he had been nearly as scared as his buddies when that .32 appeared from his pocket as though it had a mind of its own, and pointed itself at that big red-necked trucker. The room got quiet as a church while Jesse watched himself go over and pick up that money.

Nobody seemed to object. If they did, they kept their opinions to themselves. Later on that night, as Jesse lay in his bed staring up at the ceiling, he wondered if he would've had the guts to use the gun. Someday he guessed he'd find out.

A glance at his watch in the glow of the dash caused him to swear. Damn, he was running late. Those asshole buddies of his said they'd be waiting at the Shell station. They had better be ready if they wanted to catch this ride.

Sometimes Jesse wondered why he even bothered with such a bunch of deadheads. They didn't have much ambition and fewer guts. When Jesse had pulled that pistol, Ernesto, the youngest of the trio, went and crapped his pants right there on the spot.

They'd made him ride all the way home in the back of the truck. Since that day, if someone even cut so much as a beer fart, Ernesto got the blame.

In the distance, the Shell station was a bright oasis of light that drew Jesse along the now-deserted stretch of blacktop.

Farther up was a softer glow that was Crowder Flats itself. He leaned out the truck window, letting the chill night air whip his hair, and looked up into the sky. The stars were a spray of diamond dust across black velvet, and Jesse knew that when he left here, those stars would be the only thing he would miss. He'd been up to L. A.

once with his dad, and there those same stars were dim, soft-edged, impossibly distant. Here he could almost reach out and touch them.

For the first time in months he felt happy. There was a feeling of expectancy in the air; something was going to happen tonight. He didn't know if it was going to be good or bad. Truth was, he didn't give a damn either way.

Jesse turned into the gas station and slammed on his brakes, letting the pickup fishtail to a halt in front of the pumps. The place was nearly deserted. Jesus was in the left-hand car bay leaning under the hood of an old Dodge Charger. Manny and Ernesto were watching, offering advice that obviously didn't suit Jesus. He kept shaking his head no and rubbing his chin. When he stopped, there was grease on his chin.

At the next gas pump was a redheaded, scrawny teenager filling up his wired-together piece-of-shit Kawasaki dirt bike. He finished, handed Jesus two dollars.

"You owe me another buck," Jesus said, without looking up.

Elliot Cates went into his sneaker.

Jesus looked at the filthy, sweat-stained bill. "Oh man, lay that thing on the hood." He picked up the dollar with a pair of pliers and deposited it in the cash register.

The teenager walked past Jesse and kick-started his bike.

"Hey, Elliot, you little pervert," Jesse said, "what do you need with so much gas? You going out to spear some jack rabbits tonight?"

"Nah, I'm going out to spear your girlfriend. With this." Elliot grabbed his crotch. Before Jesse could get out of the truck, Elliot roared off into the night, the sound of his laughter louder than the cycle.

Over by the Coke machine an old man in baggy Bermuda shorts and a Hawaiian shirt was trying without much success to fold up a road map. His wife was bitching to him about no signal on her cell phone.

Jesse grinned into the thin, birdlike faces and saw only disapproval staring back at him. He threw the truck into reverse and punched the gas pedal, causing his truck to leap backward. The squealing tires made the old man drop the map. He and his wife jumped back into the Winnebago as Jesse slowly eased out and sauntered over to pick up the map. When he tapped on the window and offered up the map, the old man threw the camper into gear and drove away. Their receding faces looked back once. There was no disapproval on them; now there was only fear.

"You scared the shit out of that old man," Jesus said, shaking his head as he slammed the hood on the Charger. He wiped his hands on a greasy rag.

They didn't look any cleaner to Jesse. "That old fart was gonna steal one of your maps."

"Since when did you get to be such a stickler for the law?"

"It just sort of came over me."

"A lot of things have been coming over you lately," Jesus said. "You got that pistol with you?"

Jesse patted the pocket of his jacket and smiled.

"Can I see it?" Ernesto asked, his pimply face filled with excitement. His voice was high and slightly uncertain, and when he got too excited, he stammered.

"No, you can't see it," his brother, Manny, said. "We don't want you to go crapping your pants again."

Ernesto turned red. For a second it looked like he was going to take a swing at Manny, who was a year older and outweighed him by a good thirty pounds. Instead he smiled, his hand going to his pimple-ravaged face as he turned away.

"Come on," Jesse said, "I ain't got time for this horseshit. I got to be at Jake Rainwater's place in half an hour."

Jesus produced a huge key ring. In ten seconds had the place locked up. They started to climb into Jesse's truck, Manny taking shotgun. Jesse jerked his thumb at the back of the truck.

Manny's face tightened. "How come I gotta ride back there?"

"Cause I said so. Ernesto, you take shotgun."

Manny spat on the ground, but said nothing. He climbed in, wedging himself between the spare tire and the toolbox. "You want the blanket?" Ernesto asked.

Manny shook his head no. "Shit no, that thing smells worse than you. I'll take one of them beers, though."

Jesse gunned the pickup, causing Manny to spill the beer all over himself. Manny retaliated by shaking the beer and spraying everyone in the cab. They hit the blacktop with the sound of burning rubber and raucous laughter. Yes sir, it was going to be a hell of a night. One hell of a night.

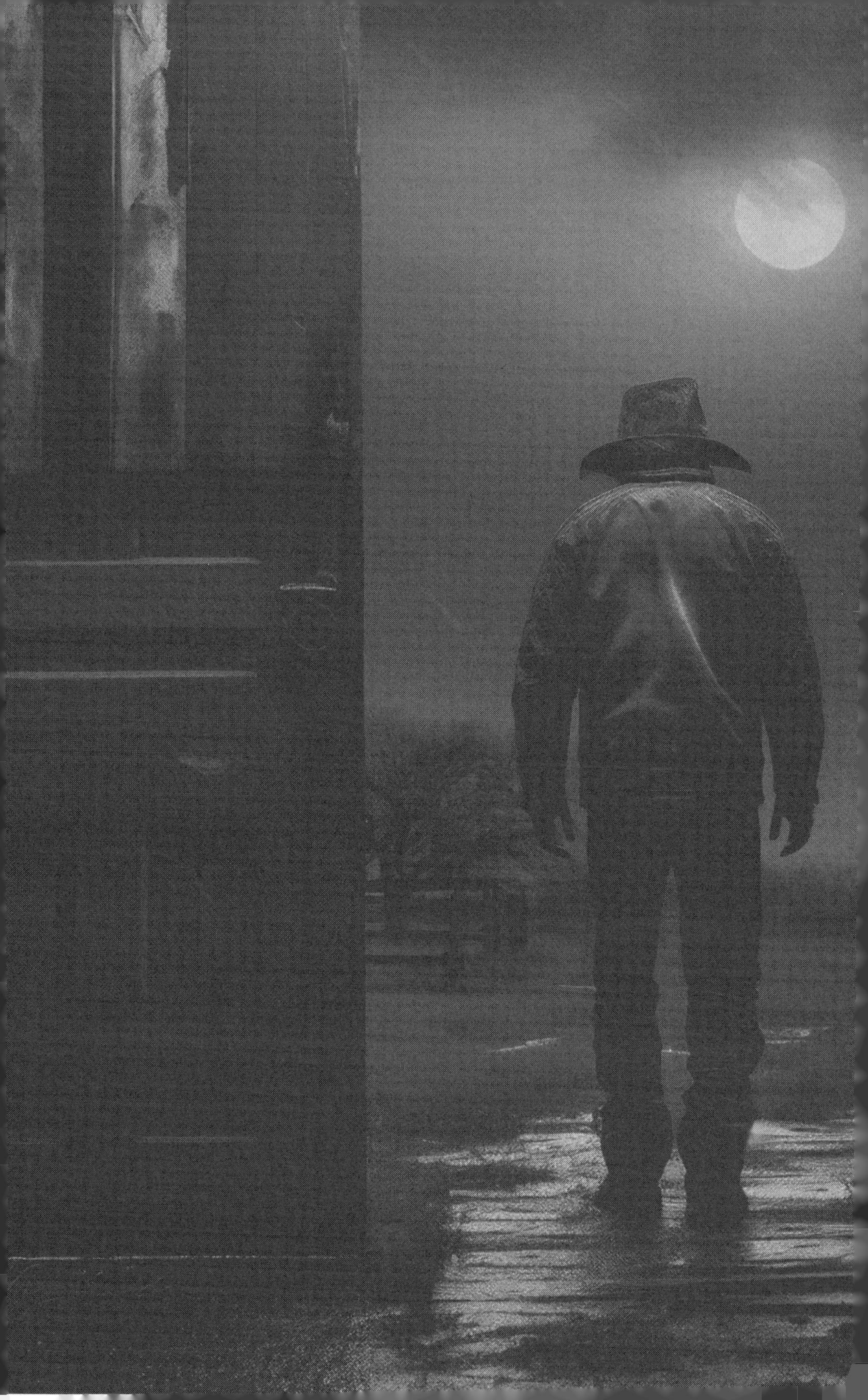

CHAPTER NINE

Amos rode toward Chester Roberts' ranch.

"Amanda, I'm drunk," he said to his horse. "Falling-down, throwing-up, pissing-on-yourself drunk." This seemed to strike Amos as funny for some reason, and he almost choked as he paused to take another drink from the bottle. Whiskey streamed from his mouth.

The clicking of Amanda's hooves was a gentle, insistent rhythm as she picked her sure-footed way along the trail. When they crossed over a ravine, a few stones, loosened from their perches, rattled down, echoing hollowly. A full moon stared down, giving everything hard, sharp edges. Stunted piñon trees, patches of wiry grass, and an occasional barrel cactus were the only things dotting the silvery landscape. They might have been crossing the moon.

The land rose gradually, finally cresting on a mesa dotted with a few scraggly pines. Not much lived here. Not much could.

Down the slope was a huge, dark depression in the earth, with long, ridged gashes that appeared reddish in the moonlight, as though the earth itself were bleeding from a wound. Amos felt his sorrow return. The crater, and that's what it was, a crater, stretched out at least ten miles, maybe more, and each day it grew, like a cancer out of control. The wind changed, blowing the smell of dust and diesel fumes back to Amos.

A low growling reached the old man as he rode the edge of the rim. Bright lights crawled around in the distance, no bigger than the fireflies he had chased as a child.

The lights belonged to huge earth-moving equipment used for strip-mining coal.

Amos grimaced. His own people, the Navajos, were raping their land for the white man's money.

Amos paused on the edge of the crater and stared out at the distant, insect-like earth loaders that crawled back and forth, holding his people's heritage in their clawed embrace, dumping it into the trucks to be carried away. Gone. Never to return.

He turned away, disgusted. Someday soon the money would be gone, but the land would stay violated. Someday, if their gods should return, what would his people say to them when asked about the sacred land?

Amos didn't think they would be pleased with the answer.

The night air was definitely taking on a chill, and Amos had to take another drink to fortify himself against it. Or maybe against the pain he felt. He knew he didn't have enough whiskey to do the job.

They moved on, Amanda trotting along the familiar trail, her smooth gait lulling Amos into a doze. Somewhere in the night an owl hooted, yanking Amos awake. A shiver passed through him. Ancient Navajo lore said that when a warrior heard an owl, a ghost or an evil spirit was nearby. Amos didn't really believe that, still it was hard to shake the teachings of youth. The old man peered into the darkness and realized he had ridden a lot farther than he had thought.

Up ahead was the reason Crowder Flats existed. A graveyard, split in two. Separate graves for the whites, one huge common grave for the Indians. Divided by a stone fence. How it came to be here was a story every school kid in three surrounding counties knew. One hundred thirty-five years ago, Crowder Flats had been wiped out, along with a small band of peaceful Navajos who had been camping nearby. Of course, the town wasn't known as Crowder Flats then. All had been massacred in their sleep, killed down to the last man, woman, and child.

All except for one. A Navajo boy—Amos's grandfather.

According to what Amos's grandfather had said about that night, the killers had appeared as though they were ghosts. They were dressed in blue, he said. And they were quiet. The wind made more sound than the blue men. As best anyone could figure out, the Navajos and townspeople had been killed by Union soldiers. They were probably deserters from General George Crook's army, headed for Mexico.

Still, no one could ever figure out how the soldiers had managed to catch the Navajos unaware. Guards were always posted. If any of the soldiers had been killed, no one had ever found any evidence of it.

The Right Reverend Jebediah Crowder and his band of followers had been the ones to find the massacre. They too had been on their way down to Mexico to spread the Lord's word to those godless Mexicans, as old Jebediah was fond of saying. The carrion birds had pointed the way to the dead from high in the sky for a day before anyone knew what had happened.

When the reverend and his people arrived, they found dead bodies strewn everywhere and the town burned to the ground. They searched in vain for survivors.

They had been stacking the dead like cordwood in the open pit when they had found one who was still breathing, a boy trapped beneath his dead mother. That was, of course, Amos's grandfather. The reverend and his followers took it as a sign that they should stop here and rebuild the town. A sign from the Lord, Jebediah was quoted as saying. Old Scratch would not have his way as long as the reverend was there to fight him.

Now all that remained from that long ago day was a white cross inscribed by old Jebediah Crowder, himself, that said simply: **Washed in the blood of the Lamb.** And of course, the Frontier Days celebration that Crowder Flats threw every year to commemorate the rebuilding of the town.

In moonlight the color of blued steel, Amos looked upon the mesa, at the Joshua trees that raised their twisted, spiked arms to the white man's heaven, at the cross of Jesus. All for the white man. But what of the red man, what of the murdered Navajos who were buried here? Did their spirits rest easy? Amos thought not.

The rock wall that divided the white side from red side was falling down in spots. Amos was the only caretaker the Navajo side had ever had, probably would ever have. Even he didn't like coming out here. The wind blew constantly in this place, a high keening sound that spooked him if he stayed very long. He kicked Amanda in the ribs to hurry her along.

There was business to take care of.

Tonight was not just another trip to Chester Roberts' ranch to chase off a few horses. Chester was gone on a stock-buying trip to Dallas and wouldn't be back until tomorrow. That meant Bobby was unsupervised at the ranch.

Martin couldn't control the boy, which meant the Ridgebacks would be running loose. They were supposed to keep the coyotes away from the stock during calving season, but that wasn't the reason Bobby had talked his father into buying the huge attack dogs. The boy was pissed at Amos.

Jesse had told Amos that the kids at school had laughed at Bobby because Amos, who was only an old drunken Indian, had chased off Chester's horses. It made Bobby look foolish in the eyes of classmates, especially Amy Warrick.

To make matters worse, Jesse said someone had let out a war whoop when Bobby had entered algebra class. Someone else had drawn a picture of a scalped Bobby on the blackboard.

That night Amos and Jesse had sat in their old trailer laughing, and Amos felt that for a moment that Jesse had been proud of him. Instead of ashamed.

Soon Jesse wouldn't have to be ashamed of his grandfather.

Amos, in his drunken logic, had determined he would make one last raid on Chester Roberts' ranch, and, this time, it would be his last. The guard dogs would see to that. He had seen the animals, huge black-and-brown brutes that could tear a coyote to pieces. Or a man. There were five of them roaming the grounds.

Being a full-blooded Navajo who no longer quite believed in the old ways, Amos had determined he would die in the old way.

In battle.

In his mind's eye, he saw the fight with the guard dogs as a way to leave this world with honor. Thanks to Jack Daniel's, he was gloriously stinking drunk. And, the way he saw it, ready for battle. Daubed across his face were streaks of red war paint. Well, not exactly war paint, the red streaks had come from an old lipstick tube he had taken off Amanda Oliveros many years ago. Tied around his neck was a razor-sharp machete. Tied to his saddle was his war-charm necklace, which consisted of obsidian, red beans, a yellow bird's head, and two black eagle feathers. He had brought the only other things that meant something to him: his horse, Amanda, and his dog, Custer. They would accompany him on his journey to the next world.

Another thirty minutes brought Amos to Chester Roberts' place. He studied the ranch from high atop the hill, looking for the dogs.

They didn't seem to be running loose. Maybe he had been wrong about Bobby. Maybe the boy wouldn't turn the dogs loose on him.

Everything looked normal. The horses stood sleeping in the corral. A single light on a pole burned by the bunkhouse, attaching long shadows to everything, except the main house, which was dark. This was Saturday night and that meant everyone was over at Jake Rainwater's place, drinking and dancing, shooting pool, maybe playing some cards in the back.

Still, there would be at least one hand here. Chester never left the ranch deserted.

Time to make a little noise.

Amos opened the corral gate and rode in among the sleeping animals. A sleepy nicker or two greeted his presence. The smell of warm horseflesh met Amos's nose. "Sorry to do this, my friends." He shook loose the rope from his saddle and began lashing the horses.

A whoop sent the twenty-odd horses bolting through the gate. By the time the herd passed the bunkhouse they were making enough noise to raise the dead. With Amos yelling at the top of his lungs, the horses stampeded off into the night.

No lights came on, no faces appeared in the doorway, no shouts of outrage sounded. Everything stayed exactly as it was. Quiet.

Amos reined Amanda in, pissed. This wasn't how he'd seen his last raid going. There was no honor in chasing off horses from a deserted ranch. Where was everyone? Where were the dogs? Their pen was open. The wind gusted, blowing the gate open and shut, making odd random slapping sounds.

Amos picked up a stone and heaved it at one of the bunkhouse windows. He missed, almost fell down. The crack of the rock against wood was gunshot loud in the quiet.

The quiet became something unexpected. The old Navajo felt the whiskey he had consumed earlier starting to wear off. His head was pounding and suddenly dying didn't seem like such a good idea anymore.

"Martin," Amos called out, "where the hell are you? You'd better get your ass out here or I'm gonna have to chuck another rock."

When no answer came, Amos finally decided his last raid was a bust. Now, more and more, all he wanted was a warm place to sleep. The cold was eating into his bones, making them ache. Cursing his gods, the white gods, he walked closer to the bunkhouse. Martin would give him hot coffee and a lecture about the evils of alcohol, but Martin would forgive him. He always did.

As Amos weaved nearer, he saw the bunkhouse door stood slightly ajar.

Had it been open when he had first ridden up? Amos couldn't remember. Calling out, he dropped his rock and weaved his way inside. He felt the warmth of the stove immediately. It felt good. The bunkhouse was dark, except for a single small light over Martin Strickland's desk. The huge room looked neat and clean as always. None of the bunks were occupied. A cup of coffee rested on Martin's desk, still warm to the touch. The chair had been pushed back as though the foreman had stood up to stretch his legs. This was curious, even to Amos's whiskey-soaked mind. He called out Martin's name again.

Only silence. The place was deserted. Sobering up, Amos felt his head beginning to pound. A few loose boards squeaked underfoot as he walked around the desk. Reaching into an open drawer, Amos fished out an almost empty bottle of whiskey and took a belt. He saw papers lying on the floor.

Someone had been rummaging around.

A quick look back outside showed Amanda standing patiently. Custer was, however, eating something. Amos sure hated to leave that warm stove, but he was curious about whatever it was that Custer was bolting down.

"Dog food." Amos looked at the busted sack on the ground. "Looks like somebody left in a hurry. Maybe they went to look for the dogs." That made sense. Suddenly, feeling very much ashamed, Amos walked over to Amanda. What had seemed like a good way to die a few hours ago now seemed foolish.

"What if the dogs had been here? They would have killed me and Martin would have blamed himself. I really am a drunken old fool, you know that, Custer?"

The dog didn't seem overly concerned with Amos's repentance. Maybe he'd heard it all before. Maybe this was the first time in his life the border collie had ever tasted dog food. From the way he was bolting the stuff down it was obvious he liked Kibbles 'n Bits better than those stringy jackrabbits he chased every day. A lot easier to catch, too.

The sound of hoof beats caused Amos to raise his head. He expected to see Martin riding up, but the hoofbeats belonged to the horses he had chased off earlier. Seemed the herd had no desire to be free, they had returned to their feed.

"Tame horses chased by a tame Indian. Nothing wild in the west anymore," Amos said with a sigh, climbing on his mount.

Custer bolted down a few more bites, started after Amos, then came back to the dog food. He would catch up with Amos later.

A kick in Amanda's ribs and soon the Broken R disappeared behind the low-lying hills.

Half an hour later, frozen to the bone, Amos rode up on the graveyard once more and paused for the last of Martin's whiskey. He'd drunk himself sober, the liquor wasn't numbing his brain anymore. Or chasing away the chill.

The wind blew harder, caused his teeth to chatter despite the burning in his stomach.

Beneath the creaking of the pines, he again heard the plaintive call of an owl. Repeated once, twice, it was a mournful sound.

Amos stiffened when the call was followed by mocking laughter. The sound seemed to come from nowhere and yet seemed to be everywhere. Amos turned in his saddle, trying to locate the source of the laughter.

It came again. Clearer this time.

The laughter was coming from the graveyard. A shadow popped up from behind the fence and then crouched down. Amos turned and rode slowly back, clutching the machete.

"Is that you, Lefty? If it is, I'm gonna cut off your other hand."

No answer. Just more laughter.

"Damn it, Lefty, this ain't no time to be fooling around." Amos tried to nudge Amanda closer, but the mare refused. Instead, she began dancing sideways, and Amos was hard pressed to hold on to her. Real alarm began burning through the haze of alcohol that clouded his mind.

The figure raised up completely from behind the fence.

Amos struggled to make out who was back there. The figure clung to the shadows along the pine trees, making it impossible to get a clear look. Something was wrong about the figure, the way it moved. Too quiet. Too quick. Amos strained to hear any trace of movement. There wasn't any. And there should be.

The graveyard was mostly loose stones. Christ, he'd almost fallen on them the last time he'd been out here.

The interloper began moving out of the shadows, toward the white stone cross that caught the moonlight. Only this time the cross wasn't bare. Tied to it was a man. The man was motionless and that was why Amos hadn't noticed him.

Amos's eyes darted back to the figure that was moving again, watching its shadowy progress toward the cross.

The figure emerged into the light.

It was unreal, a thing of myth.

Amos's eyes refused to accept that, and he turned back at the cross, to the man slumped there. The old Indian could still see incredibly well. Something was familiar about the unconscious figure, despite the black shiny substance covering his face. Yet Amos couldn't place the man. Or maybe he didn't want to.

The man on the cross moved, caused the moonlight to flash off something shiny around his stomach. It was a belt with a silver-plated buckle, common as dirt around these parts—except this one had an eagle on it. Amos recognized his own handiwork, even though he hadn't done anything like that in fifteen years.

The last one had been a wedding present for...

Martin Strickland.

The ranch foreman was slumped forward, held only by the ropes around his wrists. The wind shifted, bringing a smell Amos was familiar with.

Blood.

"Martin," Amos called out.

He urged Amanda forward. The mare was having no part of whatever was going on up there. She smelled blood, too, and squealed, a high-pitched, almost human sound, before beginning to buck.

Amos managed to calm her enough to slide off. His feet hit the ground and his knees almost buckled. Maybe he wasn't as sober as he thought.

Another whiff of blood, mixed with the smell of rot, hit him. He fought the overpowering urge to throw up.

The man on the cross stirred and weakly raised his head from his chest. "Amos," he asked in a puzzled voice, "what are you doing here? Ain't you supposed to be out chasing off my horses?" He smiled and then, as though the effort of speaking had cost him more than he could afford, Martin Strickland again slumped against the ropes. This time he didn't move.

The shadowy figure popped out from behind the man on the cross, pulled something shiny from concealment. Amos saw it was a knife. Before the old Navajo could scream a warning he knew would do no good, the knife flashed over Martin Strickland's head.

The shadow raised something high, something black and wet, and gave it a shake.

Amos didn't want to know what the figure held in its hand, but he did—it was Martin Strickland's scalp.

A scream of unholy glee undulated through the night, rising higher and higher, until Amos was forced to clap his hands over his ears. Amos felt the hair on the back of his neck rise. The cry didn't sound human.

Amos couldn't take anymore. Unable to control his roiling stomach, he spewed rabbit, corn, and soured whiskey. Still gagging, he stumbled forward, grabbed onto the rock wall to keep from falling. The rough texture of the stones bit into his skin, the pain stopping him from passing out. Unable to breathe, his knees had gone weak. He felt as though someone had kicked him in the stomach, yet his eyes never left the shadow standing near Martin.

The only thing Amos could compare it to… was a horned devil.

And then, appearing as though by magic, the five Ridgebacks gathered in a semicircle around the strange figure, standing perfectly still, their heads cocked toward it as though awaiting a command.

Amos hurled his bottle. The horned devil easily dodged the empty fifth, and the glass shattered with a loud pop.

Then the command came, though Amos neither saw nor heard anything. The Ridgebacks began moving toward him. He wouldn't have believed anything so big could move so fast. They headed for the fence with long, powerful strides, moving as though controlled by a single mind. It was an eerie sight, that had the quality of some old grainy black-and-white movie, with ghostly images racing across a dark screen. Not real. Not real. The movie seemed out of sync, jumping forward too quickly.

The dogs reached the fence.

Now Amos could hear them breathing as they sucked in the night air and spewed it back in clouds of thin, vaporous white. There was no other sound.

The dogs scrambled up onto the fence. They paused there, frozen statues in the night.

Amos backed away.

The dogs watched him, their tongues lolling from their mouths. They weren't angry or even excited.

"A war chant would be good right here, Amanda," Amos said. He gripped the machete tied around his neck. "I damn sure wish I knew one."

The first dog leaped from the fence. It looked like the animal was going straight at his face.

CHAPTER TEN

Amos knew there was no way the dog could miss him as it launched itself from the stone wall.

He threw up his machete, trying to keep the Ridgeback from his throat. His effort was only partially successful. The animal wasn't able to sink its teeth into him; instead it hit him high on the chest and knocked him back. A string of saliva hit Amos in the face, making him think he had been bitten.

The animal's breath smelled of rotten meat and blood.

The dog landed on the ground, ran past him. Then it turned and came back. Slowly. Almost playfully.

It didn't even growl.

Still reeling from the blow, Amos staggered backwards, fighting for balance. He lost the fight, tripped and went backwards over a pile of stones he'd stacked here last year. A clatter and they dislodged, tumbled down on him. Several were heavy. A couple of his ribs went with audible snaps. The pain took his breath away.

His machete was still clutched tightly in his hand, and even though everything turned black, he somehow managed to hold on to it.

Damned stones. For the last two years he'd meant to fix that low spot in the wall. The ghost of a smile drifted across his face and vanished. The odds were he wouldn't be getting around to the job this year either. Maybe never. He felt a little bit sad about that. There were so many things in his life left undone.

The blackness ebbed away. Returned. Ebbed away.

The rest of the Ridgebacks were making no move toward him. They watched from atop the stone fence, unmoving, as though waiting to see what Amos was going to do.

The old Navajo tried to sit up. The blackness returned.

The scratching of dog nails on the stones grew loud.

Amos struggled onto his stomach, tried to get to his feet. He almost made it. The blackness wasn't going away. Wobbly, he tried to find his balance.

A moment later, something heavy hit him in his chest. He flew backwards into the rocks and the pain from his ribs was grinding, sharp. It woke him up. Amos rolled away, swung the machete. And was rewarded with a yelp of pain.

The Ridgeback scrambled back, one side of its face a pulpy mess where the blade had struck. The single yelp was the only indication the dog had felt the blow.

Amos rose to his knees. The injured dog began circling him and then, one by one, the rest of the Ridgebacks jumped down from the stone wall. They did it leisurely, as though they were coming to Amos to have their ears scratched. They padded quietly over and joined the injured dog, circling Amos, just outside the reach of his machete.

The absurdity of the situation wasn't lost on Amos—the dogs were circling him like celluloid Indians in some old fifties B Western. "I'll be damned," Amos said, unable to stifle the laugh that burst from him. It held a slight touch of hysteria.

In all those fifties Westerns, the cavalry always showed up in the last reel to save the day, their bugles sounding the charge.

Amos didn't hear any bugles, just the wheezing sound of his own breath as he tried to hold off the dogs.

Each time the Ridgebacks made a trip around him, their circle grew a little smaller. Maybe just a few inches, but definitely smaller, and Amos knew that sooner or later they would close the circle. He might get one or two with the machete, but not all five of them. They were biding their time. Wearing his old ass down. Each time he raised the blade, his movements were a little slower than before. He touched his mouth with the back of his hand and saw the bloody froth on it. He was bleeding from a punctured lung.

As if to test him, one of the dogs lunged forward, and Amos swung the machete. The dog danced back out of the way. A rivulet of sweat trickled down Amos's forehead, running into his eyes, causing them to burn. He wanted to wipe the sweat away, but he needed both hands for the machete that had grown nearly too heavy to lift. He figured he could stand off two, maybe three more attempts before he collapsed.

This was the strangest thing Amos had ever seen. The dogs were somehow being controlled by the horned devil who had scalped Martin Strickland. Amos risked a look to see if he could spot the strange figure. He wished he hadn't.

The horned devil was sitting on the stone fence with its legs dangling over the edge, idly swinging its feet back and forth while it watched the dogs edge closer and closer to Amos. The strange figure was dressed in jeans, a denim jacket over a stained white shirt, with expensive snakeskin boots adorning its feet. This was no devil, It was a man in a mask, Amos saw that clearly now. He couldn't say the truth brought him much comfort.

The mask was unlike anything Amos had ever encountered in his seventy-three years; part animal, part human, part nightmare. It was large, ornate, covered on top with multicolored tufts of hair that streamed down the back. The hair looked human. Mixed in with the hair were long red feathers that sprouted upward in a fierce crest like some bird of prey. Part of a human skull came down over the cheeks of the man who wore the mask. The face beneath had been stained white, giving the entire head the look of a skeleton. The horns that Amos had seen were two serpents rising above the mask. They were red, covered with feathers, and Amos would bet his life they were carved from human bone. The man in the mask also wore an elaborate white necklace made up of small white lumps that on first appearance seemed to be stones strung together.

A closer examination revealed they were bones. Small hand bones. Those of children.

"You don't think this outfit is too gauche, do you?" the man in the mask asked. He idly fingered the necklace on his neck. "Accessories are so important. They can make or break an outfit, don't you think?"

"Who are you?" Amos asked, trying to get some air into his burning lungs. When he tried to move toward the fence, all of the dogs shifted as one, putting themselves in front of their new master.

"I guess you could say I'm a traveling man," the figure answered conversationally. He laughed at Amos's blank look. "I'm an old friend of the family. Your grandfather, to be exact. How is he? I haven't seen him in a long time."

Amos tried to get his mind around that question and couldn't. "My grandfather has been dead a long time." A small froth of blood bubbled on his lips as he tried another question. "Who are you? What do you want?"

The man in the mask considered the questions for a moment, tapping the knife he still held in his hand against the stone wall with slow measured strokes, "Let's just say I'm a man exercising his rights as a property owner." He saw the quizzical look on Amos's face and laughed again, "This property," he said, sweeping his arm back to indicate the graveyard, "was mine a long time ago and I don't care much for the way it's being taken care of now. Things are missing."

Amos followed the gesture, taking his eyes off the dogs, and one of the Ridgebacks darted in. This time Amos was a little slow in answering the charge. Teeth raked his arm and the pain was beyond anything Amos had expected. It filled his whole being, making his cracked ribs seem like nothing. He raised the machete, almost as an afterthought, and swung, but the dog moved back into the circle, content to wait.

Blood slid down the old man's arm, making the handle of the machete slippery.

"Call off your dogs," Amos said. "I won't come near this place again. You have my word."

"No can do," the man in the mask answered. He seemed almost apologetic as he explained, "This place was my home and you have been pilfering from it. I've got to make an example out of you. One that your people will understand."

"I've never taken anything from here," Amos said.

"Something is missing. A knife, a very special knife."

"Why do you blame me?" Amos asked.

"Your scent is all over this place."

Amos snorted with contempt. "That's some nose you got there, mister. I ain't been in this graveyard in over a year."

"But your friend here comes to this place often." He indicated the slumped body of Martin Strickland hanging from the cross.

"Is that why you hurt Martin, you bastard?" Amos said. "Because he came here?"

"No, not exactly, Amos. You don't mind if call you Amos, do you? Your friend Martin has been coming here for quite a while now. He's been riffling the graves for souvenirs and selling them." The knife beat a slow, rhythmic cadence against the stone wall. "I had to make an example out of him, too." The knife's beat grew faster.

The dogs had edged closer while Amos and the stranger had been talking. One of the Ridgebacks feinted in, making Amos swing the machete. Too late he saw the move was a fake to make him commit. Before he could draw back, one of the animals behind him darted in. Amos managed to alter the arc of the blade, guiding it toward the dog that seemed to be leisurely reaching out for him. Amos was too slow. More pain. His leg this time. The dog danced back, its red-toothed smile mocking him.

Amos supported his weight on the machete, fighting for balance. His right leg had quit working.

The man in the mask raised his head to the night breeze, and Amos had the distinct feeling he had caught scent of something. "You ever get down to Mexico anymore, Amos? You ever see Amanda Oliveros?"

"How do you know about Amanda?" Amos asked quietly. He was past surprise anymore.

"I guess you could say I'm a mind reader." The dusty, ghostlike figure stopped tapping on the stone fence with the knife and held it high, catching the moonlight with the silvery blade. "Why don't you lie down and die, old man. You know you're no good to anyone. Not as a man to Amanda Oliveros, not as a grandfather to Jesse."

Amos staggered beneath the words that hurt more than any bite from the Ridgebacks. For a moment he was hypnotized by the stranger's words, by the glint of light from the knife that kept dancing across his eyes. He wanted to give in. He was tired. Very tired. Seventy-three years pressed down hard and nothing was right anymore. He had done his best his entire life, only to discover it hadn't made the slightest difference. Everything was all screwed up.

The knife kept flashing in Amos's eyes.

Back and forth.

Back and forth.

"It's not your fault, Amos. Come to me and I will make everything right for you. I will give you peace." The voice was little more than a whisper now, and yet it was the clearest sound Amos had ever heard. It was mesmerizing, touching some chord deep within him. Amos listened to the words and, despite himself, he began moving toward the figure on the stone fence, drawn to the man who had hurt his son's best friend, Martin Strickland.

Once Amos had taken the first step, the second was easier, the third easier still.

The stranger in the mask was not to be feared, he was a friend, Amos could see that now. Amos wondered why he hadn't seen it right off. Just a few more steps and everything would be all right. Amos put his right foot in front of his left foot, and his new friend smiled in encouragement. Yes, he smiled. Warm. Friendly. Amos could see the white teeth gleaming beneath the mask.

"That's good, Amos. Come on, come on," the soft voice coaxed. "I've got what you want right here." The arms were open wide, beckoning to him. In one of the hands was the glittering light that would solve all of Amos's problems. The old man watched it moving back and forth, fascinated, unable to take his eyes off the silvery flame.

Amos took another step and almost fell. "My leg hurts," he said, and his voice sounded like that of a small, lost child to his own ears.

"It's okay, take your time. We've got plenty of time. Plenty of time."

Amos moved closer.

The dogs sat on their haunches, watching, their tongues lolling.

Amos was only a couple of feet away from the man in the mask when he heard the crack. The sound was distant, not connected to anything. At first Amos thought he had stepped on a dead branch.

The sound came again.

One of the Ridgebacks yelped, then went silent.

Someone was shooting, that's what the sound was. Someone was shooting. Amos looked at the dog as it fell into a boneless heap, its brains splattering the stone fence.

Another shot.

Another dog fell.

Just like knocking over ducks in a shooting gallery, Amos thought as the world began edging back into focus. Two down. Three more to go and the shooter would win a prize. Only there would be no prize. The remaining dogs turned tail and ran. Amos turned back to the wall. The light in the denim-clad figure's hand was no longer a glittering prize. It slowly resolved itself into a knife that would take Amos's life.

The man on the fence was no longer friendly, instead he seemed suddenly angry. He gripped the knife by the blade, and Amos knew the knife was about to be thrown. Amos wanted to move, he really did. He just couldn't.

The hand with the knife went back, poised, and the smile was back, teeth glinting bone white.

Another flat crack came from behind Amos.

A hole appeared in the stained chambray shirt, right in the center. A small puff of dust flew up from where the bullet struck. Another where it exited. The breeze dispersed both. The figure rocked back but didn't fall. No prize here, no prize here. The hand with the knife drew back again, slow but determined. A second hole appeared about an inch below the first. Two more puffs of dust. This time there was a small grunt, as though the man on the fence had been punched, and he went over backward, landing hard on the ground in the darkness. He lay there in a shapeless heap on his back. The head was the only part of the figure in the light, letting the white teeth catch the moonlight in a vacant smile.

Amos wanted to turn to see who was doing all the shooting, but he was too damned tired to care. He leaned against the fence and waited for his benefactor to announce himself. The smell of soured Jack Daniel's reached Amos before the frightened voice did.

"Is he dead, Amos?"

"I think so."

"Christ all mighty," Lefty said, "I ain't never shot anybody. I had to do it. He was going to kill you."

Amos could only nod.

"Do you know who he is?"

"I don't have the faintest idea, Lefty," Amos said. He watched his old friend walk closer. Lefty's face was the color of spoiled milk, and he looked like he was about to faint.

"What are you doing out here in the middle of the night?" Amos asked.

"Looking for you. I needed a drink."

"How'd you know where I was?"

Lefty laughed, a pale imitation of his normal laugh. "Shit, you don't have to be no rocket scientist to figure out where you go on a Saturday night. Especially when you get a snoot full. You always head straight for Chester's place and run off all his horses."

Lefty was still drunk and the 30-30 in his one good hand looked out of place. "I ain't never killed a man before," he repeated, almost on the verge of tears, "not even when they cut off my hand."

"It's okay, Lefty, I don't think you killed him."

Lefty looked at the figure sprawled on the ground. His voice was completely devoid of humor. "He looks pretty goddamn dead to me."

"I think he was dead before you ever shot him."

"Amos, I think you've lost your mind," Lefty said. "What makes you say something like that?"

Amos pulled Lefty closer to the fence, pointing at the dead man. "Look at him. You notice anything missing?"

Lefty reluctantly looked. "There's no—he's not—"

"Bleeding," Amos finished. "Live people bleed, dead ones not so much."

Lefty considered the implications of that statement. "If he was already dead, then why did he fall when I shot him?"

"I don't know."

Lefty crawled over the fence and gingerly pulled the mask off the still figure. "I think I know this man. It's Billy Two Hats."

"I know that name, too. He hasn't been around here in a long time."

Lefty placed a hand on the throat of the dead man. "I don't get a pulse, and yet he's still warm." The small Apache went over and checked Martin Strickland. Lefty looked at Amos, holding up a bloody hand. "We got two dead men here. What are we going to do?"

Grunting in pain, Amos slowly hobbled over the fence, knelt down, and began moving the loose stones to one side. "We could do the law-abiding thing, we could go to the sheriff. I kinda doubt he's going to buy any of this walking-dead-man stuff. He's been itching to lock me up for years. Thinks I'm crazy. This would be just the excuse he's been looking for."

Lefty knelt down and began moving stones, too. He looked at Amos, his expression quizzical. "Why are we putting these stones in a pile?"

"This is a graveyard, isn't it?" Amos said. "What do you do in a graveyard?"

"You bury people," Lefty answered.

CHAPTER ELEVEN

Jake's parking lot was jammed full when Bobby Roberts nosed his Caddy into a narrow, oil-stained spot. The reason the spot was narrow was because there was another Caddy taking up about a space and a half. The car was like Bobby's except it was red and had dusty Texas plates on it.

"Look at that, would you, boys?" Bobby said. "Damned Texans don't know how to park. They think they can just come in here and take over. Somebody needs to teach them a few manners." He got out and casually smashed a taillight on the red car with his boot.

Kevin leaned close and peered into the backseat of the dust-covered Caddy window. Lying on the seat was a cue-stick case. "Looks like we got us a shooter here. You think Jake is importing some out-of-state talent?"

"Could be." Bobby stared thoughtfully at the red Caddy and his anger disappeared as quickly as it had come. "If Jesse don't show, I still might make a few bucks tonight."

He smashed the other taillight.

"Now you wouldn't take advantage of out-of-state guests, would you, Bobby?" Nash asked with mock concern. "After all, they're gonna need their money for car repairs."

"No, I wouldn't." Bobby paused. "Oh, man, I been looking all over for one of these." Wonderingly, he stroked the side-view mirror of the other car. He looked around to see if anyone was watching him trash the Caddy. They weren't, so he kicked the mirror off and tossed it into the floorboard of his own car. "Public service," he explained. "Someone backs out, I don't want them running over broken glass and getting a flat tire."

"You're a prince," Kevin said. "The mayor should drive out here and give you a commendation."

"He would," Bobby agreed, "except he can't drive anywhere." Bobby flashed his crazy grin at them as he gave the tires on his own car a kick. "You boys never did say what you think about my new set of Goodyears."

"You stole the mayor's tires?" Kevin's jaw dropped. "The mayor?"

Bobby nodded. "Right there in his driveway. I even got the spare."

"He parks his car right by the bedroom window," Kevin said, impressed despite himself. "How did you manage to get his tires without him hearing anything?"

"The mayor was kinda busy that night." Bobby winked. "His wife was over to Springerville to visit her mother a couple of days ago, and I guess the mayor was putting in a little overtime. His secretary, Ellie Gardner, was taking some oral dictation in the bedroom."

"She was giving him a blow job? No shit?" Kevin asked, suspicious that Bobby was putting him on. He examined Bobby's face for signs of deceit. "You're lying," Kevin decided. "I don't want to hear any more." He got a few feet closer to Jake's before turning back. "How do you know?"

"Cause I heard him promise he wouldn't cum in her mouth."

Kevin thought that over, his eyes growing large behind his glasses. "Did he?" Kevin stuttered, "I mean, did he cum in her mouth?"

"The mayor ain't never kept a promise in his life. So what do you think?"

"I think he just lost another vote." Kevin laughed. They started toward the bar.

Jake Rainwater had a neon sign above the ramshackle place he laughingly referred to as a nightclub. The sign had been missing the J since '79 as near as anyone could remember. Sporadically AKES would sputter to life and light up the night sky.

"You'd think (J)-ake would get around to fixing that sign," Kevin said. "It couldn't cost that much."

"Jake ain't a man to rush into anything," Bobby said, "especially where money's concerned. Tell you how cheap he is. I heard tell he caught his third wife cheating on him and he decided to shoot her. Well, when he found out how much a gun cost, he wouldn't spend the money. He came home and ran over her with a car."

"Man, that's cheap," Kevin agreed.

Laughter, music, and loud voices floated out to greet them, drawing them ever nearer the bar.

Bobby, Kevin, Nash, and Boyce wove their way across the darkened gravel parking lot, trying not to fall into any of the bottomless potholes that waited for the unwary. "Better watch your step," Nash warned them. "Last time I was here, it was raining, and I damned near drowned when I fell in." Nash looked at Boyce to back up his story. "I told Jake he ought to have a lifeguard on duty. Ain't that right, Boyce? Am I lying?"

"Absolutely," Boyce replied.

They pushed inside and headed for the bar, yelling out greetings to familiar faces in the crowd. A three-piece country band was mutilating "Rocky Top" in the background while a few hardy souls tried to do the two-step on the crowded dance floor. The overpowering odor of booze, sawdust, cigarette smoke, and sweaty bodies filled the room; it was the usual Saturday night at Jake's.

"I love this dump," Nash said as they worked their way closer to the bar. "It's the only place I know where you can get drunk, get in a fight, and get laid all in the same night."

"I feel more like getting in a fight," Bobby said.

"Laid," the rest chorused.

Jake Rainwater, half-Navajo, half-black, half-crazy, and the closest thing Crowder Flats had to a living legend, was standing behind the huge slab of wood that served as a bar. He was old, grizzled, mean, had been shot three times, married five times, and was still here to talk about it. His hair, what there was of it, was white as snow. The five marriages, not the shootings, he claimed, were what had put the white there.

The first thing a stranger noticed about Jake was his hands; they were the size of hams. Nash swore he'd seen Jake bend a horseshoe with those hands. Made it look easy. One thing was for sure, nobody gave the old bartender any trouble.

Jake gazed over at Bobby and his companions, giving them his you'd-better-not-start-any-shit look.

Bobby just grinned back. "Evenin', Jake. Give me a *Lone Star* and try to make it a cold one, will you?" He leaned against the bar and checked out the room.

"How 'bout the rest of you?" Jake asked. His impassive face scanned them, waiting, and the toothpick that always jutted from his mouth stopped its restless flight. If you weren't female, Jake wasn't much on small talk.

"The same," Nash and Kevin said.

Jake turned to Boyce, the toothpick still motionless.

"You got any of that light beer back there?" Boyce rubbed his jaw thoughtfully. "I think I'd like to try me one of them Bud Lights. I seen it on the TV how women like men who drink that stuff."

Jake stared hard at Boyce and something akin to amusement struggled toward his eyes. Unfortunately it died before it got there. "We don't carry light beer." He pulled the toothpick out of his mouth and examined it to see if there was anything interesting on it before replacing it between his teeth. "We ain't got no white wine, or nothing with them fancy little umbrellas, neither. You want one of them sissy-boy drinks, you're gonna have to go someplace else." The toothpick began moving up and down, dancing across his mouth like a fly with one wing while he waited for Boyce to answer.

A red flush crept up from Boyce's neck and headed for his face where it had room to spread out. "Bring me a shot of tequila, then," he said, trying to salvage what was left of his pride. "Make it a double."

"Will that be with lime or without?"

"Without!"

"That's better, son. I was beginning to worry." Jake poured the tequila into a double-shot glass and sat it in front of Boyce. "First thing you know, you're drinking light beer, next thing you know, you're riding side saddle, and you don't even know how it happened. It's best to nip these things in the beginning before they get out of hand." He winked as he put the bottle away.

Boyce grinned, but he didn't look like his heart was in it. The double shot of tequila sat in front of him, waiting. "Jesus, Nash, I don't know if I can drink this stuff or not. It smells like kerosene."

"Just drink it and shut the fuck up."

Boyce tipped up the glass. A second later, a horrified expression spread across his face and he sprayed tequila all over Nash.

Nash just stood there with tequila streaming down his face. He said nothing, made no effort to wipe it away. Several drops of the liquid rolled down his forehead, gathering speed as they reached his nose, launching themselves into space. They looked like tiny kamikaze skiers going to their death as they splatted onto the bar.

The spectacle was so fascinating, Boyce was rendered speechless.

"You know what's really amazing about this?" Nash asked.

"No, what?" Boyce responded in a subdued voice.

"That I let myself be seen in public with you."

"Does this mean you want me to move down the bar?"

"I'd like you to move to another state, but a few feet down the bar will do for starters."

Clutching his empty shot glass, Boyce shifted down two barstools. When Nash kept staring at him, he moved down one more.

Jake sauntered over and refilled Boyce's glass. "You put that one away pretty quick. I told myself when I first laid eyes on you that you were a tequila drinker. Old Jake can always tell. I'll just leave the bottle."

Boyce gave him a sickly smile.

Nash ran his hand over the dark wood of the bar, staring intently at the surface, looking for something. "Jake, where's the spot on this bar, you know, where Thomas Black Eagle bled when he got killed? Is that it?" Nash touched a swirl that was darker than the rest

"You ask that dumb shit question every time you come in here," Jake said. "It's a couple of feet to your right, over there by Boyce."

Bobby laughed when Boyce moved his drink. "Jake, you're a bigger liar than Nash here ever was. There ain't no bloodstain on the bar. That's just some crock of shit you cooked up to sell drinks."

Jake seemed unoffended by the remark. "Maybe it is." He pulled out another beer, sat it in front of Bobby. "And maybe it ain't." His gaze didn't flinch and Bobby was the first to look away.

"Anything going on in the back?" Bobby asked. He took a drink to cover the fact he couldn't face Jake down.

"There's a couple of shooters back there"

"Anybody I know?"

"No," Jake answered. "I ain't never seen neither one of them before."

"They know what they're doing?"

"You mean, can you hustle them? No, I don't think so. These boys look like they been around."

"Maybe I'll go back there and see for myself."

Jake stared at Bobby with flat, black eyes. "Maybe you'll just sit your ass right there and wait for Jesse Black Eagle to show up. That's who you got a game with."

A small tic caused Bobby's right eye to twitch, otherwise his face remained deceptively calm. "You want to watch how you talk to me, Jake. My old man can put this shithole place out of business with one phone call."

"Maybe he could," Jake admitted, "but then he'd have to find out that his son couldn't cover a bet on a pool game. He'd have to find out that old Jake had to loan the boy some money. I don't think Chester would like that, do you?"

Bobby looked over to see how his friends were reacting to this. They picked up their drinks and drifted over to a table in the corner.

Jake flashed a quicksilver smile that fit him like a prom dress on an old hooker. "We're friends here, ain't we, Bobby boy? There ain't no need to get into all this unpleasantness. We're both here to make ourselves a little piece of change tonight." Jake spread his hands in a gesture of conciliation. "Am I right? Tell you what, to show there's no hard feelings, the next round's on old Jake here."

"I'll play Jesse," Bobby said, "and I'll let you back me." He looked Jake in the face and this time the younger man didn't turn away. "But after this we're quits, Jake. I mean it." Bobby pulled out some crumpled bills and laid them on the bar. "You ain't buying me a drink. I'm kind of picky about who I let buy me a drink. You understand what I'm saying, Jake?"

The toothpick poised quietly while Jake mulled over Bobby's words. He finally nodded. If Jake was upset, it didn't show on his face, but then the same thing could be said when he was happy. He sat the beer down in front of Bobby and picked up the crumpled bills, made them disappear. The toothpick began its dance again. "I was just trying to help you out, and that's the thanks I get. You sure wasn't talking to old Jake like this when you needed money to cover your ass."

"You'll get your money back tonight," Bobby said, "and a lot more to go with it. I hear old Jesse's got himself a pretty good bankroll these days."

"That's a fact," Jake said. "He won most of it right here." Jake looked at Bobby and there was something vindictive about the smile that touched his mouth. "Maybe I'm backing the wrong boy. Maybe I ought to be backing Jesse."

Bobby turned his back to Jake and watched the band for a moment while he took a long drink from his beer. "No, you're backing the right boy. You know why?"

"Tell me."

"Jesse's got a temper, worse than mine. I give him a nudge at the right time and he'll blow the money shot." Bobby turned and sat the empty beer bottle down on the bar. "Tell me something, Jake, what's Jesse doing with that bankroll of his? He sure ain't spending none of it. He's still driving that crappy old pickup."

"I hear he's saving up so's he can leave our fine burg."

"No shit." A flicker passed behind Bobby's eyes like a fast-moving cloud, leaving behind something unidentifiable. "Well, you sure can't blame a man for wanting that." He stared into the distance, lost in thought.

"Me, I like it here fine," Jake said. "Crowder Flats been good to me."

"I guess I'll be here forever, too," Bobby said, "or until my old man finally pickles his liver and I can sell the Broken R."

Bobby turned his attention to Jake, who was watching him intently. "If you're thinking you can use that little piece of information, forget about it. Chester already knows. Sometimes I think the only thing that keeps the old bastard going is knowing I'll sell the place before he gets cold."

Jake said nothing, wondering if maybe he had misjudged Bobby.

Bobby prodded the bartender with a laugh. "What do you think about that, Jake?"

"I think I'm glad I never had any kids."

The boy was a lot angrier than Jake had first thought and that would make him hard to control. Just when you thought you had everything figured, something like this had to happen. Jake almost felt sorry for himself.

Jake looked over Bobby's shoulder as the front door opened and the smoke in the bar swirled. His toothpick flickered once and then was still, like the twitch of a dying fly. "Well, up and at 'em, Bobby boy. Looks like Jesse finally showed."

Turning slowly, propping his elbows on the bar, Bobby watched Jesse Black Eagle cross the room. The two sized each other up, their friendly expressions disguising whatever they really felt.

Jake watched them with a bemused expression; he could never tell if they really disliked each other or not. They had known each other since grade school. Of course that was before Amy Warrick had come into the picture. Jake was glad he wasn't young anymore. Goddamned hormones screwed up a man's thinking.

"Looks like you brought your whole entourage along with you tonight," Bobby said with a lazy grin, nodding to Manny, Ernesto, and Jesus. "These your bodyguards, Jesse, or you thinking about starting up one of them Mexican mariachi bands?"

Jesus looked confused until Manny leaned in and translated, then he started toward Bobby. Manny grabbed him by the arm, pulled him back.

In spite of himself, Jesse laughed. "A Mexican mariachi band. That's pretty funny, Bobby. You know how we minorities have to travel in packs. It's the only way we can protect ourselves from all the love-starved white women who want to get laid."

Someone back in the crowd gave an anonymous cheer.

The hands from the Broken R drifted over and stood next to Bobby. Both groups of men watched each other warily. The crowd on the dance floor became still, watching to see what was going to happen next. The band quit playing and silence descended over the large room.

Bobby uncoiled from the bar, the grin still on his face. "As much as me and the boys would like to kick the shit out of you and your wetback buddies, Jesse, that ain't the reason we're here." Reaching down, Bobby picked up his cue-stick case. "I thought we might have us a friendly little game."

"We'll have a game, but I doubt it'll be friendly." Jesse laid his case on the bar, opened it, and took out his cue stick. He screwed the two halves together. "You ready?"

"I'm looking forward to it." Bobby headed for the back room. The crowd began drifting along, eager for some entertainment.

Jesse peeled the cover off a Steepleton and rolled a cue ball up and down its length, observing the path of the ball. It rolled true. "This one suit you okay or did you have another table in mind?"

"If you like it, Jesse, then it suits me to a T," Bobby said. "We need somebody to rack, just to keep things on the up and up." He winked. "Somebody neither one of us knows."

Bobby and Jesse quickly scanned the crowd, looking for an unfamiliar face. There were a few, because tourists had started coming in for Crowder Flat's only claim to fame, Frontier Days.

"How about you, Pops?" Bobby said, motioning to an older man in a ratty-looking leather jacket. "You got an honest face. You want to make a few bucks tonight racking some balls for me and Jesse?"

The older man stepped out of the crowd. "Thanks, son, I don't mind if I do. I could sure use the money."

"You do know how to rack balls, don't you?" Jesse asked. "Good and tight?"

The old man smiled, showing toothless gums, and Jesse was suddenly reminded of Amos. "I've racked a few sets in my day," the toothless man assured him. "Been doing it a lot lately, gettin' real good." He winked at somebody in the back of the crowd.

"Where you from, Pops?" Bobby asked.

"Texas."

Bobby smiled. "That your red Caddy out there in the lot?"

"Yep. She's a beauty, ain't she," Pops said with a proud smile. "I got her for a steal."

"Yes sir, she sure is," Bobby agreed, "a real beaut. Me and the boys was admiring her just before we came in. I'm afraid I got some bad news for you, though." Bobby arranged his face so that it held the proper sorrowful expression. "Did you know your side-view mirror is missing and both your taillights are busted? You must have been clipped by a bad driver."

"Imagine that," the old man said in an amazed voice. "I wonder how something like that could have happened. It was fine when I pulled in." He looked at Bobby and the friendly eyes went dark for a moment like blinds being pulled on a window. "Just a few minutes ago I was out getting myself a little nip from the trunk when I noticed both your mirrors are gone and all your lights are busted." The dark went away and the sun returned, causing his face to light up. "Sounds like a damned epidemic of bad drivers to me."

Nash laughed so hard beer blew out his nose.

"Say, what do they call you, Pops?" Bobby asked, fighting back the sudden rage that washed over him.

"They call me Earl, son," the old man said. "Earl Jacobs."

"Well, Earl, grab that rack and make yourself handy. I can't stand around here jawing all night about bad drivers. I got to make a little money."

"All right," Earl said. He shuffled over to the table and picked up the rack, began dumping the balls into it. "What you boys gonna play tonight, a little nine ball, maybe a little straight rotation, eight ball?"

"I think a little eight ball," Jesse said. "We both like eight ball, don't we, Bobby?"

"Yeah, Jesse, eight ball it is."

"That's a good choice," the man said. "I always liked a good game of eight ball, myself." He began arranging the balls with surprisingly deft hands.

"What about the stakes?" Jesse asked.

Earl suddenly fumbled a ball and it squirted across the table. Bobby reached out, grabbed the ball, and handed it back to the old man. "You all right there, Earl?"

"Yeah, I'm fine, son. Just got a little tickle in my chest. Must be all the smoke." He put the errant ball back in its spot.

"How about a hundred a game, to start off with?" Bobby said. "Once we get warmed up, we might want to up the ante a little. That sound okay?"

"Yeah, it sounds more than okay, it sounds almost friendly." Jesse dug into his pocket, pulled out a nickel, and tossed it to Bobby.

Bobby examined the worn coin with contempt. "An Indian-head nickel. Is this the fortune I been hearing about?"

Jesse's jaw tightened, but he controlled himself. "I thought we'd flip it to see who's going to break."

Bobby tossed the nickel to Earl, who sent it spinning into the air. The coin disappeared high into the darkness.

"You call it, Bobby," Jesse said.

"Heads."

The coin came down on the table, bounced once, rolled down to the bumper. Fell over. "Heads it is." Earl picked up the nickel and flipped it back to Jesse.

Bobby glanced once at Jake, but Jake seemed completely uninterested in the proceedings. The bartender was pouring a gin-and-tonic for some sweet young thing in tight jeans who was hanging on his every word.

"Just look at that, would you?" Kevin watched the sweet young thing wiggle her ass for Jake as she walked away. "That old son of a bitch gets more pussy than the rest of us put together."

"And him old enough to be her granddaddy, too," Boyce kicked in. "It ain't right."

"Well, if Jake only got laid once, that'd still put him ahead of you two losers." Bobby stuck his cue stick between his legs, poured talc on it, began thrusting the slick wood back and forth in his cupped hand, pushing it up farther with each stroke. The stick seemed to grow longer. "This should bring back some memories for you boys."

"It sure does," Nash said. "Throw me that talc, will you? I think I gotta go to the john."

Earl held up his hand to get their attention. "If you boys are through foolin' around, it's time to get this show on the road." He rolled the cue ball to Bobby and stepped over to say something to a young guy in a gray Stetson. The young guy laughed before slipping something unseen to Earl. The old man quickly inserted the object into his mouth and bit down. "It's just my teeth," Earl said, flashing a smile for all to see. "I'm always going off and forgetting the damned things."

Manny, Ernesto, and Jesus settled on one side of the room, Nash, Boyce, and Kevin on the other. The two groups glared at each other for a few moments. Their hostility was mostly for show, since it was Nash's Dodge Charger that Jesus was working on over at the Shell station.

Jesus was doing the work on credit.

The rest of the crowd lined up against the far wall, watching expectantly, and there were a few good natured jeers. Some money rustled as it exchanged hands.

Finally everyone became still as Bobby leaned over the pool table and dropped his cigarette butt on the floor, grinding it out beneath his boot. He lifted his hat once, sat it forward on his head.

Rituals, Jesse thought, watching Bobby. Magic to protect a man from bad luck.

Bobby leaned into the break and the cue ball was a pistol shot when it hit.

Two stripes and a solid fell. Bobby strolled around the table, eyeing the remaining balls. "The solids look like they lay out a little better, don't they, Jesse?" Without waiting for an answer, Bobby dropped the three in the corner and looked over at Jesse. "I hope you brought plenty of money with you."

"I didn't think I'd need that much."

"Speaking of money, I hear you been saving yours, Jesse. You thinking about leaving us?" Bobby dropped another solid into the side pocket with a showy hammer stroke. Then he sent the cue ball two rails and gently kissed the four in the corner good night. "What's the matter, this town not good enough for you anymore?"

Jesse said nothing.

Bobby sank still another ball. "Amy Warrick been putting ideas into your head, talking about that great big old world out there? Telling you how you got a place in it?"

"You leave Amy out of this," Jesse said, "or we can stop this game right here."

The last two solids went down and only the eight remained. Bobby said, "Side pocket, one rail," and he made the black ball vanish into the middle of the hole as though it had eyes. The cue ball came back to Bobby and paused in front of him like an eager dog waiting to do its next trick. "Sorry, Jesse. I didn't mean to piss you off. It just sort of surprised me to hear Amy would hook up with another pool hustler." Bobby laid his cue stick on the table. "Especially after her dad ran off and left her when she was little."

Jesse started toward Bobby, but Earl stepped in front of Jesse and put a hand on his chest. "Take it easy, son. He's just trying to rile you up, throw you off your game."

Still angry, Jesse tried to move Earl out of the way, but the older man was surprisingly strong. He steered Jesse back to a seat along the wall and sat him down. "I heard Bobby boy, over there, mention Amy Warrick," Earl said. "I guess that'd be your girl?"

Jesse nodded. "Bobby hasn't got used to the idea yet."

Earl started racking the balls again, sliding the triangle back and forth until all the balls were tightly bunched, before lifting it with surgical precision. "Warrick, Warrick. I think I know that name from somewhere." Earl smiled, showing a quick flash of white teeth as he pretended to remember. "Your girl, Amy, would her dad be John Warrick?"

"Yeah, that's right. You know John?"

"No, not exactly. Let's just say I heard of him," Earl said, sliding the rack out of sight. "I hear he handles a stick pretty good."

"Pretty good." Jesse smiled. "Mister, ain't nobody can touch John Warrick. He's the best."

"The best, huh?" Earl considered Jesse's statement for a moment. "I hear he comes around here from time to time."

Bobby broke again, this time sinking two stripes. "You might have to wait around awhile, Earl. Nobody's seen him in over a year." Bobby pistoned another ball out of sight.

"I'd like a shot at him, myself."

Steven Adler appeared at Earl's side and Bobby was slightly startled. He hadn't seen or heard the guy in the gray Stetson move. The guy was just there.

"You must want John real bad," Bobby said, "to interrupt a man while he's trying to shoot." Bobby stared at the guy and started to move around him, but something in the guy's eyes stopped him. They made Jake's look pleasant by comparison.

"Yes, I do," Steven said softly. "I want him real bad."

There was a sudden hunger in Steven Adler's eyes, a longing that Bobby had only seen when a man looked at a woman. "I'm sorry for interrupting, Bobby and Jesse, but I'd like to play the winner of this little contest... if it's ever over." His smile was insolent. "I've got some time on my hands and I think both of you are ready to learn the finer points of the game."

"Mister, whoever you are, you got some real cojones on you," Bobby said, "waltzing in here from Texas like you own the place."

"My name is Steven Adler," the guy with the earring said simply. "I'm the best. And I'm willing to prove it."

"Well, Mr. Steven Adler, you just park your butt over there. You're next in line."

"Consider it parked, but try to speed this up a little, okay? I might get bored and go back to Texas, then you Arizona goat ropers won't get those pointers I promised."

"Goat ropers?" someone in the crowd said. An angry buzz rippled through the room.

"It's all right, don't apologize," Steven said. "I've seen your women, I understand why you prefer goats."

This time someone in the crowd threw a beer bottle, hard, at the back of Steven Adler's head. As best as Bobby could tell, it was thrown by one of the women. He thought about telling the guy to duck, decided against it.

Just before the bottle connected, Steven turned, reached out and caught it, emptied the contents on the floor. "Thanks, ma'am, not my brand." He sat the bottle down on the table, turned and sank into a chair along the wall, leaned back, and tipped his hat over his eyes as though bored. If anyone was thinking about taking up the goat-roper comment with Steven, they didn't step forward.

Jesse stared at Steven Adler for a moment, unnerved. He too had seen Steven move and he didn't believe his own eyes. The guy was quick. Unbelievably quick.

Steven raised his hat and winked at Jesse, then lowered it again. Jesse felt a cold wind touch his back, leaving behind a trail of gooseflesh. He didn't know where these guys were from, but they sure as hell weren't from Texas.

The crowd quieted, and Bobby went back to work, dropping the rest of the stripes in short order before putting the eight ball to bed.

In the fifth game, Bobby left himself a bad lay and finally missed a shot.

Jesse ran off the next four games before scratching on a tough two-rail bank shot.

Bobby won the next one.

Jesse won the next three.

Three hours and seventeen games later, Jesse was ahead only two hundred dollars and the grind was starting to wear them down.

Both were sweating in the smoky, too-hot bar and their shirts were soaked through.

"This is bullshit," Bobby said. "This is going to take all goddamned night at this rate." He slammed his stick down on the table. "I got an idea how to speed things up, if you got the cojones for it. How much money you got?"

"Ten grand and a little change," Jesse answered after a brief look at his friends, who were shaking their heads no. They looked like those plastic dogs with wobbly heads that often adorned the back of cars.

Jesse went over to Manny, pulled a wad of hundred-dollar bills out of his jacket pocket and laid them on the table. It had taken him over a year to earn that much money, hustling, scrimping, and saving, going without. It was his ticket out of Crowder Flats. He stared at the folded bills and asked, "What you got in mind, Bobby?" His own voice sounded distant to him, unreal.

"I'll lay it out real simple. Each of us takes one turn at the table. You shoot until you miss, any ball you want, it's as simple as that. Whoever sinks the most balls wins. What do you say, Jesse, you got the guts?"

Jesse felt more than saw everyone looking at him, waiting for his answer. His mouth went dry.

"Oh, by the way, I thought I'd throw in a little kicker," Bobby added. "Just to keep things interesting. You don't make something on the break, it's all over."

Sweat dotted Jesse's forehead, but he didn't dare reach up to wipe it away.

Bobby picked his stick up from the table and looked at Jesse. "You win, you walk out of here with my ten grand. Lots of things a man can do with that kind of money." Bobby took a drink of his Lone Star, held the cold bottle against his face. "You could clear out of Crowder Flats, or you could buy more whiskey for that crazy old grandfather of yours." The familiar lazy grin spread across Bobby's face. "What do you say, Jesse?"

"I say you go first."

The grin faltered.

For the first time Jesse realized Bobby was just as scared as he was, that Bobby had been trying to make him back off, but now there was no turning back for either of them. Pride wouldn't let them.

The grin returned and this time it looked forced. "All right, Jesse, I guess that's only fair." He downed the rest of his beer. "Rack 'em up, will you, Earl?"

"You boys play rough," Earl said. "You both sure you want to do this?"

Jesse looked at Bobby, their eyes locking for an instant, and they were both eleven years old again, standing by the calf chute at the local rodeo while waiting for Bobby's number to come up. Chester Roberts had signed Bobby up for calf riding. Bobby had been scared to death on that day long ago, but he hadn't said a word. He wore that cocky grin of his as he had climbed into the chute. Even as he had pissed his jeans. He wore that same expression right now.

Why was Bobby pushing him so hard? Jesse looked into the crowd and saw the reason why. Standing there, in black jeans, a plain white cotton T-shirt, and a black hat that matched her hair was Amy Warrick. She was watching Jesse with total disbelief on her face. She had heard everything.

"Rack the balls, Earl," Jesse said, looking away from her. "Let's get this show on the road."

"All right, son." There was regret on Earl's seamed face as he bent to his task. He, too, had seen the way Amy had looked at Jesse.

Bobby made three balls on his first break and then went on to clear seven more racks, sinking 123 more balls before he finally missed.

"Looks like I'm going to have to talk to your daddy," Jesse said with grudging admiration.

"Why's that?"

"You been spending too much time in pool halls."

"That's one twenty-six to you, Jesse, and that's a lot of balls in the hole, old buddy." Bobby sank down in a chair, cocked his hat back on his head. "But never let it be said that Bobby Roberts isn't a sporting man. Tell you what, Jesse, you give me five hundred and we'll call it a night right now. You don't even have to shoot."

Jesse wanted to take Bobby's offer, that would be the smart thing to do, only something inside wouldn't let him. It wasn't macho posturing: it wasn't something he could exactly explain. It had to do with being a man, with being able to hold your head up. He stood and went to the table, leaned against it because his legs didn't seem to want to hold him up anymore. "Thanks, Bobby, but I don't think I'd sleep too good if I didn't at least give it a try."

"I'd be surprised if you didn't."

Earl dumped the balls in the rack, made a swirling pass, and the balls clicked once and then were quiet. The rack came away.

Everything was set.

Everything was waiting.

For Jesse.

Jesse placed the cue ball precisely twelve inches from the back rail, two inches off center, paused to wipe the sweat from his face with his shirtsleeve. He was operating on automatic pilot right now. Amy watched him with an unblinking stare and he tried to read her expression. It was unreadable. Her face might have been made from stone, but stone didn't have a tear running down it. Jesse dusted his hands with talc, chalked his stick, carefully going through his own rituals as though they were magic that could protect him from what was to come.

Manny, Ernesto, and Jesus were watching. Their expressions were very readable. They looked scared.

"Come on, boys, lighten up a little," Jesse said. "It's only money." Taking a deep breath, he drew back his stick and prayed he wouldn't miscue. He didn't. The cue ball slammed into the rack with a satisfying crack and suddenly Jesse knew everything was going to be all right. Only one solid fell. It was enough. He finished the rack.

And the next seven. One hundred and twenty balls down the hole.

"That's good shooting, son," Earl said. "Mighty good." He slowly dumped the balls into the plastic triangle, rolled them around until they were good and tight. "I guess you know this is the one that counts." He slipped the rack off and stepped away.

Jesse went straight into the break, putting everything he had behind his stick, feeling the shock run up his arm. It was a clean hit and the cue ball was a hammer. The balls scattered, darting across the table almost too fast to see, but nothing was falling. They danced their dance, began to slow.

Still plenty of action, still plenty of time.

The fifteen was coming down the rail, moving good. The three was coming, too.

One was all he needed.

Just one ball.

Jesse watched the striped ball turn, the number fifteen slowly appearing, disappearing, as though it were an eye winking at him.

"C'mon, you son of a bitch," Jesse whispered. "Come on." He leaned over the table closely tracking the progress of the ball, throwing all the body English he could muster as he urged it toward the pocket.

The fifteen was going to make it.

A few more inches.

That was when the three ball clipped the fifteen, stopped it.

And just like that, the game was over. At first no one could believe that Jesse had made nothing on the break. They stared at the table, waiting for something to fall, but all the balls were all still now.

"Tough break, son," Earl said softly. "I thought you had that fifteen."

Jesse didn't answer. He didn't know if he could, even if he wanted to, because there was this sudden, vast emptiness inside of him. He looked at the money for a second before stripping off a hundred and handing it to Earl. "That okay with you, Bobby?"

"Give him another hundred. He's got to get some work done on his car." Bobby grinned. "Besides, I kind of like the old bastard."

"Much obliged," Earl said. He stuck the money into the pocket of his ratty old jacket. "You boys put on a good show tonight."

Before Bobby could pick up the money on the table, another stack of bills landed beside it. "There's forty grand there," Steven Adler said, "against your twenty grand." His grin outshone Bobby's. "You made a hundred and twenty-six balls. Here's the deal: I say I can make two hundred and fifty-three balls, that's twice your count plus one, and I can do it in fifteen minutes." Steven picked up the money and fanned it beneath Bobby's nose. "I'm giving you two-to-one odds. We play. One of us walks with sixty grand. What do you say, Bobby, you got the cojones?"

It was Bobby's turn for a case of cotton mouth. The guy was fast, Bobby had seen him snatch that beer bottle out of the air like it was nothing. Could anyone really make that many shots in fifteen minutes? Bobby searched the faces in the crowd, trying to find the answer, and saw Amy Warrick standing beside Jesse. She had her arm around Jesse's waist, but her taunting expression was meant for Bobby alone.

This wasn't going like Bobby had planned.

Everyone waited for him to answer. He couldn't back down.

"All right, mister, you got yourself a bet," Bobby finally said. "You got fifteen minutes, not one second more." He pulled off his watch and announced the time. "There's no way you can sink two hundred and fifty-three balls in fifteen minutes."

Bobby was right. Steven Adler did it in fourteen.

CHAPTER TWELVE

Bobby Roberts was in a foul mood when he dropped Kevin, Nash, and Boyce in front of the bunkhouse. They climbed out of the car without a word, slammed the door.

Bobby turned off the Caddy and waited for them to say what was on their minds. He already had a pretty good idea what that was. Nobody had said more than two words on the way back from Jake's place, and now, as they stood huddled in the predawn chill, all was quiet except for a few fitful gusts of wind pushing a squeaky weather vane around.

Somewhere in the distance, the clatter of a passing train came. It was a lonesome sound.

Bobby took in the familiar sights and smells of the ranch and yet they all suddenly felt alien to him, like he had become a stranger here at the Broken R. From the bunkhouse, the smell of wood smoke carried on the night air. The outlying buildings were a solid presence. Everything looked the same but it was somehow changed. Different.

Bobby kept waiting for his friends to say something.

They held to their silence, and it had the ring of judgment in it.

Bobby started up the Caddy, put it in drive, changed his mind and slammed the lever into park. "Anybody got anything to say about tonight, go on and say it."

The three hired hands looked at each other as though trying to decide who would speak. Finally, Nash stepped forward. "That was a bad thing you did to Jesse tonight. He's been your buddy ever since he took the fall for you in high school. Everyone knows you trashed Mr. Denton's car. Old man Detention we used to call him. Jesus Christ, Bobby, Denton was the principal. They wanted to kick your ass out of school over that one, or have you forgot? Do you know what your old man would have done to you?"

"Screw the car," Boyce said. "Jesse's one of us. You backed him into a corner, Bobby. You made him bet every cent he had."

"I gave him an out."

Nash spat on the ground as though he tasted something bad. "It wasn't much of an out. You knew he couldn't take it, not with his girl standing there."

Looking from face to face, Bobby saw their anger. "Is that the way the rest of you feel? That I did wrong?"

They wouldn't look at him.

Kevin seemed more sad than angry. "You went too far this time, Bobby."

"You can go straight to hell, all of you. I didn't make Jesse bet all his money." Bobby, stung, drained his beer and threw the empty can at their feet. "I thought you were my friends, but I can see I was wrong." He ripped the Caddy into drive and punched the gas, raising a cloud of dust that swallowed the three ranch hands. When he looked in his rearview mirror, he saw they were gone, as though the wind, which had blown the dust away, had blown them away, too.

Bobby tried desperately to hold on to his anger so he wouldn't feel the hole their words had left in him, but he couldn't do it. Because he knew what they had said was true.

The sprawling two-story Spanish ranch house swam up the Caddy's lights, materializing into the Marlboro Man's wet dream, all stucco and adobe on the outside, leather couches, Western macho decorations of cowhide and steer horns on the inside. Bobby hated it. Many times when he was a kid he had dreamed of burning it down.

Once, after a particularly savage beating, he'd almost found the guts to do the job. That had been years ago, a sweaty July night. After his first rodeo. He'd been eleven at the time, scared to death, and he had peed his pants during the calf riding, embarrassing his dad.

Later on that night, Chester had beaten Bobby with his fists. Bobby was banished to room, filled with shame and rage.

He'd held on to that rage. Staring out his window that night, he'd stood there, watching heat lightning burn yellow on the horizon. Right then he knew what he had to do. Knew with perfect clarity.

In his dad's room, he stood at the foot of the bed, looking down at the man who lay there sleeping. In Bobby's hands was a box of matches. He struck one, and then another, match after match, holding them until they burned down to his fingers, and he watched the flames with bright, shiny eyes, feeling the pain. Savoring it. He smiled when the skin curled and peeled away from his fingers and the scent of his burning flesh filled his nostrils. When his flesh turned black, his smile turned to laughter. He struck every match and held them over the bed until the box was empty.

Dropping a match on the bed would have been easy, so easy. Everyone knew Chester drank heavily and smoked in bed. It would have been a perfect murder.

The next morning, over breakfast, Chester kept staring at Bobby's blistered hands, as though he was seeing his son for the first time, and Bobby knew his dad had found the curled, burned matches at the foot of the bed.

Neither of them ever said a word about those matches, but from that day on, his dad never touched him again.

Now they lived in the big house together, existing in an uneasy truce, just the three of them, the unholy trinity as Bobby called it: the father, son, and the holy ghost. The ghost being Bobby's absent mom.

Bobby cruised up to the oil slick that marked his parking spot and turned off the motor. Punching the lighter in his Caddy, he jammed a cigarette in his mouth. The lighter popped out of the dash with an audible click. Bobby guided the cherry red metal to the cigarette, dragged the smoke into his lungs while he tried to get up enough courage to enter the house.

Over the cigarette smoke, the odor of burning flesh filled the car. He looked down and saw he had ground the lighter into the palm of his hand.

It stayed there until the metal went cool.

There were two cars in the driveway, which was the reason Bobby didn't want to go into the house. His dad had returned from that stock-buying trip down in Dallas. One car was a late-model Caddy with a broken R on the door; the other was a silver BMW with Texas plates on it. Old Chester must have found more than just a good breeding bull this time out. Bobby was glad his bedroom was at the other end of the house so he wouldn't have to listen to his dad's drunken rutting.

Bobby thought about all the nights that his dad had come home drunk, of all the times his dad had beaten his mom. After the beatings came the creaking of the bedsprings, followed by the crying. Elizabeth Roberts had been gone a little over eight years now. Nobody knew where. The last Bobby had heard from her was a letter postmarked Cedar City, Utah, on his sixteenth birthday. It said she was sorry he'd had to grow up on his own, and that she hoped he'd forgive her.

Bobby loved his mom.

And hated her.

Because she had been the only one to escape this place. Sometimes Bobby wondered if he'd ever get away from here, but he didn't like to think about that too much, because if he did, his head might start hurting again. And if that happened, there was only one thing that could stop the pain—a box of matches.

Bobby said a prayer that his old man was passed out drunk or upstairs with his latest bimbo.

Things had gotten out of hand back at Jake's. Bobby hadn't meant for that to happen. Jesse and Amy were his friends, always had been. They had been drawn together by the fact they had all grown up with only one parent.

As the years had gone by, he and Jesse had become friendly rivals for Amy's affections.

Friendly, until Amy chose Jesse.

Bobby knew she would never pick him over Jesse. No changing that now. He had seen the hatred in her face tonight.

Then, if things weren't bad enough, those hustlers from Texas had made him look bad in front of his friends.

Tonight had been the worst night he could remember.

Still drunk, Bobby pushed through the front door of the house and almost fell over a chair feeling for the light switch. He froze in place when he heard the faint sound of a TV.

His dad was awake.

With a muffled "Oh shit," Bobby staggered through the darkness, headed for the kitchen. Somehow he missed most of the furniture.

With what stealth his drunk ass could manage, he eased open the fridge and grabbed a cold *MODELO*. The way his head was throbbing, he knew he'd need it come morning.

He went to shake out a smoke, realized he was out. Maybe he could sneak one from his dad. The sound of the TV lured Bobby to the family room, and he felt a ball of ice form in the pit of his stomach when he peeked in and saw the shapeless bulk of his dad stretched out on the recliner. The big rancher stirred, caused the chair to creak.

This was just great, Chester was awake. The perfect end to a perfect day.

"Son of a bitch," Bobby whispered with feeling, "I can't believe it. What else can go wrong tonight?"

But Chester didn't move again.

Bobby felt a ray of hope.

He tiptoed a little farther into the family room, avoiding loose floorboards by long habit, trying to see if his old man was really passed out or just faking it. Chester Roberts was out, his hat was tipped forward over his face as he lay stretched out on the recliner.

Bobby grabbed a cigarette, turned to head for his room, when quite suddenly, for no good reason, he felt something was wrong.

It wasn't anything he could put his finger on, just a feeling of unease. The only real light came from the stone fireplace at the far end of the room and it was beginning to burn low, so he really couldn't see much of anything. Bobby looked over at the TV, saw it held flickering black-and-white images of long-dead cowboys riding their long-vanished celluloid range. It was one of those fifties Westerns, the kind where the good guy could pull a guitar faster than a six shooter, the kind where the good guy never kissed a girl. Bobby could identify with that.

And then it came to him what was wrong; his old man hated those kind of Westerns, too.

Bobby moved closer to the recliner. Slowly, carefully, reached for Chester's hat.

"Morning, Bobby. You're up kind of late."

Bobby jumped and then started laughing with relief when he recognized the voice of the man in the chair. "Jesus Christ, Mr. Strickland, you scared the crap out of me. I thought you was my dad." He wiggled the light switch in the family room and discovered that someone had removed the bulb. "You seen the old fart tonight?"

"He's upstairs taking a little rest with his lady friend."

"Good. What're you doing sitting here in the dark all by yourself?"

"Nothing much, just watching a little TV, waiting for you to get home." Martin stared at the screen for a moment, watching the cowboys ride into the black-and-white sunset, and his voice grew wistful. "You like old Westerns, Bobby?"

"You mean that Roy Rogers, Gene Autry, Hopalong Cassidy crap?"

"Yeah, that kind of crap."

"No, I hate the things. They're stupid."

"I guess most young people today feel the same way as you. Me, I love 'em. They take me back to when I was a kid, back to

Saturday matinees… before the world changed and everything got complicated." He sighed. "Before Doralee left. Back in the old days you went to the movies to watch the good guys kick the shit out of the bad guys. You got a happy ending every time. Guaran—goddamned—teed." Martin laughed, then caught himself, as though he was embarrassed by his little confession. "Sometimes I think it's too bad real life's not like that."

Bobby was becoming uncomfortable at Martin's rambling. "Mr. Strickland, it's getting kind of late. Did you want something?"

"I'm sorry, I just wanted to talk to you for a few minutes before you hit the sack."

"Yeah, about what?"

"About this knife I've been looking for."

"What kind of knife?"

"It's from the Navajo graveyard, got a handle carved into a red snake. I thought you might have seen it. I can't seem to find it anywhere."

"That's an Indian relic. Stealing Indian relics is illegal." Bobby took a drink from his beer while he rummaged around in a cabinet for a light bulb. He found one, inserted it, flipped the switch. This time the light popped on, filling the corner of the room with eye-stinging glare. Bobby closed his eyes against it. "Can't this wait? I've had kind of a tough night."

"I know what you mean; I had kind of a tough night myself." Something was wrong with the foreman's voice. "But I really need that knife."

Bobby opened his eyes.

Martin Strickland was sitting in the recliner, dressed in the same clothes he had worn earlier today, only now Bobby could see they were crusted up with dried blood. Covered with it. There were long gashes all over his body, but he wasn't bleeding anywhere that Bobby could see. Flaps of skin hung from Martin's face like paint peeling away from a gray, weathered barn, revealing a surprisingly bright, shiny coat of red beneath.

"Mr. Strickland, for God's sake, what happened?" The words sounded inadequate. "You look…"

"Dead. It's okay, Bobby, you can say it. I look dead. I am dead." Rising up from the recliner, Martin moved toward the back of the family room, swaying as though he'd had too much to drink. He was headed to where the light barely reached, but he stopped and looked back over his shoulder, his face crinkling up as though he had thought of something funny. "You wouldn't believe what happened to me tonight, son."

Crackling noises came from the foreman's stiff clothes when he started moving again.

"Mr. Strickland, you need a doctor."

"Son, I need an undertaker. Do you want to hear what happened or not?" His voice grew suddenly querulous.

"Yeah, I want to hear."

"All right, then. You see this?" The foreman's fingerless hand reached up and touched a thin line of red that wound around his head. His hair rested on it, like a badly fitted toupee. It began sliding off and he reached up, pushed it back. "That's where I got scalped by Billy Two Hats. Son of a bitch tied me to a cross and I bled to death." He flashed a grin, showing broken stumps where his teeth used to be. "Oh yeah, I almost forgot, I got buried, too."

"What do you say we go for a little ride, Mr. Strickland. My car's out front. Maybe we can get someone to take a look at you." Bobby tried to keep his voice steady, low, like you were supposed to with someone in this condition.

Martin swept his arm out, indicating the far side of the room. "I can't run off and leave my family, Bobby, not after they've come all the way from Dallas to see me. It wouldn't be right."

Following Martin's gesture, Bobby peered into the darkness, at the couch along the wall, at the two people sitting there. Neither one acknowledged his presence.

"Say hello to Doralee and Nicky."

Bobby saw something strike Martin's head from above, run down his ravaged face. In the dark it looked like a raindrop.

Martin sat down on the couch between Doralee and Nicky and pulled them close. "You'll have to forgive these two. They've forgotten their manners, so I guess I'll have to speak for them. It'll be the first time I ever got in the last word, if you know what I mean." He winked.

Everyone on the couch wore smiles, as though they were posing for a family portrait. In the dark, Doralee and Nicky were the perfect wife and son, except that every time Martin moved, their heads lolled to the side like as if they had no bones in their necks. Nicky's eyes were milky, exposed film.

Doralee had no eyes.

Martin followed Bobby's gaze. "She was always looking at other men, so I had to tear 'em out."

"Mr. Strickland, are Doralee and Nicky... are they..."

"Dead?" Martin considered the question. "In a manner of speaking, I guess they are. It just depends on how you look at it. Watch this, Bobby, this is better than that card trick I do at Christmas."

This was madness and Bobby couldn't seem to make it stop. "I don't think I want to see any more."

"Come on now, son, don't spoil an old man's fun. You'll love this." Martin's face shifted and somehow became younger as it took on the look of a sullen teenager who is being forced to be polite against his will. His mouth twisted into a sneer. "Hey, Bobby, you getting in Amy Warrick's pants yet, or does she still have the hots for Jesse?" The voice belonged to Nicky. There was no mistaking it. "I'll bet they're doing it right now in Jesse's pickup."

The foreman's ravaged face reassembled itself into more familiar lines. "You have to overlook kids nowadays," Martin said in his own voice. "You try to teach them manners, but they don't listen."

Then the face shifted again, became softer, somehow feminine. "That's because their fathers are always out whoring and gambling. I wouldn't call that setting a good example for a child, would you?"

Bobby recognized this voice, too.

Doralee was speaking now, using Martin's throat, forcing it several octaves higher. The words were spoken softly. "I guess you already know all about that, don't you, Bobby?"

Bobby bit back the absurd urge to say, "Yes, ma'am."

Another drop from above hit Bobby, on the arm this time.

Martin put his arms around his son, his ex-wife, gave them a squeeze. "It's good to spend some quality time with the ol' family unit, but it's so hard to find the time, what with everyone doing their own thing these days. This was really fortunate that Doralee stopped by with Nicky. She found him hitchhiking just the other side of Crown Point. That's dangerous. She wanted me to give him a good talking to." Martin tousled the boy's hair. "I did. You won't give us any more trouble now, will you, son?'"

"No, Dad," Martin answered himself, again doing his uncanny impression of Nicky.

Bobby picked up the phone and stabbed at the buttons. "Mr. Strickland, you just sit right there. I'm going to get you some help."

"Too late to help me," Martin said. "The phone's dead. I cut the wires myself."

Bobby kept punching the numbers as though he could make the phone work if he just kept hitting them.

"Too late to help my family," Martin said. "They're dead. I killed them myself."

Another drop from above splattered on Bobby. The drops were falling faster now and he knew what they were.

Blood.

A shower of it.

All the time he and Martin had been talking, blood had been dripping from the ceiling, Nicky and Doralee's blood. Now there was a wide, glistening pool of it in front of the fireplace.

"I'd like to stay and chat some more, Bobby, but it's getting kinda late, and I've got to find that knife." Martin climbed to his feet and, quick as a cat, grabbed Bobby by the arm and backhanded him, bent him back over the couch. "You always thought you could take me, you little prick. Well, here's your chance."

Bobby swung at the old foreman, but he never connected.

Something was coming from Martin's mouth. Spilling out.

At first Bobby thought it was blood, but whatever was coming from Martin seemed to have a life of its own. It struck out, like a snake. The liquid was black, cold like winter rain, when it struck

Bobby in the face, it numbed him. It forced open his mouth and began pouring down his throat.

Bobby felt the coldness undulate deeper inside of him, and it was no longer cold, it was liquid fire as it crawled along his veins and arteries, spreading out in every direction, pushing his blood ahead of it. He tried to shove the old foreman off him, but they were connected now. The heat reached Bobby's brain. A sudden peace descended over him. For the first time since he was eleven, he wasn't angry.

Voices whispered to him and one of them belonged to his mom. She was just as pretty, just as nice as he remembered. Bobby saw that he was eleven and that he was standing in front of a movie theater. His best friend, Martin Strickland, who was in the same grade, stood right beside him.

Martin nudged Bobby. "Ask your mom for a quarter so we can see the new Hopalong Cassidy."

Elizabeth Roberts heard Martin and smiled. "Didn't you two already see this one?"

"No, Mom, this one is brand new."

She made a big production of digging in her purse. "All right, here's a quarter. Don't tell your dad."

They were about to start for the ticket booth when Bobby felt another quarter drop into his pocket.

"That's for popcorn and you'd better eat it, not throw it."

"We promise, don't we, Martin?"

"Yes we do, Mrs. Roberts." Martin crossed his eyes. Elizabeth laughed. "Go on, you two."

The first thing they did, once they reached the balcony of the huge, ornate theater, was to throw popcorn on those below.

"You've got a neat mom." Martin tossed some popcorn into the air, tried to catch it in his mouth.

"She's okay."

They took turns trading punches on the shoulder until the curtain finally parted.

They looked over the audience... at the black-and-white Western spewing from the projector. The opening credits were rolling and the music began to swell as Bobby watched Hoppy ride onto the silver screen. Martin was ecstatic. Bobby should have been happy, not uneasy.

He locked onto the movie. Felt the doubts recede a little.

There was a young cowboy standing in a saloon, there was music, bright lights, a crowd milling around. The young cowboy was kicking the shit out of some guy in black while everyone cheered him on. There was a pretty girl in the background who had been singing just a minute ago.

Bobby knew by the way she looked at the young cowboy that she was crazy about him. She just hadn't said it yet.

Yet something was wrong. Out of kilter.

Somebody wasn't saying their lines right, they were saying the young cowboy had done his sidekick wrong, that he had stolen all his sidekick's money.

The young cowboy turned to the audience and yelled for the director. "This isn't in the script. Who's been messing with the script?"

Bobby leaned over to Martin. "What kind of movie is this?"

On the screen, the man in black laid a gloved hand on the cowboy's arm and pulled him close. Their black-and-white faces were now only a few inches apart. "You'd better play the scene as written, if you know what's good for you."

"Screw you." The cowboy hit him.

Technicolor blood spilled from the guy in black's mouth, ran back up his nose.

Flowing like a waterfall in reverse.

"Nice effect, but a little heavy handed, don't you think? Besides, they weren't doing effects like that in the fifties."

The blood turned back to black and white. "That better?" the bad guy asked. "You happy now?"

"Yeah, I guess."

But Bobby wasn't happy at all. He had the distinct feeling that the bad guy was about to kiss the cowboy on the mouth, and that was sure a strange way for a bad guy to act.

The bad guy's hat had fallen off after the young cowboy had struck him, and Bobby saw the bad guy had been scalped. His head glistened wetly.

Bobby felt so embarrassed for the bad guy he had to look away from the screen. "I bet this never happened to Roy Rogers or Gene Autry." He watched the good guy bend over to pick up the bad guy's hat. The good guy never made it.

The bad guy pulled the good guy close, kissed him.

Bobby was bewildered. "Hey, Martin, isn't the girl supposed to do this scene?"

"Not in this movie."

Something red crawled from the bad guy's mouth, disappeared down the young cowboy's throat. And Bobby felt sudden heat.

Just like that, the saloon was on fire.

Onscreen, the edges of the old Western began charring at the edges, curling up like a photograph burning in an ashtray. Bobby saw the black-and-white flames racing toward the young cowboy, and he could feel the heat growing, becoming unbearable as it consumed everything in its path. The chandelier crashed to the floor, sending up a shower of sparks.

On the screen, onlookers began milling around. A woman screamed.

Somebody made a break for the door, a henchman for the man in black. He caught on fire before he made it, going up like a Roman candle, his screams adding to the already deafening noise.

Bobby looked around the theater to see how the audience was reacting.

The theater was empty. Except for him and Martin.

The young cowboy fought on against the bad guy, just the two of them, while the saloon burned down around them. A heavy, flaming timber slammed onto a table and turned it into kindling, killing the three card players who were sitting there. For some reason Bobby thought the players names were Kevin, Nash, and Boyce. They turned to ashes in their chairs, and the last thing to disappear were their accusing eyes. The wind blew their ashes away.

Some of the supporting players at the back were also turning to ash. The fire reached the rest.

And then they were gone.

All of them.

There was only the girl watching the good guy fight the bad guy.

Bobby knew she wouldn't run from the fire, because she resembled Amy Warrick. He was right. She burned, turning to ash without a word.

Several of the columns that supported the saloon collapsed, which caused part of the roof to fall in. More flames sprang up. The place was an inferno now, black-and-white flames burning black-and-white wood.

The flames reached the cowboy.

Bobby braced himself.

The saloon vanished without a trace.

Stone silence.

Different movie, different player. A young boy named Bobby Roberts. There were colors, bright primary colors. Reds and yellows. The scene opened on a sunny day at the fair as the camera panned in close, catching a calf in a pen, the sweaty, scared face of the young boy.

A rodeo was under way.

The eleven-year-old was about to ride his first calf and fear was a hard knot in his stomach as he climbed aboard the animal. His nerve failed. Warmness ran down his legs as his bladder let go.

The gate came open.

The calf threw the boy on the first leap.

Laughter filled the stands as everyone saw the dark stain on his crotch.

Fade to black.

Different set. Same player. Later on in the night after the calf ride.

There was only one color this time: red.

The boy caught a glimpse of himself in the full-length mirror on the wall and realized he was standing in his dad's bedroom holding a box of matches. The boy wiped the sweat from his eyes, winced at the tender flesh he felt there.

Someone had savagely beaten the boy in the mirror, causing blood to pour from the corner of his mouth. The boy was very angry.

Chester Roberts was lying passed out on the bed, just as he had been on that night long ago.

The boy on the screen looked out over the darkened theater to where Bobby and Martin sat in the balcony. "Why are we shooting this scene again? I thought we had this one in the can already."

Only silence greeted his question. In the shadows, the cameras were rolling.

"Action," Martin said in an adult voice. "You know the scene. Try and get it right this time."

Reaching into the box, Bobby struck a match, hearing the scratch of sulfur against the sandpapery side. He watched the flames spring to blue, flickering life. The match burned down to his fingers, raced up his arm. In seconds his entire body was on fire. He watched in the mirror. Blackening flesh. Incredible pain. He screamed. The sound faded before his ashes hit the floor.

Fade to black.

CHAPTER THIRTEEN

Amy Warrick and Jesse Black Eagle lay on the hood of Jesse's truck, backs propped against the windshield. Neither had said anything since leaving Jake's. The warmth seeping up from the engine felt good against the chill. The truck was parked on an outcropping of rock that jutted out several hundred feet above the Little Colorado River. They listened to the water rush by in the darkness. Behind them, in the far distance, a few lights from Crowder Flats twinkled like stars on the horizon.

"You sure your friends aren't going to be upset?" Amy finally asked. "You just running off and leaving them at Jake's."

"I think they were kind of glad to get away from me. They were afraid I was going to do something crazy."

"Crazy? You?"

Jesse laughed. "I already done my crazy for tonight, betting every cent I had on a pool game." He pulled her close. "I'm sorry for making you cry. I didn't plan for you to see the game."

"I'm sorry I turned into a girl on you, it's just that I know how hard you worked for that money. I couldn't stand to see you lose it." She laid her head on Jesse's shoulder and they watched the silver river flow away into the night, content to just be with each other. "I feel bad about what happened between you and Bobby," Amy said quietly. "I feel like it's my fault."

"No, don't blame yourself." Jesse shrugged. "Bobby and me would have come to this sooner or later. This wasn't about you, Bobby doesn't like to lose."

"Neither do you."

"You're right about that. It's a definite character flaw. Did I tell you me and Bobby are going to bump heads again tomorrow night?"

"At the rodeo?"

"That's right; we're both in the bull riding."

"I don't know why I talk to either one of you. You both act like macho assholes most of the time."

"Hey, I resent the macho part of that crack."

Amy almost smiled, but she was not so easily sidetracked. "Jesse, what's happened to the three of us? We used to be friends. Remember when we were in the sixth grade, we called ourselves the three musketeers? All for one, one for all. We were different than the rest of the kids, we only had one parent. We said we would always stick together no matter what."

"We were only kids when we made that promise. Things change when we get older. They get more... complicated."

"Maybe they do. All I know is that I feel like if it wasn't for me, you and Bobby would still be friends."

"Me and Bobby are still friends. We both just got a little carried away tonight." Jesse pulled her close. "Amy, it's not that he wants you so much, it's just that he can't stand to see you with me. To Bobby that means I won."

Amy's eyes flashed angrily. "Winning, losing, that's all you two ever think about. Sometimes I feel like a stuffed toy at the carnival, waiting to go home with the first guy who can ring the bell. Three chances for a dollar. Win yourself an Amy Warrick."

"An Amy Warrick. Gosh, I'd like to take a chance on that, but a whole dollar… I don't know…"

Amy smiled, tipped Jesse's hat down over his eyes. "You're a smooth talker, Jesse Black Eagle, how am I going to trust you while I'm away at Arizona State?"

All Amy could see were Jesse's white teeth smiling from beneath the brim of his hat.

"Guess you'll have to come home and check up on me every chance you get," he said, his smile broadening. "We'll have so much hot sex I won't be able to walk for three months, let alone look at another woman." He inched closer until the entire length of his body was pressed against her. He tried to kiss her.

"Oh no you don't," she said, giggling, "I'm still angry with you. Besides you're going to need all your strength for riding the bull tomorrow."

Jesse groaned and leaned back against the windshield. "Just remember, if I get killed tomorrow, I went to my death unloved."

"I doubt that." She kissed him, pulled away, suddenly serious again. "Jesse, what would you say if I told you I don't want to go back to school? That I want to stay here with you."

"I'd say you lost your mind." He sat up. "Doing what? There's nothing here for you, Amy. Crowder Flats is the end of the line, it's some place you end up when you can't cut it anymore. Or never could cut it," he added. He grabbed her by the shoulders and held her. "You listen to your mom and get your ass back to school."

Amy pulled away, stung by Jesse's words. She watched the river for a while. "You ever feel like you're not living your own life, that what you want doesn't count?"

"Every day," Jesse said. He tried to touch her, but she slid off the truck hood and walked to the edge of the rock outcropping. Below, the river was a silver thread sewn into the night. She stood there, looking down, the wind blowing her hair. "I feel like I'm living Mom's dream, Mom's life. Since I was small, that's all I can remember is her talking about sending me to college. Nobody ever asked me what I wanted to do."

"She just wants what's best for you."

"I know she does," Amy said, "and I want to live up to her expectations. It's a lot of pressure, maybe too much. When I was little, I used to dream about falling. Some nights I would wake up crying." She listened to the murmur of the river as though deciding whether to go on. "I called it the dream. I haven't had it since I was twelve, but the funniest thing is—I had it again last night."

"Probably just nerves. Your little brother…"

"Maybe that's it, I don't know. You ever dream, Jesse?"

"Yeah, about you. Naked."

She punched his shoulder. "No, I mean when you were small."

"I had a lot of weird dreams when I was little, mostly about my dad. I used to dream he wasn't dead." Jesse sat his hat on his knee and picked at it, his words coming slowly. "Sometimes after I woke up, I'd stay in bed all day long. That way I could pretend the dream was true. As long as I didn't leave the room…" Jesse realized he was saying more than he had intended. He put on his hat and climbed in the truck. "Come on, it's getting late. I think I'd better get you home before your mom sends the sheriff out after me."

Amy kicked a few pebbles off the rock outcropping, watched them fall. In her dreams she never heard the pebbles fall. She didn't hear them this time, either.

Shivering, she climbed into the truck.

They drove in silence.

A short time later, as they topped a rise, Jesse thought he caught a flash of something in his rearview mirror. For some reason he couldn't shake the idea that a car was back there, following them without lights. He made some excuse about checking the tires, stopped, and got out. After listening for nearly a minute, he decided his nerves weren't the best, either.

They drove on.

Steven Adler and Earl Jacobs sat in their red Caddy with the lights off, the engine silent. Earl stuck his head out the window and looked behind him at the darkened stretch of road. A big grin split his face. "You ain't gonna believe this, but I think somebody's following us." He tipped up his flask of George Dickel, took a long drink. "This thing is turning into a regular goddamned caravan."

"No shit?" Steven sounded excited. "That's great. I thought this was going to be too easy." He started the Caddy and pulled back onto the road.

After a while, the third car followed.

CHAPTER FOURTEEN

Louise Warrick moaned, called out a name.

The name was her ex-husband's and the sound of it yanked her awake. The small stucco house was quiet when Louise sat up in bed. A moment passed before she realized she had been dreaming again. John Warrick had left ten years ago.

She felt lost and vulnerable, unprepared to deal with the emotions that washed over her in her empty bed, the need that wouldn't go away.

The need she could not will away.

The phone calls from John had brought back all the old feelings, and she hated that. She ran her hands over her naked body, feeling the sweat trickle down between her breasts. The sensation wasn't entirely unpleasant. She was hot. In more ways than one.

It had been a long time since she'd been with a man.

The last man she had seriously considered going to bed with was Martin Strickland from over at the Broken R, but that was before she had gone out with him. The whole thing had been a waste of time. All he ever talked about was that slutty ex-wife of his who had run off to Dallas with a car salesman.

Martin told her about the breakup on their first date, over barbecue and beer on their way to the drive-in at Steeley Point.

The story started when Martin had gone to Harlan's Auto Salvage and Repo to take a little Chevy S-10 that he'd had his eye on for a test spin. It seemed the Chevy had been rolled by a Bible salesman from Omaha who had been run off the road by a car with no driver.

"Well, actually there was a driver," Martin said, "it was just that the driver wasn't in the car at the time. A crazy Indian name of Rudy No Horses. Caught his ass on fire and fell out, but that's another story."

Louise waited.

"Anyway," Martin said, "I thought I should drive the truck first. Maybe take it over to Jesus Martinez at the Shell Station and have him take a look. Jesus can spot a bent frame faster than he can a bill collector."

Louise agreed that spotting a bent frame or a bill collector was an admirable character trait.

"Sometimes you can end up with a bent frame when a truck gets rolled," Martin explained to Louise, who was gamely waiting for him to get to the point.

The salesman at Harlan's was agreeable about the test drive and handed over the keys.

"I should have known something was up right away from the sideways way those two kept looking at each other," Martin said, "but shit, Doralee was always looking at other guys."

Pleading a headache, Doralee said she would wait for Martin in the office.

When Martin got back, he found Doralee and the salesman gone. Along with his car.

"It was goddamn embarrassing, I can tell you that," Martin said. "Not only had my wife ran off with a guy she had known for twenty minutes, it looked like I was going to have to walk home, too."

"Did Harlan let you borrow the truck?" Louise asked.

"He did better than that. Harlan felt so bad about his salesman running off with Doralee that he outright gave me the truck," Martin answered. "One truck for one wife. Seemed only fair. He threw in a Bible, too."

Half a bottle of whiskey and one movie later, Martin swore he hated Doralee's guts. A whole bottle later (it was a double feature) he said he couldn't never love nobody but Doralee. By the time the lights came up he was passed out.

Go figure.

Sometimes it seemed to Louise that nobody had any idea what they wanted. If they did somehow manage to get it, they damn sure didn't want it for long.

Life was a messy business, Louise remembered her mother saying to her. The longer you lived it, the messier it got. For once her mother had been right.

Only Mom hadn't said how lonely it got, too.

How could so many years have passed?

Louise was a little frightened when she thought about all the years she had been alone. She would turn thirty-nine this year. No, not just thirty-nine, she was thirty-nine and alone. ALONE. She slid her hands between her legs, touching what her mother had always referred to in pained tones as her private parts, her no-no. Don't touch your no-no, Mama had told her. Ever. It's not nice. It's not ladylike. No man will ever want you if you do.

Well, right now, her no-no was the only part of Louise that wasn't soaking wet.

A woman could dry up in this godforsaken town.

Louise grimaced; something under the sheet was chafing her. She slid her hand under and came up with something gritty. A laugh burst from her as she turned to the window and identified what she held. "I goddamn knew it, my no-no has dried up, Mamma. It's got sand coming out of it."

The laughter quit and she realized it had been a while since she had found anything funny.

Dumping the sand, she thought about the dream that had brought her awake. Her hands felt their way to the nightstand of their own will and lit a cigarette while she waited for the unwanted feelings to pass. The images from the dream seemed more real to her than the memories of what had happened on that day ten years ago.

The day John had left her.

A trial separation, he said, a few months apart. That had been in July.

A week before Christmas, John had a present delivered to Amy, a pony. Mister Bojangles was what was written on the card and it had been attached by a red ribbon to the pony's mane. The significance of the vagabond name wasn't lost on Louise. She guessed that was John's way of telling her that he wasn't coming back.

Amy had never been on a horse before but she begged and begged until Louise gave in.

A few minutes later, Amy had returned to the house on foot. She had been hurt when Mister Bojangles had thrown her, a small cut on the forehead that had looked worse than it was. When Amy had appeared in the doorway, her face covered with tears and snot and blood, Louise had panicked. She remembered screaming John's name.

He didn't come.

At that moment Louise realized he really was gone. For good. That she was going to have to deal with the crisis all by herself.

Since that day she had been doing her best to raise her daughter without any help. Louise knew she had made mistakes with Amy, and she agonized over them. Sometimes she pushed Amy too hard, but she didn't want her daughter to end up in some nowhere place like Crowder Flats, smoking unfiltered cigarettes in the dark and dreaming about some man who had been gone for ten years.

She looked at his picture on the dresser. He was showing Amy how to shoot pool and he had just made a shot that was impossible. He was smiling that easy smile of his. Dark hair. White teeth. He was a good-looking son of a bitch. He had been good in bed, too.

God, she remembered their nights of lovemaking. His lean, hard body next to hers. Her mouth still went dry whenever she thought about him.

Amy said all the cigarettes that Louise smoked were really just a substitute for sex. Sublimation, Amy called it. A twenty-dollar word for fooling yourself was more like it. Louise couldn't argue with her daughter's diagnosis. Hmmmm. A smile, half-bitter, half-wry, touched her face when she looked at the overflowing ashtray. "Shit, kiddo, if cigarettes are sex, your old mama is turning into a nympho."

Louise took one last drag, pulling the smoke deep into her lungs, before grinding out her half-finished cigarette in the ashtray. Damn, this was hard for her, even though she had promised Amy she would cut back. This was about as close as she could get to keeping her promise. Lately she had begun coughing and it seemed to take longer for the coughing to stop. She wondered if she was getting cancer.

The moon poured light through her bedroom window and she stared at it, drifting back to sleep, dreaming that Amy had fallen off her pony.

The phone rang. In her half-awake state it sounded like a child crying.

Louise picked up the phone on the third ring. "Amy, don't cry. It's just a scratch—"

"Louise, it's me. I'm sorry to call so late." The voice was faint, filled with sadness. It scared her. Nine years ago she had received a late-night call from her mother telling her that her father was dead. Her mother had sounded the way John sounded now.

For a long beat, she listened to the static on the line. "John, what's wrong?"

"There's been some trouble. It's Leon. He's—"

Louise felt something cold run through her. She knew what John was going to say and she didn't think she could bear to hear it. "He's dead, isn't he? Leon's dead," she heard herself say. The words seemed to come from someone else.

"Yeah, I found him about half an hour ago. God, Louise, they hurt him bad before they killed him. They cut him, and then broke all his bones so they could stick him in the freezer. He was holding a jar of pigs' feet in his lap. There was a hand in it. I think it belonged to Dorinda."

"Why?" was all she could say.

"A cue stick." More static on the line, and this time, when the voice came back, it was as brittle as old onionskin paper. "The cue stick that I stole. I got Leon killed, maybe Dorinda, too."

"Why would anybody kill Leon and Dorinda over a cue stick?"

"I don't know, I think these guys do this stuff for kicks. They were looking for me. I guess they thought Leon could tell them where."

"Can you go to the police?"

"I called them, but I didn't say who I was. They wouldn't believe me no way. My word doesn't carry much weight since Tucson. Anyway, I don't think I could prove these guys had anything to do with it. I get the feeling they're pretty good at covering their tracks." John hesitated and Louise knew he was working up his courage to say something else. She knew it was bad.

"There's something more, isn't there?" Louise said. "You always save the worst news for last. Well, you're going to have to say it, John, you're not going to be able to send it on a cute card this time."

"There was a message stuffed in Leon's mouth. It said to bring the cue stick to Crowder Flats. That means these guys might know about you and Amy." A deep breath. "And that means they might use you to get at me."

Louise felt as if someone had stepped on her chest. She couldn't breathe. "Do you think they're here yet?"

"There's a good chance they are. Leon was damn near frozen when I got to him and that means he'd been in the freezer awhile."

"What do these men look like?"

"One's young, wears a gray Stetson, looks like Dwight Yaokam. The other is old, looks like Randolph Scott gone to seed, wears a scruffy leather jacket. They might be driving Leon's red Caddy."

"Anything else?" Louise asked.

"Is Amy there?"

"No, she went out."

"Can you call her?"

"Maybe. I don't know. She doesn't always answer her cell phone when it's me."

"Try and find her, Louise. Call her. For God's sake, try. These bastards will do anything."

"I won't let anything happen to her."

A pause on the other end. "I'm sorry, Louise, I know you won't. I'll be there as quick as I can."

Louise waited for him to hang up.

"Louise, I… I never meant for anything bad to happen."

"I know you don't, John, you never do." Louise pressed down the receiver. She walked over to the closet, pulled out the twelve-gauge scattergun and laid it on the bed beside her. Then she picked up the phone and began making a call.

Out in the corral, Mister Bojangles nickered.

Louise stiffened at the sound, but quiet resumed. "Guess I'm not the only one having bad dreams tonight," she said. She waited for Stuart Johnson, Crowder Flats' part-time sheriff, to pick up on the other end.

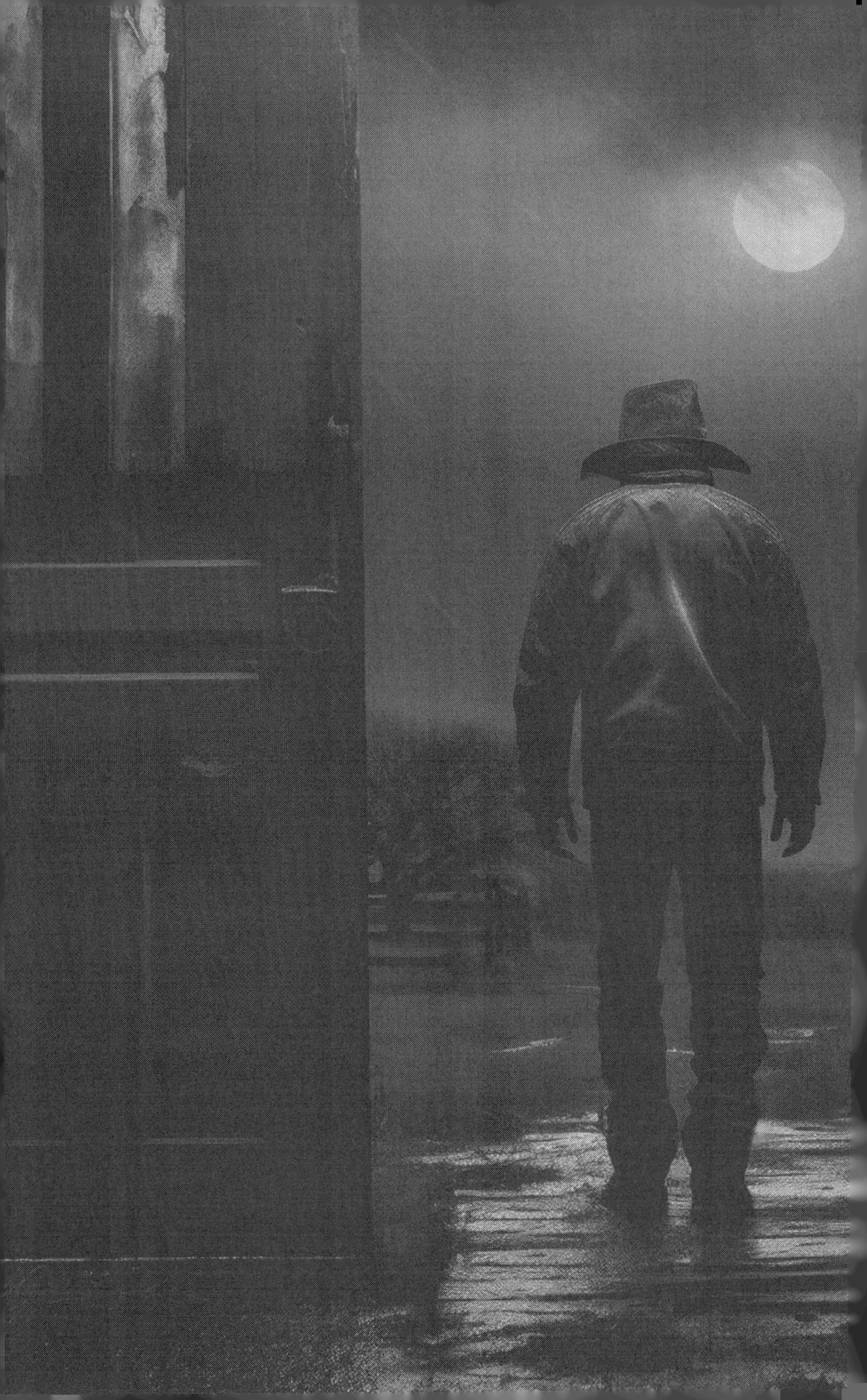

CHAPTER FIFTEEN

Crowder Flats.
Sunday morning.

Louise Warrick was scared…

…even though it was a beautiful, sunshine-filled morning. Trouble was coming to Crowder Flats. The only question left was—when would it arrive? It would come with John, she decided. It always did. Louise wondered if he was here yet. A covered wagon rumbled by, almost brushing Louise. The Frontier Days parade was under way.

The town had gone all out this year. Red, white, and blue pennants were strung from every building, flapping in the breeze. Everyone was dressed in Old West clothes, smiling and waving, but Louise barely noticed. She kept scanning the crowd of tourists, looking in the sea of shifting unfamiliar faces, trying to spot the two men who had killed Leon Wilson and his daughter.

The spectacle of the parade seemed subdued to Louise, like watching TV with the volume turned down too low. She heard a phone ring and looked around. Winced as she realized the sound was only in her head. It wouldn't stop ringing; it kept tugging at her like a child begging for attention.

There was only one way to stop it: pick up the receiver. But if she did that, then she would have to hear the bad news again. That Leon Wilson and Dorinda were dead.

Louise had loved the large black man, along with his fesity daughter. Out of all of John's friends, he'd been her favorite. He always made her laugh no matter how down she felt.

Leon Wilson, pool hall owner and teller of bad jokes. Big booming laugh. Scary looking, but the gentlest man Louise had ever known.

A man who cried at sad movies. Liked cornflakes. Drank his coffee with three spoons of sugar.

Loved his wife and daughter.

The memories drifted toward Louise like snowflakes against a window, sticking for an instant, leaving behind bits and pieces of themselves before melting away. Gone before their beauty could really be appreciated. Louise, John, and Darlene, sitting at the dining room table at Leon's house. Fifth anniversary, Leon cooking. Fine china, candles in silver holders, roses, white linen tablecloth. Leon running out of the kitchen, which was on fire.

Later that night. Sitting at McDonald's. A Formica table decorated with fine china, candles in silver holders, roses, a white linen tablecloth, eating Big Macs and laughing like crazy people while the other customers stared at them.

There had been sad moments, too.

The time Leon told the story about how his face had been cut.

The night he had called and asked if she knew where Darlene had gone.

Part of the past. Gone. All gone now.

Leon's murder seemed incomprehensible to her.

At odd moments, images of Leon's broken body in a freezer kept peeking around the corners of her mind. It was a fleeting sight. Gone in an instant. Each time his specter appeared, he would hold out a jar of pigs' feet to her. Then the bloody face would smile from the depths of the freezer, inviting her to reach inside.

The contents of the jar swirled, a ghostly image swirling behind the frosty glass. Round and round.

The hand was trying to get out of the jar, she could hear it scratching with its gold nails.

Against her will, Louise saw herself putting her own hand into the jar, but Leon and his grisly offering kept disappearing before she could touch it. Louise knew she was only prolonging the inevitable. Which filled her with a sense of futility, because each time she thought about Leon and Dorinda, the contents of the jar became more real.

Soon she was going to have to face what was inside. She didn't know if she was up to the job.

Facing things wasn't exactly one of her strengths.

Shading her eyes, Louise gazed toward the mountains in the far distance. The sun was burning off the last of the mist at their summit, drawing it upward in long finger-shaped spirals. The sight reminded her of a hand reaching out, a tired spirit trying to pull itself out of the clouds toward Heaven. But God wasn't in a helpful mood today. He brushed the fingers away before they could grasp hold.

The parade, led by covered wagons, moved past the Cates Motel and Coffee Shop. Old Charlie was on the patio in his white apron and the new white chef's hat he had broken out for the occasion. He sat a burger plate in front of a tourist and waved at some kids on the street. His eyebrows still hadn't grown back after that little accident with the barbecue grill. Dressed all in white, his pale hairless head and pudgy stomach made him a dead ringer for the Pillsbury Doughboy. He pressed his stomach and laughed.

The kids thought Charlie was funny. They waved back.

Boyce, Nash, and Kevin rode past in the stagecoach, followed by Manny, Ernesto, and Jesus on horseback. They looked game, if a little hung over, and Louise suspected they had been out late last night. She was exhausted, herself. Amy had come home a few minutes after three, and they had spent the rest of night talking about John's phone call. And the two drifters who had shown up at Jake's.

At the moment Amy was with Jesse, and for once, Louise was glad of that.

Boyce yelled at Louise, startling her, "You seen Bobby today?"

"No," Louise yelled back. She started to say something else to them, but one of the horses pulling their wagon raised its tail and deposited a steaming load in the street.

Waves of laughter rose from the sidelines. The crowd began chanting in unison, "Pooper scooper, pooper scooper."

"Looks like they're playing your song." Nash handed Boyce the shovel and broom. "Try not to step in anything this time, will you?"

Boyce swept up the mess to thunderous applause while an elderly Japanese couple pointed a cell phone at him. Taking a bow, he had to run to catch up to the stagecoach.

"Oh, man"—Kevin indicated the contents of the shovel—"that's almost as green as your face after that last shot of tequila."

"No, I'd say it's closer to Bobby's and Jesse's after that hustler from Texas walked out with all their money. I wonder where that shithead, Bobby, is hiding?" Boyce sounded worried. "You think he's okay?"

Kevin pulled back on the reins, bringing the stagecoach to a halt. "Yeah, he's fine. He's just pissed we got on his case about Jesse. He'll be here for the rodeo."

"I don't know, man. Something's going on. Where the hell's Chester? I saw his car at the house last night."

"Ain't nobody seen Martin, neither," Nash added. "God, I hope the three of them ain't getting tanked up somewhere. I don't think I can deal with that."

Up ahead, by Pierce's Merchandise, a couple of wild burros had walked out into the middle of the street, temporarily halting the procession.

Louise trotted over and chased them on across.

"Nice ass," an anonymous voice called out.

Some of the spectators cheered, a few booed. "Write 'em a ticket," someone else yelled.

The mayor, on horseback, stopped in front of her. "Anyone hear anything on my radials, Louise?"

"Not yet, Your Honor. Stuart's still looking." Perspiration caused Louise's police uniform to stick to her and she kept plucking at it, trying to keep the heavy material away from her skin. The ten pounds that she had gained in the last year weren't helping matters any. She felt as if everyone were watching her, that they saw she wasn't a real cop.

Once a year Stuart Johnson deputized her to help out with the parade. The whole thing was like dress-up when she was a little girl: "Look at me, Mommy, I'm a police woman." Even the pistol on her hip didn't seem real. She hefted the holster, smoothing down the mark where the Sam Browne belt had been let out a notch.

Something sailed out of the crowd. Landed in the middle of the street.

Louise watched the object hit, bounce once, and lie still. Smoke poured out, and she darted forward. She heard a hissing come from the smoke. Too late, she recognized the sound.

A string of firecrackers.

The first one went off, a tiny pop. A second followed. Popcorn was the word that ran through Louise's mind. Sounded just like popcorn. She knew what was going to happen. She turned, headed for the mayor's horse.

A third firecracker went off. Faster this time.

The mayor's horse rolled his eyes, showing white.

Then the rest of the firecrackers started going off, whipping their tails of sparks back and forth.

The mayor's horse squealed, tried to rear, almost unseating its rider. But Louise was there. She grabbed the reins until everything was under control.

The mayor glared at the crowd, searching for the culprit. Smiling, bland faces stared back. One, freckled and topped with a mop of red hair, was smiling a little more than the rest. The face belonged to Elliot Cates.

"Thanks, Louise, that was quick thinking," the mayor said. "You'll make a police woman yet." His dignity looked a little worse for wear.

"No problem, Your Honor. Cooking dinner, fighting off PMS, stopping a runaway horse, it's all part of a woman's job." She massaged her shoulder. Her arm felt as though it had been jerked out of the socket.

The mayor gave her a puzzled look before riding on.

When Louise turned back to the crowd, Elliot was gone.

The parade continued, bright splashes of color moving past Louise: a buckboard pulled by white horses, more covered wagons, women dressed as settlers walked by with their Adidas and Nikes peeking out from beneath long print dresses, Navajos in their ceremonial garb—one had forgotten to remove his watch—hawkers selling sparklers, cotton candy, and silver balloons.

Lots of strangers. The crowd only added to Louise's unease.

Eleven months and three weeks out of the year, Crowder Flats was three hundred and fifty-seven people, all known to her. That was the way Louise liked it. She couldn't wait for the festivities be over, all the strangers gone.

There were only a few events left: awarding first prize for the largest snake in the rattlesnake roundup—old Jebediah had been a snake handler.

That would be followed by a reenactment of a stagecoach holdup. Nash, Boyce, and Kevin would be doing the driving. Ernesto, Jesus, and Manny would be the outlaws holding them up. That would be followed by a staged hanging of the culprits. Always a highlight.

Then came the rodeo tonight. Bobby and Jesse would be competing in the bull riding. Everyone was talking about the event and the whole town would turn out to watch the two local boys go at it.

That is, if Bobby showed up. Louise had seen Jesse earlier, but where was Bobby?

A pockmarked man with an earring caught Louise's eye and she watched while he put his arms around a girl in black leather and a Harley T-shirt, running his hands under the material, cupping her breasts. Bikers. Hundreds of them. They called themselves the Legion of Death ,and they were camped at the outskirts of town. At night Louise could hear the roar of their bikes as they rode around their huge bonfire.

There was nothing anyone could do about them. All kinds of people showed up for the Frontier Days celebration.

Louise stared the biker girl's T-shirt, taking in the two smiling skeletons screwing on a black background. Right beneath a winking skull and crossbones were the words:

WARNING! SEX! HAZARDOUS TO YOUR HEALTH!

The two bikers saw Louise watching them. The man pulled his hands from beneath the girl's T-shirt, put them on the hood of a car and spread his legs as though he had been busted. The girl blew Louise a kiss. The rest of the bikers hooted. They weren't fooled by Louise's uniform—they knew she was no cop. Their laughter followed her when she walked away.

Louise fervently wished Frontier Days were over and she could get back to her normal job, dispatching.

Sheriff Stuart Johnson walked over and put his arm around her. "You doing okay, kiddo?"

"Can't we do something about the bikers?" Louise asked.

"Well, that wouldn't be very neighborly since this Frontier Days thing is all about freedom," the sheriff said. "Wouldn't be right to turn somebody away because personal hygiene isn't first on their list of priorities, now would it?" He winked.

Louise smiled, hugged him back. "I guess not, not when you put it that way."

"They just want to get to you, so don't let 'em."

"Thanks, I'm trying not to.," Louise looked into the baggy face of the old man, at the twinkling eyes buried in their pouches of fat, and tried to smile. "Sorry, Stuart, I'm not very good around people. I guess they can tell I'm nervous."

"You got to learn to smile, Louise. You have been the most serious girl I have ever known. Even when you were little." He hitched up his pants where they were sliding away from his ample girth. "You remember the first time you came into my office; you couldn't have been more than nine or ten?"

Louise shook her head no, began trying to edge away.

Stuart grabbed her by the arm. "You were all out of breath, said you spotted one of the guys on the wanted posters in the post office. You wanted me to arrest him for armed robbery." Stuart began laughing. "I went with you and it turned out to be my nephew, Cotter."

"What are you saying, Stuart?" Louise felt her face turning red. Stuart had that tone in his voice that meant he was about to deliver one of his lectures. She braced herself.

"I'm saying I did some checking on your story about Leon Wilson. You know what I found?"

"Let me guess," Louise said, fighting back the sudden urge to cry, "the cops went to Leon's house and they didn't find anything."

"Not a damned thing."

"You think I'm mistaken about all this?" Her lower lip trembled and she bit down on it. Savagely.

Stuart was still smiling, only the smile was filled with pity. "I don't know, Louise. If the cops had found anything, I might put more stock in the story."

"But since it was John, you don't believe it?"

"I'm not exactly saying I don't believe it." He gave her a little squeeze. "We both know they had to send John away for a while when he was a kid. He kept having all those crazy dreams about Billy Two Hats, kept saying Billy was a serial killer. That Billy was cutting up women with a knife. He damn near had me believing him for a while."

"That was a long time ago," Louise said.

"I know it was, but I never could put no faith in anything John said. Come to find out, John was a thief, stole Billy's pocket knife, and then made up that cock-and-bull story to cover his own ass. And don't think I've forgotten about the time he held up that liquor store in Tucson." Stuart smiled and waved at someone in the parade. "I don't figure he's changed all that much since then."

"He was only nineteen and he didn't do the holdup. Rudy No Horses did. John didn't know what Rudy was going to do, John was only driving the car." Louise shrugged loose from Stuart's arm. "So you're not going to do anything."

"I didn't say that, did I?"

Louise searched his face, looking for some sign of belief.

"Look, Louise, I didn't get to be sixty-three in this job by being stupid." The smile vanished and the twinkling eyes were dead serious now. "I asked the state boys for help, but without some kind of proof, there's not much anybody can do." He held up his hand to ward off Louise's next question. "I went on ahead and deputized three extra men just in case. If anybody shows up looking like the men you described, we'll get 'em."

A weight lifted from Louise's shoulders. "You know, Stuart, when you cock your hat a certain way," she said, "you look just like John Wayne."

"Go on with you now. I'll take over here." The twinkle was back in Stuart's eyes and Louise knew he was pleased despite all his protesting. "Get on over to Charlie Cates' place, would you? There's been some trouble at the snake pit. I think it's Charlie's boy, Elliot."

A look of distaste crossed Louise's face at the mention of the fifteen-year-old's name.

"I guess you're remembering that little stunt he pulled last July fourth," Stuart said.

"I don't call lighting the barbecue grill with a flamethrower a little stunt. His dad could have been killed. Where on earth did Elliot get something like that?"

"His grandfather brought it back from Korea after the war. Had it buried in an old trunk out in his garage." Stuart motioned to the elderly Japanese couple with cell phones out. They paused to get a short video of Stuart, who sucked in his paunch for the occasion. "You got to admit the boy showed some mechanical ability, getting that thing working after all these years." The old sheriff seemed more amused than concerned by the incident.

"Yeah, he's a real genius. I don't think his dad's eyebrows are ever going to grow back."

"Well, that was unfortunate. Charlie had on one of those floppy chef's hats and it just sort of vaporized. Don't be too hard on the boy," Stuart said. "At that age, Elliot's just a little rambunctious."

THE FIVE-YEAR-OLD DANGLED HEADFIRST OVER THE OPEN SNAKE PIT. His name was Timmy Cates and he was screaming bloody murder.

Inside the pit, there were nearly two hundred rattlesnakes crawling around. They made a constant crackling, like dry leaves underfoot. As the five-year-old descended closer, rattling sounds began, a warning not to come any closer. It grew in volume. Several of the snakes lunged at the boy's face and his screams became even more shrill.

"Put him down, Elliot," Louise said.

"That's what I'm doing, putting him down." Elliot Cates laughed. "In the snake pit." The smirk stayed on the teenager's face as he lifted up his five-year-old brother by the ankle. He sat the smaller boy back on the ground.

The boy ran over and grabbed Louise's leg in a death grip. She could feel his heart thudding against her leg. "It's all right, Timmy," Louise said. She stroked the top of the sobbing child's head. "Everything's going to be fine. You go find your mom."

Timmy turned, gave Elliot the finger before bolting.

"I wasn't really going to throw him in," Elliot said. "He asked what they ate, so I told him little boys. I was only having some fun."

"Is that a fact?" Louise asked, moving closer. She looked around to see if anyone was watching. No one was.

"Yeah, that's a fact," Elliot said. "The little turd said my snake wasn't going to win." He saw something in Louise's face and took a step back. Unfortunately the snake pit was right behind him. He couldn't move any farther. "I didn't hurt the little crybaby any."

"You scared him pretty good. He could have fallen, maybe even broke his neck. It's a good fifteen feet to the bottom of that pit." Louise took another step forward. "He'll probably have bad dreams for months because of what you did, Elliot." She punched the redhead teenager with a stiffened finger. "You ever have bad dreams, Elliot?" Her face was only inches away from Elliot's now. She grabbed him by his T-shirt and forced him back another step.

His feet found the edge of the pit and sand spilled down, causing the rattling to resume. A couple of the snakes began blindly lashing out.

Elliot looked over his shoulder; he wasn't smiling anymore. He teetered, trying to regain his balance. "I'm sorry, honest. Relax. Chill. Jesus, it won't ever happen again. Okay?"

"Why don't I believe you, Elliot?" She took another step forward, bending the teenager back over the pit. "You ever see anyone after they've been bitten by one of those big rattlers? They get real sick. Sometimes they even... die."

"You're just trying to scare me, so fuck off. You're not going to knock me in the pit."

"Is that right?" Louise let go of his T-shirt and he tipped backward, arms flailing wildly. He managed to grab hold of her arm. Her arm was the only thing stopping him from pitching into the pit, and his grip wasn't secure. Louise's skin was sweaty.

His fingers began sliding.

"You think I'm still kidding around, Elliot?"

Elliot's grip was down to Louise's hand now. "I'm going to tell my old man what you did."

Louise's hand gripped his.

Elliot smiled.

"Maybe you won't get the chance." Louise's hand opened.

Elliot started his backward plunge into the pit. He looked faintly surprised.

A third hand, dark, sunburned, reached out and grabbed hold of Elliot's shirt, held him suspended in space for a second. The shirt began tearing. The hand grabbed more material, and it held long enough for Elliot to be deposited on the ground at the edge of the pit. The shaken teenager looked down at his torn shirt, started to say something, but his throat didn't seem to want to work. He climbed to his feet and stumbled a couple of steps, fell. His legs had turned to rubber on him. Getting up, he ran. He didn't look back.

Louise turned and saw Stuart. The elderly sheriff stood there, breathing heavily, with a piece of Elliot's shirt in his hand. The expression on his face was one of shock. "Louise, what in God's name are you doing?" The voice jarred her, brought her back from the dark place.

"Something somebody should have done a long time ago," Louise said. "Teach that little bastard some manners." She shook her head, trying to clear it. The anger in her was a hard fist pounding against her temples, and when it finally stopped, it left her weak. She almost collapsed and Stuart had to catch her.

"I'm sorry, Stuart, it's just when I saw Elliot holding Timmy over the pit, I guess I lost it. He would have fallen and I… and I…" Louise began to sob, then brutally ran her hand across her mouth, stifling the tears. "Couldn't take that again."

"Louise." Stuart started to put his arm around her.

Backing away, Louise reached into her uniform pocket, produced a cigarette, but her hands were too shaky to light it. She pulled it from her mouth, crumpled it, and threw the remains on the ground. "I smoke too damn much anyway." She tried to laugh, but the sound came out all wrong.

"It's all right," Stuart said, pulling her close. "It's not your fault." He stroked her hair. "It's mine, all mine. I knew what Elliot was doing back here. I shouldn't have sent you. I guess I wasn't thinking. Forgive me."

"He was going to let his little brother fall. He was going to let… my baby fall…"

"It's all right." Stuart held her and cursed himself for being a damned old fool. "Nobody's going to fall. Nobody at all." He held her while she cried.

CHAPTER SIXTEEN

The jackrabbit was running for its life, splay-footed panic in full flight.

It had come upon two most unusual predators.

Elliot and Timmy Cates.

The fifteen-year-old and his brother leaned low over the dirt bike, weaving in and out of the stands of cactus until they were right behind the terrified animal. The teenager's torn shirt flapped in the wind, making him into a redheaded scarecrow. He was all sharp edges and gangly limbs that seemed like they didn't fit together. The vacant green eyes and smile only added to the illusion. His little brother sat behind him, holding on tight.

The rabbit, desperate to escape, threw up dust as it tried to draw ahead.

Elliot pulled up alongside and knocked the animal flying with the long pole in his hand. "Lord Doingyoursister Strathmore, the world's greatest polo player, scores the winning goal. The babes go crazy." He laughed when the rabbit went sprawling end over end, a tangle of legs and floppy ears. Elliot skidded to a halt, waited.

The exhausted jack climbed to its feet. Instead of taking off, it just crouched in the dirt, confused, its sides bellowing in and out.

"Nobody called time out. That's cheating." He prodded the rabbit with his pole and the quivering legs again ratcheted into motion. This was great. Elliot hated it when they gave up too easily.

The three of them raced across the scrub grass and out onto the open plain. The whine of the cycle was the only sound, and it was sucked up by the immense emptiness that surrounded them. A streak of blue smoke drifted out behind the bike, floating over the copper-colored landscape. Looking back, Elliot was reminded of the streaks left by the jets when they cut across the evening sky.

The rabbit began to slow so Elliot bumped him. A squeak of despair was drowned beneath the drone of the bike as the animal was sent rolling once more.

Elliot Cates and his brother lived in a fantasy world most of the time, horror movies and heavy metal were their favorite things in life. At the age when most kids were into Bambi and Disney sing-a-longs, Elliot had Timmy OD'ing on Freddy Krueger and Motley Crue.

Sarah Cates was forty-two when she'd had Timmy, and when Elliot was in the fifth grade, a kid told him that his parents wouldn't love him anymore. Elliot asked why. The kid said Elliot's parents would only care about Timmy, because Timmy was a baby. That kid had turned out to be right. As far as Elliot's parents were concerned, he was invisible.

That was the way everyone treated Elliot.

Like he was invisible.

Even though Elliot tried to hate Timmy, it was hard to hate someone who thought you hung the moon. His younger brother was the only one who didn't ignore him. The little twerp was always following him around, always asking questions. It was annoying, and yet Elliot didn't mind, because, deep down, he knew that was as close as he was ever going to get to having someone love him.

The rabbit swerved, darted down a dry creek bed.

"Oh no, bad move, Mister Bunny Rabbit." Elliot gunned his bike after it, kicking up loose gravel in a rooster tail. Tied to the back of his bike was a gunnysack for collecting rattlers. It too was flapping in the wind. In his hand, like a lance for jousting, was a pole with a wire loop on the tip. Tools of the trade. Tools that would net him the five-hundred-dollar first prize for the largest rattler.

The pole also had one other feature; it had a sharpened tip that made it perfect for spearing jackrabbits.

This one would make number fifty-seven. He was sure of the count because he put a notch on the pole after every kill.

Elliot pulled even with the tiring animal, swerving his bike, forcing the rabbit against the creek bank. The rabbit, trapped, turned wild eyes on his tormentor. It wheeled and started back the way it had come. Elliot anticipated the move, swung his bike around, pulled up even with the rabbit again.

"What's up, doc?" A laugh of pure exultation poured out of the teenager. He prodded the animal with his stick, drawing blood this time. "C'mon, sucker, don't you quit on me. Run!"

The jackrabbit put on a desperate burst of speed. Drew slightly ahead.

The bike stuttered, dropped back. A look of pure venomous hatred twisted Elliot's face. He rotated the accelerator back and forth, trying to clear the clogged carburetor. A cloud of black smoke spewed out and the bike stalled for a second.

"The rabbit's getting away," Timmy said, secretly glad.

Elliot geared down, popped the clutch. The bike lurched, almost started. More black smoke poured out.

Elliot looked like he was about to cry. The bike was losing speed. "C'mon, you piece of shit." He geared down more, popped the clutch again. The machine grunted as the engine caught, resumed its nasal whine.

"All right," Elliot said, elated. He patted the bike. "I knew you wouldn't let me down."

Elliot accelerated, standing the bike on its back wheel in a showboat maneuver. He again caught up with his quarry. "Looks like your luck has run out, fuzzball." He whacked the exhausted animal with the pole, trying to stir one last effort from it.

But the rabbit was all played out. It came to a halt, its sides quivering, eyes glazed.

Elliot rode past, swung around in a showy arc, throwing gravel high into the air. He let the bike idle while he wiped the sweat from his face. "Prepare to meet your doom at the hands of the red knight." He lowered the stick into jousting position, urged the bike forward. In his mind, Elliot was facing the black knight.

Timmy closed his eyes, pressed his face into his brother's back. He hated this part.

The rabbit seemed unimpressed by the honor accorded it.

The animal died impaled on the stick, kicking feebly, without a sound.

Wiping the blood from his stick, Elliot checked the sky.

"We'd better get home," Timmy said. "Dad wants you to wash dishes tonight."

"Shut up." The sun was beginning to set, and that made Elliot a little nervous. Time was running out. He shouldn't have wasted so much time on the jackrabbit, but he had to admit he felt a whole lot better now, not so angry anymore.

Killing something always soothed him.

Play time was over, he had to shake a leg, because ten o'clock was the deadline for entering a snake in the contest. So far he had been unable to find that really big rattler, the one that would get him the down payment on that new Yamaha he'd had his eye on for the last two months.

There would be no chance of earning that kind of money, not for at least another year. He doubted the piece of shit between his legs would last that long. That meant he could end up walking, and the possibility of that kind of humiliation was too much to even think about.

That would be worse than what Louise Warrick had done to him back there at the snake pit. Whew! Man, that bitch had gone psycho. Good thing old Stuart had shown up.

Louise had humiliated him. There was only one punishment for that; no more thinking about her when he whacked off.

Then he imagined her sweaty breasts pressing against him. Well, maybe he was being a little hasty. A couple of days off should be enough punishment for her.

Elliot pushed the bike to greater speed, ignoring the large stones that littered the creek bed.

Life wasn't fair.

Every time he tried to liven things up a little around Crowder Flats, people got pissed.

He consoled himself with more fantasies of Louise Warrick's sweaty breasts, even though he had never felt a breast, sweaty or otherwise. He stopped watching where he was going and the bike hit some loose gravel, veered off course, plowed into a patch of larger rocks.

The rear end of the Kawasaki began hopping up and down like a jackrabbit with its ass on fire.

Elliot and Timmy went one way and the bike went the other.

They swapped ends several times, but Elliot never dropped the snake pole, even when he plowed up about ten feet of the creek bed with his face.

The bike coasted to a halt, fell over on its side. Timmy started crying over a bloody nose. One of his teeth, knocked loose by the impact, fell to the ground. A smile lit his face. "Lookit, Elliot, something for the tooth faggot."

"That's fairy, tooth fairy, you little retard."

"Dad said fairies are faggots," Timmy insisted.

"Okay, fine, you got something for the tooth faggot. If you don't shut up, you're gonna have more teeth for him." Elliot climbed to his feet, dusted himself off, and walked over to his fallen steed. He gave it a savage kick. Timmy did the same, copying his older brother. Elliot's MOTLEY CRUE T-shirt, which hadn't been in very good shape to start with, was reduced to tatters now. Ripping off a part of it, he dabbed at his bleeding face before giving it to Timmy.

He righted the bike and kick-started it back to stuttering life. Everything was jake, just a little more paint missing, a little more skin. He knew his looks didn't matter. No girl had ever looked at him with anything other than disgust.

A triangular head peered at them from the bushes, tongue flickering in and out of a mouth white as cotton. A rattler, but way too small for the contest. It coiled, its tail giving a familiar warning. "You want to bite something, shithead? Well, bite this." Elliot grinned, guided his bike across the snake's back, leaving it writhing in the dust, its spine broken.

Elliot was about to head back down the creek bed when Timmy tugged on his shirt. A flash had caught the five-year-old's eye. It was far away, whatever it was. The setting sun was reflecting off something shiny. Probably metal or glass.

Gunning the bike, Elliot moved up the creek bank and tried to figure out where the flash had come from. After a moment, he did. The old Navajo burial ground.

"Wanna go to the old cemetery?" Elliot said. "See some buried Indians?"

"That place is scary," Timmy said. "Everybody says it's hunted."

"That's haunted. Shut up, will you, I'm trying to think." Elliot picked gravel out of his skin, and tried to decide if he wanted to go check the place out or not. The old graveyard gave him a major case of the creeps, even if he wouldn't admit it to his younger brother. That big old white cross made him think about church, and that made him think about hell, which was where his grandfather said he was going if he didn't straighten up and fly right.

The wind made funny noises up there, too. It sounded like somebody crying. He revved his engine. What had made that flash? Finally, curiosity won out. It could be something worth stealing.

As Elliot gazed toward the graveyard in the far distance, he saw the flash had been caused by a car. No, hold on. Three cars. They were just sitting there all in a row, nose to ass, like elephants in a parade. They were just specks, too far away for him to identify them. Elliot held his ground, looking for signs of the owners.

After about ten minutes, he was convinced the place was deserted.

Jesus, this was really weird. There was no road leading out here, yet somebody had driven these cars out into the middle of nowhere and left them. Excitement grew in his stomach. Cars had stereos. Stereos could be ripped off. And sold. For cash.

Then there were tires, car seats, engine parts, and that was just to start.

He grew light-headed at the possibilities.

As he drifted closer, guided by the white cross that rose above the graveyard, he recognized two of the cars. One belonged to Bobby Roberts, the other to Bobby's dad, Chester, but the third was a BMW Elliot had never seen before. It wore silver paint and a shiny Nevada plate.

The teenager's hopes for quick riches diminished somewhat. "That's Bobby's car," Timmy said. "He'll cut off your balls if you touch it."

"Shut up." A fly settled on Elliot's face, crawled toward his still-bleeding chin. He waved it away.

This whole scene was getting weirder by the minute, all of the cars were chained together, bumper to bumper, and he could see that the white Caddy had towed the other two out here.

He climbed off his bike and listened, not that he could hear much. His ears were still ringing from going ass over elbows. Now that they'd stopped moving, the heat was a blast furnace. Beads of sweat formed on Elliot's forehead, trickled down, stinging the scrapes on his chin. More flies gathered on him as he walked toward the cars. One crawled in his open mouth. He absentmindedly spat it out.

Rocks clattered beneath his feet. He stopped. What if someone was inside passed out in one of the cars? He scooped up a handful of small stones and fired a couple of them at Chester's Caddy. The sound was loud but nobody inside sat up. Nobody yelled at him.

He called out Bobby's name. No answer.

"Where is everybody?" Timmy asked.

"Don't know."

The sun dipped behind the mountains and suddenly, just like that, it was ten degrees cooler. In the distance, a dust devil kicked up, headed away from them.

"What's that?" Timmy asked, pointing at the small tornado of dust.

"Tasmanian Devil. He's coming for your tooth."

Timmy considerd his brother's words. "Son of a bitch don't know his ass from a hole in the ground. He's going the wrong way."

"Just because Dad says something doesn't mean you got to say it, too." The evening breeze began rocking the pines on the far side of the graveyard, causing them to creak. That was bad enough. But soon that weird crying noise would start up. Elliot wanted to be gone before that happened. Long gone.

He started to kick his bike back to life.

Hesitated.

Elliot couldn't resist looking inside the cars. Just a quick peek. A chance like this might not come along again. He inched closer, still convinced someone was going to raise up and scare the crap out of him.

The BMW fascinated him and he knew he had to look inside it first. He had only seen pictures of cars like that.

Another rock bounced off the window brought no protest, so he opened the door. Strange exotic odors drifted from inside, new leather, shampooed carpet, freshly painted metal. These were odors that Elliot had only dreamed about in his most secret wet dreams. He had to climb inside.

The BMW smelled better than the girl's john at school and was clean enough to eat off the floorboard. It had a pair of fuzzy pink dice dangling from the rearview. One said DORA, the other LEE. He sat there staring at the gauges, trying to figure out their purpose. His hands caressed the steering wheel. If he had a car like this, the babes would be begging for mercy.

Reluctantly, he pulled himself from the BMW.

Chester's car was bourbon, cigars, with a side order of dried out cow-shit. On the floorboard, Elliot found some loose change, a half-pint bottle with an inch of Jim Beam in it. He put the change in his pocket, drank the Beam. "You tell the old man, you ain't coming with me again."

Bobby's car smelled like dust, cheap after-shave, and stale beer. There was another odor, hanging in the air, one he couldn't quite identify. It smelled like perfume, but it seemed as if the perfume had been poured over something that didn't smell so good. He slapped at a fly buzzing around his face.

Man, the place was crawling with flies.

From where he stood, he saw lines of tracks leading to the graveyard and he realized someone had made several trips from the Caddy in front.

As though that person had moved something from the car. To the graveyard.

The sound of buzzing slowly seeped into his ringing ears and he looked around, trying to figure out where it was coming from. He didn't see anything at first. Now that the sun was doing its disappearing act behind the mountains, the darkness was coming quick. He flipped on the bike's light and swept it around, feeling the first twinges of panic.

Timmy pointed.

At first Elliot didn't see anything, even as the buzzing grew louder. Agitated.

The noise was coming from back by the fence.

He flashed the light in that direction, saw movement His eyes were drawn to the graveyard, to the blue-green iridescent blanket covering the stones beneath the white cross. Part of it reached up the cross itself.

Elliot's mouth fell open.

The blanket was moving by itself. Rippling in the breeze, ebbing, flowing.

The gawky teenager stared without comprehension, until he realized he was looking at blowflies. The entire graveyard was crawling with the things. The reason he hadn't heard them before was because his ears had been ringing from the bike. His light was disturbing their feeding. The flies rose in a wave, before descending.

There must be thousands of them. Maybe tens of thousands.

What were they feeding on? He suddenly decided he didn't want to know.

He bolted to his bike, straddled it. This was past weird, way past, this was getting into scary. He kicked the starter. The engine coughed once, went silent. He went to give the starter another kick.

"Hey, Elliot, Timmy, what's your hurry?"

Elliot looked around for the voice, didn't see anyone. "Who's there?"

"It's me, Bobby Roberts."

"Bobby, where you at?" Timmy asked. "We don't see you."

"I'm right here."

"Are you invisabul?" Timmy leaned around his brother with a smirk. "Elliot was in your car."

"Was he now?" Bobby's voice sounded both amused and ominous.

While Elliot elbowed his brother in the ribs, a clattering came from inside the graveyard fence, noises made by something moving rocks around.

Elliot flashed his bike light in that direction. More flies. More than he'd ever seen in one place. They covered everything.

A huge glob of them moved away from the rest. Coming nearer, the buzzing turned into a wall of sound. Frozen, the boys watched some of the flies separate from the rest, swarming their faces, crawling around on unwashed skin. Timmy began smacking at them. Elliot was too numb to even brush them away.

Something, maybe it was an arm, reached upward from the roiling mass, holding an object, slapped it against the cross. It turned into a hat.

"Be with you in a second," the voice said. The hat began beating against the bigger glob of flies, causing them to lift, revealing a man beneath. Bobby Roberts.

"Hey, Elliot, Timmy, how you boys doing?"

Elliot redoubled his efforts to start his bike. In his haste, he flooded it. The sharp tang of gasoline overrode the riper odor of Bobby as he walked closer.

"You ever have one of those nights where everything goes to shit?" Bobby asked with a laugh. He kept beating at the flies with his hat. "So much to do, so little time. There just aren't enough hours in the night." The flies wouldn't seem to leave Bobby alone. Sometimes, parts of him would completely disappear beneath their squirming bodies. "I guess you're wondering what I'm doing out here."

Elliot tried to nod. Timmy whimpered.

"Carelessness, pure and simple," Bobby informed them. "Got caught by the rising sun and I had to burrow in under those rocks back there. It's cool under the trees." His smile was a trifle embarrassed. "But I damn sure didn't count on all these flies. It must have been the dead dogs that brought them."

Elliot was unable to look away. Timmy had his face buried in his brother's back again. Elliot had to admit it was a little disconcerting talking to someone whose head kept disappearing beneath a mass of blowflies. "Bobby, don't get mad, but could I ask you something?"

"Sure, little buddy, fire away."

"How come you're all covered with flies?"

"I expect it's because my clothes are all soaked with blood." Bobby walked toward his Caddy, opened up the trunk and pulled out some clean jeans and a shirt.

"Bobby?"

"What, little buddy?"

"Did you kill somebody?"

"No... I killed a lot of somebodies."

"Are you going to kill us?"

"I expect so." Bobby began changing into his clean clothes.

He wadded up his old ones and tossed them over the fence.

Timmy whispered in his brother's ear, "See, I told you he'd cut your balls off."

The flies swarmed over Bobby's blood-crusted shirt and jeans. "I guess you'll want to know why."

Elliot nodded.

"Well, I've got a little surprise for Crowder Flats, and I can't have you two spoiling it."

"You mean like a surprise birthday party?" Timmy asked.

"Yeah, something like that."

"Are you a monster?"

"Fraid so." Bobby was completely changed now. "Less than human. I guess I'm what you'd call a vampire. It's the only term you'd understand."

"No shit?"

"No shit."

Now Elliot couldn't decide if he was excited or scared. This was definitely the most exciting thing that had ever happened to him. "You like it okay, I mean, being a vampire and everything?"

"No, not really. The thing inside me makes me do things I don't really want to do."

"Like killing us."

"That's right." Bobby closed the trunk. The sound had a note of finality in it.

"Vampires get all the babes," Timmy said. "Could you make us vampires?"

Bobby laughed, sailed his bloodstained hat over the fence, where it landed next to his old clothes. The flies descended. "You've been watching way too many bad movies, boys." Bobby's face turned serious in the bike's light, his good humor falling away. All that was left was pain, and it twisted his mouth into a crooked line. "You don't want to be a vampire, Timmy. It ain't nothing like what you think. You're better off being dead, believe me."

"Maybe we can work a deal," Elliot said. "How about we promise not to say anything about what we saw here, and you don't kill us?"

The smile was back on Bobby's face, only now it looked painted on. "You always were a funny kid, Elliot. All that crazy shit you do, spearing jackrabbits, blowing up the barbecue grill with a flamethrower. I'm going to miss you." Bobby moved around the car, started toward him.

Cocking his head, Elliot sniffed the air. There was no gasoline smell now. He stepped down, kicked the bike to life, revved the engine.

Bobby stopped. He looked pissed. "You were just stalling me, weren't you?"

"Yeah, asshole, my carburetor was flooded."

"All right, maybe I was a little hasty." Bobby backed up a step. "Maybe we can work out a deal on this vampire thing."

"Fuck you, Bobby, you must think I'm a retard. Get out of the way." Elliot revved the engine again, dropped the pole he still held in his hand to jousting position. "I mean it, get out of the way." The sharp end was pointed at Bobby's chest.

"Timmy was right, vampires get all the babes." Bobby raised his head to the night air, sniffed, and Elliot had the feeling Bobby was sniffing him. "You'd like to get Louise Warrick, wouldn't you, especially after what she did to you today?"

The pole in Elliot's hand wavered. "How did you know that?"

"Vampires know lots of things." Bobby leaned against the Caddy, seemingly at ease. "You want her. I can smell it on you."

The bike idled while Elliot digested that. "You're full of shit."

"Am I?"

"Okay, so maybe I like her a little."

"If you were a vampire, you could have her."

The possibilities played across Elliot's face. "I could really have her?"

"Absolutely. You'd be able to get any woman you want."

"Even Amy?"

The skin at the corner of Bobby's eyes tightened. "Even Amy."

"I don't know, Bobby. I think I gotta go home and sleep on it."

Bobby shrugged, raised his hands. "All right. See you boys around."

While they were talking, smoke from the idling bike had drifted toward the graveyard, sending the flies into a hovering cloud.

What they had covered was becoming visible, and Timmy was quietly tugging on Elliot's shirt.

Elliot risked a quick look, turned back to Bobby. He was still propping up the Caddy.

What Elliot had seen began to register.

Five dead bodies lying in various positions of repose.

Four of them were people Elliot had known all his life. They were pale, waxy mannequins. For the first time in his life Elliot had an inkling of what death really looked like. He tried not to look again, but he couldn't stop himself.

Elliot looked back at Bobby.

Bobby wasn't by the car anymore. He had moved.

He was much closer.

And he had both hands on the pole.

The suddenness of the move startled the teenager, causing his hand to twitch on the accelerator. The bike lurched forward.

Not much, maybe a foot.

Like magic, the pole was sticking out of Bobby's back. He looked down with surprise and his smile appeared. It looked a trifle embarrassed. "That's what I get... flapping my lips... guess becoming a vampire hasn't changed that none."

Elliot tried to angle the bike away from the cars and the fence that had him hemmed in.

While he was wrestling with it, blood, or whatever passed for blood, leaked from Bobby and ran down the pole. It was dark red, almost black in the light and slightly luminous, filled with specks of light that glittered like broken glass.

It stunk, too, worse than Bobby.

Timmy wrinkled his nose at the smell.

The black substance was a trickle at first, though, as it got nearer Elliot's hand, it sped up, moving with startling speed. The teenager turned loose of the pole as though he had been burned, and scrambled back on his bike.

The blood came to the end of the pole, paused, rose up, and split into dozens of tendrils. They wriggled with agitation, as though trying to decide whether to go any farther. They made up their mind, shooting at Elliot like a nest of striking rattlesnakes.

But their strike fell short.

All except for one tendril.

It brushed Elliot's hand, leaving behind a welt. And a trace of itself.

Inside his mind, the fifteen-year-old had a flash of something too alien to comprehend, something that was incredibly old. There were images, murky at first, then clearer, like one of those photographs that developed in your hand.

Elliot sucked in his breath when the images crystallized.

He saw a moon, bright as silver, clear as pain, riding over a stretch of desert that seemed to reach the ends of the world.

Mountains sprawled at the desert's edge, the skeletal backbone of a giant snake pushing its way up from the earth. He took a breath and looked around. The night was humid, filled with the siren call of flutes, the slow thunder of drums, the hot copper of blood, the screams of people crying out in pain and ecstasy. All somehow joined together.

Elliot found himself standing on the summit of a vast triangular stone monument. A pyramid was the word that came to him. He looked out over a clearing, with hundreds of thousands of dark-skinned people dressed in bright-hued clothing and exotic feathers. They were bowing down to him, chanting a name, and Elliot knew he was a god to these people. At his feet there were steps carved into the lofty stone triangle, leading up to him. Those steps were stained red. Blood red.

Stacked along the walls of his temple were thousands of skulls, some bleached white, some still dripping.

The sea of worshippers held out their arms to him. Beckoning. Imploring.

He moved down the familiar route to the throng waiting below, listening to them call out his name. "Huitzilopochtli, Huitzilopochtli," they screamed, their faces twisted with adoration and fear. Some began tearing at their own flesh with the knives in their hands.

As Elliot reached the base of the pyramid, they fell silent. The wind ruffling their bright feathers, their torches guttering, were the only sounds in the night.

As one, two hundred thousand people held their breath, looking to him. A feeling of expectation hung in the air, a hush so palpable he could reach out and touch it. Time ceased.

Gazing toward the summit of the pyramid, he gave a signal to the people gathered there. They were his priests, sworn to him.

Twenty thousand men, women, and children kneeled before the priests, their faces serene. They gazed down at their god with love.

He basked in their adulation a moment. Gave another signal.

And the stone knives of his priests cut out the hearts of those who knelt. The blades traced faint, arcane glimmers in the moonlight as they went about their work.

The chosen were slaughtered in a matter of seconds. Even as they died, they called out their god's name.

The priests held the severed organs high, some still beating

And flung them to the crowd waiting below.

Blood erupted from the butchered bodies in geysers of scarlet, collecting in pools, spilling down the steps, gathering speed as it went.

By the time the blood reached Elliot, it was roaring like a waterfall.

The hot liquid came in waves, striking him in the chest, then his face, covering him, drowning out the screams of his worshippers as they went into a frenzy. He was their god and he had tasted their blood.

He found it good.

Then the pyramid was gone, the jungle, the desert and mountains, all vanished. Elliot found himself back at the graveyard, looking at Bobby stumbling backward. The taste of blood lay heavy in the teen's mouth. He leaned over the bike and threw up.

Bobby, holding on to the spear that had run him through, took another step back, went sideways.

Elliot backpedaled some more, still trying to turn the bike.

The blood on the pole stopped, reversed itself, ran back inside Bobby. Run through, the lanky pool player wasn't having much luck staying upright. He staggered into his Caddy, slid down the side. He came to a sitting position with his legs straight out in front of him. The tip of the pole sticking from his back had left a serious scratch in the paint. He looked at it. "Man, this hasn't been my day."

"Bobby, listen up, you fucker, I saw something, a pyramid... in a jungle." Elliot struggled for words. "People were dying, blood was running down the steps. There must have been—"

"Fifty thousand dead. I had fifty thousand people killed over a five-day period at Teotihuacán." Bobby saw the confusion on the boy's face. "That's outside Mexico City." Bobby's face clouded with thought. "That was a long time ago, over five hundred years."

There was no way for Elliot to measure that many deaths. "But why did you kill them?"

"They're called sacrifices, little buddy. Religion and blood, they go hand in hand. Just like your face and pimple cream. At the time, I was the sun god of the Aztecs." Bobby's foot was twitching, beating a tattoo on the rocks.

"Why did you kill them," Elliot repeated. "Some were kids. Little kids."

"The natives wanted it, the killing was their idea. They believed blood was the only thing that would bring the sun back each day. So I gave them blood, all the blood they could handle. I didn't want to disappoint." He looked inward and Elliot knew that the thing inside Bobby was reliving the moment. "I have been many gods in my time, Quetzacoatl, Thaloc, Coatlicue. Many gods."

"Quetza …," Elliot faltered.

"Quetzacoatl," Bobby explained, "the feathered serpent, the god of learning and enlightenment. Pretty funny, huh?" Bobby laughed, then coughed, his face going slack with pain. "I tried to stop all the killing. Only my subjects didn't want that, they grew to like the taste of blood. And after a while so did I." Bobby's eyes went cloudy. "Gods are what their worshippers make them."

"But why do gods have to kill people?"

A faint breath. "Gods need their sacrifices, Elliot, or they die."

Bobby seemed to grow tired. His eyes closed.

Then they opened. And the old Bobby was there, smiling that old familiar cocky smile. He turned his head and examined the scratch on his car. "Oh man, would you look at that? I just had this baby painted."

"Bobby, it's you. What happened to that… thing?"

"Shut up, you two. That thing's busy right now, keeping me alive." He reached up and began pulling the pole out of his stomach, grimacing at the pain.

The wet sucking sound reached them over the idling bike.

Sweat coated Bobby's face as he breathed in shallow gasps. "Little buddies, you got maybe a minute, maybe two… before I come after you." Bobby gritted his teeth, forced out the last words. "I'd be hauling ass if I was you."

Elliot needed no further urging. He got the bike turned and he began going through the gears. Within seconds, he and Timmy were running flat out across the rocky ground, without lights. The bike took a couple of stiff hops and Elliot prayed the tires would hold.

Memory and luck would be the only things keeping them from hitting something.

The graveyard faded into the night. The last thing to go was the white cross.

A quick look over his shoulder showed Elliot a set of car lights popping on. This wasn't fair. Bobby had said at least a minute. It hadn't been a minute. The teen crouched low over the bike, trying to cut down the wind resistance, but his old Kawasaki was maxed out.

"Hurry up, Elliot, he's coming."

A second set of car lights popped on.

And a third.

All three cars all moved out onto the plain, casting around for Elliot's trail. In the distance they looked like fireflies searching out a place to land. The ground was rocky and tracks would be hard to find, but Bobby knew this country as well as Elliot.

A car horn sounded, a bray of triumph. Bobby had picked up the bike's trail.

The three cars moved in unison, headed straight for them.

"Oh man, they're hauling ass," Timmy said.

"Don't talk about ass." Looking back, the teenager mulled over those jackrabbits with a spear jammed up their asses. Not the most pleasant way to leave this world. Looking back at the bouncing shapes gaining on them, Elliot was pretty sure this was an honor he didn't want accorded to him and Timmy. Which, was going to happen if Bobby caught up with them.

Elliot kept shooting glances over his shoulder. Besides being scared, he was puzzled. Something was strange about the way the three cars were bunched together. He kept looking at them until, finally, they grew clear enough for him to realize there was only one car chasing them. Bobby's. The other two were still chained to the Caddy, and Bobby was towing them along behind.

Elliot could hear them clanking, bouncing and colliding with each other. Metal groaned and sparks flew whenever the cars hit a dip, but there was that nothing could hold back that old Caddy. The massive V8 sounded like thunder as it moved closer.

The three sets of headlights kept growing closer, telling Elliot there was no place to hide. The Caddy grew close enough to see Bobby's face now, close enough to see the painted-on grin was back in place. There was something in the seat next to the vampire driver. Whatever it was, it was slouched low, a bulky, shapeless lump.

The cars came on, rising, falling, a disembodied white wraith floating on the night, disconnected from the earth, pulled along by the ropes of light hooked to the grill.

The wraith was materializing. Growing clearer.

Ever clearer.

Bobby's bloodless face swam into focus, hair whipping in the wind, a cigarette dangling from his lip. The tip was a glowing red coal. He let out a yell, honked the horn when he saw the bike, as though he had just happened to spot a few friends on the street.

The Caddy pulled up alongside Elliot and Timmy, close enough to touch. "Hey there, little buddies, how's it hanging?"

They looked over.

Bobby had passengers with him.

All the dead people from the graveyard had been loaded into the white Caddy: Doralee, Nicky, and Martin Strickland in the back, arms around each other. Chester and some unknown Indian in a white hat up front.

Every time the Caddy rocked, their heads all lolled in unison. Synchronized sightseeing, dead style.

Elliot realized that for Bobby to load that many people in the car so quickly meant one thing—Bobby had started as soon as the bike was out of sight. He and Timmy had barely gotten out in time. That thing inside Bobby had almost hypnotized them.

"Why are you doing this?" Elliot yelled at Bobby.

"Because this is a game. I don't want the game to be over too soon." Bobby reached over, took the white hat from the Indian, and put it on his own head. He cocked it at a precise angle in the rearview. "How do I look?" he yelled at Timmy.

For an answer, Timmy shot Bobby the bird and buried his face in Elliot's back.

Bobby laughed and grabbed something from the floorboard. It was the stick used to spear jackrabbits, the same one he had pulled from his stomach. "I got it greased up, Elliot. It's going up your ass."

The two boys veered away from the Caddy and the car followed, a clanking train without tracks. Accelerating, the white car again pulled up beside them. Bobby swung the stick backhanded, catching Elliot on the nose, busting cartilage. "That's for not teaching your little brother some manners."

The pain was so intense that Elliot blacked out for a second. The bike wobbled, almost went down.

Elliot skidded to a halt.

Their follower tried to do the same, but the weight behind the car slewed it sideways, throwing huge gouts of white dust into the air before finally coming to a halt.

The headlights pinned the two boys in its glare. The dust settled on the Caddy, covering the windshield. The wipers came on, slapping the dust away with their thin arms, each stroke revealing more of Bobby's white, grinning face.

He just sat there. Waiting.

The V8 revved a couple of times and the Caddy edged closer, stopped, edged closer, stopped.

All the passengers were in whiteface now. A few flies still clung to them. One crawled from Doralee's mouth and disappeared into her open eye socket.

The Caddy suddenly roared, came straight at the bike.

Elliot faked right, went left, darting past the Caddy, past Chester's car, when Bobby cut the steering wheel. The cars behind began jackknifing. The BMW clipped the bike, sent it rolling end over end. Timmy fell clear, but Elliot wasn't so lucky. He got tangled up with the Kawasaki, while they did a little dance across the desert floor, first one on top and then the other, as though they were trying to decide who would lead.

Finally, they parted company. Elliot looked as though the dance had made him tired. He lay in the dust, eyes glazed, trying to suck some air into his lungs.

"Get up, get up," Timmy screamed. He was yanking on what was left of his brother's shirt, trying to get Elliot up. Timmy's nose was bleeding profusely from the left side, dirt had clogged his right nostril.

The Caddy swung in a wide circle until it once again faced the boys. It moved to within twenty yards, stopped. The engine revved to a deafening pitch, and the car began to sway from side to side, with Bobby standing on the brake.

If he raised his foot, they would be crushed.

Timmy tried to lift his brother to a sitting position.

Elliot managed to take in a breath, and his eyes slowly lost their glaze. He climbed to his feet, began backing away from the Caddy, never taking his eyes off it. Exhaust poured from the tailpipes, coating the backs of their throats with the taste of burning oil.

The car made no move toward them. It simply waited, headlights blazing.

Raising the bike, Elliot straddled it, pulled Timmy on behind. The Kawasaki was covered with dust, but otherwise unhurt. Elliot kicked the starter. Got only a cough. They looked toward the Caddy to see what it was doing.

At the moment, that was nothing.

Bobby was fiddling with the radio. The white-hatted head leaned out of the window. "Need us a tune for our little Western drama here, a killer tune." He poked his head back inside the car and country music filled the night. "Oh hell no, I ain't in the market for that crying-in-your-beer shit. I'm all through with that."

Something dark and shiny moved behind his eyes.

A squelch of static followed, then some rap followed by more static, and then the Stones' "Satisfaction" began thumping the speakers. "Yeah, that's the one, a killer tune. Something to get your blood moving." Bobby kept time by thrusting Elliot's rabbit pole into the dirt beside the car. "You boys all rested up and ready to go again?"

Elliot kicked the starter again. The bike still refused to fire.

The Caddy crept forward. "Ready or not, here I come."

Elliot kicked down again. And again. The bike wouldn't start.

The Caddy was picking up speed. Spitting dust from beneath the tires.

Elliot put his feet on the ground and began trying to push the bike out of the way. He could hear the music growing louder, blasting from the speakers, vibrating in his bones.

Bobby was mouthing the words to the song. "I can't get no... I can't get no... satisfaction."

The lights grew incredibly bright.

Elliot kicked the starter again. This time the bike fired. But it was too late.

Timmy had jumped off and was trying to push the bike. Elliot grabbed him, pulled him back on. The move cost too much time.

The Caddy was right on top of them.

Timmy screamed.

At the last instant, the Caddy swerved.

The dead passengers all swayed together. Rollercoaster for the dead shot through Elliot's head as he aimed the bike away from the car. They were in the clear. He jammed the gears. The bike lurched, lost speed.

The Caddy was turning. Coming around.

Elliot found the gears, started again.

Up ahead was a dry creek bed, the same one he and Timmy had traveled on the way here.

That seemed years ago now.

He gunned the bike.

They beat the car by seconds.

The Caddy, unable to fit in the creek bed, raced alongside, bouncing, smashing bushes and cactus beneath its grille. Bobby leaned out and swung the stick, almost connecting with Timmy's back. Elliot veered closer to the far bank, where they would be safe for the moment. The only problem was that the creek bed widened out about two miles ahead. He put his head down, concentrated on keeping the bike upright. Off to his right, he heard the clanking of the cars, punctuated by Jagger's plaintive cry.

"I can't get no satisfaction. I can't get no satisfaction!" Bobby swung the pole, missing Elliot, breaking the mirror off the bike. "Oh, man, that's seven years' bad luck."

The mirror bounced out of sight with a tinkle of broken glass.

Bobby was doing something in the car, something with the passengers. The Caddy veered close to the edge of the creek bed. Dirt and sand crumpled beneath the tires, cascaded down the bank.

"Hey, Elliot, you ever had a woman?" Bobby stepped on the gas, pulling several car lengths ahead. He had Doralee sitting in his lap. "You play your cards right, you can have this one. You'd like that, wouldn't you?"

Elliot kept his head down, guiding the bike into the curve ahead.

"She's quiet and she don't eat much. Perfect for a man on a fixed income, such as yourself."

Then, without warning, Bobby opened the car door and pushed Doralee out. She hit the ground, bounced a couple of times, a loose-limbed rag doll that rolled in front of the bike.

The bike almost went down when Elliot ran over her outstretched throat. Flies shot out of her mouth, her eye sockets, and buzzed away.

"Guess she's not your type, huh," Bobby said. "Funny, she was everyone else's." His face filled with manic glee. He pulled Nicky to the car door, pushed him out. "We don't want to split up the family."

Elliot dodged the tumbling body.

Martin Strickland was up next. The big foreman rolled down the bank in a shower of dirt. His hat flew off, rolled after him. His scalped head shone wetly in the light.

Taking the bike up on the far bank, Elliot managed to get past Martin.

Next came Billy Two Hats, matinee cowboy. With his white makeup and filthy clothes, he looked more like a mugged drag queen. Bobby was trying to get Billy to hold the knife he had used to scalp Martin, but Billy wasn't cooperating. He kept dropping it.

Bobby finally grew exasperated and wrapped Billy's fingers around the knife, made Billy stab himself in the chest. Right above the bullet holes where Lefty Thunder Coming had shot him.

Billy went flying.

"The cops are gonna absolutely shit when they see this," Bobby said. "Dead Indian scalps dead white man, shoots and stabs self before jumping from moving car."

Elliot leaned the bike over, barely missed Billy.

"You can really ride that thing," Bobby said admiringly. "Well, I saved the best for last." He wrestled Chester over the car's windshield and out onto the hood. Once he had Chester situated, he crammed some newspaper in the dead man's shirt. "I been waiting a long time to do this." Bobby pulled the cigarette lighter from the dash, lit the newspaper.

In seconds Chester Roberts was ablaze. The wind fanned the flames and the owner of The Broken R came down the bank like a birthday cake with one candle, landed in the middle of the creek bed.

Elliot couldn't miss Chester. There was a soft squelching sound, a moment of heat, and they were past him. The bike came out of the curve. And Elliot had to lay it down in the dirt. There wasn't time for anything else.

A red Cadillac blocked the way.

The bike slammed into the red Caddy, bounced off, leaving a gap-toothed grin in the driver side door. The impact didn't do Elliot's Kawasaki much good, either. The guy reclining on the car hood, however, didn't seem too upset at the damage. He slid off with weary ease and walked toward Elliot and Timmy. His steps were sure, catlike, and he covered the distance with deceptive quickness.

The boys lay on the ground, pinned there by the headlights, watching him come closer. Timmy's nose was bleeding again. Elliot made a sincere attempt to get up, but he was all played out. His leg felt as if it might be busted.

"You boys look like you've had a rough day," the driver of the red Caddy said. "I saw your lights and decided to see what was going on." He wore gray boots that crunched through the gravel as he moved toward them. Beneath his gray Stetson, his expression was one of mild concern. "My name is Steven Adler. Might I ask who you are?"

"I'm Elliot Cates and this is my brother, Timmy." Elliot turned to see what Bobby was doing. The white Caddy had stopped and Bobby was just sitting there, staring straight ahead. He looked scared, and Elliot had to wonder what could scare a guy who had just killed five people.

"Bobby tried to hurt us," Timmy said, his voice accusing. "It's all Elliot's fault. He touched Bobby's car."

"Bobby won't be bothering you anymore," Steven said, following the boy's gaze.

"Mister, he's already killed five people," Elliot said. "He's got something inside him. He's not—"

"Human. I know. I've been hearing a lot of that lately. It's really beginning to get on my nerves."

Elliot tried to hold on to what was left of his sanity as the meaning of the stranger's words sank in. "Jesus, are you one, too?" he asked. "A vampire?"

The Caddy's warm engine made ticking noises in the cool night air.

"Fraid so. Looks like Crowder Flats went and got itself infested with a bunch of bloodsucking sons of bitches tonight." Something occurred to the tall man as he studied their red hair. "You two look familiar to me for some reason. Did you say your name is Cates?"

Timmy nodded, wiped at his bleeding nose.

"Your great-grandfather was a rancher, wasn't he?" Steven said. "And he rode off one day, disappeared. Nobody ever saw him again."

"How'd you know that?" Elliot asked.

"I knew your great-grandfather. A friend of mine killed him." The blonde man threw back his head and laughed. The instant eyes were off him, Timmy made a break for the bushes.

Steven Adler darted forward, grabbed up the boy. Cradling him gently, the stranger dabbed at Timmy's bleeding nose with a handkerchief in his free hand. "You'll be okay, little buddy. I don't think it's broken."

Like magic, Steven produced a piece of gum from his jacket pocket, handed it to the boy.

Timmy took the gum. It was Wrigley's Doublemint.

Steven licked Timmy's blood off his fingers and smiled absentmindedly. "I'm afraid I've only got one piece, so you'll have to share. Is that okay?"

Timmy nodded, stuck the entire stick of gum in his mouth.

With his free hand, Steven took hold of Elliot and lifted him to a standing position. The guy was really strong. Elliot felt himself picked up as though he weighed nothing.

Steven ran his fingers through the five-year-old's hair, brushing the dirt from it. "Timmy, I have to talk to your brother for a minute. I need you to be brave, can you do that?"

"What are you gonna do?"

"Nothing that will hurt. I promise. I'm just going to put you in the trunk of the car."

Timmy looked doubtful. "I'm kinda afraid of the dark."

"How about if I give you a flashlight?"

Timmy thought it over. "You ain't gonna leave me there, are you?"

"No, just for a minute while I talk to Elliot."

"Okay, but I gotta go to the bathroom first," Timmy said. He began fidgeting.

Steven sat him down. "So go to the bathroom. Hurry up."

"I can't. Everybody's watching me."

A small tic appeared in Steven's left eye though his voice remained calm. "Come on."

The three of them moved away from the car lights, with Steven holding on to Elliot and Timmy.

"Don't look," Timmy admonished.

"We're not looking," Steven assured him.

The five-year-old unzipped his fly and cut loose, sending a silvery liquid arc out into the moonlit night. The sound of urine splattering in the dust filled the silence, but something was odd about the way Timmy was whizzing. There were breaks in the flow.

"Oh Jesus," Elliot said, "I don't believe this."

Steven tightened his grip on Elliot's arm. "What's wrong?"

"Nothing, Timmy's just showing off."

Steven looked into the dust and an expression of surprise settled on his face. "I'll be damned…"

Elliot looked frightened and more than a little embarrassed. "Don't be mad, mister, it's my fault. I taught him how to do that. He's been driving me crazy with it ever since."

Looking at the wet TIM in the dust, Steven picked up the small boy and ruffled his hair affectionately. "That's pretty neat, partner. Can you spell any other words?"

"No, but Elliot can spell pussy."

"Shut up, Timmy." Elliot's face turned beet red.

"I'm going to get a big kick out of you, Timmy." Steven was still laughing when he carried the child over to the red Caddy, put him in the trunk, and closed it.

Absolute darkness descended over the five-year-old before he got the flashlight to click on. The trunk was warm, smelled like dust and old rubber from the spare tire nestled there. Timmy listened to footsteps moving away while he did his best not to cry. He didn't quite succeed.

Steven led Elliot away from the car, and the blonde man was serious now. "Listen close, Elliot, I don't want to have to repeat this."

Flinching from the grip on his arm, Elliot faced Steven. He could barely look into the cold eyes.

Steven pulled him close, until their faces were almost touching. "You get your ass on that piece-of-shit you call a bike, and you go find Louise Warrick. Tell her John Warrick is to meet me at Jake's at three A.M. tonight. Tell John to bring the cue stick." Steven walked over and righted the bike, sat Elliot on it. "If I don't see your lights on the main highway in two minutes, something very unpleasant is going happen to your little brother. Am I making myself clear?"

"Don't hurt him, mister. He's just a stupid little kid."

"You do what I told you and your brother will be fine." Steven looked at his watch. "Your two minutes are running."

Elliot made the highway in a minute and fifty-three seconds. He flashed his high beams off and on several times before setting out for Louise's house.

Steven flicked the Caddy's lights off and on in answer. Then he moved to the white Caddy and pulled its passenger out. Bobby Roberts stood there, sullen, refusing to look at Steven.

"You're not supposed to be here," Steven said. "What were you doing poking around the graveyard?"

"I was only trying to help."

"Were you, really? I wonder."

"What are you talking about?"

Steven produced a knife from beneath his sweatshirt. The handle was a bright red feathered serpent, the blade was polished jade. "This is what you're looking for, isn't it? This is what you killed all those people for? This knife. You were planning to kill me with it." Steven held the blade beneath Bobby's chin, pricked him with the point. "Don't lie, it won't do you any good. I'll know the truth in a minute, anyway."

Bobby hung his head, but his voice was defiant. "I want to live. I want you to let me go."

"I can't let you go. You're a killer."

"I'm part of you." Bobby's smile was bitter. "If I'm a killer, what does that make you?"

"I haven't killed anyone. My hands are clean," Steven answered.

"Maybe they are, but I see the look on your face when I come back to you. You can't wait to feed on me, to relive everything I've done. Especially the killing."

"It's a good deal for everyone. You get to be human for a while and I get to..." Steven decided not to pursue the thought.

Bobby's face twisted up with hatred. "You pretend you're better than me, but you're not. You just don't have the guts to do your own killing."

"Is that right?" Exasperated, Steven plunged the knife into Bobby's chest. Twisted it. "Why am I standing here in the dark talking to myself?"

Bobby screamed in agony, tried to pull away.

No use. Steven held Bobby, kept sticking the knife into his body. Over and over. Until the screams fell silent.

"Don't fight me," Steven said. "You know it's useless. You've got to come out."

Bobby slumped against the car hood, his mouth working. "Let me go. Please."

Steven plunged the knife in again, held it there, and Bobby began twisting like a worm on a hook.

"No can do," Steven said. "You might get the urge to tell Earl what I've been up to. He thinks I've stopped killing. If he found out differently, he'd leave, and I can't allow that to happen. It's one of the hazards of staying in one body too long, I guess. You pick up... emotions." Steven slapped away the weakly flailing hands. "Come on out. I haven't got all night."

Wisps of smoke began pouring from the stabbed man's mouth, curling upward. "I'll go away," Bobby promised, "far away from here. You'll never see me again."

"I don't want you to go away. I want us to be together."

Bobby opened his mouth one last time, a barely audible gasp. "I want my own life. I want to be... human." His body arched in pain—and—the black substance poured out of Bobby in streams, coming out of every wound, crawling up over Steven, caressing his body with lover's arms, until it finally converged at his face and disappeared into his open mouth. A huge knot appeared in Steven's throat as the blood poured into him. Steven's eyes fluttered, became glazed with pleasure as he collapsed across the car hood.

As he relived the stolen lives. Taking what he wanted. Discarding the rest.

After a few minutes, Steven came to, and his eyes held that heavy-lidded look that comes from really great sex. He dumped Bobby onto the floorboard of the white car, then moved over to the bushes and unzipped his fly. His teeth flashed a white grin in the moonlight as he guided the black substance that was expelled from him into letters in the dust.

Steven went to the red Caddy and pulled Timmy out, showed him the letters. "Look, Timmy," he said, laughing, still flushed from the pleasure he had just experienced. "I spelled my name, too."

Timmy studied the wet letters, silently mouthing them, until a frown creased his young face. "I thought you said your name was Steven."

Steven looked at the name. He had spelled Bobby.

CHAPTER SEVENTEEN

Amos Black Eagle's trailer, 9:15 A.M.

John Warrick tasted the peyote at the back of his throat.

Amos looked on, concern on his face. "I don't think this is a good idea. You took five buttons, and peyote is tricky stuff. It can scramble your brains if you're not careful."

"He's right. There's got to be some other way," Louise said. "You're exhausted from driving all night. You go into one of your trances and things go wrong, you could die."

"I know."

"You said your heart stopped the last time."

"Believe me, this is the last thing in the world I want to do, but I have to." John looked at the people huddled around him in the bright clear light, going from face to face. Louise, Amy, Jesse, Amos, Lefty, Boyce, Nash, Kevin, Manny, Ernesto, Jesus, Stuart, and Elliot Cates. All looking at him, all pale, silent, bruised by what they had seen.

Inside the trailer were the bodies they had found in the creek bed by the Navajo burial ground.

Or what was left of them.

The savagery of their deaths was beyond comprehension.

"I have to know what we're up against, or Timmy's going to end up like everyone in there. Maybe all of us." John motioned at the trailer. White sheets covered what lay inside the door, and from where they stood, it looked like Amos'd had some company drop by, that soon the white draped figures would rise up from their sleep and ask for coffee.

But the flies weren't fooled. They knew. They clustered on the screen door. Waiting. Elliot watched them with dull fascination. He hadn't said a word since he had told his story.

John held the smooth yellowed bone of the cue stick in his hands, heard the sound of something unknown moving toward him, and he was reminded of distant thunder, like maybe a storm brewing just out of sight. A shadow swept past, darkening the morning sky before the thunder gradually faded.

Only he saw it.

"This cue stick can tell me more about Steven Adler," John said, "maybe even what he is, but I have to go into a trance. Open myself up. It's the only way."

John's gaze sought out Stuart Johnson and the sheriff dropped his eyes. Something had gone out of him, and for the first time John could ever remember, Stuart looked truly old.

John felt sweat bead up on his forehead. "It almost told me the last time. I just have to go deeper, stay longer, and that's where the peyote will help."

"That stick almost killed you the last time," Amos reminded him. "It could finish the job."

"That's where you and Louise come in. You're going to bring me back if I get into trouble."

"How will we know?" Louise asked.

"That I can't tell you, it's something you'll have to decide for yourselves." John focused on the moth-eaten buffalo in Amos's corral and he felt the wicker chair stir beneath him. It was now a saddle, the cue stick a rifle. "Something's starting to happen. I'm sitting on a horse, and it's hot, damned hot."

Louise gripped his hand.

The people around him were becoming insubstantial. He could see the three buffalo through them.

"Where are you?" Amos asked. "Are you Steven Adler?"

"Kansas, 1872, and my name is Matt Thomas," he said to the open prairie.

CHAPTER EIGHTEEN

Kansas, the summer of 1872.

Today was hotter than hell in July.

Matt Thomas, employed by the Santa Fe Railroad, sat astride his horse and stared into the distance, watching the herd of buffalo he had tracked. Beneath his new gray Stetson, sweat kept worming its way down his forehead. He pulled out an already soaked handkerchief, mopped his face, and swore at the heat that was making an unpleasant job even more unpleasant.

His job was killing buffalo. He did his job well.

He'd been a trapper, a scout, a prospector, along with a few other things he didn't particularly care to dwell on. A tall man, he'd been eroded some by the passing seasons, but like the mountains he called home, he expected to stand a while longer.

Matt waited quietly and, finally, his patience was rewarded when the herd tired of wallowing in the creek and moved out to graze. He swung down, hobbled his horse. Eyeing the huge animals, he eased out his .50 Sharps from its scabbard, along with a tripod. He hefted the gun with hands that were a little shaky. Even though the Sharps weighed nearly sixteen pounds, there had been a day when he hadn't needed anything to hold it steady. The years were taking his strength, and he guessed, maybe, they were taking his mind, because the last several nights he'd been having dreams. Bad dreams.

Looking over his horse, across the flat land, he once again he played out the scene in his mind, and fear laid its icy hands on his neck, causing a shiver to pass through him.

Remembering… a dream so much clearer than any dream he'd ever had before. Remembering… standing on a vast plain that was without life of any kind, while beneath his feet, the earth was cracked and dry, untouched by even the memory of rain. Overhead, the sky was a sullen brass color, cloudless, holding a sun that burned down much too brightly. When he stared at the mountains on the horizon, he could make out a distant shadowy figure, no larger than a speck, moving toward him. The figure appeared to be walking slowly, yet it closed the distance between them with incredible speed as though each step covered many miles.

Then somewhere, farther back, came a sound like distant thunder rolling across the plain, and Matt could make out clouds of darkness billowing up behind the walking man. A huge storm was brewing out there and it, too, was coming toward him with unnatural speed… and Matt had awakened before he could quite make out the distant figure or the blackness moving his way.

He was glad of it, because there was something unnerving about the whole thing, something that left the taste of dust in his throat.

Maybe his mind was going, maybe he didn't sleep too good at night, but right now he had a job to do. He laid the rifle on the tripod. With a motion borne of long practice, he licked his thumb, rubbed it across the bead and sighted in on the shaggy old cow that led the herd.

He squeezed the trigger, heard the flat crack of the rifle. A hundred yards away a puff of dust erupted from the animal's hide. The cow, mortally wounded with a bullet through the heart, staggered forward a few feet. Streaks of red spurted from the animal's nose before her legs gave way and she collapsed into a boneless heap.

The rest began bawling and milling around, spooked by the smell of blood, but without a leader they would do nothing.

They kept milling, and Matt kept shooting, picking off the ones standing at the edge of the herd with mechanical accuracy, until they were all dead. He felt no pride in what he had done. No shame either. A lot of meat was needed to feed the railroad work crews; he was paid to deliver that meat.

Before riding back to camp and sending out the skinners, he thought he might ride over and get himself a tongue or two for cooking. He was tired of beans. His movements were slow as he swung down. Too many winters spent wading through icy streams during his days as a trapper had stiffened up his legs. Sitting on the ground made them worse.

He picked out a likely animal, pulled out his knife and started cutting.

A huffing sound floated through the stillness, died. Pausing, he pulled his .44, straightened up and looked around. Nothing. His ears must be playing tricks on him. That old Sharps made his ears ring, sometimes for days after. He went back to work. After he had the first tongue wrapped, he started in on the second.

That's when he felt a cramping in his bowels. Time to take care of some business. Once he'd hobbled a discreet distance from the buffalo carcasses, he pulled down his pants, and squatted. Those damned beans of Corky's bound a man up something awful. This could take awhile. He hoped he didn't get his ass sunburned.

Over his grunting, that huffing noise came again. Unease curled up between his shoulder blades.

"Damn, something ain't right." He jabbed the knife into the ground, grabbed his .44 and raised up from his task.

Scanned the area.

Dead buffalo carcasses strewn all about. Carrion birds were already picking at them.

He pulled out his handkerchief, wiped the sweat from his eyes.

And saw a bull get to its feet.

The animal was covered by dust. A patch on its chest was oozing darkness, along with one from the shoulder. Both wounds were welling up like water from an underground spring.

Dazed, Matt watched as the blood trailed down to spatter the ground. The bull saw him. It sniffed the air.

"Well, looks like me and Big Dick Hendershot will be laughing on this in the hereafter."

Somewhere, far removed, came the sound of flies buzzing. A carrion bird raised its wings and screeched in triumph as it took flight with its cargo.

"Big Dick got hisself kicked in the head," Matt said to the huge bull eyeing him. "Word 'round the campfire, he had his dick in his hand. Both hands to be exact. They didn't call him call him Big Dick for nothing." The wounded animal began pawing the ground. "Now I'm not saying ol' Dick was about to throw the meat to your cousin what kicked him dead, but it damn sure looked suspicious."

Matt risked a look at his horse, calculating the distance. Too far. Besides, he'd never get the hobbles off in time, but if he could get closer, he might have some chance. He took a step in that direction before realizing his pants were still down around his ankles.

His movements were enough to goad the animal into action.

He thumbed back the hammer on his .44. Taking aim at the bull, he realized there was no chance for a killing shot, especially with his old revolver. He'd be better off throwing rocks. To make matters worse, the animal had its head lowered, protecting the heart and lungs with a skull that was massive bone and almost impossible to penetrate. Still, the head was the only target Matt had. The pistol jumped in his hand, sending a bullet smacking into the skull with a thud, a sound reminiscent of an axe biting into a piece of hard-wood. He would have taken a moment to admire his shooting—except that old bull was still coming on like a high-balling locomotive. With one bare-assed buffalo hunter looking to be the next stop.

"Old son, you done stepped in it this time." He leveled the pistol back onto its target, pulled back the hammer and squeezed the trigger again. The bullet struck home, and still the bull came forward.

The animal's ragged breathing filled Matt's ears while chewing up the distance between them. More carrion birds took to the air. Matt hoped the skinning crew found him before those birds got his eyes.

The old mountain man had three shots left. Taking careful aim, he placed them as close as he could to the first two. No good. He was going to be gored or, most likely, trampled ... when the buffalo missed a step, staggered, missed another step, and pitched forward. The old bull almost recovered for a moment, then faltered and sank slowly to its knees, a felled tree swaying in the wind, before finally toppling over onto its side. Dust geysered upward.

Several seconds passed before Matt realized his .44 was empty. He quit cocking and firing it.

Holding his unfastened pants, Matt warily approaching the downed animal, gave the carcass a kick. The bull didn't move, it had bled out. He was angry at himself for being so careless.

"Might be time to get into another line of work." The hunter took a deep breath and walked away from the bull. He almost got to his horse before his knees gave way and he sank to the ground. He yanked off his hat and wiped his forehead with a sleeve, letting his held breath pass through clenched lips.

That had been close. He stood there with the .44 dangling from fingers that twitched and jerked with a life all their own. He dropped the pistol and tried to fasten his pants. His hands refused to cooperate. The buttons kept evading his thick fingers.

After a few minutes, his breathing returned to normal and his hands quit shaking enough to shake the cartridge casings out of his revolver. To hell with the tongue, he wasn't that hungry anymore. With his pants mostly secured, he went over to his horse, bent to cut the hobbles. The rawhide thongs had been drawn so tight by the skittish animal there was no way Matt could untie them.

With no warning, the horse squealed and leaped sideways, knocking Matt onto his back the dust.

Before Matt could move, he knew what had happened. It was impossible, but the blood-splattered animal had regained its feet and was coming at him again.

A heartfelt "Son of a bitch," was all he could say. Scrambling up, he stared in disbelief at the charging animal. His hand darted into his pocket, trying to dig out more shells.

Wrong pocket. Wrong god damned pocket.

He always put them in the left pocket.

(Did he even have any more shells?)

He yanked his hand out and his pants pooled around his ankles. He pulled them up, reached into the other pocket—his fingers closed around one—

He fumbled the shell, found another.

His hand came up, his pants went down.

Racing against time, he desperately tried to reload, still fumbling with a cartridge that seemed too big to slide into the cylinder. He risked a look. The animal was nearly on top of him. Cursing his stiff joints, he managed to jam a shell into the chamber of the .44. Snapping the cylinder into place, he raised the gun and fired, all in one motion. No way he could miss. He was shooting point blank.

The bull was rocked back as though poleaxed by a hammer, caving in at the knees, yet Matt knew the slug wouldn't be enough to stop the headlong charge.

Matt attempted to throw himself out of the way, even though he was out of time and hobbled by his pants around his ankles. All he could do was watch. For some strange reason he expected the collision to hurt more than it did, because he heard more than felt something snap in his right leg.

Darkness swallowed him, and Matt shaded his eyes and looked for the walking man.

But the strange shadowy figure was nowhere to be found. Then to his amazement, he saw the blackness gathering on the horizon wasn't a storm—it was a giant herd of buffalo; countless, untold numbers of buffalo stretching across the prairie, a herd so large he couldn't see the end of it. The earth began to tremble at their approach as they swept toward him like wildfire driven before the wind, chasing the daylight from the sky.

Mesmerized by the enormity of what he was witnessing, he stood rooted on that dry, cracked earth watching their progress for what seemed like an eternity, and all during that time the herd kept moving toward him, becoming clearer and clearer. Gradually they drew near enough for him to see there was something wrong with them, dreadfully wrong. Staring at the animals, his gaze widened. Somehow, they were all wounded, terrible gaping wounds that streamed blood, until the ground was soaked, until the very air itself became filled with the sickly sweet scent of copper.

In a moment Matt knew he would be crushed in the stampede. He raised his hands in an effort to fend off the inevitable. His fingers closed around the coarse fur of the first animal—his eyes jerked open

—and he stared without comprehension at the fur clutched in his hands.

After a moment he realized it belonged to the buffalo he'd killed earlier. Three times by his count. Lying pinned beneath the carcass, he could still hear the thunder of the giant herd echoing in his head. Finally the sound died, and he saw he had been unconscious for hours, because while he'd been dreaming, the night had crept close.

He took inventory. Everything seemed to be in working order, except his right leg, which no longer felt like it belonged to him. When he tried to move, he found he couldn't. For the first time today a grim smile touched his lips.

"This is one fine howdy-do," he said to the dead buffalo. "Just fine. I can see my marker, now. Here lies Matt Thomas, bare ass naked, first man to be kilt by a buffalo while taking a shit. Probably get me in all the history books."

Matt spat blood while trying to work his leg from beneath the crushing weight. He was fighting pain so intense he bit into his lip to keep from crying out. Getting free was slow going. But after some digging with his knife, he managed to work his leg free. He studied the damage; it was bad, no doubt about that. His foot hung at an unnatural angle, and when he pulled up his pants leg, he could see red-edged shards of bone poking through. The trip to his horse seemed to take slightly less than a hundred years, and he was bathed in blood and sweat by the time he pulled himself into the saddle. He headed back to camp.

Each time his horse took a step, agony took a step, marching up his leg, and he couldn't say it was a trip he enjoyed. But at least it kept him from passing out. By the time the campfires finally swam into view, he felt as though he'd ridden halfway across Kansas. When he went to swing down, he found he couldn't lift his leg.

"Would somebody mind giving me a hand?" he said. "I think my ass is stuck to the saddle."

A buzz of indistinct voices was his answer, and then hands reached out to pull him from his horse. As they lowered him to the ground, he tried to give them directions to the dead buffalo. If they didn't get there soon, a lot of meat would be ruined by scavengers.

A bottle found its way into his hands and he tipped it up, taking a long pull. When the whiskey hit bottom in his stomach, it felt as if a fire had been built down there. Warmth spread through him and the pain was starting to recede a little when somebody grabbed his arms. Somebody else began tugging on his broken leg. White-hot agony lanced through Matt, and he did the only sensible thing he'd done all day; he fainted dead away... *and the herd of wounded buffalo passed right through him*—a dark, swiftly flowing river that could not be touched. He realized they were no more than shadows, yet the earth shook and he heard the heaving sounds they made when they galloped past. Fear drove them. Their eyes were rolled back in their heads, showing only the whites, and strings of saliva dripped from their straining mouths.

From out of their midst, the shadowy speck he'd first seen appeared, moving toward him like a swimmer fighting a strong current. As the speck neared, he saw it was an Indian dressed in gray, tattered buckskins and a stovepipe hat, like some kind of make-believe wooden figure that shopkeepers put out front to hold cigars.

No tribal markings of any sort decorated the copper-skinned body except for a blood red feathered serpent on its chest.

When Matt looked at the face, he saw it was rigid, unmoving, as though the face wasn't real, as though it was a mask meant to conceal what the figure really looked like. The Indian, neither young nor old, approached to within a few feet, doffed its hat and began capering and prancing about like some kind of puppet he had seen at a carnival when he was a child.

The effect should have been comical, yet there was nothing funny about the disjointed scarecrow who confronted him.

And there was nothing funny about the knife that caught the rays of the sun in a blinding flash.

At first Matt thought the man meant to attack him, instead the Indian placed the blade against his own copper-skinned chest and slid it downward, slicing off a strip of skin, which he held out to Matt. The bloody skin held the feathered serpent. There was still no expression on the man's face, though Matt somehow sensed great anger.

Matt turned away from the grisly offering, and when he looked back he saw the Indian now had no features at all. While he stood there, the face of the stranger began taking shape. Turning into dust. The wind started to build, blowing the dust away. Revealing what was beneath. And as the face continued to emerge, the figure walked toward him with its arms open wide, as though it meant to embrace him.

When they were almost near enough to touch, blood began welling from the corner of its dusty eyes and started rolling down the cheeks… like tears.

Matt wheeled around to run, but something held him to the spot. A quick look over his shoulder and, to his horror, he saw the face begin changing, becoming, one after another, people Matt had known in his life. All of them dead now. They called out to him with familiar voices. He saw his wife, his son, old Lame Bear, a man he had loved like a father.

Then the face steadied, became one that he was all too familiar with—his own bloodstained features stared back at him.

The figure smiled and beckoned. Matt redoubled his efforts to escape, but now they were only inches apart. The face began to melt, bubbling up like wax from a hot candle, revealing the skull beneath, revealing empty black eye sockets that watched him hungrily.

Matt fell to his knees in mindless terror. The figure stood over him, and an instant before the skeletal fingers closed around his arm…

Matt awoke to the familiar din of railroad construction: men yelling, harness creaking, pickaxes and sledges pounding loud enough to raise the dead. That was an apt description of how he felt when he sat up. Fragments of murky images from the nightmare chased across his mind, then remembering, he looked down to see his leg bandaged, splinted, that he was lying on a cot in the track boss's car.

Throwing back the blanket, he gingerly swung his legs around and sat them on the floor. Darkness obscured his vision as he fought to remain upright. After a bit, his head cleared enough he could see the purple discolorations on his ribs. They didn't feel busted, just bruised. His leg was a different story, throbbing like a bad tooth while he balanced himself and began hopping toward the door.

He peered out, wincing at the heat that sprang at him. His eyes fastened onto the track boss, a bald Irishman by the name of Charlie McAllister.

Matt tried to call out, but all that came from his throat were croaks.

They were enough.

"Well, it's about time you got your lazy ass out of bed," Charlie said, relief plainly written on his face as he walked over with a canteen. "We was about to give you up for dead. What the hell happened? Your horse fall on you?"

"No," Matt laughed, lowering the canteen, "I ran out of cartridges and I had to throw the last one by hand."

After Matt finished relating what had happened, Charlie said, "You're a lucky man. Sounds like you damn near met your end out there. If that old bull had got aholt of you, there wouldn't have been enough left for a good Christian burial. Not that," he concluded with a grin, "anybody ever mistook you for a Christian."

Matt rubbed a hand across his bristly face and looked down, trying to hide his unease. "Did Doc say anything about my leg?"

Charlie didn't answer right away, and when he did, he wouldn't meet Matt's eyes. "I got to get back to work. I'll send the doc over and he can tell you all about it. You need anything?"

"Yeah, ask old Corky if he could send over some grub."

After a while, one of the mess boys brought over something that vaguely resembled beans. Matt took one look. "Shit, ain't these the same beans we had day before yesterday?"

"Yep, the same. Corky says he ain't cooking nothing else till they're all gone."

"You try feeding them to the dogs?"

"They won't touch 'em, neither."

Matt had almost choked down the last of his chewy beans when Dr. Marigold Fraser appeared, quiet and dark as a rain cloud on an autumn day. The mournful doctor was something of a mystery. Folks in camp had their own ideas why the small, portly man had come west. Some said, back east, the doc had killed a man in a duel over a rich dowager and was fleeing the rope, some said he'd sobered up enough to get a good look at the dowager and had decided he didn't need the money that bad. Still others claimed a few too many snorts of peach brandy before an amputation had led to some slight misunderstanding about which of a patient's legs was supposed to come off.

It was a source of endless speculation. What the truth was, nobody knew.

Doc didn't say anything at first, just slapped some dust off a black suit that had more shine to it than a newly minted silver dollar. He eased his bulk into a chair that groaned in protest.

"How's business?" Matt inquired, to be polite. He knew Doc had few patients. The fact that he owned a half interest in a funeral parlor might have had something to do with it.

"Been pretty good, lately," Doc said, cleaning his glasses, "we buried three last week."

Matt glanced up from his plate to see if his visitor was kidding. Doc's face never changed expression. He slapped at suit, stirred up more dust.

"I got good news and I got bad news," Doc continued, putting his glasses back on. "Which one you want first?"

"The bad."

"That leg of yours is busted in three places," the dour man replied. "I set it as best I could, but with a break that bad and your age being what it is, I can't make no guarantees. You should be able to walk, but you can count on having a bad limp."

"What's the good news?"

"You'll always know when it's going to rain." Doc smiled—and the smile vanished quicker than a rabbit down a hole, so quick Matt wasn't sure he'd even seen it.

Matt gave up on the beans and pushed them aside. "How soon before I can travel?"

"Like I said, a lot depends on how fast you mend." Doc pushed up his specs. In the blink of an eye, they returned to their former position on the tip of his nose. "Let's just say you'll know when you feel up to moving around." With that he got up, slapped some more dust off his suit before advising Matt to keep his wounds clean.

As Doc left, Matt pulled out his pipe, letting his thoughts turn back to the days when he had lived among the Oglala, back to the days before everything had gotten fouled up between the red man and the white man. Sometimes he longed to go back, but he knew there would be no welcome for him now. Of late he had begun thinking a lot about old places, old times, and old friends.

And dying.

THE DAYS PASSED AND EVERY TIME DOC STOPPED BY HE ASSURED MATT that he was healing up good for a man his age.

Matt spent most of the time whittling himself a walking stick. To his surprise, he discovered the head of it was shaped like a snake, a snake with feathers. No matter how hard he thought about it, he couldn't find a reason for whittling such an odd thing.

He was sitting in an almost nonexistent patch of shade working on the head of his stick when Charlie McAllister came over.

"What's the good word, Charlie?"

"I talked to Mr. Simpson and he says you can stay on til you're fit enough to go back to work." Charlie waited for Matt's response, eager as a puppy waiting for a pat on the head.

"Well, Charlie, you tell Mr. Simpson I appreciate his offer. But soon as I'm able, I'm going into business for myself—the hide business," Matt added. He folded up his knife and put it away. "Way I figure, one good season and I can retire."

Charlie shook his head sadly and looked at Matt as though the older man had gone simple. His voice was earnest. "That's about the stupidist idea I heard all week. You'll get yourself kilt for sure. There's a war on, in case you ain't heard. Your hair'll end up decoratin' the lodge pole of some young buck."

"I got the answer to that," Matt said. "I'll take you with me, Charlie, 'cause it's for damn sure no self-respecting Indian would ever be caught with your scalp."

"Ain't no need to get personal." Red faced, Charlie ran a hand across his head, smoothing down the few strands of hair that still sprouted there. "I can see there ain't no use trying to talk sense to you, Matt. When you set your mind, you have got to be the most stubborn, mule-headed son of a—"

"I hate to interrupt," Matt laughed, "'specially before you get to the interesting parts. It ain't often I get a good Irish cussin', but I think I'm going to need a partner."

"You serious?" Charlie asked. "You with a partner?"

Matt nodded. "I'm slowing down. I need some help. You know anybody might be interested?"

"Yeah, I might know of someone. He's a new man, name of Steven Adler. Don't know much about him except he's been making a lot of noise about quitting. Says the work's too hard for the money. Been complaining about the cooking, too." Charlie looked more perplexed than usual. "I don't know what he's hollering about. You only work twelve hours a day, you get all the beans you can eat, and thirty-five dollars a month—just like clockwork."

THE SHADOWS WERE STRETCHING TOWARD EVENING, AND MATT WAS cleaning his Sharps when he heard footsteps approaching. He gave no sign that he noticed. When his visitor's shadow fell across his legs, he looked up. Neither said anything as they regarded each other intently.

The younger man tipped his hat back and broke the silence first. "Name's Steven Adler and I hear you're looking for a man to go partners with you."

Matt looked at him evenly, trying not to grin. The man Charlie had sent him was young. Blonde. Slender. In his fancy clothes, he looked more like a gambler than a railroad hand.

"No need to stand on formality here. The name's Matt. Why don't you sit down, Steven, cause I'm getting a crick in my neck staring up at you."

"Thanks," the young man said, tucking himself into a piece of the shade, "laying track is hard work in this heat."

Matt agreed it was.

They chewed the fat for a few minutes, listening to sounds of the camp settling in for the evening meal.

"If you don't mind me asking," Matt said, "where abouts you hail from, son?"

"I don't mind you asking. Lots of places. New York originally, now anyplace they play billiards."

"Billiards," Matt said, puzzled. "That's a game with balls, ain't it, played on a table. You use a stick."

"That's right." Steven was impressed in spite of himself. He hadn't met many people in Kansas who had even heard of the game.

"I seen a couple fellows in San Francisco playing the game a few years back." Matt moved his busted leg into a more comfortable position. "I don't think it's going to catch on. What's a billiards player doing out here in Kansas? Ain't no billiard tables around these parts."

"I don't intend to stay. I just came out here to make myself a stake."

"A stake for what?"

"So I can go back east and play billiards for money."

"You mean people bet money on a couple of grown men knocking a bunch of little balls around a table?" Matt couldn't hide his look of skepticism.

"They bet a lot of money and I'm going to be the man to win some of it."

A flash of intuition hit Matt and he spoke before he meant to. "You got cleaned out, didn't you? You bet all your money on a game of billiards and you lost." He knew his words were on the mark because a slow flush crept up Steven Adler's neck.

"I had me a little run of bad luck in St. Louis," the younger man said evenly, "but I aim to get back in the game just as soon as I make myself a stake."

"You got any family, Steven?"

Steven pulled off his hat and wiped the sweatband, looking as though he didn't want to answer that particular question. "No, not since I was thirteen."

Matt figured he'd better see if he could turn the talk in a different direction. "I reckon Charlie told you what I'm fixing to do. I need a man who can handle himself. The country where I'm headed can get pretty rough. Can happen quick, too."

There was a definite glint in Steven's eyes when he shot back, "And I know what you're thinking. You're thinking I can't carry my weight. That I'm too young. Too citified. Well, you're wrong, mister. I been making my own way ten years now, and I can handle anything that comes along."

"Is that a fact?" Matt said, unperturbed by the outburst. "Well, soon as this here thing comes off"—he tapped the splint on his leg—"I'll be leaving for the Cimarron. I'm telling you, right up front, it ain't a safe place for no white man. If we get into a tight spot, we ain't going to have time to sit ourselves down and take a vote on what to do." He stopped and fixed Steven with a dead level stare. "You got any complaints about taking my orders?"

Steven didn't drop his gaze. "No sir, I can take your orders. Anybody as old as you has got to have learned a few things about staying alive out here." He draped an arm over his leg and studied Matt with unabashed curiosity. "To hear Charlie tell it, you done killed more buffalo than Buffalo Bill his own self." His gaze dropped to the splint on Matt's leg. "Though old Bill didn't never have one fall on top of him. I got a theory about how that happened. You care to hear it?"

"I'm listening," Matt said evenly.

"I figure you got caught with your pants down."

Matt pulled his revolver out of his belt, began spinning the cylinder nonchalantly. "How you figure that?"

"Charlie said you had grass stains all over your ass."

"It was those damned beans I been eating all week. I was taking care of some business."

"And that's when the old bull caught you, wasn't it? Right when you had your pants down."

"That's right," Matt answered, growing defensive, looking around to see if anyone was in earshot. "I was having a little trouble. Beans always bind me up."

"I bet when you saw that buffalo coming at you, you didn't have any trouble."

They studied each other, dead serious.

And then Steven smiled. An easygoing smile that made him look like a kid.

In spite of himself, Matt smiled back. He couldn't help it. There was something about the kid he liked.

A little voice in Matt's head said he was a damn fool for making snap judgments, that the only reason he was doing this was because the kid reminded him of himself when he was younger. He thanked the voice very kindly when it was through, then leaned over and stuck out his hand.

"Okay, Mister billiards player, I'm willing to take a chance if you are. On one condition, though."

"What?"

"That you never tell anybody how that buffalo caught me. It wouldn't do much for my reputation. Or your life expectancy."

The young man stared at the hand for a moment. A huge smile split his face as he grasped it and shook. "They'll never hear it from me."

The Cimmaron

THINGS WERE GOING WELL AS SUMMER TURNED TO AUTUMN.

Steven and Matt were killing and skinning about thirty animals a day. The work was filthy and backbreaking, but the pay was hard to beat. Matt held up his end of the bargain on the work, though it was obvious from the halting way he moved that the doctor's words had held true; he'd never walk right again.

When they had enough hides cured to fill the wagon, they would drive to Dodge, and it seemed that they couldn't supply enough to the eager buyers.

Both men had accumulated a tidy sum of money by the time autumn drew to an end.

On December 12th, the weather was clear and warm. They decided on one last trip before the snows came.

December 18, The High Plains
Northeast of the Sangre de Cristo Mountains

THE BLIZZARD HAD BEEN HAMMERING STEVEN AND MATT FOR WELL over a day now.

The snow was getting deep, burying familiar landmarks beneath a blanket of white. It showed no signs of ending.

Steven was on his horse leading the way for Matt, who was driving the wagon.

"Whoa, hold up," Matt called out.

The younger man turned his horse and made his way back.

"You can't see where you're going in this storm," Matt said through lips that had gone blue.

"My horse does my seeing," Steven said from under his hat.

Matt considered his partner's words. "Well, my horses can't see shit."

Steven took in the pinched face of his friend. He slid off his mount. "Let's see if we can get a fire going."

The two men tried, but there was no fighting the wind and snow. It came at them from every angle, snuffing out every attempt.

Finally they were forced to give up.

Climbing into the wagon, Matt said, "Snow's getting deep. We don't find a place to hole up, we'll lose the wagon and the hides."

"I thought you were going to say we'd freeze to death."

"No, that'll be tomorrow." With those words, Matt slapped the reins. He forced the horses on through snow and ice that was falling like bullets, knowing that it was dangerous, knowing he had no choice.

SITTING HUNCHED OVER AGAINST THE COLD, MATT WAS JOLTED WHEN his team began bucking. "Whoa, you jug-heads," he yelled, pulling back on the lines.

The horses stopped, and their labored breathing filled the air with plumes of white.

"What's wrong now?" Steven shouted back.

"Team's acting strange. Grab ahold of those chuckleheads, will you? My ass is froze to the seat."

Steven was having his own problems. His horse had started crow hopping, almost unseating him. As soon as he got the animal calmed, he jumped down to grab the bridles of Matt's team.

"Something's got 'em spooked."

"Might be a panther near by," Matt said, "or maybe wolves."

Both mean scanned the snow-covered rocks above. Steven thought he glimpsed a splash of red. He looked harder. It appeared to be blood. Could be a den up there, a place for them to hole up in this storm. The younger man pawed at eyes that were nearly frozen shut. Snow blind, he must be going snow blind. Either that or his imagination was showing him what he desperately wanted to see. As though to make him doubt, the snow kicked up, and he could see nothing but white.

"What is it? You see something?" Matt yelled, trying to be heard over wind that could drown a man's voice at twenty feet.

Steven called back through cupped hands, "Maybe. Let me have a look-see."

"Thought your horse did all your seeing," Matt groused.

"I heard that." With a frozen grin, Steven pulled his Colt and plodded through the drifts on legs that had gone wooden. After a struggle up the hill, punctuated by one truly spectacular belly flop, he managed to reach the hole.

He looked down at the burrow. It wasn't his imagination. The blood he'd seen was real. The den was real. Only problem was, the opening was so small a skinny prairie dog couldn't fit inside. If it wasn't for the splash of red, he would have ridden past without a second look.

Standing in snow up to his ass, Steven stared at the hole with resentment. No way a man could fit in there.

Lifting his leg, no easy task, he gave the snow an angry goodbye stomp.

And fell through.

A moment later, he popped out of the side of the hill. The snow-covered man kicked snow out of his way.

"We got us a den," he shouted in Matt's direction. Looking at the blood dotting the snow, his jubilation became tempered with caution. "You better drag out that cannon of yours. Just in case we run up on something that don't want company."

Matt grasped his Sharps in hands he could no longer feel and clambered down from the wagon. In his whole life, he couldn't ever recall being this cold. That wind was trying to skin him alive. "Work your way inside, and see if you can light a match while I cover you."

Steven fumbled around in his pocket before coming up with one, but his fingers were so numb he had trouble holding it. He entered the mouth of the cave. After five or six tries, he finally succeeded in getting the match to light. He edged deeper into the opening with Matt following closely behind.

Once they were inside, they saw that it was indeed a cave and bigger than they first thought. They couldn't tell how big from

Steven's match, only that they were able to stand up straight. At first glance nothing seemed to be living inside, so they quickly turned and brought in the horses. With firewood they'd stored in the wagon, they soon had a roaring fire going.

"If you don't back up, you're going to catch fire," Matt observed as Steven hugged the blaze.

"I don't care. At least I'll die warm."

Grudgingly, the younger man moved away from the blaze. "You stay here and warm up those old bones. I'll get us some grub off the wagon. But first, one for the road." He backed up and stood over the flames until Matt swore he saw smoke curling up from Steven's backside.

The youngster returned a few minutes later with both arms full. "If you was to look around this mess, you might scare us up a bite while I get some snow to melt for coffee."

"More buffalo meat?" Matt asked.

"Yeah, that's all we got."

"God, what I wouldn't give for some beans. Even Corky's."

They ate in silence, wolfing down their food. When they were finished, Matt pulled out his pipe and worked on getting it lit. Soon fragrant smoke drifted across the fire. Outside the wind raged at the cave entrance, its thin keening sounding like something hungry.

"I don't know about you," Steven said, "but I didn't think we was gonna make it there for a while."

"Yeah," Matt agreed around his pipe, "I was beginning to have some doubts my own self. It must be twenty-five, thirty below out there." He gave his head a wry shake. "Guess maybe we should have quit this game a mite sooner."

Steven cleaned off the plates while Matt worked on his pipe some more. After a few minutes Matt knocked the ancient briar out and stuck it in his coat pocket. "I think I'd sleep better after a look around. Hate to have a grumpy old bear climb into bed with me. 'Less, of course—" he winked—"she was female. We got anything we can make a torch out of?"

"Under the wagon seat. Might be some poles there. The ones we used to get the wagon out of the mud. Break one in half, tie some rags to the end and dip them in some melted buffalo tallow. Should work okay."

Matt reappeared a few minutes later. "I thought you were trying to hide those poles," he grumbled, stamping snow from his feet and backing up to the fire.

After he warmed himself, he quickly made a torch according to Steven's instructions, and stuck the end into the fire. When it flared to life, he handed it over.

"Steven, my boy," he said, hefting the Sharps, "let's go have a look-see around, meet the neighbors."

As Steven held the torch high, they treaded their way deeper into the darkness, pausing for a moment to stare at some boulders that circled the floor in an almost perfect ring. Tall as a man, they didn't look natural. They appeared to have been placed there. A rusty stain rested in the middle of the stones, looking like the remnants of long-dried blood. There was something about the rocks that reminded Matt of silent old men sitting around a campfire, brooding about a secret they would tell if they only had the ability to speak.

Matt was glad to be away from the huge stones.

The cave went back a lot farther than either man would have thought. Their footsteps floated back with a ring that took some time dying.

Droppings, speckled with white, littered the floor.

"What do you think caused those?"

"Bats'd be my guess," Matt answered, a smile crossing his face as he warmed to the subject. "When I was down in Mexico some years ago, I seen bats that'd suck the blood right out of a man's body. Yes sir, do it while he was sleeping. I ever tell you about 'em?"

"No, and I wished you hadn't told me now." Despite their easy banter, the prospect of finding their way back caused the younger man's back to prickle with gooseflesh.

They had taken several convoluted turns when the torch began to flicker beneath an unexpected breeze coming from deep in the cavern. Matt shielded the light with his body. For an instant, the darkness moved in close, reminding them how far beneath the earth they were.

An anxious moment followed before the torch resumed burning. "We only got this one light," Steven pointed out.

"I can count."

"Shouldn't we be thinking about getting back?"

"What do you make of that?" Matt asked, pointing at a bulky object draped in shadow.

"I don't see anything."

A dry, rustling sound carried, like the wind blowing leaves across the ground, before silence once again descended upon the chamber. Matt readied the Sharps, prepared to shoot at the first sign of movement.

As the two of them neared the object, it seemed as though a sliver of ice had been driven into Matt's chest. An inner voice warned him of danger and his nerves were stretched tighter than wet rawhide by the time he was close enough to see what rested in the darkness.

Both men stared in disbelief. In front of them was... an Indian burial platform. The rustling sound had come from the wind moving around what was left of the blankets. Buffalo robes by their look. Everything was rotted, and that accounted for the musty smell to the place. But beneath that, barely discernible, was another odor, one that Matt had only smelled in his dreams. Whatever it was, it was sickening.

Steven was the first to speak. "What kind of Indians would put their dead in a godforsaken place like this?"

"None that I know of," was Matt's flat reply.

"I always heard they like to be buried on high ground, so's their spirits could sort of watch over things." Steven lowered his voice several notches. Something about this place made a man want to whisper. "You know, this doesn't make no sense why somebody would go to all that trouble, just to put one man back here."

There was a reason that Matt knew of, but he said nothing. He started to turn away when something caught his eye.

Squinting in the dim light, he tried to make it out. Pictures. Lots and lots of pictures. The cave wall had been painted into one huge mural.

"Bring over that torch."

In the flickering light they studied the paintings, trying hard to understand why someone would go to the trouble to draw pictures that no one would ever see. They were crude slashes of color, barely more than stick men. Large portions were faded or gone altogether, so it was difficult to make sense of what they were trying to say.

"What's all this mean?"

"It means," Matt answered softly, "we're standing in the burial chamber of a medicine man."

"What in Sam Hell is a medicine man?"

"Indians believe there are some men who can heal the sick with magic, control spirits, that sort of thing. They're held in great respect by the rest of the tribe."

"Yeah? Then why'd they stick him in here?"

"Cause they were afraid of him."

"That doesn't make a lick of sense," Steven answered. "No reason to be scared. The son of a bitch is dead."

"Indians are superstitious, that's all."

"You sure don't look convinced from where I'm standing." Steven watched the older man's face. "You sure there ain't more to this than what you're telling?"

"Come on, I'll show you there's nothing to be afraid of!"

Matt angrily grabbed the torch from Steven and walked over to the platform. Holding the light above his head, he studied the remains of the figure lying on rotting wood. Steven joined him. Both men steeled themselves at the sight. It was impossible to tell how many years the skeleton had lain there, long enough that all the clothing had rotted away long ago, along with the flesh.

The only things that still clung to the yellowed bones were patches of skin.

One had a feathered snake on it.

Matt felt as if he had been kicked in the stomach. But that wasn't the worst of it.

"Who could do something like that?" Steven asked, his face turning ashen. "Drive stakes through his hands and feet, and then leave him in the dark. I bet he was still alive when they brought him here."

Matt saw that Steven was getting scared and put a comforting hand on the younger man's shoulder. "Don't get yourself worked up, son. He's dead and the dead can't hurt you. Besides, he was killed before they brought him here. Look at his skull, it's damn near busted in two."

Something was odd about the crack, though.

"Let's get on back to the fire," Steven said, nervously licking his lips as the torch began to flicker, throwing shadows that made the stick men seem to move.

Matt needed no encouragement.

Their campfire led them the last few yards through the dark, and though neither of them said anything, both were glad to be away from the dead medicine man. They stoked up the fire while they made preparations to turn in for the night. But sleep was the farthest thing from their minds.

"Think I'll go out and see what the weather's doing," Steven said, making the first excuse. "Maybe if the snow's quit, we can get an early start in the morning."

"Good idea. Grab some extra feed for the horses. They could use it in this weather."

Steven made no effort to move.

"What's on your mind now?" Matt asked in a wary tone.

"I was thinking maybe one of us should keep watch tonight. You know... just in case there's something to what we saw back there." Steven laughed. It sounded strained.

"What we saw back there was just some paint smudges and bones." Matt's words were a curious mixture of mocking and concern. "You ain't afraid of that, are you?"

Steven looked ashamed, yet from his voice, Matt could tell his partner was still scared. "It's the way you looked when you first saw those paintings. Your face turned pale, like you'd seen your own ghost. Something bad happened back there. I don't claim to know what it was, but it just felt wrong. I think we should get out of here. Right now."

"How far you think we'd get in that storm?" Matt hunkered down and poked at the fire even though it was burning just fine. "I done told you everything I know. Will you quit bending my ear and get some rest?"

Steven looked closely at Matt, trying to gauge the truth of his words. A look of reluctance crossed his face but he finally nodded. "Don't forget to wake me up in a few hours."

Matt nodded. "Count on it."

As Steven wrapped up and prepared for sleep, Matt stared into the flames, brooding about what he'd seen earlier. There were gaps in the story on the cave wall, still he was able to fill in most of the missing pieces... because he'd heard the story once before. Back when he was young and living with the Sioux, back to a distant night when he had heard a story he had never forgotten:

There had been a raid on a neighboring tribe for horses. It had gone badly. Many had been killed in the battle that followed. An old warrior by the name of Lame Bear had been wounded, a lance in the stomach. Matt had felt pity for the injured man, and so, amidst the wailing of the women who tended the death camp, he had sat close by and listened to the fevered recounting of stories about battles fought, coups counted, as the man who had been like a father came to grips with dying.

The stories were mostly the same.

But one story had been different from all the others; one had been about a good man's sacrifice that had led to eternal damnation.

From what Matt could make out, there had been a year when the buffalo had failed to return. In an effort to save his starving people, a medicine man had struck a bargain with the *Tena-Ranide*, a spirit of the underworld.

The tribe was spared starvation, but the forces the medicine man had tried to use for good were now using him for their own purposes. Dark purposes. The man who had become the servant of death became more evil as the days passed, and beneath a hungry, staring moon strange rites were held—rites that soon demanded human sacrifice.

The old man on his deathbed said the earth had run red with his people's blood for many years.

After untold suffering, the tribe managed at last to bind the medicine man's mortal body, to hide it deep in the earth. They made great magic to seal him in his final resting place, and the fear of his evil was such it was forbidden to even speak his name.

The old man's last words were of a feathered serpent that marked the grave.

SITTING ON THE CAVE FLOOR, WRAPPED IN HIS BUFFALO ROBE, MATT WAS keeping watch. He stared into the fire, thinking about that last picture on the cave wall. Painted in blood, it was a warning in Sioux not to disturb this final prison, that whoever did was in great danger, because the only way the *Tena-Ranide* could ever have any form of life beyond this cave was if it found another body to inhabit.

Then it came to Matt what was strange about the crack in the medicine man's skull; it had been split from the inside out.

Steven stirred in his sleep, mumbled something, but after a few seconds his breathing became regular again.

Matt stared at the young man's back and thought about his own son, dead at five, taken by the cholera. His wife had followed the boy less than a year later. Something went out of her after their son had died, and Matt always thought the reason she died was because she'd simply lost the will to live.

Sometimes Matt wondered how the boy would have turned out if he had lived. Would he have been like Steven? Matt shook his head, trying to rid himself of the painful images that seemed to haunt him lately. There was no point in thinking about a past that was gone. A past that brought only sadness.

He tried to find a position that didn't cause his bad leg to ache. No luck there.

Outside the wind rose. The sound reminded him of something familiar from his past. He tried to place it. After a while he did.

Steven awoke to find Matt asleep, and the fire down to a few embers. Something had pulled him from his fitful dozing. A sound? Not Matt, not the horses. Not even the wind. It wasn't one he could place. He rolled out of his blankets, teeth chattering, and started to add some wood to the fire.

That was when he noticed the smell. God, it stank something awful, like every rotting buffalo carcass in the world. What could cause such an odor? He was about to wake Matt when he heard movement; wet slithering noises, like a snake crawling out of its skin. It was coming from somewhere back in the dark. The sounds seemed to be growing closer.

He stared deep into the cave, but he didn't see anything moving in the cold, moist darkness. Whatever was back there was still coming their way. The stench became overpowering, and his hands covered his mouth while he fought to hold down his rising bile.

All thoughts of being sick vanished when Steven got a look at what was emerging into the feeble light. A patch of blackness on the wall had detached itself from the rest. The shape looked like the shadow of a man in a top hat, and yet when Steven looked around the cave, he saw they were all alone, that there was nothing to throw such a shadow. His eyes followed the thing as it somehow crept along, possessed of an impossible life.

Steven backed away, softly called out Matt's name.

Matt didn't answer.

At the sound of Steven's voice, the thing darted across the cave wall with unnatural speed. As he watched, it abandoned the shape of a man altogether and changed into a writhing mass. Ropelike tendrils of darkness shot downward.

The younger man was reminded of a spider spinning a web as the thin shadows gathered about Matt's head and hung there, coiling and uncoiling with a rhythmic pulse that matched the older man's breathing.

Steven called out again, louder this time.

Why didn't Matt wake up? Couldn't he feel it hovering above him? Couldn't he smell the damned thing?

Steven tried once more to warn his partner, trying to speak over the gagging sounds that were coming from him. Everything began moving with nightmare slowness while the clinging shadow continued downward. It touched Matt's hat. Several tendrils entwined themselves around the older man's throat, and there was something obscene about the way they stroked the flesh.

The rest, as though they were a nest of rattlers, struck the sleeping face... but instead of drawing back afterward... they began crawling into him.

Matt cried out, began twitching like a rabbit in a snare—

—and once again the old hunter *was standing on that hellish plain* while the herd of buffalo thundered by, and all he could do was watch the Indian who now wore his face reach out to draw him close. They embraced. When Matt tried to pull away, he found that he couldn't separate himself from the clinging figure, that the Indian's flesh was still melting, flowing over him in rippling waves, crawling down into his mouth, into his throat, choking him so that he was unable to even cry out in his revulsion and fear. He realized they were merging together—that soon they would become one.

Blood erupted from every opening in Matt's body, splashed the walls, the ceiling. His eyes jerked open and he screamed. He tried to stand. His bad leg gave way, causing him to pitch forward into the dirt. As he struggled to rise, the sounds that came from him were the high, keening sounds of a man who has gazed upon something he cannot bear to see, something that has driven him to the brink of madness.

The screams broke the spell that kept Steven from moving. On his knees, he scrambled into his blankets and dug out the .44 that Matt had given him for his birthday.

The screams grew louder, and Steven was screaming, himself, when he emptied the pistol into whatever had hold of Matt. His bullets had no effect. And neither did the smoldering stick of wood he plucked from the fire. He might as well have been striking at the air. The thing was too fast.

Steven grabbed Matt, tried to pull him away. That's when one of the tendrils wrapped around his wrist. It was not a shadow. It never had been. The thing on the wall was real, solid, and cold as barbed wire when it cut into him, and for a second, Steven was able to see into the mind of whatever held him.

His whole being recoiled when he got a brief glimpse of what hell must look like.

With every ounce of his strength, Steven wrenched his arm free, stripping off the skin where the tendril touched him. The arm tingled with cold needles that somehow burned like fire. It felt as though something alive were moving inside his arm. He took the flaming stick of wood and pressed it against the raw spot on his arm. A scream followed, and Steven wasn't sure it belonged entirely to him.

Incredible pain flared for a second, but the feeling of something alive in his arm stopped.

Matt continued to struggle as the thing poured into him, his body arching backward, contorting in agony, but the fight seemed to be going out of him. He bounced on the cave floor, looking like a broken puppet being tugged along by a careless, impatient child.

Steven was reaching out with his unhurt arm when Matt raised up and looked at him. The eyes had changed—something cold, inhuman, stared out from Matt's face.

Enraged at his own helplessness, Steven grabbed Matt and shook him. Blood was still flying from every crevice of the older man's body, even his crotch. He was pissing blood.

"Fight, damn you." Steven struck him across the face.

The older man stiffened, his eyes shedding their film of darkness, and for a moment the Matt he knew was looking back at him. But the Matt he knew seemed to be dwindling away, as though he were being dragged downward to some terrible, distant place. His eyes held the pleading look of a drowning man when he struggled to speak.

At last, in a strangled whisper, blood spilling from his mouth, "For God's sake, shoot me, son. Don't let it have me. Promise… don't let it… promise."

Steven nodded, and the bitter taste of ashes filled his mouth.

The old man's struggles were growing much weaker. The thing was almost totally inside him now, and whatever made Matt Thomas human was just about gone. The friendly blue eyes glittering like chips of winter ice when they rested on Steven.

The man who played billiards for money knew what he had to do, and he knew nothing he had ever done would be as hard.

Reaching down, he picked the Sharps off the floor, raised the heavy stock to his shoulder, pulled back the hammer, and reluctantly pointed the rifle at Matt. His finger inched forward like a blind worm until it wrapped around the trigger. He gradually increased the pressure, trying to hold the rifle steady while the blood thundered in his head. His teeth were bared like those of an animal in pain as he tried to pull the trigger.

"I can't do it," Steven pleaded, his voice a grainy whisper, "don't make me. Please don't make me."

His finger loosened its grip and he let the huge rifle drop to his side.

And then the screams started; in their pain and rage, they were the most awful sounds Steven had ever heard. He couldn't believe such cries could come from a human throat. They went on and on.

Steven knew he could no longer stand by and let his friend endure such agony. He raised the rifle and again centered the sights on Matt's forehead.

A look of calm appeared on Matt's face. "Good-bye, Mister billiards player." He tried to smile. "I still say the game ain't going to catch on." And with those last words, Matt was gone. The creature was completely inside him now.

Steven squeezed the trigger. Gently... just the way Matt had taught him... and, at that moment, a part of Steven Adler died, too.

Steven dropped the rifle, started to turn away.

Movement caught his eye, stopping him in his tracks. Matt, in a pool of his own blood, was moving in broken circles the way a bug will after being stepped on. Fear flooded Steven's insides with a warm, liquid rush. The top of Matt's head was gone, and he was still moving.

Steven jammed a hand into his coat pocket and found more shells for his .44. Working quickly, he reloaded with hands that shook so much he could barely hold the revolver.

This time he didn't hesitate. The pistol jumped in his fist and a foot-long tongue of blue flame erupted from the barrel. For an instant, everything became bright as day, letting him see his shot was a good one, catching the thing that had once been Matt Thomas high in the chest. The slug's impact lifted the creature from the floor and flung it backward against the cave wall.

Steven's ears were ringing, but he heard its labored efforts to rise. He fired again. His shot went wide this time. In the flash, he saw the thing smile, showing teeth that were a startling white in the blood-drenched face. He fired again before it could move, and his next four shots found their mark, pinning it to the wall. Blackness streamed from each bullet hole, and when it hit the floor, the blackness began crawling toward him.

With a moan, Steven flung the pistol. There was no stopping whatever this was. He wheeled and ran blindly toward the horses. He heard the jingling of their harness, but they seemed impossibly distant. He mounted his horse. No time to saddle him. His horse burst from the cave, plowing through the snow drifts.

There was no moon. His animal was a shadow in the dark, and it was spooked, dancing sideways, bucking, shying away from the stink of fear on its rider. Steven was bucked off. He got up, chased after the horse. Several times he edged close enough to grasp the reins that dangled in front of him, but each time they managed to elude him.

Around and around he and the horse went in a mad dance, until Steven's footing betrayed him and a windswept patch of ground, frozen hard as iron, rushed up to drive the breath from his body. Stunned, he lay there, listening to the wind blow through the ice-covered branches, causing a tinkling noise that sounded like glass. As he watched the trees sway, he heard steps crunching in the snow. Grunting with the effort, he rolled over and scuttled sideways, a crab covered with white.

His horse was mad with fear as Steven staggered nearer. The animal must have caught the scent of whatever was behind him, because it bolted. Huge, lunging strides.

In a second, his mount would be beyond reach.

Steven, gathering his fading strength, flung himself forward. His hand touched a heaving neck, sliding downward, and he felt himself falling. The animal stumbled and the gambler's fingers wrapped around a rein, slipped, then grabbed hold. His arm was nearly wrenched from its socket by the horse's next lunge. Ignoring the blackness that danced at the edges of his vision, he held on.

A shot rang out. The horse squealed, a sound nearly human in its agony, and pitched sideways in the snow. The wounded animal was floundering, trying hard to rise. Another shot came, and Steven heard the bullet strike home. The horse let out a final death rattle before going limp.

Steven struggled to free himself from beneath the crushing weight.

"You weren't planning on leaving me here, were you, son?" the familiar voice said, moving closer. "All alone, in the cold. I thought we were partners. Remember?" Then came laughter. Obscene laughter.

Steven noticed that sickening odor was growing stronger and he tried with all his might to get loose. But he knew it was too late. Already the tendrils crawling from Matt were drifting down toward his face like cold, black snow.

The man who was trying to make himself a stake screamed and his screams floated across a vast dry prairie that had never been touched by rain. In the blinding sun he watched a medicine man draw near, and the earth began to tremble with a stain that grew dark on the horizon.

The figure stopped, and Steven saw an Indian wearing ragged gray buckskins and an Abe Lincoln stovepipe hat. The broad copper face regarded him without expression. In the distance, the dark stain had drawn close enough for Steven to see it was a herd of buffalo, but what a herd it was, an ocean of heaving flesh stretching farther than the eye could see, rippling and swelling as though torn by a storm.

On and on they came, and the world became filled with distant thunder.

Steven could feel the rumbling deep in his bones. Soon they were near enough for him to see that every animal was soaked in blood. It dripped from their straining flanks, it spilled from their gasping mouths, turning the ground red. He caught their smell, the stench of sweat and dust and blood, and worst of all—the smell of fear.

Steven fell to his knees, unable to stand upon the trembling ground. "What does all this mean?" His voice rose above the growing thunder. "Why have you brought me here?"

The skeletal figure said nothing, and the buffalo kept on spilling across the prairie, drawing nearer, while the dust they kicked up blotted out the sun.

Steven waited in the gathering darkness.

Just when it seemed they would be crushed in the stampede, the Indian doffed his hat and everything changed.

The charging herd disappeared in the wink of an eye, leaving behind desolation beyond knowing: skeletons by the hundreds of thousands glistening pale white beneath the sun, buffalo skeletons, dried and polished by the sun and wind, and among the bones, Steven saw entire tribes wandering aimlessly. They moved through the carnage, their gaunt faces bearing the specter of hunger. Their sorrow was a great cry that rose like the carrion birds on the wind. Then it was swept away. Never to be heard again.

Steven looked across the plains and saw things that defied understanding. He saw warriors sitting by darkened fires, heard the lament of the women trying to console hungry children. The red men prayed to the old gods, calling upon them to stop the slaughter, but their prayers fell upon deaf ears.

The old gods were powerless before the advance of the white man who rode upon the iron horse, sweeping everything before him.

Some things Steven witnessed he didn't understand at all. He saw Indians dressed in white-man clothes, living in white-man houses that seemed to be made of metal. There was no pride in their faces. Many were lying drunken on the street in the shadow of buildings so tall they blocked the sun. Others climbed from strange looking wagons that moved without horses and went into places that colored the night with all manner of bright lights. When they came out, the smell of whiskey was upon them, their steps were drunken.

Stranger sights awaited. He saw many of them cross great oceans to die in battles in places he had never seen, using weapons that cut men down like wheat in the field, fighting the white man's wars, and their names were not spoken with honor even though their blood was spilled just as often. Their numbers, like the buffalo, dwindled to a few, and they no longer prayed to the old gods.

They now lifted their voices to the white god.

All this Steven witnessed and more. How long he stood there watching, he had no way of knowing. One by one the strange sights disappeared, until only he and the medicine man were left on the vast plain. The wind blew over them and it was a high keening that sounded as lonely as dying.

The medicine man began to chant and, somehow, without ever being told, Steven knew it was a death chant he heard; there were no words, really, only a wavering anguished cry that rose and fell. Mourning a people who wandered a world that no longer held a place for them, speaking a farewell to a way of life that had been lost forever, lamenting a people who had even forsaken their gods.

The sad, wavering voice rose and fell for a moment longer. Then, turning his back to Steven, the medicine man placed his hat back upon his head and began walking away, each step covering an incredible distance until, finally, he was gone from sight.

In the spring the thing that had taken over Steven Adler left the cave. By summer it had moved into Arizona, feeding and killing as it went. There it found a group of Army deserters.

A week later every man, woman, and child in Crowder Flats, except one, was killed. The lone survivor, a Navajo boy who would become Amos Black Eagle's grandfather. The boy said the killers were dressed in blue.

CHAPTER NINETEEN

Jake's Place, 3:00 A.M.

The sign was off, the parking lot deserted.

Except for an old Jeep Cherokee.

Oil spots decorated the gravel. In the moonlight, they looked like fresh blood.

John Warrick sat alone at the long bar in the dark, sipping a Lone Star, waiting, trying to hold on to his anger. Anything to keep from running. The trouble was, he hadn't been able to hang on to anything—not love, not hate, not anger. Not even his life. It had all slipped away somehow. One night at a time. He was tired way down deep in his soul and he wasn't sure of what he would do tonight.

He didn't know if he would even survive the night.

The beer was clammy in his hands and, when he took a sip, it tasted bitter. Like fear.

That was the only emotion he could hang on to.

The odors of booze, unfiltered cigarettes, and cheap perfume clung to the room, bringing back memories of all the nights he had spent here when he was young. Elvis, the Stones, Ray Charles on the jukebox, all competing with loud laughter from girls trying to be women, boys trying to be men. And nobody knowing how. They had fumbled toward adulthood in the dusty seats of old pickup trucks out there in the dark, sure that once they were grown, they would have the answers.

Instead, all they had were more questions.

He and Thomas Black Eagle and Martin Strickland had hung out in Jake's back room, playing pool every chance they got, each boasting to anyone who would listen that he was the best.

But never putting it to the test. Afraid that if they did, they might not be friends anymore.

Friendship was important to them back then.

They believed in it.

In those days, they were young and their dreams lay spread out in front of them like the shimmering highway that led out of Crowder Flats.

The years had chipped away at their dreams, wearing them down to the bare bone, until finally there was nothing left to believe in. Thomas Black Eagle had been the lucky one, he had died young. Before he had seen all his dreams die, before he had become one of the ghosts haunting this place.

Now there really was nothing left. Martin and Thomas were dead. Leon, too.

That didn't seem fair, because John knew he was the one to blame for what had happened.

He should be the one who was dead.

John had Steven Adler's cue stick lying on the bar, and he tried not to look at it, even though his eyes were drawn time and again to its seductive yellow length. He felt dirty whenever he looked at the cue. Like he had been violated. Like something had been stolen from him. Moonlight, the color of dimes, spilled through the windows, caught the eyes of the serpent and turned them into fire. The red-feathered serpent lay coiled around the handle, watching him, as though waiting for a chance to strike.

He resisted the urge to move his hands away.

John was scared of the cue that had almost killed him twice. He was even more scared of the man who owned it. His stomach bore the marks of what he had gone through at Amos's, two jagged wounds where he had been gored in his dream.

The wounds had been seeping blood earlier, but Louise had put bandages on them.

In the quiet John relived his peyote vision, and again saw the herd of buffalo, heard the distant thunder of their hooves as they made their endless trek across the plains. He felt the fear, the revulsion of Matt Thomas as he was invaded and taken over in the lonely cave, the pain of Steven Adler, who had tried to end his friend's pain. John had felt the searing agony of the buffalo horns tearing into his stomach, but more than anything else, he felt the horror of Steven Adler, a man who had once been human, and was no longer. At the end of the vision, John had heard Steven's voice crying out and knew there was still a man in there who begged for release. A man who couldn't even kill himself to be free.

What could it be like to live with something alien inside of you for 146 years, making you torture and kill?

Never being able to escape?

The lean pool hustler again looked out the window, anxious for this meeting to be over. He was here to make the trade, one cue stick for one five-year-old, and then he was out of here for good. Headed someplace far away. Maybe he could convince Louise to come with him. Crowder Flats held nothing but sadness for the both of them. Maybe it wasn't too late to start over. He'd give anything for a fresh start.

He looked out the window again, saw shadows on the moon.

The waiting was eating away at his nerves, filling him with doubt. His hand touched the gleaming wood beneath his beer bottle, sought out the slight darkness there, the darkness that was Thomas Black Eagle's blood.

This was the first time John had been in the bar since the night Thomas had been killed. He wished Steven Adler had chosen another place to meet. Any other place. Sitting here in the dark, surrounded by the tired ghosts of his life, made him think, and that wasn't something he liked to do. Thinking made him feel old and used up. The past followed him around like an insistent panhandler, one who was never satisfied no matter how much money was laid in his greasy palm.

There was movement in the back parking lot, lights flashing across the window, the sound of tires crunching on gravel, and John was almost grateful that the meet was under way. At least he would be doing something, instead of waiting. Anything beat that. He moved over to the window to watch Leon's old red Caddy pull in. The sight filled John with anger.

And fear.

The car sat there idling, then went silent. After a bit, the driver's door swung open and a blonde man stepped out into the night. This time he was dressed like an Old West gunfighter. Or at least the Hollywood version of one. Everything was black, from the flat-brimmed Stetson on his head, to the vest, to the duster that whipped in the wind, to the boots on his feet. He should have looked laughable in such a getup. But he didn't. He looked scary as hell.

John tried to see if anyone else was in the car. The Caddy looked empty. Where was the blonde man's partner? Where was Timmy Cates?

This was supposed to be a straight-up trade. John felt panic, forced himself to be calm.

Even though there were five windows facing the back parking lot and the bar was dark, the blonde man's gaze found the window John watched from. The man who owned the red-feathered serpent cue smiled an easy smile and winked, as though the two of them were sharing a private joke.

John backed away from the window.

This was the man who had stuffed Leon Wilson in a freezer before Leon was even dead.

Man was the wrong word, but John couldn't force himself to think of Steven Adler in any other terms. If he did, he might not be able to go through with this.

According to what Elliot Cates had said, the thing inside Bobby Roberts was at least five hundred years old, maybe more, and it had been afraid of this man who strode so easily across the parking lot.

What could cause such fear?

John watched Steven Adler approach the bar. The blonde man moved casually, unhurriedly, and yet his eyes seemed to be aware of everything around him. His shoulder-length hair flowed out behind him, a golden mane rippling in the wind, as he moved closer. There was something animal-like about the way he walked, and John felt as if he were watching a sleek jungle cat closing in on its prey.

In this case, John knew he was the prey. Sweat trickled down his back as he waited.

The door to the bar opened and Steven Adler was inside. He was just there. Moving with uncanny quietness. The hustler's eyes probed the shadows while he sniffed the air, and John was again reminded of some huge predator testing the wind for enemies. Or prey.

He turned to John, seemingly satisfied that they were alone.

Steven went behind the bar, grabbed a cold beer. "Well, Mr. John Warrick," he took a sip, "you've led me a merry chase."

His eyes settled on the cue stick, but he made no move toward it. "I don't think we've been formally introduced. My name is Steven Adler and I think you have something that belongs to me."

John had the absurd feeling the man was going to offer to shake hands. He didn't.

They studied each other, one fair and young, the other dark and middle-aged.

"Where's the boy?" John asked.

"He'll be along in a minute. If you've held up your end of the bargain." Steven stepped over, grabbed the cue stick. He hefted it before he undid the handle and checked its contents. He seemed satisfied. "You're staring. Don't you like my get-up? I'm trying to fit into the spirit of your Frontier Days."

John tried hard to keep his face neutral, but Steven saw something there. The blonde man held John's gaze. "I've become pretty good at reading people's expressions. Had a lot of practice over the years." The easy grin faltered. "You know something, John, what is it?"

"I don't know anything. I don't want to know anything. Just give me Timmy Cates, take your cue stick, and we'll call it a night."

"You're not much of a liar, John. You saw the note in Leon's basement, so you know I killed him. You know I killed Martin, too. That's why you're here. No, it's not just hate for me or my clothes, it's something else. When I walked through the door, you looked at me like I wasn't… human." Without warning, he reached out and grabbed hold of John's hand.

John tried to resist.

His effort was useless. Steven Adler held him easily.

There was a burning sensation, and when John snatched his hand away, he saw his skin had been broken where Steven had scratched him with a knife. It wasn't much of a wound, just a tiny prick. Several drops of blood had welled up.

Raising a finger that held a drop of John's blood, Steven licked it clean. Something shifted behind his eyes. They became incredibly ancient, incredibly cruel. "I'll be damned, you're psychic, and you think you know what I am." He paused as though searching for a missing piece of information. "It's hard to read past the peyote, but I think you've told others."

"How could I tell anyone what you are? Who would believe me? No one has ever even heard of anything like you." John resisted the urge to go for the .32 in his boot. "I don't know what you are."

"What am I?" Steven considered the question. "You're the first human to ask me that in a long while. By the time most people learn what I am, they're past caring." Steven took another sip of his beer. "As I told Leon Wilson, vampire is as close as you can get to what I am, and even that's not quite right."

"You don't know what you are?"

"I guess you could call me a parasite—the ultimate parasite. I live other people's lives. Been doing it for quite a while now."

"Elliot said whatever was in Bobby Roberts has been around more than five hundred years. How many of you are there, how old are you?"

"You ask a lot of questions. There's only one of me, and as for how old I am, I don't really know." Steven reached out and touched the cue stick, his fingers tracing the snake. "Time has little meaning for me. I've lived more lives than I can count, but not all of them have been human, so things get a little murky when I think about time." He sat down on the barstool as though he and John were old buddies sharing a beer. "Sometimes, in the late hours of the night when I'm all alone, I dream about giant lizards that walk upright like men." Steven brightened suddenly. "Hey, John, you want to see a trick, a really good trick?"

"No, I don't think so."

"Come on, buddy, loosen up, don't be a party pooper. You'll like this, it's an impression. See if you can guess what I am?" Steven's face began stretching out, the jaw lengthening, almost beyond human proportion, as his lips peeled back from bared teeth. Strings of saliva spilled from the corner of his mouth, ran down, splattered on the bar. He tensed and a savage, guttural snarl erupted from his throat as he sprang at John.

John scrambled back, almost fell off his stool as he felt hot breath against his throat, but the lunge fell short and Steven Adler's face became human again.

Steven was laughing. "Good trick. Scared the shit out of you, didn't I?"

"Yeah, you did. What the hell was that?"

"A wolf."

John wiped his mouth with the back of his hand. "You become other people… and animals… how can you do that?"

"I've gotta tell you, John, it feels strange to put this into words, but here goes. I find a host and I drive out their blood, and move in. Once I do that, I just absorb their memories. It's like renting a furnished apartment." He nudged John with an elbow. "And I don't even have to sign a lease."

John saw the bodies they had found in the creek bed near the Navajo graveyard. "Don't you feel," he groped for the words, "guilt at the deaths you cause?"

"Is this a confessional? Are you a priest?" Steven picked up the cue stick, stroked it gently. "You eat steak. Do you feel guilt that a cow has to die?"

"No," John faltered, "it's just that I feel like I know a little about you, or at least the man you've taken over. I just want to—"

"Understand. There's nothing wrong with wanting to understand, I suppose. A little confession might be good for my soul." He smiled. "Supposing I have a soul." Steven raised his hand, fended off John's next question. "Before I say any more, I want something from you."

"What?"

"A game of pool."

"After all the people you've killed, that's all you want?"

"For the moment." Steven walked over to the pool tables, confident that John would follow. He began racking the balls. "I'm always in search of a good game. Any kind of game. I get bored."

"I don't want to play against you. Give me Timmy Cates and you'll never see me again. I swear it."

Steven rolled a ball down the table, watched its course. "You have no choice, John, you have to play against me."

"What if I don't?"

For an answer, Steven lazily ran the tip of the knife into John's arm before John could move back. The familiar burning sensation came and more blood appeared. Steven dipped his finger in the red line and began writing letters on the balls. He did it fifteen times, once for each ball in the rack before he let go of John. "L is for Louise, A is for Amy, M is for the mayor, B is for Boyce. I'm sure a smart guy like you is getting the picture."

"It spells lamb, you son of a bitch."

The vampire leaned close, and John used up a lot of willpower not to back away. "As in washed in the blood of the lamb." Steven wasn't upset; his tone remained conversational, friendly. "Here's the deal, Johnny boy. You don't play me my game, I'm going to break this rack of balls and whoever doesn't fall in, I'm going to kill—after

I've had my way with them." Steven leaned over, blew on the balls to dry the blood on them. His back was turned to John. "Don't you want to play now?"

John pulled the .32 out of his boot, aimed it at Steven's back.

"Don't forget I've already got Timmy," Steven said, without turning around. "So you might as well hand that over." He looked over his shoulder and grinned in John's face, showing too many long teeth. "Besides, it wouldn't be very sporting to shoot me in the back."

John fought the urge to squeeze the trigger, but uncertainty about Timmy made him hesitate.

Steven moved around the table and his eyes were shiny, slightly yellow in the light. He took the gun from John. "Look at it this way; you've got a chance to save a lot of lives. If you win, I take a hike and nobody dies. If you lose, then that graveyard on the mesa will get the blood of some new lambs. How many lambs, well that depends on you."

"What do I have to do?"

"That's more like it. I've come up with a little something for the occasion. We'll just call it a game of nerves." Steven pulled the balls out of the rack and placed them flush against the back bumper of the table. The first one in line had a red L smeared across it. The vampire placed the cue ball at the far end.

Then he did the same thing at another table.

An inkling of what was about to happen hit John.

"I can see you've done this before." Steven began chalking his stick.

"Yeah, once or twice. We take turns shooting at the balls against the back bumper, you at your table, me at mine."

"You got it. We bank the balls into the corner pocket at the shooter's end of the table. We keep doing it until one of us misses. It's mostly a game of nerves. The first one to blink loses."

John plucked a cue stick from the wall.

"Oh, one other thing before we start." Steven drained the last of his beer. "If you miss any of the balls—even one—then the game is over and that person is mine. Unless—" He produced a knife from the waistband of his belt and stuck it in the wood of the pool table—"you want to buy that person's life back."

"What's the price?" John asked, eyeing the knife.

"Nothing much, just a finger."

"What happens if you miss?"

"The game's over. You walk away with Timmy, and everyone in Crowder Flats lives happily ever after."

"Not everyone. There's six dead. Why are you doing this, isn't there any Steven Adler left in you?"

"A little." Steven's eyes looked into some dark place only he could see. "And that's the reason I've stayed with him for so long. He helps to curb some of my... nastier impulses."

"Like what you did to Bobby Roberts, Martin Strickland, and his family. Billy Two Hats?"

"That's right. The need for new sensation consumes me from time to time, and that means people have to die." He shrugged apologetically. "It's a weakness I've been unable to overcome, but I try to be selective about who I take. I find the lonely, the people with broken lives, and I try to bring them peace. People such as yourself."

John felt the words and they hurt more than wounds in his stomach, because he knew they were the truth.

"Some of your friends are in here with me. Would you like to say hello to one of them?"

"Don't do this." John tried to look away. He couldn't.

Without an invitation, Steven Adler's face again shifted and somehow began subtly rearranging itself, becoming older, broader, and Martin Strickland's voice drifted across the room. "Long time no see, John."

There was no mistaking that raspy twang.

John had seen Martin's dead body not more than an hour ago. He felt cold sweat roll down his sides.

The man who had stolen Martin's voice and face looked John up and down, shook his head sadly at what he saw. "I hope you don't mind me saying this, old buddy, but you look worse than me. And I'm dead." He smiled like he always did, like it hurt him. The cold blue eyes held Martin's familiar twinkle. "You need to quit hanging around those smoky old pool halls. You'll end up like Sparky, asphyxiated."

"Martin, is that really—"

"Yeah, it's me, or what's left of me."

John's mind refused to accept what he saw. It had to be side effects from the peyote he had consumed earlier. "This is all some kind of parlor trick." John dug in his pocket, pulled out a wad of bills, separated one from the rest. His hand was shaking. "I got that ten spot I borrowed from you last year when I was through here."

"Nice try, John. It was a twenty spot, and you borrowed it five years ago. You always did have a bad memory when it comes to money."

"Not as bad as you when it comes to women." The response was automatic, an old joke between them.

John was torn between his fear and the sudden desire to hug his old friend.

The two men stared at each other from across unimaginable gulfs.

The blue eyes lost their twinkle, became serious. "Listen close, John, I want you to do me a small favor if you don't mind."

"Name it."

"I'd sure like a drink of whiskey."

John handed him a bottle.

Martin turned it up. "Damn, that's good." He stared at John, fidgeting with the bottle.

John waited.

Martin always took a while to say what was on his mind.

After a second, Martin obliged. "Don't let that shit kicker from Dallas take Doralee back there. I'd like her to be buried with me and Nicky."

"I'll do what I can."

"That's all I'm asking."

John looked at his old friend. "What's it like in there, Martin?"

"Peaceful, that's the only way I can describe it. Real peaceful."

They stood there, uncertain of what to say. "You want another drink?" John asked.

"Yeah, maybe one for the road." He took a drink and handed the bottle back, and then the blue eyes that held Martin's soul began dimming, the voice fading, as though coming from a great distance. "Looks like I gotta go, John, Doralee and Nicky are waiting for me."

The blue eyes were almost opaque now.

John struggled with the words he had never said to any man, but he knew this would be his last chance to say them. "Martin... I love you. I'd give anything if—"

"I know that, John, and I love you, too. But do me a favor, though, don't go around telling everybody you love me. I got my reputation to think about." He laughed that raspy laugh of his. "Good-bye, old buddy, you take care of yourself. Say hello to the boys at the ranch, and kick this guy's ass. I know you can do it. You're the best." With those last words, Martin's face began coming apart, falling away a piece at a time, a jigsaw puzzle being dumped in slow motion.

He managed one last wink before he vanished completely. And Steven Adler's face reassembled in his place.

Steven's voice was cold, taunting. "You still think we're doing parlor tricks here?"

"You want to talk to anyone else? Leon Wilson, maybe. I'm sure he'd like to talk to you since you're the reason he's dead. You can tell him how sorry you are, too."

John desperately sought to change the subject; he didn't think he could bear talking to Leon. "Where's your partner, Earl Jacobs?"

"He's watching Timmy. Waiting for a phone call." Steven's eyes were steady as he glanced back at the pool table.

Something was odd about the gesture, and it suddenly hit John what was wrong. Steven Adler was lying.

Lying about Earl.

Why?

John took a stab in the dark, trying to provoke a reaction. "Earl's not with Timmy."

"Now why would you think that?" Steven's face never changed expression.

"Because Elliot said you were alone when you stopped Bobby Roberts. Because… Earl doesn't know anything about this." And John understood. "He's not like you. He's not a killer, is he?"

Steven looked like he wasn't going to answer, then for some reason known only to him, he relented. "No, Earl is different, but he'll be like me someday. Exactly like me. The virus I put in his blood takes a while to kick in."

"Earl doesn't know what you really are, does he? Or what's going to happen to him?"

"No, and you try to tell him, I'll kill you, and then I'll kill the entire town."

"Why did you pick Earl to stay with you? I think I know the reason." John was beginning to put it all together, feeling his way by instinct. "Because he reminds you of Matt Thomas, the only real friend you ever had. That old man was like a father to you."

A mask shifted across Steven's face and his eyes went flat. "Bring that bony white ass on over here, John, I got a jar of pigs' feet. Would you like one?"

John looked Steven squarely in the face and this time he didn't flinch. "You let Matt down; you let him die in that cave, because you slept too long and left him alone."

"Help me, John, it's cold in this old freezer." A scar rippled down the smooth white skin, and when Steven Adler smiled, only half of his face moved.

The hustler moved nearer the vampire. "So you found a replacement for your partner in Earl Jacobs, but there's one problem—Earl is too much like Matt Thomas. He's a decent man who wouldn't like what you're doing if he ever found out." It was John's turn to smile. "You're a lot more human than you want to admit."

The muscles in Steven's face clenched and unclenched. "That's right. You've got this all figured out, John. Can you figure out what's going to happen next?"

"You're going to kill me and take the cue stick."

"Maybe. That depends on how well you shoot pool."

"Let's get this over with. Timmy's mom is waiting."

Steven watched him, calm now. "You humans are always in such a hurry, you never take time to savor the moments."

"We have to hurry. Our moments are numbered."

"Take that as a blessing." Steven Adler held his stick by the handle and it looked as if he had grabbed a snake by the head. When he spun the yellowed bone between his hands, the snake began crawling.

Around and around, slithering up the handle, going nowhere. The sight was mesmerizing.

John tore his gaze away from the snake, stepped up to the table, took a deep breath, and bent to shoot. The one ball looked a mile away. In his sweaty hands, the stick felt like lead.

He stepped away. A lot of people's lives were on the line. Reaching for the talc, he sprinkled the white powder along the length of his cue stick, then he slid the wood through his fingers until it was smooth like glass. He lifted his hat, sat it back.

The rituals had to be followed or the magic might go away. Again he stepped up.

And this time he didn't hesitate, he drove the cue ball into the yellow ball, the one with the L on it.

The white ball jumped to the left and the one started its solitary trek to the pocket.

The shot was off a fraction.

The ball kissed the rail once and wobbled a little, ran to the edge of the pocket, hesitated.

And finally fell.

"Not a very auspicious start." Steven sank his ball easily, barely even looking at it. "I hope you'll do better on your next shot. I'd hate to think I went to all this trouble for nothing."

The A came next.

"A pretty girl, Amy," Steven said. "She looks a lot like her mother."

John said nothing as he punched the ball out of sight. His hands did their job, independent of thought, of emotion.

Nothing else in his life had ever worked, except his ability to shoot pool. It had never let him down. It didn't let him down now.

He dropped every ball in the rack.

So did Steven.

They went through another rack. Then they did it again.

And again.

And again.

They did nine racks without stopping.

Steven fished the balls out of the belly of the pool table, dumped them into the rack. "I have to say I'm impressed, John. You're quite a shooter, the best I've seen in a while. Most don't make it past the second or third rack."

John said nothing. He slid a hand beneath his jacket, touched the wet slipperiness spread across his stomach and saw that his fingers came back red. When he looked down, he saw a patch of darkness that ran all the way down his leg.

More blood.

Laying his stick on the table, Steven walked over and tore John's shirt open. He lifted the bandage, stared at the oozing wounds. "Looks like you've sprung a leak, buddy. That's a shame; the game can't be called on account of pain." Steven prodded the wound with a stiff finger, watching the lean hustler double over in agony. "What happened, Johnny boy, you look like someone stuck a knife in you?"

"A buffalo gored me in a dream." The room was tilting, and John had to lean against the table when Steven released him. "Most people would say that's crazy, but I guess you know what I'm talking about."

"Don't try to play games with me. You won't like the way they turn out."

"I need to sit down." John's hands had gone numb, and his stick clattered to the floor.

Steven picked it up, handed it back to him. John was barely able to close his hands around the cue.

The blonde vampire watched calmly, his eyes taking in the blood dripping onto John's boots. "You're bleeding to death. If you don't get to a doctor very, very soon, my friend, you're going to be very, very dead. Tell you what I'm going to do. You pick one of those balls, say with somebody you barely know, and you give it to me."

Steven took John's stick from him and laid it on the table. "And I'll see you get to a doctor myself."

John made his tongue work. "It's your shot."

They did six more racks before the cue slipped from John's hand, causing him to finally miss. It was Timmy Cates who didn't go down.

John folded up, slowly slid to his knees in front of the table, his face bathed in sweat. His jeans were now completely soaked with blood. There was a pool of it at his feet.

"Looks like your leak has turned into a gusher, Mr. Warrick." Pulling the hustler up from the bloodstained floor, Steven half dragged, half carried him over to where the knife waited. "What's it to be, do we stop here, do I take my prize and go home? Or do we keep playing?"

John's head felt like it was too heavy to lift, but he managed to meet the icy blue eyes. "We keep playing."

"Then you've got to ante up."

John laid his hand on the table.'

The vampire worked the knife out of the wood. "Are you sure? A finger is a precious thing to a man who makes his living with his hands."

"Do it."

"All right, you're the boss." Steven pulled out a cigarette lighter and began heating the blade, running the flame back and forth along its length. A tongue that licked a red glow in its wake. "We don't want you losing any more blood. Which finger?"

"The little one."

"Good choice. That's the one they all give up first." Steven tested the knife. It wasn't hot enough to suit him so he continued holding the flame to the blade. "One time I played this guy in Reno. Ten grand against one of his fingers. I think he owed a lot of money to some loan sharks." Steven tested the knife again and still he wasn't satisfied that it was hot enough. "The guy just wouldn't quit, he kept thinking he was going to get back in the game. You know, I walked out of there with every one of his fingers, every last one. Can you believe that?"

John spread his fingers.

"I'd suggest you give me Louise. She's got cancer. I don't think she'll live more than another year."

"You're a liar. Louise has never been sick a day in her life."

"She's got lung cancer. You might as well give her to me."

"Take the finger."

The blade was glowing cherry red now, and Steven put the lighter away. "It's your fault she's got cancer. She smokes too much and thinks about when the baby was still alive. She knows you blame her."

"Our son fell off the back of the truck while Louise was trying to take his picture. It was an accident. I don't blame her." But John knew that was a lie, he did blame her. The words sounded hollow to his own ears.

"Last chance to save the finger."

John looked away.

The heat from the knife reached John and it almost felt good, because he was so cold. A shiver passed through him as his hand was grasped, held. The knife touched his finger and he heard the crunch of his bones when the blade passed through them. He heard a slight sizzle, smelled the sickly sweet odor of his own burning flesh.

Then it was all over.

Just like that.

His finger lay there on the table like some kind of undersized Vienna sausage.

But it wasn't all over.

The pain caught up with him. Coming in waves. Drowning him.

He curled into the fetal position on the floor, holding his injured hand under his armpit, making mewling noises as he crawled across the pine boards. There were no words to describe how much his hand hurt.

Steven knelt beside him. "It's the heat from the knife you feel, not the loss of your finger. Don't worry, the worst of the pain only lasts for a few minutes."

John's consciousness began going grainy at the edges, slipping away. Just before he blacked out, the sudden image of a cabin in a clearing strobed on the inside of his eyelids, and he saw a dead man and woman lying on the ground. Then the scene was gone before he could get a good look.

The sawdust on the floor filled John's open mouth, choking him. He threw up and he felt the wounds in his stomach tear some more.

Something wet and cold struck him in the face, brought him back. He saw Steven Adler standing over him with a fresh beer. The vampire pulled him up until they were face-to-face. "The clock is ticking and we don't have time for rest breaks." He handed John a cold beer to wrap his injured hand around. "The game is waiting. We play until I miss, or until you run out of fingers."

They did three more shots, and John missed.

Kevin this time.

The little finger from his right hand joined his left.

Steven placed them side by side. "Two down, eight to go. I'll make a necklace out of them."

John tried to pull away from the knife waving in front of his face, but he couldn't find the strength. The blade caught the light, fading in and out, and John realized he was no longer seeing the present. He was watching something that had happened a long time ago.

The knife was reflecting off a kerosene lamp.

Shadows danced on the wall.

John realized something about the knife had jump-started him, had taken him to this distant place in time.

He felt his legs go limp and his eyes rolled up, but there was no escape from what was in his head. He was hot-wired into this.

Going along for the ride.

He was standing in a clearing looking into the door of a dirt-floor cabin. There were two boys sprawled in the corner and he could tell from the odd angle of their heads they were dead with broken necks. Steven Adler was crouched on the floor in front of a little girl.

His knife kept catching the light as he worked.

The whole thing only lasted an instant, but John was sure of what he had seen—Steven Adler crouched over a little girl with a wet knife in his hand. Her high-pitched screams carried on the night air.

Another strobe.

He saw a young Earl Jacobs ride up to the cabin, walk in. The screaming started again. There was a pistol shot and the screaming stopped.

Another strobe.

John was back in the present. Despite the blade hovering inches from his eyes, he spat in the vampire's pale, grinning face. "You skinned her alive, you son of a bitch, you skinned her alive. She was just a little girl."

"What little girl?"

"The one in the cabin. The one Earl found."

"Oh, that little girl." He held the cue stick under John's nose. "Her skin made the leather on the handle of my cue stick, her red hair made the snake. Little boys and girls around five are the best. Their skin is very supple at that age. I always wanted to see if I could skin one who was still alive." Steven wiped the spit from his cheek and hauled John over to the table, deposited him face down there. "You've got a lot of spunk, John, and I admire that. I really do, but you'd better save it for the game." He handed John a cue stick. "It's your shot."

But the cue slipped from John's hands, fell to the floor with a clatter. He crawled across the green felt, leaving dark stains in his wake, until he finally collapsed. His hands no longer hurt. Nor his stomach. In fact, right now, he couldn't feel anything.

"Come on, John, I'm waiting."

John tried to move. Couldn't.

Steven picked the stick up, broke it across his knee as though it were a matchstick and tossed the pieces on the table. "Looks like we're all through here. Game's over." He grasped John by the hair and lifted his head, exposing the throat. The stained knife was still in his hand. "I guess the time for us to part company has come. Any last words before you join your dead friends, or do you just want to whisper them to me later?"

"You didn't beat me." John tasted his own blood in his mouth. He choked on it, swallowed. "You're not the best. I am."

"We'll have eternity to debate that." Steven placed the knife under John's outstretched throat, hesitated, and then the blonde vampire smiled a sad smile. "You showed a lot of guts tonight, and I'd like to let you live, John, I really would. But some day you might work up enough courage to come after me. With what you know, you might manage what so many have tried to do and failed."

A bullet poked through the window, tugged at Steven's shirt and shattered the jukebox across the room. An instant later, the sound of a shot followed.

"Looks like your friends are trying to save you. Too bad they're too late." He pulled the knife across John's throat with a swift economical motion, and let the hustler's head drop back to the table. A pool of blood formed, began running toward one of the pockets.

Steven knelt beside John, whispered in his ear. "Since you played so well tonight, tell you what I'm going to do. I'm going to let you stay dead. We'll call it professional courtesy." The vampire placed the knife back in his belt and eased out into the night, looking for signs of the would-be sharpshooter. Dawn was almost here and he had to hurry. He reached the Caddy, unscrewed the cue stick, tossed it in the seat.

The bullet that punched through Steven's back splattered the dust beyond the car. He stared at it wonderingly before turning, before looking at the man in the door holding the .44, his .44; the one Matt Thomas had given him so many years ago. "Earl, what are you—"

The second bullet caught Steven in the leg and he had to grab hold of the door to keep from falling. "I had to kill him. He had my cue stick. I can't live without it, you know that."

"We don't have time for any more lies. I found Timmy Cates at the graveyard and he told me what he saw before I gave him back to his dad. Amy and Jesse told me you were here, so I decided to ease over and see what was going on. I heard everything you told John." Earl's face was filled with determination. "Maybe I could live with most of what you do, maybe even pretended I don't know what you are, but I couldn't lie to myself about the little girl. Not the little girl."

Steven made an effort to move toward Earl.

The pistol belched flame and Steven's other leg crumpled, the kneecap blown away. He slid to a sitting position in the dust, his back propped against the car, his leg cocked at an impossible angle. Almost faster than the eye could follow, he produced John's .32 from his boot and pointed it at Earl. He pulled the hammer back. His finger tightened on the trigger, but his hand trembled and, after a long moment, he lowered the gun. "Well, how about that? Couldn't pull the trigger. I guess John was right, I'm a little more human that I thought."

Earl walked over, took the gun from Steven's hand.

The wounded vampire didn't resist.

Bobby Roberts' Cadillac pulled into the parking lot with Louise behind the wheel, Jesse and Amy beside her. They went into Jake's and came out with John between them.

"He's lost a lot of blood, but he's still alive," Louise said. "Don't ask me how. We're going to try and get him to the doctor in Holbrook. I don't know if he can hold on that long."

Earl watched as they laid the injured man in the backseat and drove away. "He's pretty tough. I bet he hangs on." Earl turned to Steven. "You did a piss-poor job of cutting his throat."

"Did I? I guess my heart wasn't in it."

Earl sat down beside Steven.

"What do we do now?" Steven asked.

"We wait."

Across the rapidly graying night, a stage coach approached the bar. Boyce was doing the driving. Kevin, Nash, Ernesto, Manny, and Jesus were on board. They pulled into the lot, threw on the hand brake, and piled out. "Is John all right?" Nash asked. The horses were hot from running and steam rose off their bodies in the chill air.

"Don't know," Earl answered. "He was still alive when Louise took off with him to Holbrook."

"Is this what you wanted, Earl?" Boyce asked. "It's as close as we could get to a wagon on such short notice."

"Yeah, that'll do fine, boys. Much obliged for all your help."

Steven Adler shifted beside the car, made an effort to stand. "Did you sell me out to the humans, Earl; did they promise that you could live among them like a normal man?"

"No, they didn't make me any promises, but I made them one."

"And what was that?"

"That I'd stop you."

The men gathered around Steven Adler, staring at him with equal parts of curiosity and hatred on their faces.

"Well, it looks like you caught yourselves the boogeyman." Steven regarded them calmly. "What are you going to do now that you have him? Have you come to extract your vengeance, to punish me for the death of your loved ones?"

"No, we've come to lay the dead to rest," Nash said.

"The people you grieve for suffered in life. I gave them peace."

"It's not up to you to decide who should live, who should die," Kevin said.

"And who are you to decide I should die? I've been on the earth longer than the race of man; I have fed on your kind since the beginning. I am the eater of souls." He grinned at Kevin. "I may have yours before the night is over, my young friend." He made a lunge at Kevin, who jumped back.

The .44 in Earl's hand centered on Steven again.

The vampire's cold blue eyes tracked the gun. "Matt Thomas gave me that for my twenty-third birthday. How did you happen to come across it?"

"I found it. I talked to Timmy, Amos, Elliot, and everything kept coming back to the Navajo graveyard. Time and again, too many times for it to be a coincidence. There had to be a reason, and I finally figured it out. Your home is close by the graveyard."

Moving incredibly quick, Steven crawled snakelike on his stomach toward Earl and made a grab for the .44.

But Earl was ready. The pistol jumped in his hand and a hole the size of a dime appeared in Steven's forehead. The long blonde hair fluttered once, as if a gust of wind had caught it. Flecks of gray matter splashed the Caddy door, ran down. "Well, I'll be damned," Earl said wonderingly, staring at the stain on the car. "I finally seen a bat. After all these years I finally seen a bat." There was no joy in his voice.

The vampire began writhing on the gravel like a snake with a broken back.

Walking over, Earl pulled Steven's knife from his belt. He grabbed blonde hair, held the blade in front of Steven's face. "I don't know if you can hear me or not, but you try to come out of your body and I'm going to stick you with this." Then he nicked Steven in case the vampire couldn't see the knife. Smoke boiled up from the wound and the vampire screamed in agony.

Earl picked Steven up, threw the vampire over his shoulder, and dumped him on the top of the stagecoach. He then pulled out a set of handcuffs that Louise had given him and fastened Steven's hands to the rail.

"You're taking a little trip, in case you want to know," Earl told him. "You're going home."

They all drove to the graveyard in the coach.

Earl slung Steven over his shoulder and walked toward a hole in the cliff wall. "There's a pyramid in there, right inside the mountain," Earl said, "or at least the tip of one. The rest goes down into the ground. Don't ask me how far, 'cause I don't know."

"Where did the hole come from?" Boyce asked.

"It's the entrance to Steven's home and it's protected by a stone slab that must weigh better than a hundred tons. Looks natural as hell. It slides up and down. The whole thing is controlled by counterweights." Earl pointed at the cliffs above them. "You have to climb that rock face over there to get to the lever. No human could ever make the climb."

"How did you find it?" Jesus asked.

"I used to be a pretty good tracker once upon a time. I seen where some footprints went up to the cliffs and then just stopped. That didn't seem right, so I did a little climbing myself."

They walked inside.

Boyce's flashlight found a hole leading down. There were steps carved in the stone.

"This is it," Earl announced. "Home." He laid Steven at the edge of the hole and paused. "I figured out what was really in that cue stick of yours."

The vampire tried to mouth the word "What?" but he had no voice.

"It was your salvation, it could have saved you from your evil side. You told me you had to have a taste of it to stay alive. But that wasn't true, was it? You had to have a taste to keep from killing."

Steven closed his eyes, unable to face Earl.

"The voices in your head made you do bad things, only you got to where you liked the voices in your head. You got to like the bad things. So you quit taking it. You knew right from wrong."

Steven looked in the pit, tried again to speak, and this time he was able, even though the sound was muddy. "Don't do this. We were friends once. Kill me."

"You're right, we were friends once, but what you did was wrong. I'm not going to kill you. That'd be too good for you."

The substance inside Steven Adler poured out of the hole in his head, spit in two, and stretched upward toward Earl. In the dark, it looked as if the vampire had suddenly grown horns.

Manny, Jesus, and Ernesto made the sign of the cross, backed away.

Earl lifted the blonde vampire high above his head, and the duster that Steven wore spread like dark wings as he was thrown into the pit waiting below.

They never heard him strike bottom.

Outside, Earl pressed a button on a remote and a series of explosions occurred. The cliffs crumbled, fell.

"Dynamite," Earl explained. "He'll spend eternity beneath those stones."

"Wouldn't it have been kinder to have killed him?" Kevin asked.

"Yes, son, it would have." Earl strode toward the coach in the predawn light.

They gathered around Earl as he climbed up in the stagecoach and gathered the reins.

"You don't have to go," Manny said.

Boyce seconded that sentiment. "You can stay with us for as long as you want."

"I appreciate your offer, boys, believe me I do, but this is the way I got into this, and this is the way I'd like to get out." Earl began turning the coach. "A long time ago, I used to drive a wagon from town to town, selling snake oil. Had me a worthless white dog that wouldn't do any tricks." He smiled down at them. "It wasn't much of a life but at least it was mine."

They appealed one last time.

"No, it's time for me to go. I had me a good life, so don't you worry about old Earl."

With those last words, Earl pointed the stagecoach toward the desert, due east, and he drove into the rising sun.

And legend.

EPILOGUE

Crowder Flats, the Navajo Graveyard
Two Years Later

The day was gray, chilly, with rows of dark clouds running across the sky like some endless train, sometimes hiding the sun for several minutes at a time. When the sun did pop out, it held no warmth or cheer. Rain had been threatening for a week, but had never materialized.

Amos Black Eagle and Lefty Thunder Coming had just finished laying flowers on the unmarked grave, weighing the wreath down with stones to keep the wind from blowing it away.

They stood back to check their work.

The wind rose and the wreath began flapping.

Amos laid another stone on it. "There, I think that'll hold."

"I don't know." Lefty sat on the stone fence, lit himself a smoke, and listened to the wind sigh through the pines. "The wind don't ever let up around here."

"I know what you mean. Sometimes I think I hear it calling MY name."

"Me too."

They stared across the gray landscape, each lost in his own thoughts.

Lefty was the first to speak, and he repeated the names of the people in the unmarked grave, his voice taken by the wind. "Billy Two Hats, Martin Strickland, Doralee Strickland, Nicholas Strickland, Chester Roberts, and Bobby Roberts." After a moment he added, "May God have mercy on your souls." He turned to Amos. "I wished they could have had a proper Christian burial."

"I do too, Lefty, but nobody can ever know about what happened here. They just wouldn't believe it. This is one burden we're going to have to carry all by ourselves. We're taking a chance even putting down a wreath."

The small Apache's face was eroded with sadness and he raised up his bottle of Jack Daniel's and took a long drink. "I keep seeing them, Amos, not alive, but the way they looked when we found them in the creek bed. Martin scalped, Doralee without no eyes, Bobby all cut up." He shook the bottle, as if to assure himself it wasn't empty. "If it wasn't for this, I don't think I'd be able to sleep at night. I don't see how you quit drinking."

"It wasn't easy, but I made a promise to Jesse."

Lefty took another drink. "You heard from him lately?"

"He's coming home for Thanksgiving." Amos smiled proudly. "College boys always need two things, money and something to eat. He's getting a little uppity; he told me we can't have corn on the cob."

"Amy coming with him?"

"Yeah, then they're going out to Missouri to stay with John and Louise Warrick for a couple of days at the farm." Amos instantly regretted bringing up that subject.

"Missouri, that's a strange place for those two to end up, if you ask me. John doesn't know anybody in Missouri, and he damn sure don't know nothing about farming." Lefty took another drag on his cigarette and jumped down off the fence, dusted off the seat of his pants. "You know, I still can't figure out how John pulled through that night. My cousin knows a girl who dates an orderly at the hospital over to Holbrook who was there when John was admitted. My cousin says John should have been dead when he came in."

"How come every time something happens, you got a cousin that just happens to know what's going on?"

"I got a lot of cousins," Lefty answered, unoffended. "They hear things."

"Things like John was down to his last pint of blood? You bring that up every time we come out here, and I gotta tell you, Lefty, that story is sure starting to get on my nerves."

"I been thinking about this," Lefty insisted, "so hear me out, okay?"

Amos watched the sun dip behind the mountains, flashing off the large white cross before throwing the graveyard into sudden shadow. A shiver passed through him. "All right, Lefty, tell me what happened."

"Who was the first person to see John that night at Jake's?"

"Louise."

"Amy?"

Amos was becoming exasperated. "All right, who was it?"

"Earl Jacobs."

"So it was Earl Jacobs. What's your point?"

"I think Earl Jacobs and John Warrick are the same person, or at least…" Lefty floundered, "a part of Earl somehow got inside John. I think Earl did that transfer thing on John before he went outside and killed Steven Adler."

"I think you scrambled your brains with that whiskey," Amos said.

"Well, then you think about this. John and Louise had themselves a little girl, and everyone says that John and his new daughter are inseparable. They said they never seen nothing like it."

"That's your proof?"

"He's got himself a little white dog that he's been trying to teach tricks to."

"I got a dog, too. His name is Custer. I been trying to teach him to protect my chickens for the last five years." Amos paused, became suddenly still. "You hear that?"

"No, what is it?"

"Sounded like voices." Amos shook his head, laughed uneasily. "The wind's making me hear things."

They moved nearer to the dynamited cliffs and Amos placed his ear against one of the stones. His hearing wasn't what it used to be, still, there for a second, he thought he heard a faint voice. Then it was gone.

This was crazy. Steven Adler was dead, buried under tons of rock for the last two years.

"Come on," Amos said to Lefty as they moved away from the rocks, "let's get home. Jesse's and Bobby's old running buddies are coming over for a while."

"That'll be good. Give us a chance to catch up on what they're doing these days." Lefty watched the pine trees dotting the hillside sway in the wind, and he listened to their murmuring voices for a moment. They too sounded sad. "I heard tell Manny, Ernesto, and Jesus finally got themselves that little gas station over in Albuquerque."

"Yeah, they did. They're all equal partners."

"Hell, those three can't agree on anything. They'll never get anything done."

Amos couldn't argue with that. "You hear anything from Boyce and Nash?"

"Last time I talked to them, they were still trying to buy a piece of the Broken R. They said they're going to raise beef for the Japanese. I think it's just crazy enough that the bank's going to go for it."

"Too bad Kevin didn't live long enough to hear that."

The grizzled Apache ground out his cigarette butt beneath the heel of his boot. "Kevin lives through all this, only to die of a ruptured appendix seven months later. God takes him at twenty-two and leaves two old farts like us. It doesn't seem fair, does it?"

"No, it doesn't, and I can't give you any kind of answer. I wish I could."

They said nothing for a long while.

"I heard tell Boyce got himself a girlfriend," Lefty said, brightening a little.

"Now, you don't expect me to believe that, do you?" Lefty got a twinkle in his eyes. "I think this calls for a bottle of tequila."

As they walked toward the pickup, Amos nudged Lefty with an elbow. "What do you say, after everybody leaves, we play us a little pinochle? I'll give you a chance to win back part of that ten million you owe me."

"Sounds good to me." Lefty grinned. "I'm gonna kick your butt. I feel lucky tonight."

"You say that every night."

They climbed into Amos's pickup; the one Jesse had given him, and drove away.

Soon after the taillights vanished into the twilight, the wind rose and the wreath worked loose from its perch and sailed across the hard ground, flipping end over end like a tumbleweed, until it finally fetched up against the rocks that covered Steven Adler's grave. The wreath became trapped there.

And even though the wind blew hard, the wreath remained wedged in the rocks as though it belonged there.

It stayed there until it became dust.

ABOUT THE AUTHOR

Gary Raisor is an American horror author best known for the novels Less Than Human, Graven Images, Sinister Purposes, and his extensive short fiction work. He was nominated for a Bram Stoker Award for Best First Novel for Less Than Human in 1992. He also edited the anthology Obsessions with stories from Dean Koontz, Kevin J. Anderson, F. Paul Wilson, Dan Simmons, Joe R. Lansdale, and featured the story Lady Madonna by Nancy Holder, which won the Bram Stoker Award for Short Fiction in 1991.

Raisor has written numerous short stories, beginning in the 1980s in Night Cry Magazine and The Horror Show, working his way into a lot of "Best Of" anthologies. Today, Raisor concentrates primarily on screenplays and comics.

CEMETERY DANCE PUBLICATIONS

We hope you enjoyed your Cemetery Dance Paperback! Share pictures of them online, and tag us!

Instagram: @cemeterydancepub
Twitter: @CemeteryEbook
TikTok: @cemeterydancepub
www.facebook.com/CDebookpaperbacks

Use the following tags!

#horrorbook #horror #horrorbooks
#bookstagram #horrorbookstagram
#horrorpaperbacks #horrorreads
#bookstagrammer #horrorcommunity
#cemeterydancepublications

SHARE THE HORROR!

Cemetery Dance Publications Paperbacks and Ebooks!

BAD MOON RISING
by Luisa Colon

In Gravesend, Brooklyn, sixteen-year-old Elodia is an outcast at school, at odds with her father, and longing for her mysteriously absent mother. Lonely and isolated, Elodia knows that something unspeakably terrible has happened to her—she just can't remember what....

"Twisty and disturbing, Bad Moon Rising is an ambitious, moody meditation on the cycles of familial trauma. Luisa Colon's impressive debut is sure to get under your skin."
—Paul Tremblay, author of *The Cabin at the End of the World*

EVIL WHISPERS,
by Owl Goingback

Robert and Janet should have listened to the local legends. They should have heeded the warnings about the black water lagoons. And they should have listened to their daughter when she told them about the whispers in the woods. Because now, it's too late. Krissy's disappeared, and whatever took their little girl is coming back for more...

"Goingback's unflinching prose spares no gory detail, and the author maintains a solid sense of dread throughout. This is not for the faint of heart."
—Publisher's Weekly

THE NIGHT PROPHETS,
by Paul F. Olson

Universal Ministries was the fastest growing religious group in the country, but Curt Potter joined it to meet his father, Reverend Arthur Bach, the charismatic founder of the church. But Curt and his fellow initiates make a shocking discovery:
That the church hides a dark, horribly secret...

"If you are looking for an action packed, blood soaked, character driven tale that just happens to be a vampire story, you need look no further than The Night Prophets. Enjoyed every minute of it."
—Literary Mayhem

Purchase these and other fine works of horror from Cemetery Dance Publications today!
https://www.cemeterydance.com/

HORROR DNA

MOVIES
COMIC BOOKS
MUSIC
BOOKS
VIDEO GAMES

IT'S IN OUR
BLOOD
horrordna.com

Made in the USA
Middletown, DE
22 March 2024